THE PROMISE

SEED

THE PROMISE SEED

ISBN 978-0-9970326-7-3
Library of Congress TXu 2-108-832
All books are available on Amazon.com & e-books
Current publication is solely the property of Words-with-a-
     Mission   Follow us on:
Linkedin, Facebook,Twitter, Pinterest
www.wordswithamission.com and our blog

Thanks for the Phillips County Museum for permission to use the photograph of the Fairview grain elevators

Additional Books by Author

Violence and Hope in a US Border Town (2008) Prospect Heights, Ill.: Waveland Press & Amazon.com

To the Mountain and Back (1994) (anthropology classic) Prospect Heights, Ill. Waveland Press and Amazon.com

The Biocultural Basis of Health, (1980/1987)L. Moore, P. Van Ardsdale, J. Glittenberg, and R. Aldrich. Prospect Heights, Ill. Waveland Press.

Out of Uniform and Into Trouble. (1972/1982) C. De Young, M. Powers, and J.Glittenberg. Mosby; Slack Publishing, NY, NY. (nursing classic)

ACKNOWLEDGMENTS

Living with amazing people taught me much about the world and our human frailties and strengths. From early years on the windy, challenging prairie to my international work across all continents, I found a mix of robust saints and wobbly sinners–I being one of them.

To the hundreds of students that I've been privileged to share your learning, I thank you all.

To the many storytellers in my own family I owe much. Crafting a tale to tell was part of my everyday life as Mom told real stories and some made up. She was colorful and funny. Dad was part of a clan of gifted men who reaped laughter and slapping of knees, as they shared adventures of their farming worlds. My five brothers, sisters, and spouses, each has been a gift to me.

And most of all the children and grandchildren I've been blessed with: you are my well of creativity. And surprisingly God sent me a miracle later in life, my Beloved Joel, a faith-filled man who gives me goose bumps every time he enters the room. He, a grammarian, a wordsmith, has made this novel a better read.

This is a work of fiction.

Historical events such as the Extended Homestead Act, Sand Creek Massacre, Dust Bowl, Great Depression, and WWII are real but the characters and situations are purely fictional.

DEDICATION

This historical fictional novel is dedicated to people around the world who join together in halting the destruction of our resources, who deeply respect all creatures, and who honor this magnificent Mother Earth.

INTRODUCTION

The mysterious spirit of the Cheyenne sweeps through this novel set in the pioneer west. What is the message blown in the wind? Can naïve Homesteaders rally the harsh land to produce enough food for survival? Will the love they have for each other and faith in the Promise Seed be enough to secure life? Will the Spirit of the Earth be sufficient to sustain all things sacred against harsh weather, ruthless people, and a secret so important even the grave cannot contain it?

TABLE OF CONTENTS

. . .

FAMILY TREES

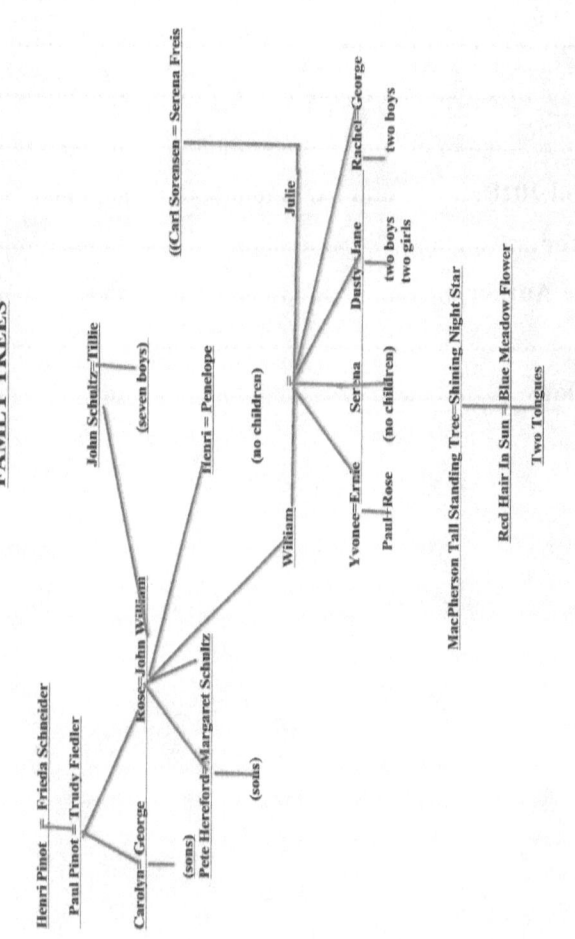

PART I

THE COVENANT

Chapter 1

TWO WORLDS BLEND

Listen to the land, it speaks to you; it tells you its secrets.
Red Sun in Hair, Cheyenne Spiritual Leader, 1910

March 21, 1983

The smell of freshly brewed coffee wafted through the dining room of Betsy's Café as the rain continued its patter on the roof. Who'd guess those coffee-drinking farmers were millionaires–some even multi-millionaires? A dozen or so old timers came most mornings to Betsy's Café in Hopetown, Colorado, just sitting–talking–and keeping their caps and muddy work boots on. No worries like their parents had–those risk-taking homesteaders at the beginning of the 20th Century. Yet out on the open, windy prairie of eastern Colorado, they needed to stay connected, to check up on everyone in this daily ritual.

"Sure wonder where Hank is. He's usually the first one here, especially since his ole lady passed," one muttered.

Hank Schultz, the handsomest, richest bastard in these parts was not well liked by most.

"He sure changed his ways after he married that rich widda. Why I remember when Hank got ex-communicated from the Lutheran Church, 'cause he was chasing and fornicatin 'n adulteratin with ev'ry woman–single or married," another reminded them.

"Yah, 'n I never played poker with him–too risky–cheatin 'n all," retorted one. "Some folks don't forget," chimed in another, "like when he did some finagling to get Widda Rose's homestead. Folks don't forget about those things–even if they happened a long time ago."

"Nope, sure don't forget–" sighed several others, sitting with their beefy arms crossed in front of blue bib-overalls, red-faced from years in the blazing sun.

If they only knew they were talking–about a dead man.

–

In a machine shed about ten miles away on the old Schultz homestead, shadows looked real in the day's grayness. But there was no doubt that a horrible accident had happened. An old man's body was pasted against the wall like a fly hit with a swatter. He was squashed into place by the hood of a green and yellow John Deere tractor–not a sound–no motor running. As if he were trying to hold back the oncoming tractor, the dead man's outstretched arms–a crucifix–were splayed against the ancient wall. Above the victim's head, hardly to be seen was a strange object–a red arrowhead on a black shaft–the Cheyenne Red Arrow of Revenge, plunged directly into the one original Homestead wall of that shed. With eyes bugging out and his mouth agape, forming a scream, the dead man's tale was lost in silence.

The machine-shed door stood slightly ajar, but nothing was out of place. Each tool hung in perfect order–that made the scene even more sinister. Only the west wall of the shed had been hit.

The room grew cold, and a whisper was heard. "Remember, Mama Rose had insisted, when we rebuild this shed let's keep one wall–the west one–just as it was–sod–as Daddy built it so precisely in 1909. He squared each block, so it would stand for years to come knowing the livestock couldn't survive underground as we had to–in the dugout. The shed sheltered horses, cows, and pigs through blizzards and the blazing sun. We did survive. Never forget how much work and prayers went into building our homestead." A wind swished through the room–it was cold again.

Only this wall remained as a symbol of struggle and triumph going on now seven decades later.

Perhaps this accident had its beginning long, long ago.

March 21, 1909
Mother Earth, Father Sky

Inside each raindrop swims the sun.
Inside each flower breathes the moon.
Inside me dwell ten million stars,
One for each of my ancestors:
The elk, the raven, the mouse, the man,
The flower, the coyote, the lion, the fish.
Ten million different stars am I, but only one spirit,
connecting all.
Nancy Woods, 1993 Spirit Walker

"The homesteaders are coming, but I can't wait as the ancestors are calling. It's March 21st; it's spring again. It's time to bless the land, keeping our covenant as always." Beating a drum the man began to chant–whispering–almost silently–then louder.

The strange figure–facing the sun–danced–moving up and down. From nearby, his song was heard.

"Mother Earth, bring power to this land that has slept for four moons under the welcomed blanket of snow, awaken it for all, and open the rivers of ice to flow sweet waters again.

"Father Sky, bring cloud spirits filled with healing rain–fill the night sky with light, the moon to shine, the stars to poke through the black cover, and the planets to move.

"Great Spirits bring life to all creatures and leaves to grace the trees, bushes, and all plants. May seeds planted in Mother Earth open to their newness. Lighten the waters for fish at sea; may they explore with joy the depths of the ocean's bottom. Awaken four-legged and two-winged friends, creeping crawlers and eight-legged earth dwellers after winter's long sleep. To the one who slides on his belly, may he hold his tongue from harm and whisper only in defense. Mother Earth, Father Sky, may all who dwell upon this land rejoice. May they live in harmony and with honor.

Then facing the East the silhouette chanted, "Great Spirits of the East bring warmth for seeds that growing roots may reach deeply into Mother Earth."

Facing the South, a prayer was heard, "Great Spirits of the South bring power of new life, silence storms, keep the rain gods happy and clouds weeping ice and whirling winds, far from this place."

Turning to the West, the plainsong continued, "Great Spirits of the West make happy the winds that bring clouds, keep them soft and whispering through the night when Father Sun is sleeping."

Then to the North, "Great Spirits of the North, hold the cold for time of winter, keep stars close to Mother Earth, guide the traveler toward unknown destinies, protect two-legged mothers and fathers, and cherish each child born from their seed.

"We, the Cheyenne, promise to honor this land, which is sacred for all."

The silhouette reached for grass and pulled up some, kissed it, smelled the freshness of spring. "Yes, it's time for the new ones to come. I saw them at the Land Management Office. This land is the place where ancestor spirits dwell. I stand on sacred land that will belong to them–where once Brother Buffalo roamed without fences, giving us, Cheyenne, food, skins for moccasins and tepees, strings for our bows, fur hides for warmth. Once Brother Coyote kept us from harm with his tricks, and the meadows were filled with grass and flowers. Bless this land"

Far off to the east–maybe a half mile–two tall men mounted their horses and rode slowly across the open prairie, each straight in his saddle. Even that far away, you could see the taller one sat stiffly, upright with reins held tightly and close to his chin, while the other, a bit shorter, seemed part of the horse's saddle–relaxed.

As the sun rose higher in the sky the taller one yelled, "Hurry up, John, we got 'ta go."

"Just wanted to see our land, to touch it, to feel the strength of the soil."

"Jeez, John, you're so dang sentimental about the land–get on with it. We've got money to make. This entire mumble jumble about the land–sometimes you really piss me off."

The taller rider stiffened again, "I wanna git our plows right now 'n dig up all this ole sod, plant, plant, plant, grow wheat 'n corn like at home in Iowa. 'N trees–got to have those–this damn sun 'n damn wind 're killing me. Got a fortune to make–but not by poking around 'n 'feeling the soil'–for god's sake–I sometimes can't believe we're cousins!"

"That's OK, Gus, we both want to make a go of it. We just may have different ways of doing it, but we'll do it."

"Yah–you in a hundred years. Dang, you're such a peewee. Hey what's that sound? Look over there–what in the devil is that? Someone on our land! Let's ride over 'n make 'em skedaddle." Gus touched his gun in the holster.

About a half mile off on the flat prairie a silhouette rose against the skyline. No, two silhouettes, one a horse and another–perhaps a man–his hair seemed long and blowing in the wind. The closer the two men rode–they could hear a drum beating. "Wait," urged the shorter one, "wait–let's see what's happening."

"Dang, John, we got 'ta git goin–got to get our stuff from the train."

"Just listen, will you? Maybe this is important–listen!" They slowed their horses and listened.

As the riders came closer and closer, the red-haired figure raised one hand in greeting. *In the Land Office yesterday I saw the new ones, one, a handsome man without wrinkles, with warm, brown eyes–like my mother, Shining Night Star–and caring hands. He speaks with a deep, melodic voice. The taller one does not speak.*

"Hello," said the shorter one, as he dismounted from his horse. The taller man, slid stiffly to the ground holding tightly to the reins. He didn't speak.

"Hello," repeated the shorter man.

The tall, red-haired man standing by his pinto pony nodded. He said "Hello," precisely, like an educated man, yet he looked native, but red-haired.

The shorter man spoke, "I am John Schultz from Iowa. My claim is a half section–here–and south of here." Pointing to the taller man, he said, "And this is my cousin, Gus Schultz. His claim is just west of here."

The taller man, with harsh face and eyes, gave no greeting. "What 're you doin out here?" demanded Gus in a strained voice.

"I am here to learn who you are and to ask the Great Spirit to protect the land. Every spring I come here to bless it and give thanks. It had been my grandfathers', grandmothers'–belonging to the whole tribe–home to our countless buffalo–now long gone–as well as my people, the Cheyenne." *John—seems a nice man—and the other one—probably, too.*

"I am Gregory MacPherson," continued the old native in a clear, strong voice. "Everyone in these parts calls me—Old Timer, as I've been here a long, long time," moving his moccasins ever so slightly outward.

Yes, thought John William, *you are an old timer as your face shows many summers. Your hair is long, red with many streaks of gray. Eyes are brilliant blue, but look as if they have seen countless years of life. Your leather jacket is worn and old, and the moccasins on your feet are ancient. Yet you move like a young man of twenty—like the wind.*

"Tell us more," urged John.

"I've come to bless the land for you, as it once belonged to others—and now you are the keepers. I am asking for kindness from Mother Earth and Father Sky to help you homestead."

"So, you know all about the Homestead Act?" inquired John William.

"Yes, I went to see President Lincoln about it before the War of the States," the piercing eyes projected resignation.

Gus looked disgusted. *Gads! Some stupid Injun—doesn't look all Injun—probably a damn half-breed—trying to convince us he's some chief—ha! Says he saw President Lincoln!!* Gus touched his holster.

Old Timer noticed the movement and watched carefully. The shorter man, with wavy hair and silken eyes, continued, "Thanks, we'll need all the help we can get. This is a new challenge for us—been farmers in Iowa. We heard about the new Homestead Act. Land is scarce in Iowa, so we decided to take a chance and start all over again. Our families are coming soon. I have a wife and three children, and Gus has a wife and three sons."

Old Timer nodded his head, as if in approval.

"Gus and I are here with plows and horses, to build dugouts this year, then real houses—turn the soil—plant crops."

John sensed Old Timer shudder.

"We hope to have this all done soon, but we'll need some help. Do you know of any young men we could hire to help us? Sure could use some help."

Old Timer brightened a bit. "Yes, there are always some men looking for work, back in Alva or even Hopetown, I'll ask around. When do you want to start?"

"As soon as possible—a week?" Gus nodded in agreement. "Union Pacific won't charge us anything to bring all of our stuff, like beds and farm machinery, some livestock–every thing by train! I guess the old Union wants us to help settle on this land–keep it from cattle rustlers and train robbers."

Old Timer wanted to add, *"And the wild Injuns–those savages!"* But he kept his mouth shut–nodding silently. He knew all too well about the "generosity" of the railroads.

Gus looked stern and angry.

The Indian thought, *Gus doesn't want John even talking to me– Old Timer.* A shudder went through the tall redheaded Indian. *How sad to break the skin of Mother Earth protecting us all and keeping the sacred rain in place for grass and all growing things.* Old Timer knew about the desperate need to fill the desolate land. Having vast stretches of open range was dangerous to the Union Pacific, so they gave free transportation–free to all naïve families coming to build new lives on dry, semi-arid land. The U.S. government was also pushing the risky chance to survive.

"I have been here long before the homesteaders came. I am Cheyenne and Scottish," said Gregory. He continued, "This land is crusty, but also fragile. It needs to be handled carefully. Weather is harsh with withering winds, blizzards, and the hot breath of the devil in the summer. Prairie fires are feared. They jump around when the wind changes–leaping like flaming deer–can catch a whole bunch of fighters. They're hard to put out–no rivers to stop the fire, no trees, just prairie grass. Look out for tornadoes and lightning storms, as they also make this a dangerous place. Many have come before you, but failed, so returned to the east. Some newcomers tore the sod so cruelly that it will never heal,"

Old Timer lowered his head. "I know the ways of Nature. Maybe I can help."

Gus looked skeptical. This screw-loose old codger probably wants us to leave so he can have his land again–*I ain't goin to fall for that.* The tall, redheaded man–looking somewhat like his father-in-law Papa Paul, fascinated John. *Some how I know this is a messenger, sent to us–maybe he is an angel. I know he's a very learned man.* "We'll listen to you. Giving up all your land, that must be hard for you," queried John.

"Not really," said Old Timer. "I know all that happens is according to the Great Spirit's plan." He looked to the sky, light and very blue. "We all walk this journey for a short time, and our paths are guided by the Great Spirit. We know that all is planned for us already." He looked content.

"Oh, jeez, not you, too," said Gus; he grimaced, as he turned his horse as if to leave.

"Maybe you can teach us more about the land and the Great Spirit," said John, looking with disgust at Gus.

Gus waved his hands in the air, "Come on Cuz, it's time to go back to Alva to check on all our stuff." *I really wanna git away from this old, weird Injun.*

"I'll come by in a week to see how you're doing," Old Timer said. *Maybe I can help–especially the kinder one–to survive on the prairie. I will come often to this land to bless it–perhaps blessing– will save them.* Then the ancient Cheyenne/Scottish man mounted his pinto pony with grace; he seemed to glide onto the bareback–he rode away like a quiet spirit.

John noticed that Gus was looking angry, "You want to go by your claim–now?"

"What? You want me to do that blessin stuff on my land, too– all that mumbo jumbo. Let's get outta here. It gives me the cold shivers. Go!" And with that Gus jumped on his horse, and began to trot across the plains to Alva, Colorado, fifteen miles to the north.

John followed; it took until the afternoon to arrive.

As they sat down for coffee at the train station's café, the owner said, "This is a tough place to live, and the only way we make it is to help each other, to stay connected. Yah, this a tough place to live," cautioned the toothless train agent.

The cousins looked at each other–sort of in doubt–maybe it wouldn't be as easy as they'd thought. Time would tell, but to hear that warning–twice in a day–was a bit foreboding.

"I'm going to ask a few more questions, if that's OK," said John, now more curious about their homestead than before. "Met an old fella out on our claim about three miles south of Fairview; he called himself Old Timer. Said his name was also Gregory MacPherson. What do you know about him?"

The agent, laughed, "Yeah, that would be Gregory. He's a great man, in my estimation. We call him Old Timer for respect, but his Scottish name is Gregory MacPherson. His Cheyenne name is Red Sun in Hair–for his red hair–just call him Red Sun. His Cheyenne mother was Shining Night Star, daughter of Old Gray Wolf, a spiritual leader of the Cheyenne–now they're all gone. Old Timer's father was Dr. Christopher MacPherson, a fine doctor who came from North Carolina around 1820. His first wife had died in childbirth; the baby was stillborn." The agent shook his head, "Sad. So he joined the Army to be a doctor on a western post– that's how he got to Bent's Fort."

As the agent finished his sentence, a woman of about fifty walked through the back doorway. Eyes shining excitedly, pushing aside her lanky husband, said, "Let me tell the story about him–it's such a romantic one." Her eyes grew dreamy and her mouth held a wide smile, "The story of Doc and his Cheyenne bride. You wanna hear it?

Both cousins replied, "Of course. We've got time."

As if she'd told the story many times before, the gray-haired woman began in a stage voice, "When Shining Night Star was about twenty, a smallpox epidemic swept across the Plains; she caught the fever. Her father, Chief Old Gray Wolf, feared his daughter would die like all the others had (shuddering for emphasis). In Bent's Fort, near the Cheyenne winter hunting grounds, was a small hospital. Doc MacPherson treated many Indians from all tribes, but the Cheyenne were his favorites, because they were so spiritual."

The storyteller's eyes became misty; "They say Shining Night Star was beautiful, with large, soft brown eyes, a happy maiden with many young Cheyenne braves in love with her. When she became ill, her people cried, 'Take her to the Fort'. So her parents did. The Doc told them that Shining Night Star was gravely ill, her fever very high, and they gave her water and bathed her often to lower the fever. Her face was filled with pox–sometimes they said she didn't know where she was. Her parents feared she'd gone to the Other Side. Then one day the fever broke. Through her tears Shining Night Star saw Dr. MacPherson for the first time. He had saved her, and she loved him–and he–her." The narrator even choked a tiny bit at this point in the tale.

She continued, "When it was time–three months later–for them to return to their Cheyenne village, Dr. MacPherson asked for Shining Night Star's hand in marriage. When Doc proposed, he supposedly said, 'I have seen the beauty beneath your scars, and I love your sweet heart and tender ways. Will you be my wife and live with me forever?' The gray-haired one sighed–then continued." She answered, 'Yes, my beloved Chris, you have made me whole again.'

"The tribe was happy and gave Doc an Indian name–Standing Tall Tree, for he gave people life." Then the taleteller put her head down as if to pray.

"Soon they married and then came their son Red Sun in Hair or Gregory, his Scottish name. He had the red hair and blue eyes of his father, but the strength and grace of a Cheyenne warrior, just as you saw him today–now nearly 80 years later." She punctuated the statement with a swoop of hands into the air.

Without pausing, she continued in a pensive, haunting voice. "The good doctor and Shining Night Star stayed at Bent's Fort for twelve years. When it was time for Red Sun to go to high school, they wanted him to have a good education, so they moved to North Carolina–where Doc had his medical education. Red Sun finished college there, but he didn't study medicine; he studied botany instead, as he loved prairie flowers and herbs.

"Shining Night Star lived in misery for seven long years, as she was never accepted by the people in North Carolina. With her dark skin and pocked face, some locals even said, 'She's dark as a blackie." The taleteller's face turned into a nasty grimace, "Shining Night Star was beautiful to her people and to Doc. So they returned to Bent's Fort."

Her voice then turned into an ominous whisper, "It was called the Month of the Freezing Moon, November 1864. Shining Night Star was going with some of her tribe to a ceremony in the winter at the southern part of the Colorado Territory. Red Sun went with his mother, as he was now a spiritual leader, following his grandfather Old Gray Wolf's legacy. Dr. MacPherson stayed at the Fort to care for the sick. The tribe, numbering about 300, led by Chief Black Kettle, stopped for the night on banks of the Sand Creek with the United States flag flying above their tents. This flag was a symbol that the Cheyenne were guaranteed to be protected by the U.S. government in their travel to the ceremony."

Her eyes looked downward as she continued, with tears now streaming from her eyes, "Suddenly without any warning an army of soldiers attacked the resting Cheyenne. Red Sun quickly mounted his horse to ride further north to warn other tribesman and gather warriors. The army, led by Commander John Milton Chivington, a weasel, raped, scalped, and killed over 150 helpless people; some say more. One was Shining Night Star, who ran carrying a child in each arm to escape the brutality. She was caught and stabbed many times, yet she held the children under her to protect them. The soldiers left her for dead.

"When Red Sun returned with other warriors, he found his mother dying, but still breathing and protecting the children. She whispered, 'Take the children. Tell your father that I love him with all my heart and also you, my beloved son, and that I will wait for him at the gate to the Great Hunting Grounds.' Then she turned her head and died."

The historian, now crying, continued, "Red Sun's heart was burning with anger and hatred toward the soldiers. He returned to Bent's Fort to shield his father and grieve for his mother.

"Do you now want to hear what then happened to Red Sun?" The old woman was even more excited, barely standing still.

Both John and Gus were fascinated. "Yes," they replied.

"The story is–strange, but true," she continued in a slightly ethereal voice, "Before the MacPherson's moved to North Carolina, Dr. Chris had built a home near the North Platte River– actually right here where the town of Alva is. Those were the summer hunting grounds for the Cheyenne, where there were abundant buffalo, small wild animals, and plants. As they grew older, Dr. Chris could no longer work the long hours of a physician, so they moved here to rest and only returned to the reservation for ceremonies. Shining Night Star loved their prairie farm and told Doc, 'when I die, bury me here.' So Dr. MacPherson, Standing Tall Tree, wrapped his wife's body in a white buffalo robe, and with a tribal entourage, carried Shining Night's Star's body in a wagon, all the way from Sand Creek to their prairie home. In a special Cheyenne ceremony they buried her. Doc guarded her grave, putting new flowers on it every day, even finding something to put there in the winter. One day about a year later, Red Sun found his father's body stretched across the grave holding in his hand a key marked 'Gate to the Great Hunting Grounds'. All the Cheyenne chiefs and many of the nations came to honor the man, the white doctor, who had saved so many of them.

"All this time Red Sun knew he wanted to be more Indian than white. In the Cheyenne Village he'd grown up with a maiden called Blue Meadow Flower. He wanted to marry her even then as a little boy! They are–like wolves–that mate for life. So the young chief brought Blue Meadow Flower as his bride to live on the prairie farm." Again the romancer looked heavenward, as though savoring a lovely memory.

"On the little farm they grew fruits, vegetables, and raised some livestock. It was like a garden on the prairie. Soon they had a baby, named Two Tongues, who could speak both English and Cheyenne–Two Tongues. He was bright and energetic–and loved by his parents. Two Tongues was a beautiful child with coal black hair like his mother and blue eyes like his father." The narrator sighed.

She continued, "In March of 1865, Red Sun went to Washington DC to ask President Lincoln to set aside land for the tribe in the Oklahoma as a reservation. Lincoln did do that (but it wasn't official until 1869). This land was to protect them from any further massacres. Red Sun was a tribal leader–as you probably noticed already.

"But while he was gone, a storm came out of the northwest near Alva with large black, angry clouds bringing rain and hail, but also a tornado. The snaking evil struck part of the town, and then the garden farm. The sucking wind tore off the roof and flung it far into the field. It picked up Blue Meadow Flower and his son.

"When the storm was over, neighbors searched for the mother and the little boy. Finally, late in the evening, both were found–the two–lying on top of an undisturbed haystack. Not a scratch on them–just like they were asleep, but they were dead. Blue Meadow Flower was holding her son, cradled in her arms, and he was resting on her breast (tears flowed, again). They both died at the same time looking peaceful, so it was said. All this happened almost fifty years ago!

"When Red Sun came home and found them, he rode his pinto pony over the prairie for days and nights, crying softly for his wife and his little boy, Two Tongues. He wanted to stay close to them–to be connected with them spiritually. Old Timer still lives right here, on his garden farm.

"That's why in March, like now, Red Sun remembers when the tornado came. So he rides the prairie, blessing the land to honor his parents–and Blue Meadow Flower–and–little Two Tongues. He decided to give up his hatred for the white people and instead to help them honor the land. You may hear Red Sun chanting early in the morning, as he gives thanks to Mother Earth and Father Sky. He is a wise man and respected both here and in our nation's Capitol. You'd be smart to have him as a friend."

"Well, that's quite a story. We know now why he asked if he could help us–he wanted to bless the land for us," said John looking a bit shaken. "Thanks for telling us the story." The two men turned and walked away quietly.

Gus looked stressed and upset. "I'm not quite so sure. You know, John, you're a college graduate, n you don't believe all this hokey, pokey–blessin stuff–and talkin to Mother Earth 'n Father Sky–do ya? Ugh!"

The station supervisor, overhearing the comment, stood up straight and retorted, "Maybe you do have degrees, but you'll find this prairie will teach you many lessons–more than any university! And Old Timer is the best teacher around."

"We'll try hard, you know that," called John. The two cousins left to go back home–to their land on the prairie.

Gus didn't say a word.

Chapter 2

PRAIRIE LIFE

January 1909

When Congress passed the Extended Homestead Act of 1909, thousands of risk takers spent hours learning about getting a place of their own–yes–on the Great American Desert.

"Look, it's only about an inch on the map from Iowa, across Nebraska, and into that tiny little corner of northeastern Colorado," Rose said.

"To homestead–it's the only way. Just think we can get nearly a whole section of land–FREE! A way to start over," replied her husband, John William.

"We'll be rich as ole Rockerfella', barons on the prairie," laughed Cousin Gus. "Do you suppose we'll need to fight Injuns?" Gus' wife Esther moaned.

"Nah, they's long gone, put out on some fenced in place in Oklahoma, where they'd belong. Good riddance, I'd say," said Gus smirking.

"We need to sell our family land right now–Papa Paul said he'd buy us out. The prairie land is free, but there'll be other expenses. Like hay for the livestock 'til we get our crops, and buildings. Gee Whiz–just a lot to do," John said.

"Yah, it's our chance–maybe the only chance we have to get outta this hole we's in. The family farm is gettin smaller 'n smaller, 'n Dad doesn't let up on me at all, always pushin for more work. We've got three half-grown young men for god's sake! I wanna be rich some day 'n that's not gonna happen in Storm Lake, Iowa!" Gus snorted.

"But where will the boys go to school, way out there? I don't see any towns around on the map at all, 'cept that little dot for Alva, the town where the Union Pacific lands us," whined Esther.

"Just may have to teach them ourselves, Esther. We can do it. Maybe our kids will become governors and senators, and we'll be the Ladies of the Land–living in mansions," laughed Rose. Thus began the saga of how the two Schultz families trekked across Iowa, Nebraska, and into the northeastern part of Colorado to become homesteaders, conquering the expanse of open territory known as the Great American Desert.

"Millions rushed to get rich in the Gold Rush of 1849 but no one stopped to live on this desert," said John William. "Now's our chance."

Others had more lucrative motives to settle the land. The railroad magnates, J P Morgan and P H Harriman, didn't want to cultivate the land, but had to save their trains from stampeding buffalo, a few marauding Indians, and roaming bandits. So they offered free transportation to families to move all their belongings from the east and to homestead on the prairie. Thus the vast space would become populated and a safe passage would be opened from coast to coast. Morgan and Harriman were no dummies.

Settlers knew little about the prairie except that it had been inhabited by millions of buffalo thriving on the prairie grass and providing food and shelter for the nomadic Plains Indians. However, no one else wanted to live on the dry, treeless and. To entice people in to come developing the desert, Congress extended the Homestead Act by doubling the amount of land given from 160 to 320 acres. Anyone, even a women, could stake a claim, and improve on it, plant crops, build a house of 12 X 24 feet, (dugouts counted as houses), and survive for five years. Then if they persevered, by the end of those five years the property was legally theirs.

The two Schultz families took up the quest and in spring 1909 began their homesteading.

March 21, 1909

Every bone in John's body ached. No trees shadowed the first rays of the sun, so morning came quickly. Four horses were neighing, snorting, and demanding attention. Burt and Babe were John's horses and Bell and Charlie–Gus's. They had survived the 28-hour trip in the Union Pacific boxcar crossing onto the prairie. Gus was still sleeping in his wagon, heeding the warning folks had given them, 'Sleep above the ground, as rattlesnakes are waking up and moving around now that the weather is warmer. Look out for them critters.'

"Makin coffee n the biscuits will be the usual," sighed Gus, as he rose reluctantly. "Won't it be good to have the women folks here to fix us real food?" For weeks their diet had only been coffee, biscuits, and jerky.

"My stomach will never waste another meal, once we get beyond this junk!"

"No argument there," replied Gus. "How bout our abundant buffalo chips. Whatever you want to call 'm, they stink!"

They'd been warned that the only firewood–fuel–on this treeless prairie would be the buffalo chips, so they'd gathered as many as they could. The millions of buffalo had been gone almost fifteen years, so the supply was very thin. Buffalo chips burned hotly and breakfast was quick.

"'Nough to get us goin," reminded Gus.

The stench of the fire made each cough. They spat into the air–putrid, dried buffalo turds–but the heat was welcomed.

Gus raised his arms to the sky, and shouted, "Think of it–it's–all ours!"

"But this wide openness puts me on edge. If there's just was one tree I'd feel better. Sort of like you're exposed to everything. Even the sounds are eerie–like the coyotes we heard howling last night. The howls seemed to echo and echo. Do we know what we were getting into?" John pondered again.

"'Nough of that! You're creepin me out. Here we are with all of our dreams 'n we're goin to build dugouts 'n grow crops." Gus laughed, "Sittin here, 'n this dry, rough prairie grass nothing to speak of–like where's the water? We're really in a desert! There's no way of goin back now. 'Member when we saw all the fliers.

FREE LAND, ours to own–just go west 'n homestead. We believed 'em, 'n here we are–our chance–if we can just survive. Makes you wonder how the Injuns could have survived," said Gus.

"That's right, but they didn't–and that's why they're gone. They're gone 'cause of our guns and horses, don't you think?" John asked.

Pulling up some tough prairie grass, Gus replied, "Nah, I think it's survival of the fittest, you know like Darwin wrote. Superior species will survive 'n we're just that–superior species. Can't deny it–the Injuns just wasted all this land. They wasted it, 'n we're here to finally rescue it from total extinction."

"Not as simple as that," answered John. "They were here thousands of years before us and had a balanced way of living. They didn't need railroads to race across the continent. Just can't see what the rush is all about, do you?" asked John.

"Think God gave it t' us to start new towns and cities, ones more advanced with great buildins, homes, churches, schools, not wide open prairies just filled with jackrabbits, gophers, coyotes, 'n snakes. No, we're to conquer this prairie 'n build a bigger, better way of life. It's our responsibility. If we just let it lay here–we ain't done our duty. God said 'Conquer the earth'," commented Gus.

"Maybe our duty was just to stay put in Iowa and not invade this land. Just imagine how it would be to have some outsiders come and take over your land. Can't get my mind around how that would feel–like if someone, somebody strange, would just march in and take over our Iowa farms. And then force us off the land, moving everything and us to some far-off place with a fence around it. Doesn't seem quite right, does it?" queried John.

"Why, John, you sound tetched in the head. Look, we got work to do. We need to first survive, then multiply 'n thrive–to break this dang virgin land 'n open the soil to grow lots 'n lots of food for everybody. Just imagine a hundred years from now, what this might look like–real houses 'n barns, with livestock growin fat from the land fed by our crops. Not just naked Injuns 'n teepees. 'N think 'bout the schools 'n churches we can build, not like the illiterate, heathen Injuns," concluded Gus.

"Not sure I agree, Cuz," remarked John, "you know they have a belief in the Great Spirit. And they have worship; it's just different than ours. Now that's all gone. Even wondered if we've been duped. Like when we were crossing Nebraska, I had to ask myself, 'How did this homesteading stuff begin?' Yeah, I know Lincoln signed the Homestead Act in 1862. We weren't even born then to get in on the rush. But this land–this prairie–is the leftover land that no one wanted. What's the real motive behind the deal? Was it to just get more farming done on this American Desert, or were there other reasons as well?'

He continued, "Remember the Alamo? That was just to keep the land for the United States and not to let Mexico keep any of that land. Now this seems like more of the same."

"We'll be opening the West for railroads and new communities," reminded Rose when they first began making plans to homestead. Nothing seemed to lessen their excitement of becoming good farmers of this land stretching from the Missouri River to the great Rocky Mountains. All that was needed would be strong, courageous young families to respond to the call given in the 1909 Extended Homestead Act–Free Land! Free Land!

The young mothers were eager to leave, to bundle all belongings–including six children, two cows, two dogs, dishes, bed frames, bedding, cook stoves, wash tubs, cooking utensils, more dishes, and plenty of flour and root vegetables, and plus hay for the livestock–onto an emigrant train. Only memories of beautiful homes, good schools, and even concert halls in Iowa would be left behind. Nothing could halt them, as they were total optimists. Would they to be disappointed?

No, thought John.

I know that my Rose, soft and tender, an artist with her violin, always laughing, is ready for new adventures. I've loved her since grade school. I was in the third grade and she in the first. Her flashing black eyes and shiny black hair made me happy. Best yet she was talented, playing the violin even then. Rose, tiny, could be fierce when encountered on the playground. Once I saw her tackle a big kid who was picking on a smaller one. 'Don't you ever hurt him again, or I'll bloody your nose,' I'd heard her yell.

We'd been sweethearts all through high school. Rose played her violin while I sang at all types of gatherings. We seemed to be one–the music–part of our breathing. We both went off to college after graduating from Storm Lake's high school–we both went to the University of Iowa. I studied architecture and Rose the violin.

Been married now 14 years–we're happy. Our three children are healthy,

John continued thinking, *Gus didn't go to college but worked hard on the family farm; he'd married a neighbor girl, Esther, soon after high school. We have different goals in life. Gus wants to be wealthy like his father, and I want to build beautiful things, like churches, schools, and concert halls. We want different things in life,* John thought.

Gus held up some turf; "I wanna be rich, John! I really don't care if anybody else is. I'll get mine first–even before you, Cuz! You're too dang kind-hearted," Gus laughed, "You'd give away your first glass of water–if there was one!" He laughed; they laughed together.

"Let's don't talk about water. I'm so thirsty I will just spit air; 'n the horses, glad they had water in Fairview when we came through. Gotta get those wells dug. Time we get busy. Just hope our women folk can tolerate these places–these mud houses with vermin of all kinds, dark, 'n leaky if it rains. If we can last for even a year, if we can just hold on 'til we can real houses built, ugh!" Gus said.

Was it a mistake? Would they survive? Each had different dreams, different ways: John, the dreamer, Gus, the schemer.

Gus thought, *How can I become king of all–from horizon to horizon–buildins like in Chicago–maybe even tall buildings– wealthy business men wearin suits of success, 'n drivin a new automobile built by Ford. 'N our sons, Mark, Matthew 'n Peter. Esther may be a problem–she's weak–not like Rose–Esther has always been so frail–complain'–having cramps–and whining–we'll see. Survival of the fittest–yes, that's me.*

However, when finished the dugout was still a dump, whatever the precision of the walls! Dark, damp, and creepy. Two tiny windows barely let in light; any additional light came from two dim, kerosene oil lamps. A smoke stack for the potbelly stove went straight through the roof. Nails pounded into scarce timber planks held a few shelves against the wall, for garments, bedding, dishes and pots and pans. An outhouse stood a few yards below on a slight depression near the front door. Rising simply as a lump in the prairie, the dugout home was hardly visible from a distance.

"Can't wait until I can build a proper house," said John.

"For now it'll keep the family safe from storms and the cold and heat. It'll work," remarked Old Timer, nodding his head in approval.

They built the same type of dugout on Gus' land. "Gads, don't know about Esther livin below the ground; she gets spooked by most everythin," Gus said, shaking his head. Next the hired men helped them built sheds from sod for the livestock and chickens.

'Cain't have 'em live below the ground like us humans," said Gus.

"Couldn't have done it without Old Timer's young men," reminded John. "Yup, you're right 'bout that," replied Gus.

"Just glad we had some money from the sale of our farms, or we could never have made it alone."

"You've been very fortunate, as too many homesteaders come without enough funds, so they don't make it. It still will be very hard, as sometimes the first crops don't produce. You'll be lucky just to make it through the first year," reminded Old Timer.

The morning breeze sighed–only whispers on the vast, unsettled prairie could be heard as the sun peeked over the unbroken horizon. It was still chilly in the oblong, dimly lit dugout home. John stumbled around in the dark. No aroma of coffee could be whiffed, only the stink of buffalo chips.

"Today's the day," John shouted to the mud walls, "the family arrives. I can't wait." He pulled on his long underwear and sang at the top of his lungs, "With someone like you, a pal so good and true, I'd like to leave it all behind and go and find–" His laughter resounded, as he remembered the song he'd sung for Rose–thinking he'd soon hold her in his arms. He'd even taken a tub bath the night before, scrambling to get enough heated water from the little potbelly stove.

He wished for a mirror. *Wonder if I've changed! It's been six weeks since I've seen my beloved Rose and the kids. Oh, God, please keep them safe.* With that and a few bites of jerky and leftover coffee, John fed the horses and hitched them to the wagon that would pull his precious cargo back across the trail from the train station. "Let's go!"

Babe and Burt, pulling the wagon, seemed as excited as John and began their trot immediately across the prairie to Gus's place.

A dim trail had formed, connecting the cousins' houses. Gus was ready to go with his team and wagon. "It's been a long time, right?–Cain't wait to see my boys–'n Esther–hope she's in a good mood. The snakes might spook her, 'n the bugs–but the dugout's good 'n sturdy. We'll see."

Gus went first, followed by John. The teams knew the trail to the train station, and didn't hesitate to trot. They arrived in the early afternoon.

"It's sure goin be different with the women folks 'round. Let's go buy some eggs and milk if the store has any. They'll need a lot more, but this'll be a start," Gus grinned.

Just then a distant whistle signaled the train's arrival. After a wait of about fifteen minutes the cousins could see their kids and then their wives getting off the train. John's kids ran toward them with happy looking faces and crying out, "Daddy, Daddy, Daddy." Even Gus's sullen sons smiled. Hugs and kisses and even tears were shared, as the families tumbled together. While the men went about the business of unloading belongings from the train, the wives and children ate at the cafe–perhaps their last 'civilized' meal for a long, long time.

"We'll have to come back several times to get all of the household goods, books, and farm equipment, but for today we'll take the bedding and clothes, and some things needed for washing," explained John.

Gus said, "Look at my boys–almost men." He was right, as his sons were tall and already teenagers. Gus continued, "You didn't plan it right, John, havin a girl first–what good is she?"

"Oh, mine's pretty good, just as she is," and John squeezed his nine-year old daughter, Margaret." He remembered Rose's many miscarriages, and the anguish weighing heavier with each loss. But, Margaret was a full-term baby. Joy–boy or girl–joy!!

"She won't help much on the homestead! Your young'uns Will and Hank–are too little to do much of anything. How old are they anyway?"

"Well, they'll grow. Will is six and Hank is three. They'll learn, but first they need to be in school."

"Maybe Rose will have to teach 'em all–she did go to college–Esther never did."

"We'll have to talk about that some more, but now's time to head home."

Flowers were blooming in the unbroken prairie; their color and fragrant sweetness welcomed the families. The land was graceful with waving green grass, thick with small, wild animals just right for hunting: prairie chickens, grouse, cotton tail and jack rabbits. Soon the sunset and the stars showed the way. The clear, open night skies displayed vast seas of almost touchable stars. And the wind–never stopped blowing, sometimes so hard it was difficult to stand upright. It was dark when John turned the wagon onto their trail and halted in front of the mound of dirt–their dugout house.

John went ahead to light the lamps. But with so much new to see, no one heard the gasp as Rose went down the steps into the dugout. Her eyes told the story of shock, disbelief, and fear.

"It's not exactly a castle," John William said quietly as he held her hand, standing on the earthen floor and hoping for more light.

"It's a wonderful, safe place, and I can see how carefully you made the walls." Only the whites of Rose's eyes shone in the dark– but her gut turned inside out–trapped like a rat–oh my God. Little Hank clung to his daddy's neck and put his cheek on John's chest. "I feel kin'a sick, Daddy."

"You'll be OK, just take a deep breath, and pretend you're in a rabbit hole. Pretty soon you'll be able to see lots of things," John urged.

"It's so dark," little Hank began to cry.

So it was for the first week; each day became less scary and more intriguing, as the children learned chores and got work done. The wives took on the challenge of making their dugouts livable. Inside, the simple, earthen floor also made a welcome home for worms, bugs, and spiders. For the women, the first priorities were food, water, and safety. All was unfamiliar to them; in Storm Lake it was easy to find flour, lard, eggs and milk, but here there was no supply. You had to grow it yourself or do without. The first year, it was mostly–doing without.

Fairview was three miles away and only a cross road on the prairie with a sod Lutheran church, a sod schoolhouse, and a sod grocery store. A larger town, Hopetown, with a population of about 100 people, was about ten miles west. There stood another sod schoolhouse, Catholic and Lutheran churches, a grocery and hardware store with a few staples like salt, sugar, and kerosene oil for lamps, a blacksmith shop, and a pool hall for men. In a small room on the main street a doctor had his office to set bones, stitch up cuts, and treat fevers and bleeding. He kept a few medicines and bandages, and oh, yes, he also delivered babies at home, as well as did a couple of midwives in the area.

Chapter 3

LIVING LIKE GOPHERS

The only source of knowledge is experience.
  Albert Einstein

The first month passed like a blur. But by the second month, life was no longer so exciting. July was hot and fierce summer storms brought lightning and thunder. The horses and cows needed more water than they had in their buckets, so the men brought large metal tanks in the wagons, and filled them with water pumped from the windmill. The tanks supplied the horses with water and the kids, a swimming pool.

Rose wrote her first letter to Papa:

May 20, 1909

Dearest Papa,
We are fine, but miss you very much. John William and Cousin Gus work from daybreak to setting sun. Gus's sons work beside them, and our Will tries hard, but he is only six years old. Hank wants to work, too, but he is still so little. There are rattlesnakes and other problems out in the fields. Every day they plow more and more of the sod and plant seeds and a few tree saplings. They say they have never seen such hard soil—nor have they lived where there are no trees. Papa, it is beautiful, but sometimes almost frightening to see the sky from horizon to horizon—so open—so flat. You can see for miles and miles, all around. The stars are huge, bright, almost touching the ground. John says, 'God has blessed this land with His great love for the earth.'

We are happy living in what is called a "dugout"–hardly a real home, but a shelter from the elements. Other creatures also like to share these mud houses with us–like bugs, spiders, and snakes. The dugout is carved deeply into the hard soil–and has a tarpaper roof, raised up on sod. It's hard to explain. It'll be cool in the heat of the summer and, we understand, warm in the winter. We had a couple of rainstorms that didn't get us wet. Sometimes rain does cause mud to come down from the roof, and if there is hail sometimes it breaks through. We have to carry water in from the pump. The windmill works all the time, as the wind never stops blowing.

Old Timer, a Cheyenne Indian–a friend, says it has been very dry this summer. He worries about prairie fires, which usually come in the early spring. That must be very scary.

I cook outside so we don't have so much smoke in the dugout, wash our clothes on a washboard. We have a hole in the ground for our toilet. Our real house will not look like this, John promises. By next January we will order our lumber, for frame houses. Until then we will make do in these "homes."

Our horses, Burt and Babe, are jewels that pull wagons and plows. The rough roads and trails are very bumpy, and when it rains, the ruts turn into rivers. The horses seem content with all the grass to eat. The grain is planted and is growing already. Harvest is still two and a half months away. John bought another milk cow from one of the families who live near Fairview because the kids need milk. We now have at least three-dozen chicks in some pens. The dog keeps the coyotes from getting them, but the hawks are also a threat and have to be shooed away. The hens should be laying eggs soon, and a few roosters will be ready to eat as well.

Right now we depend on all the wild animals we can kill and eat, like prairie chickens, pheasants, and rabbits. It's not like buying meat from a butcher. I must be very brave about these things. I'm using all the ideas Mama taught me about cooking with little. I try to use fresh things every day, but over the winter that will be impossible.

Margaret is quite happy. As soon as we arrived, she planted the seeds you sent–onions, peas, beans, carrots, potatoes, and turnips. Will helps John William by carrying things for him, like water when he works outside. But little Hank is into everything–has such a temper–has your mother's red hair.

Only Cousin Esther is fretful, crying a lot, and homesick. She hates living around snakes and bugs and with all the wind blowing. I try to comfort her and Gus does, too. I wish so much for the violin, to play some music, and we could even dance. John William plays his mouth harp at night, and we even sing hymns with it. Remember how I used to play Mozart for the cows in the barn? You laughed and said you knew it made them give more milk!

We have to stay healthy and happy–and in God's good hands. I wish you were here to see the miracle unfolding before our eyes. Yes, Papa, this is ours, a chance to begin. God has blessed us, and we give thanks every day.

We miss you so much. Wish all the family our best, and we pray that someday soon we will meet again.

Your loving daughter, Rose

As he read the letter, Papa Paul lowered his head. As he prepared for bed in the basement of his eldest daughter, Carolyn, he thought. *I watched John William and Gus leave Iowa, but they didn't know that I wanted to go with them. Oh–for a chance to start over. When I left Germany, the Valley of the Rhine, I took a little sack of dirt, just to smell it now and then. When we finally found land in Iowa, then I was happy again–just to touch the earth–early in the spring.*

Sometimes it was hard, but I knew the earth, and it knew me–we were connected. I watched which seeds were the hardiest, looking at each grain, seeing if it was full and smelled strong. I would even chew a few and see if the strength to grow was there. Neighbors would ask. 'What do you think, Paul? Are these the best to save as seed crop?' They'd ask questions after questions. I helped when I could–looking over the seeds–feeling the energy. Grandpapa taught me to feel the bad ones, the dead ones. I could see the low vitality in those that would not reproduce. Oh, I love to feel the seeds–then watch in the fields which ones really did the best. Yes, I know I was a good farmer–and our crops were the best around Iowa. If I could only be with John and Rose now. Paul turned his head sadly to his empty pillow, feeling unwanted and, very lonely.

Protected by God's good grace, there was no hail that year; within minutes such a storm could wipe out a year's supply of wheat or corn. Fortunately the crops grew fast, and a small harvest began the first of August. A winter's supply of hay was ready for the livestock. The soil was virgin, rich, and energized. The gardens flourished and provided potatoes, squash and dried beans to last throughout the winter. Root cellars would hold them. Rose said, "And in case of a tornado we're to run to the root cellar. That will save us."

Neither Rose nor John complained, as every night they would read the Bible, sitting by the oil lamp, reviewing the day and the blessings they had. "Yes, I know we could sit around and complain, but what good would that do? We're pioneers who will triumph; yes, we do miss our families and we could cry a lot, but I'd rather sing and have you read me love poems," laughed John.

Rose responded, "I'm too tired to think of anything, but just fall onto our mattress and sleep. But, I like to dream about what our real house will look like. It will be two-storied and have a big pantry to hold all our food. Oh, to really bake again! And, I'll plant flowers especially yellow roses by the front gate. I love yellow roses, darling. They are always so happy, just like you, and the fragrance is the sweetest in the world."

Although Rose never complained, she felt so closed in by the earth house. *No air and no light–like a coffin,* she thought.

Under the warmth of their goose feather coverlet cuddling together as they did every night, John reminded her, "One thing we must always protect is the seed crop. Without that we'll have no crops next year. We'll keep the best seeds that we have so that we continue to have good crops. Keep them in this sturdy box that we'll call The Promise Seed. It will be our connections from one year to the next. We can't let any mice or rats get to that box, so we'll keep it right here by the steps and touch it every day as a blessing."

One morning in October, frost made sheen on the grass. "Soon snow will close us off from the outside world," worried Rose.

The first major snow storm came in early November, and nearly buried the dugout. John pulled snow off the tar roof with a rake. After that came a blizzard, blowing snow so hard, at a horizontal level. No one could see the horses and cows in their shed. The chickens were protected by the thick sod wall and lots of straw. By the end of the storm, the door to the house would not open until the sun came out. The family was held captive for three days under ground.

"Let's hope we don't have any more of those." pleaded Rose, as she felt so closed in the earth house. No air and no light.

"We'll make it to spring," promised John, "then we'll have our new house!"

Margaret and Will had played every game they ever knew and became restless. Hank was sick with a cold most of the winter. When eating, he'd scream, "No more MUUUUUUUSH." The sympathetic looks he got showed that everyone else felt the same way. John William rocked and sang to him, but the cries continued. It was a trying time, locked up forever it seemed in that dirt house, with a tar roof about to blow off. The nights were long–very long– and the lamp oil was in short supply. It was dark most of the time. Rose told stories and more stories about living in Iowa. John sang. He noticed that Will had a special voice–already–at age nearly seven–a clear voice with an excellent ear for pitch. When Will would sing, Hank would wail–he was jealous.

Things stayed simple and orderly. Margaret helped her mother set the table with the few dishes they had for daily use, and brought the milk jug in from the storage sod-shed where it rested in a pail of cool water. The snow cave stored other food like salted meat and root vegetables.

"It's been almost six months since we've had any fresh vegetables. I'm so hungry for a fresh tomato or lettuce. And we haven't seen anyone else for a whole month. I hope everyone is still alive!" cried Rose.

"We'll make it, just a couple of months, and it will be spring," John reminded them all. "We'll survive!"

Thanksgiving came and went, and Christmas Eve. They celebrated it in the dugout, pretending that it was a manger scene, but that seemed sad, and pretending didn't make it better. In time even festival days faded into dim memory.

Chapter 4

PRAIRIE FIRE

Even when the way goes through Death Valley, I'm not afraid when you walk at my side. Your trusty shepherd's crook makes me feel secure. Psalm 23 The Message Eugene H. Peterson

At last, spring was in the air. You could feel the earth awakening. The sighing of the morning breeze was the only sound on the vast, unsettled prairie as the sun peeked over the unbroken horizon on that clear equinox day in March 1910. It was still chilly in the dimly lit sod house. Dawn was just spreading light across the eastern horizon–'red sun in the morning–sailors take warning!' John smiled remembering the old adage.

But this was a day to rejoice, as it was the beginning of spring– March 21st. Soon Old Timer would come and bless the land. Hope he comes soon, thought John. He could feel the breeze hurrying to waken the sleeping earth.

"This is the day," he shouted. "Yes, Gus and I are loading up the lumber for our houses." He laughed, as this was the day he had been waiting for. Lumber ordered in January was to arrive March 21st and so the telegram said, "Lumber arrived!"–Such a sweet message.

"Just getting the lumber will make me feel like we are on our way to a real house–out of this tomb. Old Timer says we had a very mild winter; hardly any snow fell. Perhaps that was good, as we still needed to patch the tarpaper roof many times. Old Timer warns that the ground is too dry for seeds to germinate. He worries that we won't have a crop at all. Guess he should know as he has a degree in botany and has lived here for a long, long time. The ground fairly crackles as you walk on it, even from the house to the horse shed. But we've done a lot our first year. So it may be O,K," he reassured himself.

We'll work as a team—finishing the insides of our houses by June, as well as plant all the crops. That gives us three months—a lot to do. But oh, Rose and the kids will be so happy. She hasn't said much about the dugout; she shudders, as the spiders are coming out now and then worms and all kinds of bugs! Every inch of the inside of that mud house is full of insects, and they are coming to life now that it isn't bitter cold. Rose never complains, just takes her hot iron and squashes each one she sees. What a strong woman she is!

Walking briskly to get the horses hitched to the wagon, John noticed that Babe was fidgeting, moving her head up and down and snorting loudly. "What's up girl? What's bothering you today?"

Burt, too, seemed restless, so John filled their water tanks from the well and gave them more hay to eat. Noticing they were still jumpy, he said, "Perhaps there is a coyote or rattlesnake around. I'd better look; something isn't right!" John William gazed around feeling something in the air, "What's that?"

He saw way off on the horizon—a faint haze—fog—or maybe even fire? Looking closely he was certain something was not right, but what was it?

Thinking ahead, John thought, *I'd better harness up Babe and take the wagon with a plow, take a look out farther in the field. As he did, he saw that indeed there was a fire—far, far off on the southern horizon—perhaps five miles away. I'd better check in with Gus on this one, as I can't tell if it is coming this way or going farther south.* He turned the wagon around, got out, opened the dugout door and called down to Rose, "Honey, I'm going to go over to Gus's and see if they know anything about a prairie fire. I'll be back as soon as I can. Keep an eye on it, and if you have to, go to the root cellar—or keep the blankets wet to stamp out any flames,"

"Be careful, John, be careful," Rose called. And she heard him call, " I'll be back soon."

The wagon bounced on the dirt trail to Gus's. John realized that although he'd heard of prairie fires, he had never experienced one. Indians feared them even more than tornadoes.

Several other neighbors were already at Gus's house; it was the closest to the fire. They'd seen the haze and smoke on the horizon. "Best take our plows and shovels and go down to see what we can do, if it is a fire coming our way," they all mumbled.

"I'm on top of it, pull out your wagons. Hope you all brought plows and shovels; we may have a lot more to do than we think. Never fought a fire before, but have heard that it can be very dangerous. We have to plow a fire strip at least twenty feet wide and that takes work. Let's go," John shouted. So they did.

"Some places were already plowed and planted for the season–that'll help, but we need to cut through some fences." John yelled, as his wagon headed toward the fire.

"Don't get too close," called Gus, "'member the winds can switch directions."

As they got closer, they saw several other wagons and men hurriedly plowing about ¼ mile north of the fire, but it seemed to be spreading closer and closer. The sky darkened, covered with black smoke; the winds wailed. Flames soared 30 feet up, marched left to right, and swirled back again. They engulfed everything and anything with their conquering force. The smell of smoke and rising heat were overwhelming, but the men–continued on.

John William pulled off a plow and hitched it to Babe. He began frantically plowing at a parallel line to the fire. Watching as he went, John stayed at a safe distance–the other men did the same, scooping with their shovels and yelling back and forth, "Look out if the wind shifts, so we don't get trapped," one called. Babe was nervous, jerking her head this way and that, trying to see the danger.

John kept saying, "Good girl, Good girl." The blinders on her halter helped; even with the overwhelming odor of burning brush, she couldn't see the flames that came closer and closer.

"Fall back–farther away," one of men shouted. "The wind is shifting. Turn back toward the north and get out to a safer distance!" By now the flames were reaching forty feet high and the heat was truly fierce. Men, horses, and wagons began their retreat.

The wind shifted again, moving flames away from the fighters. John moved toward the receding flames to make a bigger swath of plowed ground. It was hard to manage the plow on the hard, dry dirt. Again the wind shifted, and this time the flames swirled right back toward John and Babe. Babe saw the approaching flames and reared up frightened and screaming; she tipped the plow over and John with it. Struggling to pull himself up, he let go of the reins momentarily.

Feeling the slack, Babe bolted and ran wildly away from the flames–the plow bounced along. The flames followed their own path, swirling higher and wider and the rising wind brought them into a big circle. John was caught in the middle–flames whirling round and round the brave young man. His black silhouette jumped around, but became smaller, and then–fell.

The strong winds swallowed up his screams of pain and fear. "Oh, God help me, help me–save me–Lo I walk through the valley"–and no more words came from his mouth. Soon only the wind was heard, high, screaming, and as if–laughing. Flames continued their hungry path, burning everything–even John William. There was no way others could save him, as flames were now covering at least a half-mile in width and gaining strength.

Suddenly out of the north flew a figure on a pony, a figure with a grisly face and long red hair. "Back, damn, you, back, Mahoe, I call on you, back damn you, back!! The man on the pony went from side to side, yelling as he went, "Back, damn you, back, Honeheveho–help me, your brother." Flames continued, but then slowly they began to sputter–and–lessen. Wind lessened, then stopped, and reluctantly the flames fluttered–and–petered out. Smoke became a thin layer, lifted, and was–gone.

Shuddering, the firefighters stopped in their tracks and with mouths wide open. They said nothing, but they knew they'd seen a miracle. Why had the wind and flames suddenly stopped?

Old Timer raised his arms to the sky and with a loud scream yelled, "Why, why Mahoe? His face contorted in anger, then slowly eased, and his head dropped to his chest. Only his lips moved–as if in prayer. Then slowly, picking its way through the remaining smoldering embers, his pinto carried him to John William's blackened body.

Slowly Old Timer dismounted and slid gently to John's side. He picked up the still-smoking corpse, covered with black soot, eye sockets empty, hair mainly gone, and skin falling from his hands and arms. "My brother, my brother, my beloved John, why, why, why?"

He held John to his heart, "I came as fast as I could, my beloved brother; I'm so sorry I was too late," great tears streamed down the ancient's face, as his hair covered John's face. Carrying him as a cradled baby, Old Timer brought his body to the closest wagon, Gus's, and gently laid it there.

The evil thing had spanned half a morning. The men took shovels and pounded out the remaining embers and hot spots. They could not bring themselves to even look at John Williams' body. All stood silently. What could they say? They had lost their friend, their cousin, and could only bring his burned corpse back to Widow Rose.

It was the saddest day of their lives. How quickly a life was snuffed out in this relentlessly cruel land. They remembered the verse from Matthew 6:30; "If God so clothe the grass of the field, which today is and tomorrow is cast into the fire–" Gus took off his jacket and placed it over John's face, and the wagons moved together to John and Rose's homestead. Old Timer rode his pinto slowly beside the wagon; his face was like stone. They trudged to Rose's dugout. How could they speak? What could be said?

Rose and the children had seen only distant flame and smoke, had placed wet sheets over part of the roof. "Daddy, Daddy," cried Margaret as she saw Babe bounding over the sod with the bouncing plow behind her. Babe panted and snorted loudly. Rose couldn't see her John! Will hung closely to her, as they saw, in the far distance, Gus's horse pulling a wagon, and Old Timer riding quietly beside it. The ominous sign–they did not hurry.

"Where's Daddy?" screamed Will.

Margaret's mouth was open. No words came out.

Rose only stood stiffly looking toward the coming wagon. "I know, I know," her heart was breaking–"I know my John was burned, but maybe he still lives–maybe he does. Oh please, dear God, don't take my John away. Oh, please, dear Lord, we love him so–." She was hardly breathing when the wagon arrived, carrying the body of her John. Gus couldn't say a word. Old Timer's face was covered with soot.

Only Old Timer dismounted and came to hold Rose. "He's gone, my dear, dear sister Rose; he's gone." His old, worn-out body shook violently; he cradled hers to his heart. He sobbed wildly.

"Please, Lord, let him hold me one more time. Please, Lord, just one kiss goodbye." Quickly Rose climbed into the wagon and uncovered John's face, now charred and black, all hair gone. She gently touched the places where his mouth and mustache had been, and the sockets where his eyes once had looked upon her with gentleness and love.

"My John, my John," was all she could say. "You are always in my heart–you are not gone."

Old Timer held back, as the memories of losing his wife and son came back to him.

He couldn't breathe. Sorrow knows no ending.

Gus gently lifted Rose out of the wagon and carried her small frame down, down into the dugout. The shock was too much for all of them, as they looked around the tiny room. The morning sun stood halfway up the sky, full and promising, but there was no promise in this Schultz house–the spirit had died. How would they manage? Soon wagons of neighbors and Cousin Esther and her sons came–all with sympathy too hard to even express.

"We'll take care of the arrangements, Rose." And so they did. The burial next morning was simple and quick. That morning had an overcast sky, as if it, too, was sad. As if the whole world were connected, even the birds seemed absent, and the wet-fire smell of dew on the ashes made a mockery of yesterday's tragedy. The coffin, a box quickly hewn with soft blue satin material Rose had brought with her to make a dress for Margaret now lined John's final resting place.

She placed beside his burned body a small, dried, yellow rose that had been in her wedding bouquet, now the only symbol of her love for this magnificent soul mate, gone before his time. The simple coffin contained the dust of a well lived, but short life.

Standing beside it, Old Timer slumped over, looking well over one hundred years old. John William's dreams of the homestead would now take shape in the hands of Widow Rose and his children.

Cousin Gus offered a prayer and a Bible reading from Job 14. 'He springs up like a flower and withers away, like a fleeting shadow he does not endure.'

As the group continued crying, little Will's voice began to sing, "Abide with me, fast falls the evening light; Hold Thou Thy cross before my closing eyes–shine through the darkness and point me to the skies, in life, in death, Oh, Lord abide with me." His voice, strong and showing signs already at age seven that Will was to have the same baritone voice of his father. He led the group of mourners, who raised their voices in unison.

As the small group of mourners left the little cemetery about four miles from John Williams' dugout–now only Rose's–she threw herself upon the fresh grave, crying, barely speaking:

"John, John, my beloved husband–my soul mate". Her children stood nearby, quietly. Seeing them, she rose, got into their wagon, and went home.

None of the men ever talked about the unbelievable action–that miracle of Old Timer–how he'd shouted against the flames–and they died down triumphs between this half-breed, Cheyenne-Scottish man and the powers of the Spirit.

So the men knew–they knew what John William always knew–this was a very special man living in their midst. In the next years they would see more.

Chapter 5

ROUGH EDGES

Out of suffering have emerged the strongest souls, the most massive characters all seared with scars. –
Khalil Gibran

Fresh morning dew against her cheek couldn't soften the rough straw she huddled on. Curled in a fetal position, uncombed black hair drifted down her back spreading like a dark blot against the golden hay. Wide eyes stared at nothing–blankly into the growing gold of dawn. Turning slightly she wrapped her shawl yet more tightly. Sobs rose deeply within her chest. Grasping at handfuls of straw, she groaned, "No, no, no–it cannot be. John William come back. John, John, my beloved John William–our dreams have just begun. You can't leave. John–my John," she twisted deeper into the hay.

"We have no way out. No, John, it cannot be. Come back, hold me tightly, sing to me. Your body–the only one I've ever known–each curve, each muscle, your soft brown eyes, your laughing lips." Wails began to rise from her open mouth–high and into the morning dawn–the wail heard throughout time and around the world when loved ones die.

"I'm lost. I will never find my way again." She spread prone across the straw mattress, as if it held her John. "Brown eyes always fixed on me since in first grade. We were never apart. You held me when it thundered. You smiled and gave me hope when I first began to accompany you as you sang the Schubert songs. We danced as one, seeing only each other–everywhere–any time–in the ballroom, the kitchen, the field. You were my melody, my rhythm–you were my North Star. As our bodies joined as lovers/husband

and wife, we were not two but one, united in our passion–our faith."

The sobs began again, "No John. No, come back!" Each child when born was your creation. You'd call each name: Margaret, William, and Henri; each has half of your soul and half of mine. No, John, no. We were to walk together into God's sunset, not this–not now–"

Her wails rose higher and higher into the morning. The wind was the only audience, and it didn't cease to blow.

"Wind–Damn you, DAMN YOU," she shouted. "Where do you come from? The devil? From HELL. You caused my John William to die, because of you, damn wind; the flames circled and leaped. No one could control you, Damn Wind!"

Rose thrust her head deeper and deeper into the straw, somehow hoping to obliterate the whining sound of wind. The smell of smoke wafted sadly in the early morning air, marking a memory of the prairie fire that yesterday had scourged out life in this windswept, treeless hell.

Finally, the moon walked across the sky. Rose sat up, straightened her hair, wrapped her shawl around her body, and emerged slowly up the stairs of their dugout–their home. Behind her, the three children still slept on their blankets–hoping to waken from their long nightmare and find it wasn't true. But 'Daddy is dead.' Darkness had gone, and no one moved; no one ate, they just–slept. Hoping to forget. Then a new morning challenged them.

Deathly silence embraced the earth; no coyotes howled, no cows mooed. Just silence. One figure stood in the lingering dawn, a man with long flowing hair; his arms raised heavenward, chanting and praying by the graveside. He moved silently as a whisper; no one came by there. He stood three days and three nights, continuously praying, then went away. Three days had passed.

Sky met horizon as a thin grey line–not fog–not cloud, but the last drift of night.

Morning yawned. No wind, just silence, just quiet–except for the faint crunch of moving feet across the crust of the barren prairie sod. A tiny silhouette–like a semi-colon–moved slowly, slightly unsteady. Perhaps it was one who had too many slugs of whiskey the night before. The slouched figure continued across an unseen path toward a shed of some sort. Head covered; no features could be seen. Coming closer the figure grew larger, enough to show a face in shadow, shrouded by a woman's shawl. It was a small woman, of about thirty-five years. Bent over, eyes piercing through the dim–a mouth drawn tightly into a thin line. Approaching the shelter, a pair of horses raised their heads, nostrils flared. The smaller chestnut's eyes looked sad, the head dropped close to the ground, sweeping the straw. Not a sound was heard.

Suddenly the silhouetted woman threw open her shawl. She raised one hand holding a pistol and pointed it at the chestnut horse. The shawl fell back; unruly black hair splayed across her shoulders. Eyes glowing like red coals in a settling fire, she hissed, "Babe, you betrayed me." The chestnut neighed softly, eyes filled with terror. A slight smell of smoke still hung about her glossy coat.

Long, slender fingers that once held the violin bow looked strangely unfamiliar as they unlocked the trigger's safety catch. Tendons stretched tightly like steel. The pistol barrel rose upright beneath her jaw.

"I won't feel a thing; you will see me die just as you did John William," the woman whispered. "You will be the first to witness my answer to this unforgiving, god-forsaken land."

The chestnut pranced slightly to the left–then to the right. Nostrils flared and the head rose and fell as if nodding to say, "Yes, yes."

Sobbing now the woman cried, "God help me; there is no hope–my John is–gone. Our dreams are dead. All I want is to close my eyes and let the angels take me to his side."

The gray line of morning became wispy gold as dawn broke. At that moment a smaller silhouette dashed across the horizon, crying out ,"Mama, Mama, Mama. Don't do it."

Startled, the woman glanced quickly at a small boy standing in front of her–perhaps all of seven years old. His soft chocolate eyes were brimming with tears, young lips trembling; his body shuddered.

"We love you, Mama; we need you, Mama," his small voice whispered. Her outstretched hand still grasped the pistol that cuddled her lower jaw. He knew the bullet was a second away.

"Go back, Will, go back. I can't live. I must go; go back!" the woman rasped.

"No, Mama; no, Mama. We need you. We're all alone."

A breeze suddenly swished dark leaves in front of the woman. The horses stirred, and the boy's voice echoed against the morning sky–"All alone–all alone– all alone–"

Gently, the small boy reached up and took the pistol. He methodically emptied each chamber and placed the bullets into his pants pocket. His eyes still brimmed with tears, as he took his mother's hand. He looked older now, perhaps nearly grown up. Will led his mama back across the path to the small dugout. She walked stiffly, as if in a trance. Inside a smaller boy and a young girl still slept. The grieving woman slipped downward on the steps and then turned and tenderly touched–the wooden box marked– The Promise Seed–then to a straw mattress on the earthen floor. Will laid down beside his mother, as she drifted off to sleep.

For the rest of their lives neither spoke of that dawn. They would keep the secret between them, although Will's eyes would never forget the image of a pistol under his mother's chin. Even as he grew very old, sometimes at night, you might hear Will cry out in dreams, "No, Mama–we're all alone."

Chapter 6

SEND FOR PAPA

Heroic responses in ideals and conduct are a choice of regal dignity in the presence of new Earth and Heaven.
Helen Keller, *Let Us Have Faith*

When the telegram arrived, Papa Paul hesitated to open it. Telegrams in 1910 were only sent when there was a death or other catastrophe. Bad news travelled fast. Paul lived with his eldest daughter, Carolyn, her reluctant husband, George, and three whiny adolescents. Not a happy situation, but one he had to tolerate. The son-in-law, George, had no ambition! He was a lazy bum, delivering mail–never getting a callous on his lily-white hands. Besides that, George seemed to resent having Paul around; feeling this old man of almost eighty was a nuisance–in the way. (This in spite of the fact that Paul had bought the house for them) Paul slept in the basement, for peace and quiet, they told him. *Yes, to keep me quiet,* thought Papa.

'Come, help; John William died in fire!' Rose said in the telegram. His heart pounded. *How could it be; he was barely forty.* Paul sobbed loudly. *But quite a risk taker, and so in love with my Rose,* he pondered. *They could dance and laugh whenever, as in his mind he remembered them, twirling around the living room, gazing into each other's eyes. Now John is gone; how can she survive?* Paul reflected.

"Yes, I can help!" he shouted into the empty room. He continued, "What a chance I have to help–to teach those grandchildren the smell of the earth, the touch of the seeds, to honor this gift from God. I know I can still lift more than most men, and certainly more than those who are eighty, like I am."

Peering into the bathroom mirror he saw the face of a man grown old, his beard and hair still auburn red with flecks of white. His gnarled hands, once the strongest in the country, were still broad and tawny, nimble. Paul stood tall, upright, with a proud, sturdy stance.

"I can still work the fields, drive a team of horses, and butcher a pig. I can help! and–I will."

Towering over 6'4", even at his age, Paul was unaccustomed to being viewed as a nuisance. His strength of body and character were known throughout Iowa–big, tall Paul. His flowing light auburn hair and beard had only slight speckling of gray and white, and his piercing blue eyes were steady and fearless. Seeds of a German mother and French father had produced one child, Paul, known in the Rhineland as a French/German bastard.

Being a half-breed would not stop this gifted young man. Half Breed!–instead of cowering in fear Paul triumphed over discrimination, and became a man of unusual wisdom and talent. His father, Henri Pinot, a short Frenchman, came from a family of musicians–violinists. Paul's mother–Frieda, Germanic, tall, elegant and shrewd, came from an agricultural family of prestige and wealth. This young redheaded woman was smitten by the amorous musician; he was totally in love with this aristocratic creature.

Dressed in the latest fashion, the statuesque beauty held every eye as she entered the concert hall to be enthralled by the concertmaster, her beloved husband, Henri. They were a favorite couple in the social circles of Strasburg, Austria.

So it was natural that all expected their son, Paul, who even at the age of nine played the rare and valued Steiner violin passionately, would someday take his father's place as concertmaster.

However, Paul's heart held a different dream, that of being a horticulturalist. The rich earth of the Rhineland and the careful mentoring of his German grandfather had taught him the generative qualities of seeds, discerning which were best for abundant crops. Although the area was to become famous for grape growing, it was also a place of wise farmers who studied the cycles of planting, the patterns of rain and wind. Being the early scientists of farming, especially of seed crops, Paul's kinfolk became rich.

Even as an adolescent Paul's height, strength, and special knowledge and love of seeds made him a renowned 'seeds' expert. He would sit for hours examining seed saved from one year to sow the next. Paul knew that farmers depended upon careful sorting and saving of the best seeds–year to year, the seed crop, the promise seed.

Mentored by the best in the Valley, Paul carried this knowledge with him as he immigrated to the New World. "I must join my cousins, but Mama and Papa, you'll soon come to the land of promises. Yes, you will!" The plans were made.

Young Paul, at age twenty, shared the risk-taking character of his parents. As young people in love, his parents, Frieda and Henri, had married outside the norm–a French groom and a German bride. "Yes, dear son, some people will call you a French bastard, they will hurl insults at you, but you must not be afraid–take a chance–follow your dreams and your loves."

So Paul left to begin farming in the New World, expecting that soon his parents would follow. However, that reunion never came; both parents died in a tragic fire that razed their elegant home. Fortunately Henri's fine violin–the Steiner violin–was kept at the Conservatory and was not lost. Paul's childhood friend, Trudy, would soon carry it to America, carefully. At age 21 they married and settled on the rich farmlands of western Iowa. She endured miscarrying two sons, but birthed and raised daughters, Carolyn and Rose.

Papa Paul remembered Rose: small, almost five feet tall, and not the prettiest of his two daughters, but the strongest. Her strength was in her eyes, so black and perceiving, and in her voice, soft and mellow, convincing–like a melodic mourning dove. And her small hands with long, tapering fingers were built for the violin–that she loved so much. Such a rush of feelings–mixed–for he really cared for Rose–his tiny, fragile–sweetest child–now mother of three and 37 years old–and a widow.

Thinking of the tragedy, Paul grieved the loss of John William Schultz–his son-in-law–his true son. John, too, was good–small and lean–but lightning fast in his movements. *He is–was–such a happy, laughing man,* Paul remembered.

They were never afraid to try new things–like homesteading," he recalled firmly. In spite of loving Iowa, they were the first to go and take advantage of the 1909 Enhanced Homestead Act. Cousins Gus and John William could even compound their acreage by cultivating next to each other. After farewells, the Schultz cousins set off for the West, taking a Union Pacific train that would carry them and their families to their homesteads. Earlier pioneers made a strenuous journey over dirt roads, sometimes trails, to reach their destination. Trudging against stiff western winds and even blinding blizzards, it took nearly a month to cross Nebraska to reach the northern corner of Colorado. Now the train took only 28 hours. Cousins John William and Gus arrived on January 17, 1909 to stake their claim, and then returned to gather equipment and their horses.

I will come in one week was the simple telegram that Papa Paul sent to Alva, Colorado. From there it was carried by coach to Fairview–finally picked up by Gus and taken to Rose.

It didn't take Papa Paul long to prepare to leave Storm Lake. Saying good-bye to family and friends took only a few days. Packing a steamer trunk was more difficult, as Paul knew he would never return–not at his age. Carefully he placed the Russian winter wheat seed and corn that surely would grow on the newly turned sod soil. He wished he could bring tree seedlings, but knew that would be hard, and they might not grow–he'd wait and see.

Paul packed photographs of his beloved Trudy–gone now three years–dying from cancer. He smiled back at her smile and laughed remembering the many sweet times of touching her soft, loving body, and kissing those tender lips. Then his breath came in sobs as he touched the Steiner violin–the violin played by Papa Henri in the Strasburg Conservatory–the orchestra–Papa and Mama–now gone more than fifty years. Their photographs were old and faded, but still you could see the triumph of will–Mama Frieda–looking with great love at her husband, Henri.

Paul paused for a minute as in his mind he heard Trudy playing their love songs: *I with my violin and Trudy with her piano. Duets brought us together for a lifelong love and marriage of 54 years. How we loved–Brahms, Mozart, Beethoven. Oh, to hear Trudy again as her beautiful long, tapered fingers would glide smoothly over Chopin's etudes. She embraced and played gracefully complicated Bach fugues.* Paul looked down then placed Trudy's photograph in the trunk.

Paul thought Carolyn was the beauty. *She looked like Mama Frieda, with her red hair and blue eyes. She had no musical talent at all. My eldest daughter was content to bake, cook, and clean house. Rose was just like her grandpa Henri, small with dark hair and dark eyes and the minute she touched the violin, you knew she would be magnificent. I'll carry the Steiner violin safely, not putting it in the trunk at all. Yes, I'll take some tools, like hammers, a carpenter's square, chisels, folding ruler and–.oh, I'm sure that John William had all of these, but it would be good to have them.* Paul smiled to himself thinking of building again.

"I pray that you will come and see us soon," he said tenderly as he hugged his daughter, Carolyn, and the grandkids, then shook hands with George. He never looked back as he heart was already in the northeastern corner of Colorado.

Chapter 7

PAUL REMEMBERS

Never shall I leave the places that I love.
Never shall they go from my heart
Even though my eyes
Are somewhere else.
Nancy Wood, *Spirit Walker*, 1993

Des Moines disappeared as the train chugged onward–stretched always westward–on and on–but Papa Paul didn't sleep–too excited as he watched the terrain slip by. Houses, barns, pig pens, stacks of hay, now and then unique little towns, but made with standard shapes–a water tower, a small church steeple, and a main street–nothing more. *Who are the people who live here? What kind of lives do they live? So barren. Have they libraries and concert halls?* He couldn't stop thinking about the rich cultural life he left behind in Storm Lake or even his childhood life in Strasburg, with exciting gatherings of intellectuals and musicians.

In Storm Lake, Iowa–the Pinot home–was also considered a model of good taste. After Paul left for America his parents would have approved of his wife, Trudy, and their successful lives as agronomists–farmers.

Mama Frieda and Papa wanted me to continue my studies as a violinist, but they also wanted me to follow my dream to become an agronomist like my Uncle Rudolph and Grandpa Schneider. I guess it's not so different that Rose, wanted to be a pioneer–a homesteader. Sad, though that her mother, Trudy, can't see our spunky daughter facing life's challenges in such a triumphant, powerful way. But, she would be sorrowful to know that Rose is now a widow–living in a–a dugout!

His thoughts continued on, as he recalled, *I wanted to pass on all that I knew, but that was not to be to sons, or even daughters. Until Rose. She was so different, so interested in life. Her delivery was easy, but they wondered how the tiny infant with black hair, short nose, and a dot for a mouth would survive. And, she was not pretty, no way to lie about that. Her face was too long and her piercing black eyes were too close together to be considered– pretty. But by the third day of life, Rose surprised everyone–for she actually smiled–not just a gas grimace–but an actual smile. Her smile seemed premature, but it became her mark of life–smiling.*

But there was also something urgent about her movements–like she wanted to be on with life–'Let's go!' she seemed to say. Her hands had the same long, tapered fingers of Trudy. We named her Rose because of her rosebud mouth, and the bloom that she gave to me at forty-three and Trudy at forty-one–a late in life baby we called her–but she was all ours.

Even when she first began to walk, she wanted to touch the piglets, the lambs, and the calves. Rose was never afraid of chickens and even would sing her little songs to them, as she placed her hands under their soft bodies to gather eggs from their nests. Trudy and I knew we had a cherub. She just loved every one, even when Carolyn didn't want to play, Rose would put her arms around her big sister and say, "That's OK, another time," and kiss her sweetly on the cheek. Never a night would go by when saying her prayers that she wouldn't ask for blessings on the cows, pigs, horses, and even the homeless cats. She worried about the strays.

Now she is a widow. I can't imagine Rose without John William. When they first met in grade school, Rose would say, 'I love Jooooohnnn William', stretching out the tones of his name. John was one of the youngest of the eight Schultz boys. He was a nice kid who grew up to be a prince of a man.

I remember the first time I saw him with Rose on the playground. He seemed just like an ordinary eight-year old, playing rough with the guys. But he was always careful around the girls, not rough like some. Then I heard him sing in the Christmas program at church–he might have been head high to my belt buckle, but could he sing "Silent Night"! His pure tones and uncanny volume bathed the sanctuary. The whole Schultz family was singers, but John William had unusual talent. I had hoped he would study and perhaps become an opera star. Yes, John had a future.

Rose and John William became Sunday school sweethearts when only ten and eight years old, always laughing and walking together. She began playing the violin, took lessons from me. John William became known as a fine singer, so soon they were performing together at weddings, funerals, and high school events. I remember that he always protected her–making sure that she wore warm boots and scarves in the winter.

Rose. Paul's eyes filled with tears. *I just can't imagine her without her John William. And the music, touching the piano as her mother did, was a natural, but when Rose took my violin, my Papa Henri's, it was there I saw the spiritual connections–those rich tones! And her tapered fingers knew the touch of each string. My breath is just gone, thinking of those moments when we played as a trio, Trudy, Rose, and I. Carolyn was always a good audience, but had no interest in music. We played often in the churches and at school, but the best times were in the evenings at home, after the day's work.*

Their love connected two powerful families–the Pinot's, mine–and John's--the Schultz's–both well-respected, successful farmers. But, farming came first. John's papa, Mr. Justin Schultz, was a taskmaster with his sons. He never questioned the singing talent, but he also knew that John William was unusually gifted with his hands, building sheds and chicken coops with intricate yet efficient workmanship. Wasn't surprised when Justin sent him off to become an architect. 'There are always buildings to be built, and we need someone who has that understanding.' Justin demanded. So, John William left for the university soon after high school and Rose followed him. She studied the violin and, of course, teaching.

When they graduated John said, "I want to marry Rose," *and she, of course, said,* "Yes." *They married in September. The whole community came to celebrate–food and drink, dancing and laughter–always the two were laughing.* Paul's eyes fill with tears, remembering.

They lived on the Schultz farm in a tiny house. You could hear the violin and John's singing after the chores were done. Rose was a strong worker–in charge of the chickens and getting their eggs to market. Only the family knew that Rose miscarried five babies, each one only a few months in the womb. She and John never talked about that, just continued loving life, and then came Margaret, William, and finally Henri or Hank.

Rose, Rose, I pray that you will have years to live, for the children, for me. I don't know how your emptiness will be filled, but if I can help, missing that part of you, that part of your soul is harder to bear than anyone can tell you. The Lord tells us to "Cast all your cares upon me and I will give you rest." Indeed He does. I'm still missing my Trudy. Cancer made her body not her own. Oh, the pain she had, I just wanted to take it from her! She endured those two years of long suffering without hope, but never gave up. I held her in my arms the last hours, rocking her like the angel she was becoming. My tears caressed her cheeks. 'Don't cry, Paul,' she said, 'I'm just going to the mailbox. I've heard there's a message for me. Jesus sent it long ago, the day I was baptized. I'll wait for you, and we'll sing our way to heaven.' She began humming "Blessed Assurance Jesus is Mine" and I joined in as much as I could without choking up. She ended the song, by singing in full voice, "Oh what a foretaste of glory is mine." And she closed her eyes never to open them again.

More thoughts and concerns kept swimming through his mind while the miles flew by. In the river valleys the trees were beginning to show buds–but of chartreuse green. It was nearly April.

Union Pacific chugged its way westward, the landscape slowly grew desolate.

This seems like the end of the earth!

It wasn't the end of the world, but rather the vast open prairie of eastern Colorado.

Chapter 8

PAPA ARRIVES

Live for something rather than die for nothing.
George Patton

The train pulled into Alva just as dawn was arriving. There was Gus, huddled up in the cold–waiting. Without ceremony they shook hands and gathered up Paul's few belongings. The open wagon cut across the fifteen miles to John William and Rose's dugout–now only Rose's. Winter had pocked the road with ruts and unevenness.

Cousin Gus didn't talk much–never did.

"Really sad 'bout John William. I'm glad you could come 'n help. I'll help as much as I can with my three sons, but we're behind in gittin our house up 'n the crops in. You can ride Burt, Babe, Bell or Charlie the horses, 'n come ask fer help any time."

Papa thought about riding a horse again. *It's been a long time since I actually rode a horse–guess these old bones won't crack if I fall off. This is really like starting over–I've go to do it–for Rose.*

Traveling in the horse drawn wagon was familiar, but the ruts and unfinished trail made it a sore trial. Bouncing wildly after several hours, they finally passed by a cluster of buildings, a hamlet called Fairview. Then they headed south again. It was evening–barely light as the wagon pulled up to Rose's dugout.

What a shock! Paul had seen photographs of these hovels of dirt but had never stood in front of one. Why you couldn't even call this a house. It was just a pile of dirt with a tiny window and door stuck into the heap. Inside it was brutal. Dark, walls of sod-dirt, two small windows hovering in one wall and on the other wall–a door, there was no floor–any way not a real one but a hardened dirt–an earthen floor–not really a house–only a shelter.

A small figure appeared at the door–could it be Rose! She looked so small in the twilight, smaller than ever, just a wisp of a woman, with red eyes and shaking hands–and no smile. She was barely thirty-seven now. That laughing adventure called–life was now--tough. Her black-socketed eyes wore a heavy, new look–a hardened determined look, her mouth–a thin line. She clung to Papa.

"Papa, you're here," she cried, "we need you."

"I'm here, I'm here–to help." Tears streamed from his eyes, as his arms enfolded his youngest daughter. Funny how that word, "help" means to give your all; not to question when asked of friend, neighbor–or daughter. It was the rule of life–these are the connections of being human–you help. Do unto others as you would have others do unto you, God's great commandment.

Papa thought, *Life on the prairie will be different from my lush, tree-dotted Iowa. The patterns of weather vary, and the time to plant, too. The seeds will look different–how fast can I learn all of these before planting season. Neighbors will have to be the teachers, as Margaret is too young, so are Will and Hank. A harvest this year? Gus says it's too dry, no rain, and the wind, and still threat of more prairie fires! Perhaps the seeds won't sprout.*

"We'll make it–we'll make it," Papa said, aloud. "God will provide; He has promised."

Gus said goodbye and headed back to his farm.

Papa picked up his daughter and sat in the rocking chair, cuddling her like a baby, and began rocking and rocking. No sound other than the creak of the chair was heard for two hours. Enfolded like a hand in glove, the tension left her face as she closed her eyes and slept, perhaps for the first time in a week. Father and daughter, like mother and son of the Pieta, were one to each other. Tenderness flowed like a powerful stream, unlike any other force in nature.

She awoke and saw his face and flowing beard, and said, again, "Papa, I'm glad you're here," but Rose didn't smile. "I have some biscuits for you and some tea on the stove."

The house held a strong, acrid smell, that Papa knew was from the buffalo turds. In the middle of the one room were blankets on straw mattresses. A curtain separated the sleeping areas, and the children were already asleep in the dark of early night.

"If you have to go, just step outside. Tomorrow when it's light I'll show you the outhouse. It's not safe to go alone now, as the rattlers are coming out."

After tea and biscuits, Papa got ready for sleep–he was exhausted. He fell to his blanket laid near the potbelly stove. But trying to sleep the first night in Colorado, Papa Paul was restless. There was no air to speak of. Mud house–a blanket on a straw mattress and insects crawling all over–snakes outside–*Gads, this is savage. My old body can't take much of this.* But his mind continued over and over again, thinking–*vacant, dry, open space– end of the world–no wonder the government wanted to give it away. Farm it? Can't be done. No rain and the blasted wind–no wonder railroads gave the morons free transportation to bring everything out here–I mean everything–free–free–free. No turning back–home–Iowa, Indiana, Ohio–or wherever. Stuck–have to stay.* Dread swept into Papa's head–over–and over he heard. *It can't be done, can't be done–can't be done.* But he then heard that still small voice–God's voice repeated, all things are possible, only believe.

All things are possible over and over again in his mind. *Indeed on the river-less Volga Steppes, the Russian farmers knew their seeds–their tough, resilient seeds–and they believed. They made a fertile valley that fed the masses in Europe. They triumphed.* He remembered those resilient seeds–*the Russian winter wheat seeds they are with me--in my baggage!*

Only believe!

Chapter 9

REALITY

Finally sleep came, and quickly–morning right behind it. Papa lay quietly for a few minutes before waking up. He could hear Rose sobbing softly in her shelter beyond a simple blanket hung on a string. Rubbing his eyes, recalled his promise–"I will come and help." Papa rose and built a fire in the potbelly stove, the first he'd done with prairie turds. *Ugh– they stink, but they do warm the house.* He heard the others stir.

Rose, up with puffy, red eyes, grim mouth, cried, "Papa, Papa." and hugged him fiercely. Margaret and Will brought sleepy eyes to greet Papa Paul and Mama, and went out together to the two-hole outhouse. Then each brought back a bucket of water from the pump and dumped it into in a reservoir on the side of the blacktopped cook stove that sat against the south side of the house.

"We cook out here, Papa, so the house isn't full of smoke," said Margaret.

Margaret fixed the usual breakfast meal–gruel, simple–mush– thin–and milk–fresh from the cow, and thin hard biscuits–and thin coffee. Everything–thin. No one said much. All tried not to cry. Papa's eyes filled with tears–remembering. Facing the loss of John would be a lifetime of sadness. He said firmly, "We need to go on– work–that helps."

Papa said, "I must first visit the grave, John's resting place."– over whelmed with tears again–"John, my beloved son."

It took about an hour on the trail to reach the cemetery, already filled with several tombstones and a few small wooden crosses. John's newly dug grave had one on it. As they gathered, Rose threw herself on the grave and cried loudly, "John, John, come back, my love."

Papa stood quietly. When she arose he held her to his chest. "I know, I know."

Slowly they left, leaving the prairie winds to caress the softly settling dirt mound above the beloved husband.

"Tomorrow I want to see the whole farm," said Papa. In the still-young morning Paul walked with Will and Margaret out into fields. He asked subtle but important questions: Which way does the wind blow? How does it feel when rain is coming? Tell me about the clouds. He walked swiftly, head high, and back straight. "What do you see?" he asked.

"Our field–where we will plant and harvest," Will said. "I can see a hundred miles."

"Keep looking, listen to the land. Learn from it. It speaks to you–listen–it has a spirit, and you are connected," Papa reminded him.

"Look, there goes an antelope," cried Will.

"And a hawk after some prairie chicken," whispered Margaret.

"Look close to the clump over there–a bull snake." Will was excited. "And listen for the birds' songs, and the way wind talks to you."

Margaret smiled, "It tells us that a storm is coming, a thunder storm is coming. So we better not do wash today."

"Listen" Papa said. "This prairie is not dead but alive. Before you touch the soil to plant seeds, listen to it. Let it know that you love it. Hear its rhythms, and remember there are others who live in this vast place–respect all–leave some for others. Don't be greedy, just take what you need and be grateful."

"You sound like Old Timer," the children laughed.

"Who is Old Timer?"

"He's our Indian friend; he will come by later. He loved our daddy." Both of them looked away sadly.

"I want to meet him. You have a lot to teach me. When I was about your age, my Uncle Rudolph took me one summer to the Volga Steppes. That's a place in Russia much like this–treeless and flat. I asked uncle "What grows here?" He answered, "Food for hungry people–the bread basket of Europe.""

Papa stopped walking, standing straight as in a trance. "That's it! This place, this prairie is like the Steppes of the Volga Valley!

Now I remember! Now I can teach you something I learned long ago as a young boy in Russia."

Papa seemed suddenly excited and rushed off into the tough grass around the dugout.

"Now I remember! I remember that winds blew all the time–and little, little or no rain. We had to plant seeds in the fall not in springtime; to let the first grains go to sleep over winter, and then sprout up again in spring, and to be harvested in the summer. Yes, yes, that is it! Not to give up! Not to give up." Papa was laughing now, as he pulled up some prairie grass and smelled it, and chewed it.

Will and Margaret followed his example–smelling and chewing the grass. They, too, became excited. Papa scraped the surface of the sod with a stick and reached for a pinch of soil. He put it into his mouth, tasting it, and looking heavenward.

"Good, good, soil is strong, but we must go very carefully, children. The soil is rich in minerals, but hard with clay, not like the loam of Iowa." Papa kept talking excitedly about what he saw and felt.

"It's a fragile land. Too much of anything will ruin it–kill it. Yes, kill this desert. I remember what Uncle Rudolph said, 'Treat it like a fine, but frail lady; treat her kindly.' I remember now how tender uncle was when he talked to the land, patting it gently. If we follow that plan–this gentle plan–the frail lady will be fertile for you and your grandkids."

Will and Margaret laughed, "Our grandkids?"

Papa couldn't stand still, but walked around the farm, examining each gopher hole, and looking for coyote scat.

Margaret went back to the house to help Mama. Will saw little Hank outside the door, crying. "You didn't wait for me," he wailed. Will ran back and tried to pick Hank up, but he was a big kid.

So Will and Hank trudged along beside Papa, "I'm a big boy, too, Papa," Hank looked up at his tall grandpa.

Papa picked up the sturdy redheaded, four-year old and gave him a big hug. "I know you are, and you're going to be Papa's good helper."

"Yes," stomped Hank, as he pushed his big brother, Will, aside.

The three of them and also their mutt dog, Rex, were usually together. "We love Rex, as he is King, and he protects us all the time," said Will.

"But he likes me best," cried Hank, as he pulled at Rex's collar.

"He loves everyone," remarked Will, as he patted his little brother's head. His hand in Hanks as they walked carefully. They saw no creeks or lagoons, just flat land.

"This flat land makes it easier for us to plant and harvest grain. In some places homesteaders have to chop down forests before starting to plant, and in other places they have to remove tons of rocks and stones. Don't you think this will be easier to farm?"

"Yes, but did they have water, too. Daddy always talked about there wasn't enough water for the seeds," Will claimed.

"You're right young man. We'll have to depend upon clouds to bring us rain. Most of the time there's enough rain in spring and summer and snow in winter. But, sometimes there are droughts, when there is no rain for a whole summer and no snow in winter. Sometimes these dry spells last for years and years."

"How do the seeds come alive then?"

"Most of the time they are very puny. Often don't live. So you save your seed crop–protect it like precious gold, and then plant it when you have enough moisture–like rain and snow. Seeds are the soul of your crops. Sometimes you have to let land rest, until there is rain."

"But what do you do then for food and hay for the livestock?" asked Will."

"You learn to be very careful–to plan ahead for that day and then feed livestock carefully. Hope we never have to deal with that problem," Papa Paul warned. "My uncle showed me the way people saved their crops on the Volga Steppes. They kept the best seeds in tall metal bens called silos or grain bins. These bins kept rodents like mice and rats, out–so they couldn't get to the seeds and eat them. And you had to keep the bottom sealed so mice couldn't sneak in."

"Let me show you Daddy's Promise Seed Box," Will quickly took Papa Paul to the stairway in the dugout. "Here's where Daddy kept the seed crop, and planted them last fall; he was very careful."

"I'm glad you understand this, son, as you will now be the keeper of The Promise Seed."

"Me, too," shouted Hank to Papa.

"Yes, you, too, young man," Papa said.

Food was scarce in the Schultz home. Every meal was about the same–mush, eggs, milk, and biscuits. The garden sprouted vegetables from seed planted after the last freeze in May–to stave off hunger in the winter. Then there was hunting. Papa didn't own a gun, but Will did. Even at seven years old he could shoot straight, and shot two rabbits while walking with Papa that day.

"This'll make a good stew."

"Proud of you, young fella–you're a good shot–and pretty young to do that."

"Yes, Daddy taught me how to be careful and take cautious shots," Will's eyes filled with tears remembering his dad.

"This land is full of rabbits–but rabbits also love gardens!" Papa reminded them.

Will matter-of-factly replied, "We don't share our garden with the rabbits or our chickens with the coyotes or hawks. Rex barks so loud that he scares off the coyotes."

"That's good," laughed Papa. "We'll keep a fence around the garden plot, but someone needs to be on guard for those fragile vegetables.

"Daddy built this shed as a chicken coop–so we could have eggs and chicken stew," said Will. "One half of the coop is for chickens and the other half for storing farm machinery like the plow, disc, thrasher, and harrow." Papa looked at his small grandson and shuddered thinking of the weight of responsibility this young person carried. *I wonder how he will grow up–not too soon, I hope*–thought Papa. John had died scant weeks ago–but work went on.

"What tough, hard work this is!" acclaimed Papa. "The land is so dry. It's surprising that anything grows." But, lo and behold, seeds had germinated into sprouts with unfurling green leaves.

"The season is short–maybe only a dozen weeks from when the winter wheat begins to sprout to harvest? The timing seems perilous, if rains are too heavy and roots are not yet set, they may not mature. Somehow we have to listen to the land; we have to hear its spirit."

"Papa," said Hank, "there's water 'neath the ground? Like–do you feel that?"

"You listen and you smell. You have to be very quiet and not think of anything else but the land. You have to be still to feel its rhythms, to hear it speak to you."

"Like a person?" queried Hank.

"No, you have to feel its voice, more like a song bird. If you listen you will hear it, and you will feel it in your bones. Just be very quiet and feel it."

"I don't feel anything but the wind," claimed both Hank and Will.

"You will, if you let yourselves go. It takes time to learn any new language; don't be afraid. It's a gift God gave us farmers. Probably he gave this feeling to Adam–or was it to Eve?" He laughed–even in sorrow, Papa laughed.

"Most important of all is that you love the land. You treat it kindly with respect as someday you will your wife."

Will chuckled, not imagining that scene at all–at age seven. But he listened to Papa.

He stayed in step with Papa. Hank was now going to sleep on Papa's shoulder.

"I can't feel much, I'm honest," Papa replied. "I have to get to know the moods of this land, and I have to feel its heart and soul. I have to be connected."

Will wanted to feel it in his heart, too.

"We need to talk to Cousin Gus to see how they are working their land. Let's hitch up Babe and Burt and go visit them, OK? I haven't seen his place yet."

Papa called Rose, who bundled up Hank and Margaret and put her coat on. Paul and Will hitched horses to the wagon and off the five went. The trail to Gus's was still barely passable after the winter snows. When they arrived Papa was surprised to see what Gus had done. He had been very aggressive, plowing up his entire half section of land, when he was supposed to leave half fallow–to rest.

Papa challenged him. "The reason for the rest period is so that it can get rejuvenated–just like people. We need to rest and think about things."

"Well, I'm 'n a hurry, no need for this rich land ta rest," Gus replied rudely. "We'll see."

They didn't stay long, as Esther was having a sick spell–like she usually did. Gus's young sons were out in the fields plowing and harrowing. Back home, Papa Paul said, "Gus's attitude disappoints me."

"I know. John William was always concerned, because Gus doesn't have the same goals as we do. He wants to plow everything under and plant all of it at once."

Papa said, "Who is this Old-Timer you always talking about?"

"Just have to think about him, maybe call out his name–Old Timer, and he seems to appear. It's sort of spooky, but he just comes.

"His dad–Dr. MacPherson–was the military doctor at Bent's Fort, and his mother was Shining Night Star, a Cheyenne spiritual chief's daughter. He's half-breed–half Scottish and half Cheyenne–his Scottish name is Gregory MacPherson and his Indian name is Red Sun in the Hair. He was a Cheyenne leader–guess he still is. Red Sun–even met with President Lincoln about the time of the Civil War when he argued for Indian rights and protection from white invaders.

"His wife and small son were killed in a tornado. Old Timer is a widower, too–must be at least eighty years old–like you, Papa. He has blue eyes and red hair, like you do!" Rose was startled, as she realized the similarities between these two powerful men.

"Maybe we have a lot in common–and we're both half-breeds, and both widowers." laughed Papa. "How can I meet him?"

"We'll just call him. A year ago when John William called him, Old Timer came with five hard-working young men who helped build the dugouts, the windmills, and put in the wells. The neighbor men believe Red Sun stopped flames from burning more of them–but it was too late for John." Rose stopped talking, as her eyes filled with tears.

"I want to meet him. He sounds like an important link with the land," responded Papa.

She continued, "Old Timer seems to know a lot about the land and especially about horses. He told us that Babe wanted fresh grass, not hay, and that Burt was happy to eat hay. Old Timer just goes up to the horse and looks into their eyes, and they seem to understand each other. It's really strange.

"You can't hear him come up to you. He's just quiet. But I love him–so did John William. He 'straight talks' and says that land is a sacred gift. Mother Earth and clouds hold the presence of his ancestors. He talks to them, not like a crazy person, but just as if they were standing beside him. He's fast–rides a horse like the wind.

"Gus used to think he was a kook. Thought he was too superstitious, always looking at the clouds and sky. But when the prairie fire surrounded all the men–then Old Timer came flying on his pony. He began shouting and chanting. The flames stopped coming, and the fire died out! Gus even looks at him differently now–like maybe he does have special powers. Yes, you must meet Red Sun–Old Timer. Let's call him now!"

"Let's get to work–we need to start building a real house." Papa took a hammer and saw as he walked toward the pile of lumber, the lumber that John William was going to pick up in Alva, the day he died. Neighbors had stacked it neatly beside the dugout; now was time to begin building.

Chapter 10

HALF-BREEDS

You and I are sons of one religion, and it is spirit.
Khalil Gibran

Just then over the trail you could see a cloud of dust rising from a pony and rider. Within minutes, there was Old Timer–just as Rose knew he would come.

This was meant to be, they both thought.

Two sets of deep blues eye met and stared at each other; the uncanny feeling was overwhelming.

"I'm Paul Pinot," uttered Papa.

"I'm Gregory MacPherson or Red Sun in the Hair," answered Old Timer.

They stared in disbelief, for each could have been the other's twin. Paul was slightly taller, with broader shoulders, and hair less red. Old Timer had higher cheekbones, and his skin was a darker bronze. Both had intensely blue eyes.

Old Timer seemed to be engrossed in studying Paul's face. "My Brother," he proclaimed.

Paul grasped his hand, "Yes, my Brother."

"Most folks around here call me Old Timer, but it looks like now there may be two old timers!"

They both laughed.

"May I call you Red Sun, then?"

"Of course," laughed Old Timer, "and I'll call you Paul."

"Thanks for taking good care of my son, John William and my daughter, Rose." Red Sun only nodded.

Paul remarked, "It's time we met."

Red Sun replied, "Indeed."

"Do you drink coffee?" asked Paul.

"Do you smoke a pipe?" asked Red Sun.

Thus began a friendship, two old half-breeds–Paul, a half-breed French/German and Red Sun or Gregory, a Cheyenne/Scotsman. The friendship lasted to the ends of their lives.

Two days later Red Sun returned, but this time with another pony; this one was for Paul. "Thought you might like a pony of your own. Your other horses are fine, but they are mostly for work, like plowing. This is Angel, and she is. It's a custom of Cheyenne people to give a friend a pony, and I'd like you to have her."

"What a beautiful roan horse, and larger than usual. Hope she can hold my big frame. Thanks so much for the generous gift," Paul said.

"She likes a challenge, is gentle, and courageous. Angel will obey anything you tell her, but love her lots. She's a fine lady." With that Red Sun gave her a gentle pat on the rump and handed over the reins.

"Thanks. Never ridden bareback before," Paul said.

"It'll become second nature to you, but it may take some time. Only ride for ten minutes a day at first, then gradually increase, or you won't be able to walk."

Both men laughed.

"Thanks so much. A horse of my own."

They tethered the ponies to a stake near the house and sat outside with cups of coffee.

"Come sit here and tell me about yourself. There's much I don't know about the Cheyenne tribe and you. I understand you studied botany at the University of North Carolina. That's fascinating."

"And I want to know more about you–the Seed Man. John William had great admiration for you. He told me that you were from Germany and are a great violinist."

The exchange started early in the morning and stayed alive into the evening. The two half breeds had much in common, especially about their understanding of the land and of nature. Both saw networks connecting all living creatures, and Red Sun even saw spiritual connections between clouds, rocks, and the soil.

"Each has a soul, a bond with other souls," began Red Sun.

"I see that as energy," responded Paul, "with God, the Triune God, as the all-knowing connector between."

"That is one way to look at it," said Red Sun. "I feel that each of us has to be true to how God–the Great Spirit was revealed to us, like you, through your family's history as Lutherans from Germany. You need to be true to how God was revealed to you–

"For me I have two faiths in a way; the way of my father, a Presbyterian, and my mother's people, the Heevahetano'o, the Southern Cheyenne, who speak an Algonquian language like our cousins, the Arapahoe and Apache. We believe in many spirit guides, and some which inhabit animals. Our prayers are for guidance and protection, and we have many forms of Blessings. Mahoe is our word for God: you have Father, Son, and the Holy Spirit. God guides you, as Mahoe guides us. You have angels, and we have spirit guides."

"Tell me about your powers over nature, like the fire that Gus tells me you put out with your chanting. Is that true?"

"Yes and no. It's like if you pray, and your God answers your prayers. I am only a man, a person of faith, so when I ask for power, such as halting the flames, Mahoe sends spirit guides that squash the flames. I also listen to the messages sent by these guides. As soon as I knew that John William was in danger, my pony flew as fast as the wind, but we were too late. The guides send messages like when I knew you wanted to meet me. I came when I heard. "Do you hear such as well?"

"No, I don't think so, but I have not trained my mind to do so. Perhaps if I train, I can hear. I do feel energy, like the energy of promise in the seeds that I feel like a warmth."

"Yes, that's very similar to my guides. Perhaps we are more alike than different." Both men smiled.

"We have ceremonies throughout the year to put ourselves back into harmony with Mother Earth and Father Sun. One is the Sun Dance; it comes during the summer solstice. My mother, Shining Night Star's father was the great Old Gray Wolf, a renowned leader of the Cheyenne. As his descendant, I am considered one of the tribe's spiritual leaders. He trained me to be a leader of the ceremonies and also to be a medicine man. I use prayers and herbs for healing and carry a medicine bundle with me at all times in case some one needs my help. Of course, I know much about white man's medicine as well, as my father was a physician. But help doesn't come from me, but through me; the power is in the Healing Spirits hands, and they are many."

"That's mysterious. I've heard of the Sun Dance and learned that some of the rituals are very painful. Is that true?"

"You have heard only about those who use those rituals for punishment, but they are very rare. They remind me of the Los Penitentes de La Fraternidad Piadosa de Nuestro Padre Jesus Nazreno. Such people are a part of the Catholic beliefs but are an ancient sect that mutilates themselves during Holy Week as retribution for their sins. Los Penitentes are not like the usual followers of Christ that celebrate His resurrection and forgiveness of sins. And like the Penitentes, some indigenous people, only men, mutilate themselves during the Sun Dance as punishment rather than seek forgiveness and harmony with all creatures. I celebrate the Dance as a sacred ritual that unites the whole family, the whole tribe. It is holy and a blessing to make all land new again. We Cheyenne humble ourselves through ceremony to become ready for the Sun Dance. We use various Blessing Ways in this cleansing and a bringing of cosmic energy connecting us to the Creator–Mahoe.

After finishing a final cup of coffee Red Sun brought out a pipe and filled it with tobacco. He said to Paul, "Pipe smoking is a special ritual we use to connect us in a mission. Tobacco is sacred, and smoke that rises goes to Mahoe, with our requests and prayers. Would you smoke a pipe with me?"

"Of course, if you believe this is correct for me to do."

"Yes, you are a spiritual Brother. Others who might make fun of the ritual are not allowed to smoke it."

"Sort of what we Lutherans–you know most Germans are either Catholic or Lutheran, so that's what most of us immigrants are. It could have been other denominations that settled here in Colorado. We believe that one who doesn't believe that the body and blood of Christ are in the bread and wine at the Communion table should not eat or drink it. It is a sacred ceremony."

"Exactly right."

With that the two men smoked the pipe; it further bonded them into a partnership with the land and with each other.

"One other important ceremony I'd like to tell you about is the meaning of the Sacred Arrows. The eagle is the bird that soars nearest to Mahoe, closest to the Sun. It is believed that the eagle is the connection between man and spirit. A special arrow is made with an eagle's feather as a fletching on its spire or shaft. The feather gives the arrow stability to hit its mark.

"Sacred Arrows are used in many ceremonies. For instance the White Arrow is used to proclaim peace between tribes, but the Red Arrow is the symbol of revenge and war. The Red Arrow has blood on its fletching, the eagle's feather. It is only used when an enemy has broken some sacred covenant and deserves death, either of the body or of the spirit. You may never see a Sacred Arrow–either white or red–but they are powerful symbols of the Cheyenne."

"Tell me about your love of music and of farming. How do they mix?"

"That's a good question. I see that music is a rhythm of patterns in sound and that farming is the same of patterns in the soil and the seed. Each is part of God's great plan to bring harmony to the world. When I play the violin, and I will for you, I feel a spiritual connection with all musicians before and after me. I feel a communication far beyond my own words. Music speaks to the soul, and it expresses all human emotions: sadness, joy, anger, and passion. It reaches all parts of the world–to the rich or the poor. It is a universal language. To me the violin is like the human voice, so when I play I can speak my feelings and those of others, like the composer.

"To me being a farmer is like being a link between the Creator and the people. Through my hands I make the soil ready for seed that the Creator has made. With care in planting and tending the fields I am the mediator between these to great forces. The harvest is the fruit of both. The new seeds produced are connections between generations–the old and the new. I see my role as the mediator or an instrument; it's a sacred calling."

Red Sun began, "That's a very good description of how I see my role, too. And we've lived such long lives that we've passed this knowledge on to the next generations,"

In the next months and years Red Sun and Papa Paul rode together, talking and uplifting each other. They also got to work. Old Timer brought his young men to help frame and finish the house that John was going to build. Neighbors and especially Gus came, as well, to help. Within three weeks the house was in place. Because John had completed the architectural plans, the house was structurally strong and rooms unusually large. It became a model for other houses, to replace other dugouts.

"Surely John's hands are in each of these rooms, for this was his dream," Rose remembered.

Chapter 11

SEED MAN

I think that in life we need to be a little like the farmer who puts back into the soil what he takes out.
Paul Newman

The harvest came, the winter roared in as well, but in their new house above the ground, it seemed shorter and even held some happiness. One evening in April, Papa heard the sound he was longing to hear, the violin. Rose was playing in the barn for the cows. The melodies were as fresh as years ago, and her talent remained as before, but the best sign was that her sorrow was lessening, and she, too, was coming back to life.

Spring also brought hope. Hope that the rains would come but not too much and not too early, that they might feed, but not wash away the tiny sprouting winter wheat. Last year's crop had been one of the best. Farmers saved the good seed for the next year's crop. They had done research at the end of harvest. Papa Paul reminded them, "We must each share a portion of our best seed crop and mix these seeds about every two-three years–that way we breed for stronger seeds and better crops, so we have the most fertile seeds."

The farmers did just that, meeting at the grain elevator that stored their crops. They met to learn more about the promise of good seeds. Mama Rose, Will and Hank were among them–but Gus was not. When asked if he wanted to come, he said, "I already knows 'nough."

Papa held fistfuls of seeds, examining each grain, looking for striations and markers. Then he bit into the seed, "Look this is a good example of a possible puny seed." He showed it around to all the farmers.

"These seeds are not plump and almost white in color." He put that handful of seed into a box marked 'Experiment'. "These seeds I'll put into a special plot to experiment to see what they do produce; sometimes you're surprised. You don't want to mix these until you know. They may be a new strain, maybe a real treasure, but right now you don't know."

"Yah, yah," the farmers agreed. "Paul, we can see why y' 'ah called the Seed Man." "Yah, Yah," all echoed.

Papa Paul laughed, "I learned it all from my grandpa–he was one of the best farmers in Germany. He'd studied horticulture at the university and did experimental farming on the Volga Steppes in Russia. Have you heard of them?"

"Nah, nah," murmured the farmers.

"It's a place in Russia. The geography is like what is around Fairview, treeless, no rivers, little rain–and lots of wind."

The farmers sat in awe of the great Seed Man–they never had an expert before, and here was the best.

"When I was a little boy, about seven years old, my uncle took me to see our family who had been brought to the Steppes by the Russian government–actually encouraged to go–with free land, just like here with the Homestead Act. You all came because of free land. Those Russian farmers became so successful in growing special wheat that the Steppes became known as the "Bread Basket of Europe." They produced enough wheat on that barren land for all of Europe. And even today that land is still fertile, still produces bread for all."

"Gee whiz, whatta ya know!" muttered the farmers again, looking surprised to find that this land–their land–could do the same.

"But lotta work doin all this checkin and keepin records an stuff." grumbled a couple of men.

"I just wanna throw seed in 'n hope for the best," said one younger fellow who seemed in a hurry about everything.

"In the long run, young man, it won't pay off. You'll find that you will wear out the soil real fast and that sooner or later your crops will get puny and stay that way. All kinds of insects eat up some crops. Maybe you'd have good crops for five to ten years, and then they'll become weak."

"Don't think I'll stick 'round that long 'nyway," chided the younger man.

"You don't have kids," remarked another man. "If you did, you'd think different."

"Nah, I just wanna make some money and move to a warmer place–without the wind."

"That's too bad in a way, young man," Papa continued. "Out here what you do on your land affects all your neighbors, like if you don't hold the land down, and it blows and blows, you blow lots of dirt onto your neighbor's land. Some is OK, but lots will drown out the seeds from coming up. So we need to think of that, too, we are our neighbor's keepers. And we're–all in this together."

The young man slouched down in his chair, and didn't say anything more. Papa continued with his demonstration.

"These are good seeds," he said. "These are the best. Now take two scoops from each box–that'll be just right–and put it into your Promise Box for this year. Mark it so you know. You have to keep good records of what grows and how; be your own experts," Paul laughed.

"Yah, yah, uh huh" and with nodding heads, the weather-beaten farmers agree. "You'll need bushels and bushels of seed crop."

Papa Paul continued, "Know which is the best seed and move it around some in the field. At the end of harvest pull out your ledger and write all of these things down–like what kind of seed you used; how much rain; how many bushels per acre, all that stuff, like a business man."

A couple years later, one farmer said, "You've got ta watch how Widow Rose does her land. Why it's laid out nice and waving, not so straight as mine. Guess it protects it from the wind. She always seems to have the best crop around. We've got ta plant trees like she did, as they're really holdin the ground as windbreakers. She sure learned a lot from Papa Paul. For a woman, she's pretty good."

Chapter 12

WILD WOMEN

What the caterpillar calls the end of the world, the master calls a butterfly.

Richard Bach

"Dolly and Ginger, these are the gentlest ponies of mine. They'll be easy for you to ride. They'll be patient, too, but you have to talk with them, tell them they are beautiful. Women like that, you know," Red Sun smiled. Neither Rose or Esther was a vain woman, but they had a sense of humor, so they laughed. Leaving his ponies behind, Red Sun rode off.

"Why didn't Old Timer stay and teach us how to ride?" Esther shuddered a bit.

"Oh, Esther, we're pioneer women; he thinks we can do anything. And we can! It's 1913, so we can ride horses, too." Rose laughed. "So, let's do it. Let's surprise them all. Let's be Cowgirls," Rose crinkled her nose, and her eyes sparkled.

"Get the bridles on, then the saddles. But we'll have to work together on the saddles so they're not too loose. We could end up with our heads on the ground. What have we taken on," Rose exclaimed excitedly. ''Come on Esther! Let's try at least to get the bridles on."

"OK, but your horse is smaller than mine. Look at me, I can't even reach her ears!"

"Just throw it over Ginger's head. She'll know what you're doing."

"No, she'll know I'm afraid."

"Just keep saying, you're a beauty, I love you! Just sing a little."

"Rose, I'm not like you, I can't carry a tune. She'll buck and run away if she hears me let out a squeak."

"What are we going to do? We want to be independent women and ride with the wind, like the men do. We don't want to just sit like lumps in a wagon–or just stay at home cooking and cleaning all day. Someday we may even get rich!"

"Don't think that will ever happen, but you're right! Let's try again."

Esther face whitened. "Maybe we'd better wait 'til Gus and Papa return from town."

"You're probably right, but we can do it ourselves. I'd like to ride into town and shock them. We'll look like some English sophisticated queens," laughed Rose.

"Ha," reminded Esther, "We can't even hold on to the reins. We'll look absolutely stupid."

"Yes, but if we could just ride a little bit every day, then some day, we'll do it right, then we can ride into town," Rose replied. c

Feeding on Rose's mood, Esther came over to Dolly, Rose's smaller white filly, to help her get the saddle on. Dolly's eyes almost looked like they were smirking–if horses' eyes can do that. Both women, dressed in pants borrowed from a son, with cowboy hats tied on, gave great oomph's and heaved up the saddles. They were heavy. Finally they were firmly attached to the horses.

"Check my cinch belt," asked Esther, never as confident as Rose.

"It needs to be tighter or the whole saddle with slip around." Rose yanked on the cinch belt while telling Ginger how beautiful she was and how gentle–hopefully.

"That's really heavy, poor Dolly, and then there's me," moaned Rose.

"Oh you can't weight over ninety pounds. You're so tiny. I'm the monster."

"You're just taller, not fat at all."

"Who could get fat out here, when we work like slaves all day, just making bread, the garden, and then all the clothes to wash. It's a job for six women!" responded Esther, somewhat bitterly.

"You're right, I agree, but we do have freedom, not like the ladies back in Storm Lake who have to go to all those gossiping Ladies Aid meetings. I like my freedom," Rose said.

"You're right, but, oh, I miss the nice clothes and stores and the–."

"Enough of that," laughed Rose, "or we'll never learn to ride straddling these horses."

"Now what would the ladies of Storm Lake think of that? Scandalous I'm sure," laughed Esther.

"Just try to get on."

Their huffs, grunts, and final leaps showed that there was no lady-like way to mount a horse. Each horse neighed slightly, looking pitiful as the women hung on to the saddle horn, as if to say, "What now, we've been reduced to this humility!"

"OK, now that we're on what do we say, something like Hi Ho–or Giddy-up?"

When awkwardness was gone, the women sat high in the saddle, pulled their hats downward, and Rose was the first to say– gently–"Giddy-up." Dolly began to walk smoothly toward the grassy meadow. Esther's Ginger followed–also gentle.

After about a quarter of a mile Rose yelled, "Maybe we should get them to trot?

"How do you do that?"

"You give them a little poke with your shoe in the ribs, not hard–just a signal."

"OK," and Esther was first. Ginger began a slow trot–Esther yelling as she bounced up and down. "Ouch, ouch. That hurts!"

"Stop, stop, stop," Esther said pulling hard on the reins.

Rose also stopped.

"That was rough! Let's just walk back, OK? We had our first ride. I'm pretty stiff and my bottom feels like a rock hit it. Ouch. Ouch," Esther groaned.

"Mine, too," cried Rose.

So two elegant horsewomen slowly walked their horses back to the stable and tried to dismount, with legs flying over the saddle and settling on the ground.

"Oh, I'm so glad we didn't try to ride into town, looking like a couple of cats clawing onto these poor ponies," noted Esther.

"You're right. We'll have to practice much more," concluded Rose.

With that they began to take the saddles off and together hung them on the hooks in the stable, and the reins, the same.

So they did.

After putting the saddles away, they walked, rather stiffly into the house where Rose prepared cups of tea. "I think we did quite well," said Rose.

"You didn't even try to trot your Dolly," laughed Esther.

"You're right. I saw how you were bouncing up and down and yelling every time you hit the saddle. There must be a better way of doing that. What do you think?"

"I've seen men ride like they're part of the saddle, and they have all that 'stuff' down there," Esther giggled.

"We'll have to learn that trick, but right now my bottom feels just broken–ooooh," she grimaced.

"Don't know how Papa and Red Sun ride bare back. They don't have anything to hold on to. Oh, the men 'll soon be back, let's get to our sewing, OK?"

Just about then Papa and Gus rode up the dirt road in the wagon, came in and asked, "What have your lovely pioneer women been doing all day?" seeing Esther and Rose huddled over their sewing.

"Oh, just sewing and a few other things," Esther said with a faint smile.

Over the next two months, the women met to practice and learn more about riding. They watched the men syncopate their smooth saddle lifts, as their horses trotted and galloped."

"You have to use your knees more," said Rose, "and not let the bounce be high, just a part of the saddle and horse."

One day the men commented often how stiffly Esther and Rose walked around the kitchen.

"It's as if you hurt your bottom," commented Papa Paul.

"Oh, I'm just stiff from working in the garden, I guess," Rose concluded with a smile.

One bright, cloudless day, the two nonchalant horsewomen followed Gus and Papa's wagon into town, at a safe distance. They rode with smoothness and confidence. In Fairview the women saw the wagon hitched near the hardware store. They, too, hitched their horses to the rail and proudly walked into the store.

The looks of surprise were worth all the secret practices! Gus and Papa Paul gasped when they saw Rose and Esther, in riding pants, cowboy hats tied down, and ruddy faces from the wind.

"How did ya get here?" cried Gus.

"Oh, just a couple of cowgirls decided to take an afternoon ride," laughed Esther.

Papa Paul looked shocked, "You don't mean you taught yourselves to ride straddle?"

"Absolutely, if men can do it, we can, too!" Rose replied.

"Let's see how good you're in putting on the bridle 'n harness," doubted Gus.

Checking it out, he said, "Wow, you did really good Now tell us, who taught you all these things?"

Both Esther and Rose claimed, "You both did. We watched you all the time, getting ready for the ride, but we didn't do it well at the beginning."

"No, the saddle slipped off once for me, but Ginger stopped right away."

"You were lucky," said Papa, "as sometimes horses get spooked, and they rear up and sometimes even run away, pulling you under their bellies–not good. Can hurt you really bad, or even kill you."

"I noticed that Dolly likes to play jokes as she sometimes seems to poke out her belly when I'm cinching up the belt, so I have to wait a few minutes 'til she let's out the air again," Rose said proudly

"You're learnin, that's good. Watch out for rattlesnakes. If you hear one, stop, look. Be careful as your horse may rear up, or may even panic. You have to keep on the horse 'n manage the reins– holdin tight but not too much as that'll fright the filly even more. I've had happen twice," said Gus.

"Another thing is watch for storms. Lightning is bad out on open places, and if you're on your horse, lightning likes to strike higher objects, and you're–it. Get down in a gully. 'til the storm passes by," warned Papa Paul.

All four pioneers headed back home, the women on their ponies and the men in their wagon. When they reached the bend in the road, Esther and Ginger headed westward, and Rose on Dolly, eastward.

"I'll call you tomorrow morning," yelled Esther, as they now had a multiple party line telephone.

"That's fine, we'll plan our next ride," said Rose.

Each felt more empowered. Through the fall and until the snow fell the women rode almost daily. They found ways to use their time well, like inspecting fences or watching for signs of problems in the fields. Rose felt confidence build in her mind, but Esther remained troubled about the prairie and not being close to her family in Iowa. She was constantly homesick, and even became nauseated and weak–especially in the mornings. It didn't take long for her to recognize that she was pregnant.

"Oh, what a shock," she told Rose one day. "I thought I was too old, now that I'm forty, but a baby is on the way. The boys are teen-agers. Don't know what they'll think at this age. Probably that Mama and Daddy don't do those "things" any more," she laughed.

Chapter 13

AN ANGEL

In the end, it's not going to matter how many breaths you took, but how many moments took your breath away.
Shing Xiong

A good time to be born–April 19, 1914 Marie was born almost five years to the day that Gus and Esther had arrived to homestead. Gus, an aggressive farmer, never allowed any land to fallow–to rest. He also moved Rose's boundary stakes a time or two to take a slice of her half section.

"She'll never notice 'n she doesn't need as much land. I'll just take a little here and there. She's just a woman," Gus sneered.

Papa Paul warned him many times that the soil would gradually become weaker and weaker unless he let it rest. However, this day was a time to celebrate, not to worry. Maria Schultz weighed–7 pounds 3 ounces–by estimate using a chicken weighing scale–and a really beautiful baby.

Even at birth you could see that she would become a gorgeous woman. She had no hair to speak of, but her eyes were the darkest blue–probably soon to change, but still a startling sight. Within a week she was smiling.

Gus's heart simply melted–and her three big brothers couldn't resist running in to see Marie as often as possible. They even missed school days, if she so much as had a tiny whimper. Naturally Esther was content–she had her daughter. Some days she did nothing more than sit and rock this tiny angel.

Summer came and went, as Maria grew even more beautiful. Strangers would stop and rave about her looks, and she'd smile. Tiny dimples and loads of dark brown curls added to her charm. By Christmas Maria was beginning to stand, and on her first birthday she actually walked to her daddy, giggling all the way. No one could believe how this baby changed Gus. He became a tender, loving person, even sharing this little creature with Red Sun–who came as usual to bless the land in the spring.

"Sometimes it takes a child to change a hardened heart," Red Sun reminded them.

But again Gus refused to let the land rest. "I've got 'lot of responsibilities now–have to make it fast. Glad I have three big sons." His sons never complained; they worked constantly.

"We don't have time for school or playin. We're buildin the farm," said Matthew, the oldest. Summer came and went.

An early hard frost hit at the start of October, foreboding signs of a tough winter ahead. Clouds of doubt spread among the farmers, as they'd had a meager harvest, but hoped as always for a better one next year. The seeds for the Russian winter wheat were in the ground, and it was time to reflect and slow down. It was also a time when folks began to get colds–just seemed to go hand in hand. But this year it seemed worse.

Besides colds, whooping cough–that dreaded disease that took young children overnight–gasping for breath–was going around.

It was unusual for little Maria to get sick. She was such a strong toddler, running around, talking, and jabbering, laughing. What a joy! The night she became sick seemed days long. Her fever rose higher and higher. Both Gus and Esther bathed her in cool water, trying to bring down the fever. Her cough grew steadily worse. Gus phoned the doctor, the only one in Hopetown yelling, "Come quick–our Maria is sick."

About a half-hour later the doctor arrived in his Model T Ford, one of the first in the county. He rushed in with his bag and examined Maria, who by this time was breathing heavily and sometimes gagging with her eyes rolled up and back.

"Help us, help us," cried Gus.

Esther just remained silent–almost comatose. Suddenly the room became quiet–no breathing–no cursing–nothing. Maria was gone. The wee body was quiet; her blue eyes shut. Her brown curls, dampened with the heat of the fever, clung like a downy crown on her head. Gus pulled her to his heart and sobbed uncontrollably–gasping now and then for breath.

"Where 're you God? Where 're you? Why take the angel so soon? I hate you!" The doctor closed his bag and left.

Esther sat shocked in the rocker where she had held her baby girl for many hours. She resembled a stone.

The brothers left the house–walking all night about the fields.

No one could talk about this loss, although Rose, Papa, and Will tried. No one could help. Time didn't heal. Gus and Esther didn't celebrate Christmas that year. Gus seemed to have gone crazy; he worked all night sometimes–walking in the fields– plowing more land. He seldom spoke to anyone–even his boys. Esther would go to Rose's house and just sit there staring out the window. Rose let her grieve–as she knew all too well that no one could take away the pain of losing a loved one.

Chapter 14

HEALING POWER

Be strong, do not fear; your God will come. Isaiah 3 5:4

Spring came late that year and a huge blizzard hit the plains on what would have been Maria's second birthday. Everyone was isolated for a whole week; snow piled and drifted, burying the up-wind sides of houses. Finally the wind stopped, the sun shone and snow melted. The Schultz boys began to plow and harrow the fields. Weeds had sprung up as fast as the winter wheat, so work of separating the two–wheat from weeds–was important in the early stages of planting.

All three sons, now 17, 15, and 13, were hard at work. The snow was gone, and the sun's warmth was welcomed. Matthew, the eldest, was in charge of Mark and the youngest, Peter. They were similar to Gus, not speaking as they worked. Matthew yelled at Mark to come and help lift some lumber that had been left in the field last fall.

"Come get these damn 4X4's off here so I can plow! Right now!" Obediently Mark ran over with a wheelbarrow to a pile of about twenty boards.

"Why did we leave these here, do you remember?"

Before he could get an answer, Mark yelled, "Oh my god, I got bit! Oh, Oh–help me, a rattler sprang up and bit me on the neck."

The rattler had been hiding under the wood, awakened by the movement and heat of the sun. As it began to slither away you could see it was a smallish rattler, maybe a youngster. Young rattlers were known to be even more venomous than adults. It escaped into the field before anyone could smash its evil head.

"Dad, Dad," yelled the two brothers, as they rushed to Mark's side.

Within a minute they'd put Mark into the wheelbarrow and were rushing the teenager to the house. The puncture marks were clearly on his throat, next to the jugular vein. The pain was excruciating, but Mark tried to be brave. He knew the consequences–and knew his chances weren't good.

"Pray for me, quick!" was all he could say before he fell into a coma.

The venom worked that fast.

Just then over the road they could see a pony galloping at full speed. It was Red Sun. He rode right up to the house, jumped down, ran inside without knocking, and squatted beside Mark.

Within a moment his hands were on Mark's neck, pressing against the wound and praying. "Grandfather, help this young warrior, the one who travels on his belly has done evil. Take away the poison–throw it to the skies–keep this heart beating." Red Sun looked worried, as he continued to hold fast on the wound.

"Run, run. Go to my saddlebag, and find my medicine bundle. Bring it here! We must hurry." Matt flew out as fast as he could, found the bag with many small jars and herbs in woven sacks, and rushed back in to Mark's side.

"Here, Red Sun!" he shouted.

Red Sun reached for the one small jar, and Peter opened it for him, the Cheyenne medicine man held his hand over the wound.

He was chanting and calling, "Prophet Sweet Medicine. Oh powerful medicine spirit guide, we ask for your power and strength to heal this young warrior, Mark Schultz. Give him your power over the poison. Keep him breathing. Give his heart strength to beat away the awful poison of the fangs." Mark had lost consciousness by now, and his breathing had become rapid and shallow.

Red Sun smeared a small amount of an orange ointment over the punctures and raised his left arm up to the sky. "Grandmother, Healers of All, give power to the medicine. Call on all your helpers to save this young man."

He continued chanting, as Gus came running in.

"Get out of here–you weird ole 'half breed!"

"No," shouted Esther, "he's our only hope." She actually stood between Red Sun and Gus; her nostrils flared and fire was in her eyes. "You old doubter of God–get out of here yourself!"

Gus was shocked; he'd never seen Esther so mad. He stood back.

Red Sun ignored the threats and continued to chant. Sweat formed on his brow; he felt power gradually return to Mark.

Slowly Mark's eyes opened and his breathing slowed then became normal.

"What happened?" whispered Mark looking around, "I felt like I was floating."

"You were, my Brother. You were floating on the power of the Great Spirit. Just lie still and breathe deeply."

"Did I go to sleep?" he asked fretfully, "'cause I had a dream that I was running and running, and there was Maria. She was laughing and walking. She looked so pretty. I ran toward her. I didn't want to leave her, but she waved goodbye. And then I woke up to see you, Old Timer."

"It wasn't time for you to go, young warrior, you still have work to do," answered Old Timer quietly. Esther was clinging to her son and sobbing. Gus stood with awe in his eyes. He got down on his knees, hugged his son, and began to sob deeply. After a time he got up, put his hand on Red Sun's shoulder, and could only say, "Thanks, Old Timer."

Red Sun got on his pony and rode off.

This story was told over and over again throughout the county. There had been other unusual–perhaps miracles that happened during those years. Red Sun never took credit for any of them; never charged a fee and refused any gifts. He would only say, "You must believe, that's all, believe in the power of God–the Great Spirit."

Gus walked out into the noonday, staring at the sun peeping at the edge of a cloud that nearly touched the earth. "Dear God, thanks for savin my son. I knows I've done wrong. I knows I've not been faithful. I knows I cheated Rose; I knows I cheated the land. Maria was my angel 'n now you nearly took my Mark. It's time to leave this land. I knows it. It's time to start over again. I ask for forgiveness."

Esther was in favor of moving back to Iowa–"Let's go home, to old friends and the good life; I've never felt at home on the prairie."

Papa said, "I'll give you a dollar an acre and five hundred dollars for your equipment and livestock and another two hundred fifty for your house. That'd be one thousand seventy dollars."

"Make it even eleven hundred, 'n it's all yours," bargained Gus.

"You're a hard man, Gus, even after what you've been through, but I'm glad to buy your place and bring it back to life," was all Papa said. He was glad to have Gus move back to Iowa, as Papa knew he'd already ruined the good soil.

It would take another decade to heal it.

Rose was sorry to lose her friend and companion, Esther. They'd shared so much sorrow, but maybe it was time for joy.

Before summer arrived, the Gus Shultz family was headed back home–Iowa–as they'd never really left it. Will and Papa began to rescue Gus's half section. Hank looked on, never lifting a finger unless he had to. Papa registered Gus's homestead in Rose's name, as she was the one who loved the land.

PART II

LOVE &

CHANGES

Chapter 15

JULIE, FROM DENMARK

You are a child of God.
Marianne Williamson

"Come here my little darling," Carl, a tall Danish fisherman, said as he lifted up Julie Serena, his three-year old daughter. "Good-bye and angels keep you 'til I come back."

"Don't wan 'ou ta go; I miss 'ou, Dadda."

"You take care of Mommy, and I'll be back when the sun comes up, OK?" He gave her a longer goodbye kiss than usual. "I love you, dearest daughter."

"Lov 'ou too" and Julie gave her daddy another hug, as he put her carefully into bed.

Carl stood looking at his golden-haired toddler. How he loved her, so vibrant, so much like Serena, his wife. He knew that she would grow up to be the beauty her mother was. Serena was tall, lithe, and a caring nurse who had the gentle skills of a healer. She also was an artist whose paintings of the sea were quite well known in Denmark. Her flair for color and movement were matched by her own free lifestyle.

They'd met in Vejle one summer, five years before, when Serena happened to visit an aunt and stayed after falling into 'crazy love', as she would say.

So it was. The two lovers would find places to skinny dip, feeling free as the fish he would catch. And, so he caught her–his mermaid. Their moments of lovemaking were scorching and yet tender, as both were expressive Danes.

"I love to worship your glorious body," she'd tell him, as her gentle hands sculpted his back and buttocks. And he would admire her perfect nipples, on transcendent breasts. "God must have loved you very much to give you such creations." Locked in free and frequent love making, they seemed oblivious of the world around them. When pregnancy began, Carl was uncertain if he could share his love of Serena with another creature, but there this creature was, closing her toddler's eyes and soon fast asleep.

"A miracle to have two loves," he said, as he left the Julie's room for his dangerous task of the night.

Serena was also courageous–sharing a fisherman's risks as his wife. When they first married, Serena begged him to leave the sea, as "I know too many who are now widows who lost their husbands at sea. I don't want that to happen."

Carl, however, loved the feeling of the brisk breeze and roar of waves crashing about him. "It's my life. I won't be lost at sea–if so, I'll come back as a water spirit, and haunt you," he laughed. So Serena quietly accepted that her love might be cut short, but for now it was complete.

He kissed her gently, then passionately. "I'll be back by morning. This is just a tiny storm, and it brings the fish out in droves. It's a good night to fish; this is mild. We have the best chance for a big take tonight, as the wind is from the north and that means the fish will be in schools, easy to catch." Laughing at her silly fears, Carl swung Serena around and around, kissing her neck and nibbling at her ears. With that he left, giving her a last, deep kiss and pinch on her bottom.

"Can't wait 'til I get back," he laughed. Serena held on to his hand, longer than usual.

Carl loved the ocean. He lived in a tiny villa Vejle, Denmark on the shores of the North Sea; the nearby waters were always unusually rough. Many generations of Sorensen's before him had been courageous fishermen, the first to reach out to hold down the sails or to pull in nets filled with fish. Descended from Vikings, Danish men were stouthearted. Sailors often belittled the risk, for they loved the wild sea and the adventure of pulling in the catch. However, too often the rolling waves and angry gales were fatal. The village Lutheran church and churchyard were filled with symbols of naval bravery and naval loss. Instead of the crucifix at the altar, there was a swinging lantern, a symbol of hope.

As Carl ran to his boat, the night appeared stormy. Lightning flashed and winds blew fiercely.

"Please don't go out tonight, Carl," he'd heard Serena call to him. "It's too stormy; I can feel the worst is yet to come. It's raining so hard now, what can you see out there?"

"I'll be back before morning. I love you," he'd called back.

"I love you, too, Take care–" he felt her hand still cling to his. Serena worried all night, as the winds only became stronger.

Hurrying out to the wharf, Carl admitted the sea was angry and that lightning was always a worry. But he trudged onward, joining his crew of nine.

Taking his post as captain at the wheel, he yelled, "All aboard. Launch."

Outward they went with their sails full and the wind stiff. About two hours out to sea, just as expected they encountered a huge school of fish, and their nets filled quickly.

"We have our full load, let's go home," shouted Captain Carl. "We can be home before morning."

Turning around, the wind whipped the sails suddenly into an almost horizontal level. "Look out. Grab the lines and pull hard. Hold On!" shouted Carl.

Another giant jolt of wind hit the boat again, and two men slipped overboard. "Help! Help! Two men over board, men overboard!" yelled the Captain.

Then yet another sudden jolt, and wind quickly twisted the boat yet another quarter of a turn. Carl lost his hold on the wheel. Twisting and turning and turning again, Carl slipped and slid overboard, yelling, "Watch the wheel, watch the wheel" as another sailor took over the helm. Throwing out lines as quickly as possible, the other seven tried to reach their comrades, while the boat twisted at yet another wild angle. Hopelessly they lost control. Tossed by waves and hammered by winds, they couldn't spot their friends in the boiling, rolling deeply dark sea.

"Over here, no, over there."

The confusion continued. Lightning flashed rapidly, but no one could be seen. Calling loudly, "Carl, Peter, Christopher"–over and over again. No answer was heard, waiting and waiting for a response. There was none. The crew tried for hours to find the lost ones, but finally knew the toll had been final. Three men lost at sea.

By dawn the sea had calmed, but still there was no sign of life. Waves were gentle, holding quietly the secret of the night. The wrathful sea had swallowed Carl and two others in the dark. Only seven returned in the quiet morning. The message stormed out to the whole town, and flags were flown half-mast. Everyone in Vejle soon knew the fate of Carl and two others–'swept over board and out to sea' were the tidings given at the funeral.

Two other widows and Serena sat as stone figures in the little church. Julie was held to her mother's heart. The small fishing town of Vejle was accustomed to these fatal events.

Yet Serena walked out to the sea every night, continuing to hope that somehow her Carl would return. Grief stricken, Serena knew that she would receive a two hundred dollar death benefit from the fishing company. It could never replace her Carl–but it could buy two tickets to America–not for her–but for daughter, Julie, and Aunt Mary.

"I could never cross this hateful sea that took my beloved. I will stay behind, just in case he comes home someday. And I don't want my Julie to grow up to the same fate–a fisherman's widow," Serena cried sadly.

She and Aunt Mary made plans; Mary and Julie would sail across the Atlantic. They would join another aunt and two uncles in a small town, Storm Lake, Iowa. Serena pretended to be happy, but held a heavy heart; "She will have a new beginning, in a new home."

But before the plans were complete Serena grew deathly ill. The doctor listened to her lungs and declared she had pneumonia. He also knew that she was grieving for her lost soul mate. Sometimes that's a fatal condition, the wise doctor thought. Serena's fever rose higher and higher, perhaps from all the cold, damp nights she had spent looking seaward, waiting, hoping.

As she lay dying, little Julie held her hand.

"Mommy's going to be with Daddy in heaven. We both love you and know that you will be okay with Aunt Mary. Daddy and I will be with you in your heart forever." Serena closed her eyes while still holding on to Julie.

"Sa sove i Jesu navn (So sleep in Jesus name)," were her mother's last words.

"I love you, too, Mommy 'n Daddy," said Julie, as her eyes swelled with tears, but she let go.

As the years went by, Julie would never forget those final moments with her mama. At the end of May 1908, she and Aunt Mary left to board a steam ship crossing the Atlantic, and a train headed for Storm Lake, Iowa.

The Danes throughout history were a resilient people, resisting invasion, composing unforgettable music and writing charming children's fairy tales. Generally Danes had contentment and lived in a land of sufficiency, not because of the favored environment but rather because of being robust, risk-taking, and hard-working people. Tall and generally slim, Danes lived healthy lives on small, productive farms. They didn't suffer from the potato blight, as did the Irish. But too many crowded onto the small, peninsula jutting into the North Sea. When the New World opened to immigration, Danes were among those eager to bet on their futures as Americans.

One who left the old world was feisty, bubbly four-year old Julie Serena Sorensen.

As the party sailed from the Copenhagen harbor, bound for America, Julie held onto the railing; her golden curls, bright blue eyes, and enchanting, dimpled smile faced the rhythmic waves. She watched them push past the dock. A cloudless sky predicted an easy voyage. This young orphan would live her life like that first trip, unafraid, facing the wind and any other challenge that came her way. Julie would take challenges in her stride, accept the inevitable, triumph, and move ever forward. Perhaps it also was that Julie was unusually precocious.

"Come on, Aunt Mary," Julie cheered, "let's go watch the waves from the big ocean. Look, we can barely see the shore any more! We're on our way to America!"

Aunt Mary had mixed feelings of leaving her warm, thatched roof house and the yard where chickens ranged freely. In her fifties, Mary would manage to find her way in America, but always with more caution than the bright, courageous, spirited–but ever so tender Julie.

Chapter 16

ALONE

Because of deep love, one is courageous.
Lao Tzu

Storm Lake, Iowa was known as Little Denmark, for many immigrants were from that Scandinavian country. They were a serious, hard working, and Lutheran. The rich soil was similar to Denmark's, but farming took hard work and a community of support. Each family reached out to new immigrants. "Being connected with others is the only way to survive." So Aunt Mary and her niece found they were welcomed. Everyone spoke Danish, but their children would be English speakers. "We're Americans," they would declare proudly.

School wasn't a challenge for Julie. She not only learned English quickly but also listened to recitations of all the upper grades in that one-room schoolhouse. Soon she was a helper for the teacher. Settling in Storm Lake, Aunt Mary worked as a pie maker for a local baker.

"We love our little house, don't we, Julie, and so many new friends." But, that winter, Aunt Mary became seriously ill, "Weak lungs in our family," she said sadly.

"Tanta, Tanta, please don't die. I'll be all alone," cried Julie.

Within four days, Aunt Mary died. "Pneumonia," the doctor said.

Julie was now really alone.

Uncle Chris and wife Karen already had six children. Their house was crowded. "Guess we're the only ones she has left; we have to take her in," Aunt Karen sighed.

"Yes, it's up to us. We're her only family."

So they made a place for Julie behind the door of their three daughters' bedroom. She had only a blanket to sleep on, and her cousins were not happy to share anything with her.

"We don't like you," they'd say.

Sometimes they'd hide her dress for the day, and Julie would wear the same one over and over again. Her male cousins were equally as taunting, sometimes swiping her homework and teasing her as she walked to school, alone. Aunt Karen never said a thing to correct the meanness. Uncle Chris was always working away from home.

Julie ignored her cousins; in time their bullying stopped, but they were never friends.

By age fourteen Julie had grown tall and lean, her blue eyes beautiful, and her head topped with curly blonde hair. Her actions were quick and definite; she wasn't shy. Her chores were many. She did more work than any of the cousins. Beyond her outward characteristics, Julie had a generous heart. "Let me help you," she'd say to an elderly person as they tried to rise during the long Lutheran church services.

Julie was a natural observer of human behavior. *I must stay alert, she'd think, as so many things are happening, and I'm alone.* She used these skills to remain aware of her surroundings. This awareness would save Julie many times in the future.

Aunt Karen never talked with her. She would just give orders, but never said thanks. In fact, the only person Julie could talk with was her teacher, Mr. Jensen. He was a kind man, with little hair and a big mustache.

"Mr. Jensen, may I ask you a question about hired girls?"

"Why of course, Julie; why do you want to know?"

"My uncle wants me to become one. It's hard to live with all his kids that need so much, and I don't have a mom or dad."

"Oh, I hope you don't do that. You are the smartest pupil I've got. I need to talk with your uncle

"I don't think he'd like that. He's pretty stern."

"But, Julie, you're just half way through high school. Why, you should go to college; you have that much ability. You are very smart."

Julie was surprised to hear praise, but she'd never known anyone who had gone to college. "How could I ever do that?"

"There are ways; I must talk with your uncle." Mr. Jensen looked concerned. That evening when he came to talk with Uncle Chris and Aunt Karen, Julie wasn't in the room. She could hear raised voices, and once heard Uncle Chris shout, "You're putting nonsense into that girl's head. She's a burden and needs to make her own way. We can't keep her anymore."

Julie heard the door slam behind Mr. Jensen, and soon uncle came into the parlor where she was doing her homework. His face was red, as if he were angry.

"Listen missy, (not even calling her by namc) you are leaving here as soon as school is out. That's just three more weeks, and you'll be a hired girl. No more talk about college, do you hear? I'm putting an ad in the newspaper so someone will hire you."

"Yes, Uncle Chris," was all she answered.

Chapter 17

LOCKED UP

Yesterday is but today's memory and tomorrow is today's dream.

Khalil Gibran

Three weeks had passed, and school was out. One morning a fat man in a 1920 black Model T Ford came to the door. He didn't smile.

He said. "I saw in the newspaper you have a girl you want to hire out. Did I come to the right place?"

"Yup, I have that one right here," answered Uncle Chris. "What's your name?"

"I'm Peter Pedersen and I live in Norfolk, Nebraska, about 100 miles from here." He was a big man, with a stomach that stuck way out, and beady black eyes.

Julie thought, *I don't like the way he looks me up and down, as if I were some cow he might want to buy.*

Mr. Pedersen looked her over–front and back–nodded to Uncle Chris, "Does she work hard?"

"Yup"

"Does she get up early?"

"Yup, like the rest of us; we're up at dawn." "Huh," was all he muttered.

"Does she eat a lot?"

"Normal."

"Yup," the big man from Norfolk, not smiling, said, "you're going to be my hired girl, so bring along all your things. I'll pay you a dollar a week. You'll have a room of your own and can eat what we have." He never smiled.

Uncle Chris didn't ask another question of this stranger. No one said goodbye.

With that, Julie packed her few things, moved out of her uncle's house, and never saw him, Aunt Karen, or her cousins again. She was now a hired girl. Julie turned sixteen that month, but no one knew she had a birthday. Her home was now Nebraska.

"It'll take us about five hours to get there," and that's all Mr. Pedersen said for many miles. He seemed like a stern man.

After about four hours he broke the silence; "My wife is Sophia, and she's going to have another damn kid."

Julie said nothing, not knowing if he expected her to say anything. So she kept quiet. Once he glanced at her, looking at her arms and feet, as if wondering if she could do all the required work. Julie sat up erect and alert.

Then she spoke, "How many children do you have?"

"Too many," was all he mumbled, looking straight ahead.

Although she was hungry and needed to go to the toilet, they never stopped until he pulled into a lane and went down a long, long road to a big white house. In the dark you could see a barn and other sheds. It looked quiet–and way out in the country. Julie could see only a couple of dim lights of farmhouses in the distance.

Sophia, Mrs. Pedersen, came to the door and merely said, "Go to your room and put your things away."–never smiling either.

A door stood open, down a dark hallway. Julie walked briskly. The room was tiny but had a window to the west. A small dresser held an oil lamp, no mirror, and a single bed had a dark gray coverlet on it–no chair.

The closet, yes, it's big enough for my two dresses, two skirts, and three white blouses, my brown winter coat and two pairs of shoes–one for church–if they go. Better than I had at Uncle Chris's. Julie sighed sadly.

"I've saved some supper for you and Mr. Pedersen, and the toilet is off to the left." Sophia didn't smile–not once. She looked very sad–and very pregnant.

"Thanks," replied Julie.

Why she's so sad–and where are the children? Julie thought. Soon she would learn, and in dismay began her plan to escape.

"We expect you up at 4:00 AM to fix my breakfast and feed two kids before they leave for school. Then you'll do the chores in the house, whatever is needed. Have supper ready for me by 6:00 PM and the kids when they're hungry. When you're done, you can go to bed." Mr. Pedersen said, not expecting an answer.

He never mentioned any day off, going to church, or anything. Don't know what a 'hired girl' is all about, but this doesn't sound good, thought Julie.

So began Julie's life as a hired girl.

Every morning Sophia stayed in bed, weak and tired with her pregnancy. She would quietly get up after Mr. Pedersen left for the barn and fields. Sophia remained quiet most of the day, sometimes staring out the window and, Julie thought–crying. *Don't think she ever plays with the children–doesn't even talk with them. How strange. I wonder why?*

I work all the time, by myself, cleaning, cooking, doing the wash and playing with the two little ones. So tired when I finish about 10:00 PM then up again *at 4:00 AM. I never hear any laughter. How strange.*

"Don't you want to sit down to eat?" Julie asked the two older children, as she had their supper ready for them.

"Nope, we just stand and eat in the kitchen, so it's faster."

Mr. Pedersen came from the fields about 6:00 PM, ate his supper by himself, then went into the parlor, and read with a some booklet on the second coming of Christ. He had a battery-powered radio and would listen to it until around 9:00 PM, and then he went to bed. Sophia was already there. This was the pattern–day after day–night after night.

Julie cried herself to sleep every night–she missed Mama–and Daddy.

Mama, Mama, why did you have to die–like Daddy did? And Aunt Mary, too. I hate it here. Mr. Pedersen is so mean; he talks in a loud voice and yells at his kids all the time.

But things were about to change. The Pedersen's seldom went anywhere at all–but about once a month they'd dress up–all four children and go to the Lutheran church in a small town about four miles west of the farm. Without a mirror in her room, Julie combed her hair the best she could, and put on her Sunday, blue-flowered dress.

The second oldest son, Andrew, looked at her and smiled, "You look really pretty, Julie."

Mr. Pedersen raised his hand as if to slap the boy, and said, "You keep your eyes off of her and mind your business, or you'll get a smacking from me."

His face was livid red. Andrew hurried upstairs and didn't come down until the family was ready to leave for church. No one said another word, but Julie could feel Mr. Pedersen's eyes looking at her bosom, that showed up perky in her Sunday dress.

At church Mr. and Mrs. Pedersen mingled with a few folks. One roly-poly woman walked over to Julie and said, "Hello, I'm Mrs. Thompsen, and I've heard that you're from Vejle, Denmark."

Startled, Julie could hardly remember where she'd been born; it had been a long time since she even talked with an adult in Danish. "Why, yes, I was born there, what do you know about Vejle?"

"My family came from there, the Julian Olsen's. Did you know them?"

"No, I was only four when I left for America with my Aunt Mary. My mother and father both died in Vejle. My aunt died, too, after we'd settled in Storm Lake, Iowa."

"My goodness, girl, you've had a hard time. How old are you?"

"I turned sixteen about the time I moved here."

"Well, you're sure a pretty one," Mrs. Thompsen's laughed heartedly. "Bet you have a lot of boyfriends."

"No, actually I haven't met any young people, 'cause I'm the hired girl for the Pedersen's."

Was that a shadow I saw cross Mrs. Thompsen's face? Julie thought.

"Just call me, Hilda, please. So, you work for Mr. Pedersen." It seemed that Hilda took a breath in as she spoke those words. "How did he find you–so far away?"

"My uncle put an ad into the newspaper advertising that he had a niece available as a hired girl."

"Where was that?"

"Storm Lake, Iowa."

"Oh, my, my–that's interesting. That's a long way from here." her voice seemed to wander off, and her eyes became wide with a look of fright. "So you don't have any kin around here. No one to keep an eye on you, and–."

Julie wondered what this mysterious reaction was about. *Did Mrs. Thompsen know something about the hiring of a girl so far away–.that she, Julie, didn't know?* Julie suddenly had goose bumps on her arms. *I need to tell someone about how violent Mr. Pedersen is, but I don't know this woman very well, so I must keep quiet.*

"How does he treat you?" Mrs. Thompsen seemed to whisper.

"I guess OK. I've been there now for almost a month to help Mrs. Pedersen. She is due any time now." Julie felt her face grow red, as if she was hiding something–and she was.

"You should be getting out, every week! There are some really nice dances for young people in Norfork. What a shame you don't get out. You should come and visit someday–we can talk about Vejle." Hilda seemed to be sending a message.

Suddenly Julie felt a rush of warm tears about to slide down her face. "I'm doing OK." She quickly gained control of herself. *I must NOT cry; I must be strong.*

Hilda looked at this young teenager with concern, "Are you sure?" as if she might know something about the Pedersen's.

Just then Julie saw an arm reach out and grab hers. It was Mr. Pedersen. Sternly he said, looking at Hilda in anger, "It's time for us to go."

Mrs. Thompsen called out, "Come over sometime. I live just across the field to the north. You take care."

Everyone hustled into the Pedersen car, but Peter looked back disgustedly and said, "That ole busybody." Everyone in the car kept silent.

The days and nights streamed onward. Now and then Julie would recall what Mrs. Thompsen had said, "Just remember if you ever need to talk with someone, I don't live far away, just across the field to the north. I'm always home and have time to talk."

Strange, this woman must know something, thought Julie.

Early one Monday morning after Mr. Pedersen had gone into the field to work, there was a knock at the front door. Opening it, Julie was surprised to see Mrs. Thompsen with a plateful of cinnamon rolls.

"I know the baby is due any time now, so thought maybe you'd like a little something special. How are things going?"

Sophia–just stared into space before answering in a quiet voice–"We're doing OK. I'm glad Julie came to help, as I'm not strong any more."

Then Mrs. Thompsen looked directly at Julie, "And how are you?"

"I love the children; they need lots of love," was all Julie could say, knowing the shouting and hitting that went on every evening. *I'm afraid to tell her, afraid of what might happen to the others and me.*

"I'm sure you do love the children, but you also need to have a life of your own. Do you have time to go to any social things at church?"

"No," answered Sophia sadly–"as it's time for the baby to come, maybe after the baby is born."

"Well, if you want to get some fresh air sometime, I know it would take you only about fifteen minutes to get to my house. Do come over sometime soon." Mrs. Thompsen's words seemed to hold some mystery.

"Thanks, I'll remember that." Julie's eyes showed that she understood the hidden message.

Each day seemed the same monotony. One morning Sophia came into the kitchen, shaking as she held a cold cloth to her face.

"Are you OK, Sophia? " Julie inquired.

"I'll be OK, don't worry."

That afternoon her water broke. "I'm in labor," Sophia cried out. Julie called the midwife. She knew about babies, but had never seen a birth. When the midwife came, she took over the birthing, and Julie stayed with the other children; she heard groaning and then a baby's loud cry.

"It's a girl," declared the midwife.

"Oh, no. Mr. Pedersen wants no more girls!" Sophia cried.

When Peter came in from the field, he screamed, "Another damn kid. Another damn mouth to feed!–and another ugly girl," plainly ignoring his beautiful, tiny infant daughter.

Shocked by such angry words, Julie was taken back, then felt anger rising. She stayed nearby the bed, gave Sophia water, and held the new bundle of baby. She was soft and smelled sweet; Sophia named her, "June," as it was the month of June. Peter never looked at the baby nor touched his wife. He went out to the barn– alone.

Julie became manager of the house, cooking, cleaning, and caring for the baby, a sweet little mite. She loved June, the tiny, fuzzyheaded baby, even holding her when she wasn't fussy. Sophia breastfed the baby, holding little June closely, kissing and playing with her toes. When Peter would open the door, coming in from the fields you could feel tension rise as she held little baby close to her heart.

"Suppose you think that baby will save you, you bitch." He yelled in front of all the children. They cowered, as if expecting to be hit.

Julie, tensely as well bravely said, "That's not right, Mr. Pedersen for you to say that. The baby is yours, too!"

With that Peter stepped in front of her and raised his hand as if to slap Julie's face. Julie knew he didn't mean he would only slap her. She wanted to escape, but she couldn't leave poor Sophia or her five children.

Chapter 18

ESCAPE

For two tense years Julie went about feeding the family and doing all the household duties. She saw no way to escape. Baby June, now talking and trying to do everything, was beautiful and precious. She would run to Julie the first thing in the morning, to hug and kiss.

Julie loved June so much. *I wonder what her life will become. This isn't a good situation. How can I tell anyone?* Julie knew she must never be alone with Peter, so kept close to the children. One night, Julie swore she heard scratching on her window. *It doesn't sound like an animal; it's so repetitive, like some person is scratching a knife on the windowpane. I wonder. I'll check in the morning to see if I can see footprints.*

Sure enough–there they were, right under her bedroom window–large shoes worn by a large man–a peeping Tom or an intruder. *Now I'm worried that he might be hiding in my closet some night or? I want to run away–now.*

But thinking ahead, Julie waited until Peter had gone to the fields. She pretended to need something from the tool shed next to the house, where she grabbed a claw hammer. She lifted it to feel its heft, and gage her arm's strength. *Could I bash a man's head with this?*

Perhaps, but it would be a hard thing to do. Tucking the hammer in a fold of her apron, she left the shed. No one saw her, so Julie crept back into her room and placed the hammer in a tight spot between the mattress and the wall. *Just in case, I can grab it and swing it as hard as I can, then run out across the field to the Thompson's or somewhere.*

Each night she touched the hammer to see if it was still in place–it was. As it was harvest season, Peter was in the fields most of the day and late into the night. Somehow the house seemed more content. Sophia even laughed several times. Before long it was fall, and soon another winter began. Peter was inside many days, busy keeping his books. Christmas came and went –as barren and joyless as any Christmas Julie had ever seen, but her fears were fading. Little June was speaking in baby sentences. Julie checked to see how much money she'd had saved with her wages of a dollar a week. With so few chances to spend she had saved almost –enough to get away.

At church one Sunday Mrs. Thompsen said, "I want you to come over for Easter dinner–surely they will let you do that?"

"I'll ask and see if I can come."

To her surprise, Mr. Pedersen, said, "Yes." This would be her first day free after more than two and a half years. So after Easter services she put on her walking shoes and cut across the field to Mrs. Thompsen's. Fritz, her husband, was even more roly-poly than his missus, and their sons and families equally so. They laughed and told jokes at the table. Julie had forgotten how "normal" families interacted. After the table was cleared, Hilda said, "Fritz will drive you back to the Pedersen's before dark, so let's just sit and talk."

Julie remained loyal to the Pedersen's. She didn't reveal the dark secrets of continual abuse and fear. However, she must have given Hilda a reason to say, "If you ever want to leave the family, just come straight across the field, and I'll take you to safety–like the train, so you can go west. Have you thought of that?"

"Why, yes I have, but I don't know any one in the west."

"I have friends in a little, prairie town called Fairview, Colorado. Mrs. Olsen, a friend, is Danish, too. Oh, she's a dear one, and generous. Let's make a plan."

"I hate to leave little June."

"If you knew what I know, you'd go right now!"

Puzzled, Julie didn't ask anything more. "I'll go in September after the harvest is over," she answered bravely.

"Good," answered Hilda, "but if you decide that you must go earlier, run fast across the field; it's safe that way." Mr. Thompsen drove Julie home; all was quiet when she entered the house.

I will leave in September, thought Julie. She slept soundly that night, knowing that her escape was planned.

About a week later she heard a scream from the Pedersen's bedroom, like none she'd heard before.

"You bitch, another damn kid–how could you do this–you're just a slut–a whore–who's the father? Why do you do this?" Peter's rough voice was yelling loudly. And then Julie heard not slapping, but pounding–like a fist in the stomach.

"Ahhhh" she could hear Sophia moan.

"I'll get rid of that bastard," he shouted, as hc pounded more.

Sophia's voice trembling and screaming "Stop, stop, you are hurting me."

Horrified, Julie could hear muffled cries, as she knew Sophia was being raped!

"Don't, don't you're hurting me." Sophia screamed. Then more slaps.

Julie couldn't stand it any longer. She pounded on the door. "Are you alright? Is everything OK?" she called out.

Peter yanked the door open and–naked, with his penis still erect, grabbed Julie's arm. He shouted, "You want some, too, come here and lay down by the bitch, and I'll give it to both of you. How would you like that?" His eyes were red with anger, as he reached out to grab her. Sophia, shrunken in the background and naked, held a pillow to her chest.

Though caught off guard, Julie stood firmly. She looked him straight in the face and said in a loud, clear voice, "You don't want to do that–there are laws."

Her hate-filled eyes held his squarely, as he stood back, shocked by her strength and courage.

"You'd better back off right now, or I'll pinch off that tiny little peepee of yours with my long fingernails."

She stepped back horrified.

"You'll get yours later," he sneered.

Shocked, Peter backed off and gained his composure. "Why you little bitch–always coming on to me–I could see you wanted something from me–all along."

"You're mistaken. I just want to take care of your wife and your children, but you are a vile man! Sophia, I feel sorry for you and the children." Julie turned around and walked straight to her room, realizing that Peter was a man who abused his wife when she was pregnant. Luckily Peter did not follow, and the house became quiet. She knew better than to wait any longer, and needed to leave very early in the morning, straight to Thompsen house. She wouldn't forget what she had learned as a "hired girl." *This isn't a safe place. Please Jesus, I need help. You have promised to always be with those who love yo*u, Julie thought.

That night Julie kept the claw hammer next to her in the bed. Long before dawn the next morning she quickly prepared breakfast. She grabbed her already packed suitcase–and left the claw hammer behind on her bed–a symbol of her courage, gratefully she never had to use it.

Julie ran straight across the field to Thompsen's house, never looking back, with her money tucked into her blouse. She rapped rapidly on the door. Even though it was still dark, Hilda answered and said, "I was hoping you'd escape soon." Julie then sat down and began to cry–the first time in almost three years. She told a story of horror.

Hilda put her arm around Julie's shoulder and said, "I wish we had laws to protect children and women–and maybe some men, too. I've seen abuse in my family, so I could sense what Sophia was going through, but she'd never reach out. They had another hired girl about a year before you came who just disappeared. No one knows what really happened to her–I've always thought that Mr. Pedersen had something to do with her disappearance–don't know–just a feeling. Sophia was pregnant then, too." Hilda continued, "Let's make plans to have you move to Colorado–to be with my friends. OK?"

Julie nodded.

"We'll send a telegram to the Olsen's at Fairview to see if they can help."

Julie stayed safely in the house while Mr. Thompsen sent the telegram. In two days a reply arrived. *"We will help. Come, Julie."*

"I know you'll be happy there. The town even has a Lutheran church, and you'll soon find a good man to marry!" Mr. Thompsen laughed.

The next morning roly-poly Mrs. Thompsen packed cinnamon rolls and cookies, and hugged Julie goodbye. Mr. Thompsen put a blanket on the Model T Ford's floor that covered Julie, just in case they encountered Mr. Pedersen. Arriving safely at the train station, Julie took the Union Pacific that crossed Nebraska into the northeastern corner of Colorado.

The wide-open prairie would become her home.

Chapter 19

GOING HOME

You know the place where I am going,
John 14:3

Both Papa Paul and Red Sun were old, now in their late 90s. Hard workers all of their lives and still vibrant; each had begun to wither and shrink. "I'm going home soon, to be with my Trudy," Papa proclaimed one day.

Red Sun responded, "Yes, it's time for us both to go. I celebrated my last Sun Dance and left lessons for those who will follow."

And so it was. One September morning Rose tried to waken Papa, but found that he didn't respond. He had died during the night. "He looked so peaceful, just sleeping," she remarked. Then she found, under his pillow an envelope addressed to:

Jesus Christ, My Savior, Heaven's Gates.

Inside was a short note:

"Goodbye to all. Dearest Trudy, I'll meet you at the mailbox. I'm coming Home."
Signed,

Your beloved husband,
Paul.

Hundreds came to honor Paul Pinot as the man who had given these homesteaders a promise–the Promise Seeds. Red Sun stood by his brother's grave. Will, now a young, grown man began to sing, "I Love to Tell the Story of Jesus and his Love." He added, "Papa lived his love for Jesus every day and that's how he told His story. Then Will broke into his favorite song, "Abide with me." All joined in to finish the song, "–hold Thou Thy cross before my closing eyes. In life, in death, O Lord, abide with me." Hank stood to the side, looking upset and left out.

Several weeks later, the body of Red Sun in Hair was found on the grave of his beloved Blue Meadow Flower and his son, Two Tongues. He had in his hand a key marked "The Great Hunting Ground." Hundreds, too, honored him, and the stories of his healing and power lived afterwards. On the Cheyenne reservation, a Blessing was held for the dead, and a White Sacred Arrow was sent high into the sky as a reminder of the passing of this faithful spiritual leader. His medicine bundle was handed down to one of the young leaders who had shown wisdom and healing powers. The sacredness of the ceremony was shared with all Cheyenne people.

"This is our way of connecting with all of our ancestors and with Mahoe," chanted the new chief, Running Bear.

After the memorial service Rose, Will, and Hank returned to their homestead. "Just look at our farm," said Rose, "can you remember how it looked in 1909, so barren, so colorless, and now alive with grains we planted, trees to give shade, yellow roses, and all the livestock. Look at our new Fordson tractor. Indeed, we are blessed." She took up Papa's violin and began playing, as she knew Papa and Mama were now together.

Then she finished, she merely said, "It's time to go to work." And so they did.

Over the years Papa, Red Sun, Rose, and Will had become the team that changed the prairie. Their crops and livestock were the best in the county. From horizon to horizon, their land was fertile. Rose's reputation grew as a smart widow with uncanny knowledge of the land; she had become a well-to-do pioneer woman. She had even become a voice for women.

"We cannot build a strong nation when half the population's voice is silent. We must be allowed to have more rights." Rose was even invited to the Governor's mansion to celebrate the national passage of the Nineteenth Amendment.

Governor Shoup said:

"Rose Schultz you have paved the way for women of all ages and are a role model for those to come. You have triumphed over many challenges."

With Papa Paul gone Will, now twenty-two, was head of the house. He was wise beyond his years, and although only completed the third grade, he was a quick learner. Margaret finished her elementary schooling. She taught in a country school, until she fell in love and married a neighbor boy. Hank, always headstrong, selfish, and arrogant, had by age 20 become a problem of long-standing in school and at home. He was tall, like Papa, handsome beyond words, and intelligent. Young girls fell for the charming seducer, Hank. Young men were not so charmed, "He's a bully and a womanizer; no one trusts Hank Schultz."

Hank's grasp of numbers and completed high school education let him take over as bookkeeper for the homestead. He was accurate, but also cunning. While going through the records left by his uncle, Hank discovered that indeed Gus had cheated Mama Rose.

I can see how he must have moved the fence posts very early when the land was first settled. He probably did this right after Daddy was killed. That ole bastard, taking from a widow yet, but then again, he saw that it could be done. Maybe I can figure out some way, too, Hank paused. In his mind began to see ways in which he could put aside money from the accounts and into other banks, like at Ogallala, Nebraska. *They'll never know. They're so trusting and stupid! They deserve to lose the money.* As time passed his schemes became more and more calloused and evil.

Chapter 20

RULES TO LIVE BY

As Julie was getting to know the Olsen's, she also was learning to live in her new Colorado home. October–time to relax, have fun, and socialize. The harvest was in, winter wheat planted, and snows were yet to come. But what was there to do? About fifty families now dotted the prairie, meaning about three hundred people–not bad, but the pickings for romantic partners remained very slim. Often you saw double weddings, as siblings married siblings of a neighbor or friend. Then their children were double cousins–and so on–pretty soon in some way or another, everyone in the area was related.

"This could be sort of scary, but folks have good memories so that those marriages weren't "too" close–"Don't want any idiot kids," the women of Fairview would say.

The majority of homesteaders came from the Midwest, primarily German or Scandinavian heritage, so everyone sort of "looked" alike. Big, blonde, and good meat eaters. Over their quilting bees in the basement of the Lutheran church, the older women, keepers of the culture, would talk and talk, making sure that the community stayed connected and "pure ".

You'd hear the old women say, "There are all sorts of rules, like looks aren't as important as 'can she cook', 'can she have babies', 'does she look after old Papa and Mama'. And 'is he a worker' and 'does he drink'? Oh, everyone drank some–men folks that is–but just home brew, and not during the week. No drunks in our family.

"But if he has traits such as bein smart with numbers, that's good. Does he keep his machinery clean and in good shape and does he get his crops in on time?

"No daughter willingly marries into a lazy family. And no hussies in our midst. Oh, no. We count the months before the first baby comes! And it better be nine months–well–some babies just naturally come 'early'.

"Boys are encouraged to look for a girl who showed good traits, such as her prize-winning bread or cakes at county fairs. And is she generous–helping her old grandmother and raising a good flock of chickens. It helps if she had good tits, too, as breast feeding is a requirement–makes for a good mother."

They'd continue, "Oh, you've got to watch out for certain features –like crossed eyes–or being too short–or too fat. No one wants a weak, frail baby in the family; everyone hopes for strong, sturdy boys or girls. Life on the prairie is hard work, work, work. You needed to be a rugged, sturdy pioneer–and honest. A cheat, schemer, or stingy person is to be avoided. You look for someone who is moral, upright, and reads the Scriptures–that's really a plus."

These rules were passed on from one generation to another. That's just the way it was.

Religion defined the rules of being a pioneer, and around Fairview you needed to be Lutheran, since it was the only church around. Some Catholics lived in Hopetown–the bigger town. You dared not marry outside your religion lest you receive shame and rejection.

In these parts no one ever saw a Jew, and seldom a Baptist or Methodist. "Those folks just don't live around here." A couple of families–like the Ottos–were atheists. Survival of the fittest, you measured by a narrow yardstick; that was best. Rules for living on the prairie were strict–to break them meant that you would be given the cold shoulder–even snubbed. Family, neighbors, and community kept eyes-open and order in this harsh, unbending desert.

Church was the center of social life. On Sundays the buggies arrived early–and by 1919 in Model T Fords, always black–began to park by the church. Folks would pour in after morning chores–and stayed 'til time to do chores again toward evening. No doubt one came to hear the sermon, but more important was being with family and friends that you mightn't see during the week. Sunday School was for children and confirmation instruction for adolescents. Adults sat through an hour-long sermon–in the Lutheran church by a German-speaking, serious preacher or maybe even a Norwegian or Swedish one.

Women were just to be seen, not heard, never in the pulpit or at any Council Meetings. They must dress in nice clothes, but not too fancy ones, longish skirts, no high heels, and never any makeup–like lipstick. Red lips only invited devilish, peculiar thoughts from men, even the old cougars.

The back row was a place of honor for mothers nursing their infants–a whole row of exposed breasts and sucking babies. It was a proud place to be–and if you quietly slipped out to go to the basement with a crying baby–everyone understood. In the Catholic Church women could be dutiful in cleaning the sanctuary and, of course, the priest's quarters, even if he had a saintly housekeeper to do his chores and make his meals. Baptism, confirmations, weddings, baptisms, and funerals were events that defined the cycle of life.

Potluck dinners–yes–those wondrous feasts of fried chicken, dumplings, baked beans, ham, German potato salad, JELL-O salad, and pies, pies, pies–cakes and cookies, too. The best came out of each woman's kitchen, bare as it ever might be. Now was the time to bring out butter and the biggest eggs you had, to make sure that cake would stand taller than any other; and its frosting thick and swirly. You could see women eyeing, comparing each competitor's offering with their own. How sad to see your dish untouched when Tillie's went first.

Some critics looked and compared how much each one brought; "Look at stingy Mable."

"Can you believe it–she brought only one tiny pie. What a shame–and her eight rangy kids are always first in line, too!"

But just the thought of an upcoming potluck could make mouths begin to water a week beforehand. Mission Sundays were the best of all. The president of the Synod came from Denver, that big city, and dinner went on for hours, with women folk piling up the dishes and washing them while the menfolk sat and smoked a pipe–talking about the price of wheat and hogs, comparing the best seed and worrying about the lack of rain. More pies, cakes, and hot coffee came out in the afternoon after hearing again the call to give generously to missions in far off countries–like Africa or even

China. Everyone stayed 'til evening–"Waitin 'til dark to do the milkin 'n sloppin the hogs."

But both preacher and priest claimed that one other major event featured the Devil as invited guest, and whose main feature was–temptation–The Saturday Night Dance–in the school gymnasium. Every weekend in the fall you could hear fiddlers and drum begin playing from around 7:00 PM–on and on–for two and a half long hours.

Around 9:30 PM, before the last dance, you smelled the coffee and saw cakes and pies roll out. Most of the time young children were tucked among coats piled up on the stage, where they fell asleep, despite the laughter and music. Older children began dancing as soon as they could–or they chased around behind the stage curtains, always getting yelled at by irate parents.

Here was where the unmarried began to court and choose their future mates. If you weren't chosen by age thirty you were delegated to the category of spinster–old maid–or old bachelor, and you never tried coming to Saturday night dance again. Why relive such a painful experience of rejection?

Chapter 21

COURTIN TIME

No one ever fell in love gracefully.
Connie Brockway *The Bridal Season*

Saturday night called to Hank like a siren in the wind. He never missed, except when he and some buddies travelled to Ogallala, Nebraska. That's where they met up with dance hall girls for a weekend. They would stay the whole weekend, doing whatever can be imagined with dance hall girls in the wee hours. Will had never gone on one of those weekend jaunts. "I just like the girls here in Fairview," he'd say.

Eldest son, William, had responsibilities–since he was only seven when his daddy died. Papa Paul had bought Gus's homestead for Mama Rose, so there was even more work to be done. Many mothers hoped that Will might attach to one of their daughters, as he was the most prized man in the area, but his work always came first.

Tall, handsome, romantic Hank made a sharp contrast to Will. He loved the girls and would dance with each and every one.

"Can't leave any out, you know, might break their hearts," Hank bragged.

No doubt every single girl in the area would love to be Hank's girlfriend. His dark auburn hair and bright blue eyes were always flirting and admiring the figure of each woman. Hank's face was that of a movie star–sharp straight nose, full lips, and the cheekbones of a prince. He also knew it–prancing around, looking to see who was looking at him.

"Ooooh I just swoon when he puts his hand around my waist," sighed Leatha Heyman.

"I hope he asks me twice, then I'd know if I am sort of special–'cause he seems to like us all," said Ramona Liedle.

"That's the problem, I think, he flirts with all of us–and the guys sure don't like him–he just steals anyone's girlfriend–just because he can."

"My mama doesn't want me to ride in his buggy, 'cause she thinks Hank is 'fast.'" Myrtle Andersen confessed.

And they all giggled, imagining kissing Hank and letting him be 'fast'.

"Let's see, Myrtle, my lovely, I haven't had the pleasure yet of swinging you around the floor; would you give me just one dance?" Hank's eyes looked up and down her robust figure.

"Oh, Hank, of course," her face grew red with anticipation. Off they went, round and round, Hank smiling as if she were the only one for him. He held her closer than most guys did, and brushed his cheek on her forehead. Myrtle didn't resist.

"Wonder why Will seldom comes? He's the best dancer of all, and when he sings, my heart just melts," Ramona said.

"You're right," the others chimed in.

"Oh, he's such a hard-working man. Never seems to leave the farm. And with the Schultz's having a whole section to farm, and Papa Paul gone, he's real busy. You know, of the two brothers, Will would make the best husband," Myrtle said, even though her heart was still pounding from the dance with Hank.

"You're right, but Hank makes me twitter," the girls joined in laughter again.

About that time the door to the gym opened and Mr. Olsen, a married man who lived north of town, walked in with a stunning, tall blond girl, perhaps nineteen years old. She was smiling and looked friendly, but somewhat shy.

"Thought I'd introduce our new hired girl," Mr. Olsen said. "This is Julie Sorensen from Iowa; she just moved here at the end of the summer."

Julie looked shy, but said in a nice, quiet voice, "Pleased to meet you." Each young woman filed by to introduce herself and welcome Julie.

Anne, who was also shy, asked, "Would you like some punch? I'll get you some."

"Thanks, I'd like that." Julie's heart was pounding as she looked around, feeling like someone on display. She hadn't been with so many young people for over three years –and certainly not with openly friendly ones.

Oh, God help me–I feel so afraid–all these new people, and I'm not a good dancer–why have I come? Her simple print dress seemed just right for the occasion, and her shoes were plain, like all the others. She seemed to fit in–but she was too pretty to be liked–right away.

Ramona was more confident than the others said, "Tell us about how you got to come way out here to be a hired girl."

Julie began to tell how her former employer didn't need a hired girl anymore. She didn't reveal that she'd run away. That story would be her secret.

Just then Chet Schmidt, a young man with a big nose, walked over. "Hello, I'm Chet, and I would like to dance with you."

"Oh, I'm not a good dancer, but if you teach me, I'll try." Julie said, looking both petrified and resolutely brave.

They went onto the dance floor with Chet teaching her the two-step. They stumbled a couple of times, as Julie looked at her feet and tried to move with the rhythm of the drum and fiddle.

"I'm sorry, Chet, I'll get it soon, and I like music. Do you live here?" she asked.

"No, I live on a farm about twenty miles south of here. We have cattle and some wheat."

"Did you grow up here?" Julie asked.

"Yup, all my life, right here. I've been to Sterling–a couple of times, that's a big town about fifty miles west. It's really big and has an auction for cattle. Maybe you'd like to go to a farm auction. I like 'em a lot 'n you get ta' see new people–'n buy really good chili." Chet smiled, so you didn't notice his large nose–as much. The couple continued dancing around the gym.

Chet took Julie back to the gaggle of girls, who were pondering the coming of this beautiful competition. Just then Hank returned with Myrtle and was startled to see this new creature–Julie.

"Oh, my dear," he said, as he bowed, "I have not had the pleasure. You must have come directly from Venus for you are so beautiful." His heart was beating so fast you could see his shirt move up and down with the rhythm of his breath.

"Hello, I'm Julie Sorensen, Olsen's new hired girl."

"Well, new hired girl, will you give me the pleasure of this dance?" Hank smiled and even forgot to thank Myrtle for last dance; she looked slightly abandoned.

"I have to warn you, I'm just learning to dance, so you'll have to show me how."

"Oh, my lovely, I'll teach you a lot of things–and show you my best side." Hank whispered seductively in her ear.

Hank held her at arms length, but thought *Oh how I'd love to hold her–really in my arms–and kiss her tenderly and then passionately and maybe even give her a lift in my buggy back home–and maybe–maybe, oh–she is so sweet to see–. Maybe – maybe.*

He tried to keep the rising lump in his trousers a secret.

Julie looked right past it without noticing; she had eyes only for her feet, trying hard to keep up with Hank.

"My lovely, just look into my eyes and feel the rhythm. You don't need to look down there–I'll carry you along–there–there, see how much better that is, see how we just seem to fit together and float. You'll get it soon, dearest one," Hank said, almost swooning himself. This tall, lovely, well-formed creature felt new in his arms, unlike the others. She was slender, strong, and completely alive.

They danced the next three dances together while the other young women waited and waited for a turn. Hank didn't want to let go of Julie's soft hand, but at last Robert, another tall farmer, tapped him on the shoulder, "Say buddy, don't hog this new creature, my turn, OK?"

Hank knew the rules of the dance floor and reluctantly left Julie to Robert's rough farmer hands.

Six other young men came by turns: Frank, Bill, Ernie, Sam, Jim, John and then Chet again. Each seemed entranced with this beautiful new woman in their midst. With each new partner Julie enjoyed dancing more and more. She relaxed and began to laugh. Her cheeks dimpled as she smiled and her sky-blue eyes sparkled. She was coming alive, forgetting the pain of her past.

At last Hank tapped Chet on the shoulder and held her at length saying, "It's my turn again. Ooooh, Julie, I want to dance with you for the rest of my life." Hank's eyes, those blue-violet eyes, were

filled with passion, and his voice trembled as if he really meant it–
this time.

Julie looked seriously into his eyes, seeing his male passion
building, "You're really a fine man, Hank, and I hope we can
dance a lot more on Saturday nights." Although she saw that he
was very handsome, she had no special feelings for him–*just not a
man for me–only a friend*, she thought.

"And maybe I can come to the Olsen's house soon and take
you for a buggy ride. What do you think?" His face was red now,
and he seemed flustered–not the usual cool-hand Hank.

"I really am very busy; Mrs. Olsen has such a large family. I do
get Sunday afternoon free after church. Do you go to church,
Hank?"

"Oh, well–I haven't for some time, but yes, I go to church and
would really like to go with you." Hank thought, *I'd have to give
up a weekend run to Ogallala–and those wild, wiggling dance hall
girls that I love to spend the night with–her.* "Maybe I could pick
you up in my buggy, and we could go on a ride together." Hank's
heart was beating so fast now that he was afraid she could hear it
pounding.

"Maybe we could talk about it next week, and I can see what
Mrs. Olsen has for me to do. I help her get the children ready for
church and then have dinner for them at noon." Julie looked
interested, but not smitten.

Hank could tell, as most of the young women would look at
him with glassy eyes and lips ready to be kissed. He knew the
difference–*Julie is not interested–not yet–but later–I hope,* he
thought.

Julie looked up and saw Mr. Olsen in the doorway. "Oh, Hank,
I see that Mr. Olsen's here to take me home. He's good to me."

"Julie, I'd like to take you home–and be good to you, too,"
Hank said wistfully.

"Maybe next time, Hank, and thanks for the dance lesson,"
Julie said lightly.

"Please come next time, and I'll teach you to Charleston,"
Hank said breathlessly.

Julie turned and went to the gathering of young women and
said, "It was good to meet all of you, and I hope to see you again.

Bye now." They all responded politely but secretly wished that the charming newcomer had never come.

"Did you have a good time?" asked Mr. Olsen, as they climbed into his buggy.

"Oh, it was so much fun, and I got to meet many people. I liked them all and hope I can come back on other Saturday nights," Julie said.

"Absolutely, yes, there are many fine young people in our community. I suggest that you keep a little distance from Hank Schultz; he has a reputation of being pretty fast with women. He has an older brother, Will, who is solid as a rock, but seldom comes to the dance. Their dad was killed in a prairie fire, so Will quit school to help his widowed mother run the farm. Then his grandpa came from Iowa to help after the accident, but he died a couple of years ago. So there's a lot of responsibility for a young man. Will is very well liked, quite a singer, and also a good dancer, so I'm told. Everyone likes Will. He's trustworthy and that's important on the prairie."

Julie didn't say much, but she assumed, from the lack of words about Hank's honesty, that he probably wasn't.

The dance broke up soon after Julie left, and people went their own way. Hank hopped into his buggy and headed homeward, but his heart was singing, "Julie, Julie, Julie."

Shucks, I've never felt like this before–just can't get over how she felt in my arms, dancing, and how her lips were just inches from mine. I think I'm in love–in love–. No, get a hold on yourself, Hank; it was just a first meeting. But my heart is just pounding thinking of her and how she smelt and felt in my arms. She's the most beautiful woman I've ever seen. None of my little dance-hall gals measure half as pretty. I just must see her. Maybe tomorrow I'll just ride over to the Olsen's and see her again, Hank thought, as he smiled.

Chapter 22

FALLING IN LOVE

Have you ever watched a leaf leave a tree? It falls upward first and then it drifts toward the ground, just as I find myself drifting towards you. Beth Kephart *Underover*

Will said. "What's going on? When did you get in last night? How was the dance?"

"I feel like it is a beautiful morning, the birds are singing, not a cloud in the sky. I feel like I could fly!"

"Wow, is that you, Hank? What happened to you?"

"Oh, I just met an angel. Her name is Julie; she's Olsen's new hired girl."

Mama broke in. "Yes, I met her in the grocery store with Mrs. Olsen a couple weeks age. Julie. Yes, that's her name, a lovely young woman. Mrs. Olsen says she is the best-hired girl she's ever had. Julie laughs and plays with the children all the time. Says she can cook like a professional, especially baking Danish things. Guess she's an orphan or something and came from Denmark when she was a young child, with an aunt. Maybe you should go and visit her on Sunday. That's usually the day off for hired girls," Mama said casually.

How I'd like Hank to get a nice girl–not one of the floozies he sees in Ogallala or where ever he goes on Saturday nights, and doesn't come home until wee hours on Monday morning. I'd like him to go to church, too–who knows–maybe.

Mama Rose didn't even think about Will having a girl friend, not for one minute. Maybe she didn't want that to happen–she needed him to manage the farm.

Hank dressed up for church and rode along with Will and Mama Rose. His eyes eagerly scanned the congregation, looking for that blonde angel. He didn't see her. So disappointed, he wanted to go home right after the sermon, but Mama Rose and Will had friends they wanted to chat with. On the way home, Hank said, "I'd like to go to the Olsen's and see what happened to Julie, and why she didn't come to church today."

"That's fine; I'm just going to rest and listen to the radio, do what you want," said Will.

Hank made certain he was clean-shaven, then cut a few of the last blossoms of the season from the rose bushes. He found an old newspaper to wrap them in, thinking *Never done this before, but guess this is what you do–oh, the thought of putting these beauties into her lovely hands.*

As he left with the buggy, Mama looked down the road and said, "I've never seen Hank quite so smitten, have you?"

"Never noticed, Mama," replied Will.

When Hank arrived at the Olsen farm, he tied up the buggy and walked gingerly to the house, holding the roses lightly in his hand. When he knocked on the door Mrs. Olsen appeared. "Why, Hank Schultz. How nice to see you on a Sunday afternoon; please come in."

He stepped into the large country home's hall parlor. "Hello, how are you, Mrs. Olsen?" he asked.

"I'm just fine, but if you are here to call on Julie, she is upstairs caring for three sick children who have high fevers, as they caught the stomach flu. They all got sick, so she's been with them all night, poor dear. Shall I take your roses –I guess they are for her. She can't come down, as she is just exhausted."

Deeply disappointed, Hank handed the flowers to Mrs. Olsen. "I'm sorry to hear that. I just met Julie last night at the dance and thought perhaps she could go for a buggy ride with me, as she said Sunday afternoon was her free time. It's a beautiful day, and I thought I'd show her some of the countryside."

"That's kind of you, Hank, and I'm sure she'd love that, but not today; she's had no sleep. I'm sure she'll be glad that you called." Mrs. Olsen didn't seem eager to call Julie or make future plans. *I really don't trust Hank. I've heard stories about his passions. Best to keep Julie safe until she knows him better– besides she really didn't get any sleep 'cause the kids were vomiting all night long.*

"I'd best be on my way, then. Please tell her how sorry I am that we couldn't go for a ride today–maybe another Sunday?"

"I'll tell her. Would you like to take some cookies for your ride back home? Julie baked them."

"I'd like that very much." *Just think, eating something SHE baked with her own lovely hands.* Hank's face grew red just thinking of the act. As he left, Hank looked back once, hopefully to see Julie's face in one of the windows. He didn't.

Three weeks went by without Julie attending the Saturday night dance or even church on Sunday. Mama Rose cleared the mystery at breakfast one morning, "I saw Mrs. Olsen in the store yesterday, and she told me that her whole family had been sick. Said that their hired girl, Julie, had a touch of pneumonia, but is recovering nicely. Guess they had to get the doctor to come and see her. It's rare to have pneumonia at this time of the year. Maybe Julie needs to get adjusted to the new climate."

Hearing that news Hank's heart nearly stopped, *What if she died before I got to see her again!* The thought twisted his face into a grimace.

"Are you OK, Hank?" asked Will.

"I'm OK, just surprised that a young person like Julie would get pneumonia."

The next Sunday afternoon Hank decided to make another visit to the Olsen's. This time he saw Julie, looking quite thin and very pale.

"It's good to see you again, Hank. Yes, I was quite sick, but better now."

"Do you think a ride in the buggy and some fresh air might make you feel better?"

"Why, thanks, I think that would be a good idea! I need some sunshine and would like to see more of the farms around here."

Hank's heart was pounding. "Better put on a wrap and something on your head," he said tenderly. Soon they were seated in the buggy, and the horse began a gentle trot.

"Let me show you some of the newly planted winter wheat and how it grows this time of year." Hank said. "My Papa Paul was the pioneer who changed the ways of farmers around here. Instead of planting wheat in the spring, we plant it in the fall, and then in the spring the seeds sprouts again–full and sturdy. The wheat is very fine–for baking, not just feed for livestock. Papa was quite a hero around here 'cause of his expertise with seeds." Hank wanted to brag more about his family, to impress Julie.

"Tell me about your family?" he asked.

"There's not much to tell. My father was a fisherman, and he was lost in a storm when fishing one night. My mother was sad, and I believe that caused her pneumonia. She died a year later, so I came with my Aunt Mary to America–to Iowa. She died, too. When I was sixteen I started working as a hired girl. That's all there is." She didn't tell him of her many losses during those years, nor of the cruel man she'd worked for as a hired girl.

"I heard about Mrs. Olsen from another Danish woman, who was a neighbor in Nebraska. The Olsen's needed help and sent for me. They have six children and another on the way. I like living with them and all the children."

Hank wasn't really listening, as he was staring at her bosom; it lifted with each breath and her nipples stood out when the breeze blew against her chest. "That's quite an interesting story and shows how strong you are–as well as beautiful." His mind then wandered to her lips, full, pink, kissable.

"Tell me about your family, Hank"

"Well, there are three of us Schultz kids. My sister, Margaret, is married to Pete Hereford, and Will is my older brother. My Mama Rose is a widow, and Papa Paul was my grandfather who came from a family of violinists in Germany. I don't play a tune." Hank laughed. "Margaret and Pete live just a few miles away and have two kids. Will is 22 and shorter than I; he does the farming with my help. I keep the books, since I'm the smartest and most educated." His mouth was in a grimace and his eyes glittered, a startling sight to Julie.

Hank didn't share more about Will, as he had always been bitterly jealous. Once he'd nearly killed Will–and would have, if Papa Paul hadn't been there to grab the pitchfork from his hands. They'd been tossing snowballs back and forth. One ball smacked Hank right in the face. Furious, Hank grabbed a pitchfork and Papa said, "Put that down!" Just in the nick of time. There'd been other times when Hank had wanted to kill him–because Will was always the favorite with Mama Rose and Papa Paul–always working and getting praise. *Makes me sick*, thought Hank.

"I was valedictorian of my class; could have gotten into any university because of my good grades, but I decided to stay home and help build the family fortune. As I said, I keep the books for the farm."

Julie looked surprised to hear such bragging, and thought Hank was joking, but realized, no, that was how Hank actually felt.

"Look as far as you can see south and west–that's how much land I want to own some day. I want to own more than anyone else." Hank's chin looked sharp, determined; his eyes squinted toward the sun. "And sometimes you have to be rough, just to get it all in place."

Julie shuddered as if she'd heard the devil speak. Uneasy, she asked, "You mean to cheat or hurt someone else in getting your fortune."

Hank laughed, as if he had been telling a joke, "No, my dearest Julie, I'd never hurt anyone–unless they deserve it, or are too dumb to figure it out." He laughed again and looked at the sky.

Julie felt uncertain; was Hank joking or did he really mean it?

Hank then took her hand and kissed it gently. "But with you, my lovely, I just want to give you the world and watch your smile as you receive the gifts you so deserve to have."

Feeling uneasy again, Julie laughed–hoping to break the more serious atmosphere. "Well, dreamer, until then you best get me home, so my bones don't crack from the cold air."

"Oh, my little darling, I hope you haven't a chill, here is a blanket I have in the back. Let me put it around your shoulders." As he did, Hank let his hand slowly caress her breasts, as if accidently.

Julie stiffened up, "I think we'd better go now."

"Yes, my little rosebud," Hank persisted, letting his hand slide slightly down her leg. He leaned over to Julie, and said tenderly, "When can we see each other again?"

"I think it will be some time before I can get out; I'm still pretty weak," responded Julie. She didn't want to be brutally honest, but she felt this would be the only time she wanted to be alone with Hank. *He just is too fast for me–I was warned and they were right–he's fast.*

"Thanks for such a lovely afternoon, Hank. I best go lie down again." She didn't invite Hank in for coffee and cake. When they reached the Olsen farm Hank helped Julie out of the buggy, holding on to her arm just a little too long.

"Until soon, then my, lovely." Hank kissed her hand gently, turned, and left. *I want her.*

He took the reins and began turning the buggy around, going home, singing all the way.

Chapter 23

RIVALS

Oh, believe, my lord, of jealousy, it is the green-eyed monster, which does mock the meat it feeds on.
William Shakespeare *Othello*

"Mama, I'm ready to go when you are," said Will. "Buggy's all set." Will and Hank had been talking about getting a real car–a Model T Ford.

"Seems they're pretty reliable, sometimes cranky in the morning, but Henry Ford says everyone should have one by now–it's the roaring 20's," Hank had chided.

"I'm always the first to try the newest and the best," said Mama Rose, "and times are changing. We now have the Fordson tractor, and it plows faster than a horse. Next is the Model T." Mama's black eyes flashed with excitement. It was October 1923 and the War had been over almost four years. The stock market was booming and life seemed good.

But right now Mama and Will were on their way to Fairview to sell eggs and milk. They had over 100 chickens and five milk cows–how different from their beginning–now almost fifteen years ago.

"Our farm is growing so much that we may need to hire some more hands," said Mama.

"We will." Will looked across the fields of green. Wheat covered nearly the whole section of land. "If we get enough snow and rain, we'll be set," Will said.

Each Fall before planting the winter wheat Will and Mama blessed the land, just as they had when Papa and Red Sun were with them. They continued with the same spiritual ritual, a call to the heavens and then sprinkling water on the land near the old homestead livestock shed, the west sod wall of it still standing. Then in the spring, they would repeat the call for God's blessing and to give thanks for keeping the family safe.

"We'll build our new livestock shed right here," said Mama Rose pointing to the spot of the original sod building, "and always keep part of that sod wall, just in case we forget all the work Daddy did." Her eyes still formed tears when she thought of her beloved John William.

Then Will would chant, "Father in Heaven, Great Spirit, we ask Your blessing on Mother Earth and all the creatures who live above and below."

Mama would take a handful of soil, kiss it, and toss it high into the air, saying, "We are honored to be keepers of Your land, Father in Heaven. We ask that the sun be strong, the winds gentle, and the rains soft to give birth to the seeds we have planted."

The seeds she held were seeds-of-the-seeds, The Promise Seed that Papa Paul first brought to the homestead from the Volga Steppes of Russia. The power remained strong, and. the fruit of that seed continued. Farmers came from miles around to see the superb fields of grain begun by the famous Seed Man–Papa Paul.

Each summer when harvest was finished, Will, Mama, Margaret, and her husband Pete would gather at the graves of Papa and John William. They sang, "Praise God from Whom All Blessings Flow." Will's booming baritone sounded just like his dad's. Then Mama Rose always went to John William's headstone and kissed it, saying, "I love you, John William–now and always."

Hank, the bookkeeper for the farm, had little interest in this "silly hocus-pocus stuff," as he said. "I just want to see the bank balance," he'd say, "that's all that counts."

"Yes, I'm ready," called Mama as she came dressed modestly but not in black. "Let's buy more potatoes for the winter; we didn't have a good crop of them this year."

Will hitched up the wagon and drove into town. He stopped at the hardware store, and Mama Rose went into the grocery store. There she saw Mrs. Olsen and Julie Sorensen.

"Good to see you! How are you feeling now, Julie? My son Hank said you had pneumonia."

"Much stronger, thanks," Julie said. Just then Will came through the door and joined them. Julie's eyes lit up seeing the older son. She felt a twinge in her chest, like a flutter of a bird. He looked quite different, a tiny bit shorter than Hank, chocolate brown eyes, and his hair was golden brown and wavy, almost curly, but such a bunch of it–it almost stood straight up. She nearly laughed, as he probably wasn't aware of his ridiculous crown.

"I'm glad to meet you, Julie. I've heard about you from my brother Hank. Welcome to Fairview."

"Did I hear correctly? What a marvelous voice, you sound like a radio announcer." Julie held out her hand, and their fingers touched–like an electric shock. Julie thought, *Does his voice sound like someone I remember from–like maybe–Daddy?*

She continued, "Well–I'm glad to meet you, too. I heard that you are a great singer–at least some girls at the dance told me that." Julie laughed and looked him straight in the eyes. Julie watched his smile spread across his face, and saw the most perfect white teeth and warm, full lips.

"Well, I wouldn't say I'm great, but I do love to make a loud noise," he said shyly. She noticed he had huge, rough farmer hands and that he was tall–over six feet.

Will's face was rugged, as if he'd been in the sun, a lot, and he had a rim of white around the top of his forehead, like he wore his hat outside while working.

"Perhaps I'll hear you sometime in church," Julie commented.

"I'd be pleased to share a hymnal with you," Will said, again shyly, nothing like the bold Hank. "Best be helping with the groceries, good to meet you." He moved quickly toward the sacks of potatoes.

Once the buying was done, Will and Mama headed homeward. "What did you think of Julie?" asked Mama.

"Oh, Mama, don't think I ever saw someone so beautiful as she is, so–soft. But I couldn't think of a thing to say–I'm not good around girls, like Hank is–I just stumble for words. Gee Whiz, I'm just better talking to cows and chickens," he laughed.

Mama remembered how Will had to quit school in the third grade to cultivate the fields with Papa Paul. He had never been around girls much, just his older sister Margaret. He was also very bright, perhaps smarter than Hank. *Why didn't I ever think about Will having fun, dancing, and maybe falling in love? Why didn't I?*

He's always been my right hand. Oh, I feel I've been so selfish, Mama thought.

"I think you'd better go to the Saturday night dance and get acquainted with some girls. You're 24 now and time to think about having your own family. You could live in Gus's house–and–"

"Mama, Mama, oh, Mama," Will laughed, "I think I can do my own courtin."

They both laughed. Will was so easy-going that Mama really didn't worry about him. Sure enough, next Saturday night both Hank and Will decided to take the buggy into town to go to the dance. Hank wore a new, blue shirt that showed off his blue eyes, and Will wore an old, nicely pressed, white one.

"Look at my boys," Mama said.

The music was playing when they arrived. The young people were gathered into two groups–the girls on one side and the young men on the other. Several older couples were dancing. When the fiddlers saw Will arrive, they called him, "Hey, Will, how about singing with us?"

"Sure 'nough," he answered. Will jumped nimbly onto the stage and sang "Red River Valley" (Kerrigan 1896) Every one clapped; his voice was velvet and strong. He saw Hank dancing with every girl.

Then the door opened and in walked Julie. Will's voice cracked a little, just seeing her, but he kept singing, as he watched Hank take Julie onto the floor and keep his hands around her waist–dancing only with her. The other girls looked around for other partners.

Will took a break from singing and moved toward the group of girls. He took Ramona's hand and whirled her across the room. Awesome, light on his feet, and gentle.

"Care to try the Charleston?" asked Will.

"Let's do it," laughed Ramona, and so they began, and everyone else stopped dancing just to watch the two.

Will then tried it with each girl willing to take floor with him. Everyone was laughing and having a great time–except for Hank, who sulked quietly to the side of the dance floor.

Then a waltz began, and Hank took Julie's hand–"You are really getting good, Julie. I mean it. I could dance with you all night–all night. How about another buggy ride?"

"I think that will have to wait. You know it's really getting colder out now. Maybe in the spring time," Julie resisted.

"I'm planning on buying a Model T Ford; what do you think of that? Won't have to worry about cold wind in your face then!" said Hank.

Just then Hank felt a tap on his shoulder, looking around he was stunned to see his brother Will.

"Well, Brother, it's time to share this young lass with your big brother. I've danced with every lady here, but this one."

"Oh, I guess I don't have a choice, Will. I know the rules," Hank looked grim.

With that, Will took Julie by the hand and floated across the dance floor to the music of the night. Julie believed her feet didn't touch the ground, as his rough hands were gentle and tender, but different from any others. Her heart was pounding like never before. *What is this I'm feeling? He's just a regular guy.*

His voice was deep and real–"You are learning so fast. I love to dance–more than even eat–hope we can try the Charleston sometime." He held her close to his chest, and Julie could actually feel his heart beating.

"I like dancing with you, Will. You seem to just carry me along."

"No, it's us–together–it's different when you are in rhythm with someone–."

Will stopped in the middle of the sentence, afraid that he had blurted out something really stupid. He felt so much at this moment–as if he and Julie were made from the same clay, together.

"I think I know what you mean," Julie's voice quivered.

Just then Will felt Chet's tap on the shoulder, so he let Julie go to the man with the big nose.

The dancing ended exactly at 9:30 PM. After having coffee and cake, Will and Hank said goodnight to all the girls and finally to Julie.

Hank asked, "Will I see you in church tomorrow?"

"I certainly hope so," Julie said looking at each Schultz boy, but her eyes dwelled on Will.

The next two weeks were repeats. The Saturday night dance and Sunday church service gave both Will and Hank a chance to see Julie. It was easy to see that both were falling in love with the same woman.

But Julie was falling in love with only one–Will.

Hank began to notice that whenever they both came into a room, Julie's eyes would look straight at Will. He noticed her blush when dancing with Will, but with him her face was like stone. *Can it be that Julie would prefer Will to me? That has never happened before, and it won't with this one either–how could she prefer that naïve farmer over me–a business man intent on being the richest man in the county.*

But the more he tried to win her over, the more she seemed to resist and cling to Will. It was made more obvious when she asked Will over for Sunday dinner–at the Olsen's. Hank's heart was broken–deeply, truly broken. He could barely look at Will at breakfast the Monday morning after that dinner. He knew the signs–the happy smile, the twinkly brown eyes, the bounce to his walk.

Will was in love.

Mama knew the signs, too; after Will had gone to feed the livestock and milk the cows, she took Hank aside, "It's hard when you both are in love with the same woman. I can feel your heart breaking, Hank, my dear son. But God has chosen one beloved for each of us. Love is hard to find and harder to define. Like my John! I loved him in first grade, and he did me, too. I could never love another. Somewhere there is another love for you, Hank. You can try all you want, but Julie is in love with Will, and he with her."

"You're right, Mama, but you're wrong, too. I'll never stop loving Julie," Hank said sadly. He was right; all of his life he never stopped loving Julie, but he did move on to find another mate.

Will, on the other hand–every hour–every day. His feet barely touched the ground, as he walked out and unhitched his horse and got into the buggy–barely breathing for the sweep of passion that overcame him. He wanted to shout it from the rooftops–but what would he say–*"I'm in love!"*–

Julie, in the meantime, knew she was falling in love, too, although she'd never had these feelings before, so she asked Mrs. Olsen about the Schultz family.

"You want to know about Will. I can see how you two look at each other. Let me tell you what I know. When Will's father, John William, died in a prairie fire, his mother, Widow Rose asked her widowed father from Iowa to come and help. That was Papa Pinot, an old man even when he came. He taught Will so much about farming and keeping the covenant with the land. William would make a great husband." Mrs. Olsen laughed.

"Now Henri, we call him Hank, is the most handsome young man around, and he knows it," she laughed again. "Hank's smart and witty. He was valedictorian when he graduated a couple of years ago. All the young single girls are crazy about him. Even my little Daisy, who is only 16, has a crush on Hank Schultz.

"They say he's "fast"–you know tries to–you know–. The men folks don't like him very much, but they do respect him for his business sense. They already elected him director of the grain co-op–he is clever. But the men, I've heard, are jealous because–he's–done it–with all the loose women around here and in other towns as well, and likely some you'd be surprised at." Mrs. Olsen shook her head and put her hands over her eyes–ashamed for saying such a bad thing.

"Well, I know which one is my favorite," Julie responded, laughing, and blushing at the same time.

"You could never find a boyfriend better than Will Schultz. Every mother in the county would like her daughter to catch that man–what a jewel," Mrs. Olsen continued, "I don't think he ever had a girlfriend–not even one–."

Friday evening the phone rang at the Olsen's house, and a man asked to speak with Julie, "If she isn't too busy, thank you, this is Will Schultz speaking."

Julie came to the phone, and breathlessly said, "Hello."

"Hello, I want to thank you for such a good Sunday dinner. I really liked coming to your house." *God, I sound so stupid–like a baby.* "I'm just wondering if instead of going to the dance tomorrow night if you might like to ride into Hopetown to see a movie. You know they have them now."

"Oh, I'd like that," said Julie, "I've never been to a movie."

"Well, neither have I. Guess we'd both be risking ourselves to do something new," he laughed.

"I think that would be fun."

And, so began the first date of Will and Julie. Each weekend it seemed to be the only thing on their minds. Hank was left out, and soon went back to spending his weekends in Ogallala. Mama Rose was left alone–just as she knew she would be sooner–or later.

Their first kiss took place under a canopy of stars with a full moon rising rich and lustrous over the treeless eastern horizon. Will sang in his rich baritone, "'With someone like you, a pal so good and true, I'd like to leave it all behind and go and find, some place that's known to God alone, just a place to call our own–"

Many, many times over the next years Will would sing or hum that song to Julie–just as his dad, John William had sung it to Mama Rose. The heavens always seemed to open in Julie's heart a way of knowing that all would be OK–even in spite of all the problems that would loom ahead– *'a place to call our own'*–would ring through her mind and she'd smile.

Chapter 24

A WEDDING AND MORE

They are no longer two, but one. Therefore what God has joined together, let no man separate.
Matthew 19:6

Will and Julie married on April 22, 1924, in the living room of the homestead. Mama Rose, Margaret and Pete, their two children, Hank, the Lutheran pastor and his wife, and all the Olsen's witnessed this joyous event. Altogether twenty people filled the small house. If Julie could have noticed she would have seen that Hank was pale and quiet. He left soon after the ceremony to go out and sob to the cows.

How could I have lost her to Will–of all people, Hank thought.

The first night of their married life Julie wore a maiden-white, satin gown. She was quiet, tender, and naive. On her gown was a tiny rose pin. "Mama gave this to me before she died. She said, "Wear this on your wedding night as a symbol of love and cherish the moment when you become one."

They were virgins, with no experience of lovemaking outside of their passionate kisses. Julie had not known what it meant, 'to become one,' but now she did. It was more than the physical act of lovemaking, but a covenant–a promise–of becoming one in spirit and heart. Each gave them selves completely.

Will said, "You have made me–so loved–and now we are one," as he felt her body beneath his in their marriage bed.

Julie's response was, "And you alone have my body, you alone will know me inside as well as out."

The first night was more exploratory than completion, but each was satisfied with the new experience. Subsequent lovemaking became more and more exciting as the couple found new ways of expressing their joy. One night they walked into the field and lay together on a small haystack. As they placed their bodies closer and closer, and their rhythms became more intense, the stars seemed to explode and the night sky became irrelevant.

Julie's passion matched Will's at every turn. They were made for each other. Days and nights were filled with coupling at every opportunity. At noon one day, Julie moaned, "I want you–more, more!" during one passionate session. Neither had heard the knock on the door, nor the whisper of Hank's entrance into the house. He stood silently watching the wild movements of each and the groans of satisfaction. As quietly as he had entered, so he left. Hank turned outside the front door and vomited.

"How could she do that? How could she!" he uttered under his breath. His face was ghostly white, as tears streamed down his cheeks. Hank didn't visit unannounced again.

Julie and Will made Cousin Gus's homestead their home. No one had lived in it for seven years, so it needed a lot of repair. Julie busied herself daily painting walls and sewing new curtains.

One evening Julie raised a new challenge. "I've been thinking that, since we live so close to the high school in Fairview, that maybe–if it would be OK with you, I'd like to finish my schooling. Before leaving Iowa I had only two years of high school."

"Why, darling, I didn't know that! I think it's a great idea."

"I could ride Pepper–or even drive the Model T.

"Do it. Maybe you can teach me some things, too?"

They laughed and hugged. "I'll be your teacher–for a change," said Julie.

When classes began in the fall, Julie sat with the other students. She wrote quickly and accurately. Arms filled with books, she studied every night. After church in mid- November the teacher, Mr. Wingert, called Julie and Will over to the side.

"Mr. Schultz, I have to tell you honestly that I have never met a student as bright as Julie. She absorbs everything. Her reading is far, far ahead of the other students. I wish she were able to go to the university; she is more than capable. She has already finished most of the work for a junior year. If she continues she will have enough points to graduate in May–from high school."

Julie looked down, rather embarrassed, "I just love to learn, Mr. Wingert. Thank you for teaching me."

Will looked proudly, "I knew this all the time. She remembers every little detail about farming and calculates math in her head. Does she recite poetry for you? She knows hundreds of poems by heart."

"Well, I didn't know that, but I'm not surprised."

"Do you know that she can draw and paint?"

"No, I didn't. Why not bring some of your work in for me to see?"

"They're mostly seascapes, so beautiful. Don't know how she has that memory, for she was little when she left Denmark," said Will.

"Sometimes childhood memories stay with you forever." Mr. Wingert remained puzzled for he had never encountered such a gifted student. *What to do about this? I haven't a clue–no teacher worth Julie's brilliance is out here on the prairie.* He didn't forget this unusual student, Julie.

Julie did indeed master all the points to graduate in June. As class valedictorian she gave a stirring commencement address about following your dreams and giving thanks to people who helped you along the way. Standing before the community crowd, her blue eyes radiated the power of learning. Her black robe mocked the joy in her heart, and she thanked her husband for supporting her.

"My husband is the reason I stand before you as a graduate. He is my well of creativity, my motivation to learn. His generosity to every living thing is an inspiration to all. Each person who passes through our lives leaves a seed of promise or a seed of despair. May you be as fortunate as I to have received so many seeds of promise in my life. And let us remember as well that we, too, may leave behind us seeds that are negative–like jealousy, selfishness, sadness, or positive ones, like–hope, generosity, joy. You have a choice; you can make a difference."

The crowd exploded in applause. Hank had a front row seat; he felt the sting of guilt, for he sowed many negative seeds. His heart pounded just looking at Julie, standing tall and beautiful with her valedictorian medal. He still loved her–always would.

Soon Will and Julie would be passing on the promise seed, as Julie had become pregnant. Ernest Schultz, their first child, was born on September 26, 1926.

"I adore him," Julie held him to her breast, while Will caressed his tiny head.

"He is truly is a wingless angel," Will paused, "he is our promise seed between your mom and dad and my parents and all those children that will follow; he is the beginning of the next generation."

Ernie's soft brown eyes showed an unusual intent; he smiled often, but always looked around, sizing up the world, just like Mama Julie. He was destined to become a leader.

PART III

EVIL

Chapter 25

THE GAMBLING MAN

There's a lure in power. It can get into a man's blood just as gambling and lust for money have been known to do.
Harry S. Truman

A little over two years had gone by since Will and Julie's wedding and birth of Ernie. Hank continued his old pattern of going weekly to Ogallala, helping on the farm episodically. The October moon rose, red, round and close to the earth. Brisk air foreshadowed the coming winter winds, and snow, and quiet time. Around 9:00 PM one Saturday night Mama Rose heard an unusual sound–a horn honking–right outside the kitchen door.

In a moment Hank came bouncing in, laughing and wiggling a set of keys. "Mama, look what I have, a 1924 Model A Ford–a real beaut!"

"How did you get that, son?"

"I won it fair and square from Mel Otto, that old, fat pig farmer."

"But, how?"

"Just a couple hands of poker–honest and all. He's so dumb, deserves to lose a good car like this."

"But son, you know it isn't right to gamble. It simply isn't right. Now what is he going to use. He's got a big family, you know. Winter's coming, and he'll need his car. It isn't right to take away a man's Ford. Now how could you do that?"

Hank laughed loudly, "Ah, it was easy. We played for a no-limit pot. Six guys started, and the bids were the usual. Gradually the stakes grew higher and higher. I lost a bunch at first–on purpose–that gave ole stupid Mel some hope that this was his night. The pot just kept getting bigger and bigger.

All but the two of us dropped out. They sat there–dumb–with their mouths wide open as the pot got huge–like a thousand dollars; we were like fighting bulls. Each raised the pot more and more. I knew I could win, because I had a Royal Flush–nothing beats that. Finally Mel couldn't raise another dollar, so he put his car keys in the pot. Ole Mel was sure he had me! He called it and put down a Straight Flush–7, 8, 9, 10, and Jack of Hearts–and dropped his jaw when I put down a Royal Flush a 10, Jack, Queen, King, and Ace of Clubs, clubs, can you believe it! I clubbed him to death."

Hank was now doubled over with laughter.

"He did put up a fight though, said he'd see me in hell, saying that I cheated. "Whoa now," I said, "You know the rules. You put your car up for the pot, and I won it fair and square He kept shouting that I'd cheated and wanted a show down with fists or pistols."

"But big Ben Bennett stepped right in–he's the best attorney in the county, and said, 'No, I'm witness to the deal'.

"Ole Mel got madder and madder and raised his fists at both of us. Others left the pool hall–expecting a show of blood. I was ready–being 6 4" to Mel's puny 5' 10"–no match. So he put his fists down, looked right into my face and said, 'Just you wait–Hank Schultz–you'll regret this some day–just you wait. Someday I'll see your blood all over the place!' He was practically screaming.

"Hah, he's always been a hot-tempered son of a bitch–whoops–didn't mean that, Mama."

"Son!! Don't talk like that. He's a good pig farmer–you know that–he works hard and keeps his place real clean."

"You're right about that, Mama."

Mama Rose was still angry. Her black eyes were flashing. "Since you were kids, there's been bad feelings between you and Mel. Remember the fight you had in the 7th grade, and you came home with a black eye and bloody nose?"

"Yah, but things changed after that. That stinky, old pig farmer. Some neighbor took him home last tonight–still shaking his fists at me. And I drove away–with a car. But I plan to trade the ole Ford for a new Studebaker, something more fitting for the King," Hank continued to brag.

"I don't like that–son–you know I want everything you do to be honest and kind, but you seem to feel that whatever you want is yours. It really isn't. God gives and takes away. Remember your Ten Commandments, son. Do unto others as you would have them do unto you," Mama said.

"Aw, Mama, you know that God gives to those who ask, and I asked for a car!" he smiled triumphantly, remembering two nights before Polly married Mel Otto, *that I–the King–had her to bed–she wasn't all that bad–either–wanted more and more–guess ole Mel found out about it and backed off for a day.* Hank skipped upstairs to his bedroom still singing and laughing all the way.

Rose hung her head in shame, concerned about how poor Mrs. Otto must feel now, as she had just given birth to a baby daughter and lived a long way from town. It's a sad situation, she thought. *I'm ashamed of my heartless, youngest child. Why is he so selfish? Didn't I teach him like Will and Margaret? Papa used to say that Hank reminded him of Frieda, his aristocratic, redheaded mother who also seemed to be selfish–Papa tried to help Hank many times, but Hank would just walk away, laughing. He always wants his way and to hurt others.*

"Sad, sad, sad." Rose muttered to herself.

The next morning, Hank said at the breakfast table. "Think I'll go over to Scottsbluff and see what kind of trade I can make. Will can come over and do the chores as he always does–anyway."

Again Rose looked down as she cleared the dishes and began her morning checking on the livestock, especially getting eggs from her chicken flocks. She had no way to drive into Fairview without Will coming over, but he would be here within the hour, as usual. She could always depend on Will.

Rose's favorite son was Will, as he loved the land. But Hank was the cleverest, to the point of being distrusted. Rose had often wondered if somehow Hank was siphoning off money, the way Gus had done.

Rose had confronted Gus on two occasions for moving the boundary stakes at night. She believed he'd taken at least ten acres of her land. When she confronted him, Gus said, "What do ya mean I'm takin your land?"

"I mean you've been moving the boundary stakes on my land, over and over again. I can see where you covered up the old holes.

I placed a stone on the edge of my land months ago, and now that stone is way on your side of the line. That is stealing. I'm not afraid of you–never have been. You stop that–or I'll take legal action. Now get off my land."

Gus was astonished at the power of this tiny woman. Those black eyes blazed as she talked, and he knew he was caught. *But how did she know? How did she figure this out? She really is sharp. I'd better do somethin.*

"I just thought I'd help you out. You have so much land now to cover, and if I help you–we both benefit."

"How is that? I think you must be joking. How does your stealing help me?"

"Oh, I was going to give you the cash for the crops from your land." He shied away from revealing all the other things he had done to fill his pockets.

"We're relatives. I will always honor you as flesh and blood but never do this again. Or, I will call the men of the town together, and they will handle you the way they would any horse thief. Do you understand?"

Gus knew that being shunned in the community was worse than any prison sentence. He could only nod and look away. That night he and his sons moved the stakes back to where their original places. They knew the power of Widow Rose and her unrelenting drive to do the right thing. The situation was never mentioned again.

Sometimes I wonder about Hank, as he always seems to have money. Where does he get it? We always share and share alike, but–I just wonder–shaking her head, Mama thought.

Two days later as Hank drove a new, yellow Studebaker with shining chrome into the yard, he waved and honked the horn. Mama Rose and Will said nothing–and Julie looked away in shame.

Can't believe Julie's still not impressed with me! Look what she could have had if only–Hank didn't even finish his thought.

In this car he would become more admired, and more hated, as a dishonest, but an available bachelor.

Chapter 26

A WIFE FOR A KINGDOM

Persistence and determination alone are omnipotent
Calvin Coolidge

Still boasting about his win, Hank gathered up a change of clothes, toothbrush, and razor, and–headed for Nebraska–about ten miles east. Fence posts and telephone lines flew by–going maybe 45 miles an hour. The dirt spun around him. Hank looked straight ahead, putting distance behind him. As he pulled across the state line, Hank had a wave of sadness that overcame him, so he pulled to the side of the road and turned off the engine and began to think.

No, I haven't always gotten what I wanted. I was just a little guy–just three–when we moved from Iowa. I don't remember much of living in the dugout–'cept what Mama tells me. Then Daddy died, I didn't even get to see him in the coffin to say goodbye. I loved him so much. He used to take me on his saddle horse–Babe– and we'd ride into the wind. No one noticed that I missed him more than anyone, but I do remember.

The kids in parochial school teased me about my red hair– called me Carrot Top, so I had to learn to fight hard. Will wasn't there to help me. He was doing farming at home. I needed to fight alone, until I grew and grew and my hair turned auburn–not a carrot top. Then I got to be the tallest, best looking and the smartest in class, but I needed to be Number One–all the time.

Lot of times I felt lonely–alone, as Papa talked with Will all the time, about farming and stuff like that. I was left out. Girls liked me fine, because I knew how to make them get really hot, and their kisses led to other things. They would whisper, 'Oh Hank, Oh, Hank'. I really didn't love any of them, until Julie, and now she is my sister-in-law! That's not fair! Some day I'll get even with Will. He can't have her!

Sitting in late afternoon–looking out across the empty land, the sadness overwhelmed Hank

Sometimes I think about the time I was confirmed in the Lutheran Church. I really felt the presence of God then and I remember my Bible verse and when the pastor put his hands on my head and blessed me. He read my verse, out loud. I still remember 1st Timothy 6:12–remember as if it were just yesterday! 'Fight the good fight of faith, lay hold on eternal life where unto thou was called and confess the good confession in the sight of many witnesses'. Then his eyes filled with tears.

I remember the temptations that came my way. No one had them the way I did, I know for certain. Even as I was walking out of the church that day of my confirmation, there sat Mary Jane with her big tits hanging right out there for me to squeeze, now that was too much.

Then I remember a few years later when mama was crying telling me that the preacher had come to our house and asked her to get me to change my wicked ways of doing 'it' with all the pretty women. She and I talked until the moon came up about all the Ten Commandments and how I should keep each one holy, I thought I did, but I told her I was going to try to be better and that made her happy again.

Then later when I was older, Brother Will came and he too was crying telling me that I wasn't going to be with him in heaven unless I repented my ways and didn't sin against all the Commandments. I told him I didn't break one rule–not one. When he questioned me about doing 'it' with all the girls I said that I never committed adultery as no one was a married woman (oh, maybe one or two were) and cheating and stealing, I never did that unless someone was too dumb to notice. It was their fault not mine.

But the worst was when the three elders stopped me at church one Sunday about four years ago, saying that they would need to ex-communicate me unless I stopped going to Ogallala to sleep with all the dance hall girls. I said, 'You're just jealous–and these women need to talk with me about their troubles. It's the Christian thing to do; you know to help your fellow man–or woman. Without my talking to them, they'd probably be living on the streets right now. Shame on you guys! You're just jealous.' Guess I told them, but they sure didn't want to hear it. I knew they didn't like my answer.

So when they came to our house about two years ago, and asked to meet out in the barn, I knew it was over. They told me that I had hardened my heart to the Devil and I was fornicating– fornicating!!! Now they had to do their holy thing and ex- communicate me. No longer could I take the Sacrament of Holy Communion, and they would not offer me a funeral in the church if I should die. Fornicating maybe–but never adultery–they were just jealous.

Wow–that was rough. I never told Mama or Will, but I think they knew, as I never went to church with them any more. That was hard, as church was the only time I got to see my beloved Julie in her beautiful dress and looking like an angel. So that was the end *of my life as a Lutheran.*

Big Hank was now crying. No, he was sobbing. Great sobs leaped from his chest in staccato beats. *It can't be true, it can't be true, not my Julie. Now getting it from Will-not me–Big Hank. No, it can't be. His kisses on her lips–no, no, no. Having his baby–no.* More sobs came, and snot began to creep down to his lip. He didn't even see the car pull up behind him and park. The knock on the side window startled Hank. In the dim light of dusk–he could see the burly chest–the gun in the holster. Hank didn't recognize the rotund face, not smiling, and heard the voice. "Open up! What's the matter with you?" Then he saw the badge–a sheriff's badge!

"Sorry Sheriff, I was just trying to get my bearings. I'm trying to decide whether to go to Red Cloud or to Ogallala."

"Well, either way, you should have your lights on. Sittin here in the dark like this, you could get hit from behind. Let me see your license, mister," the hefty man said.

Hank was embarrassed being seen with red eyes and snot on his lip, but he pulled out his billfold and gave his license to the sheriff.

"See you're from Fairview–not far down the road. See by your papers that ya haven't had this car very long–just a couple of days. Right?"

"Yes."

"This is a nice machine. Don't see many Studybakers around these parts, How'd ya come by it? How much did you have to pay for it?" The sheriff was now curious, wanting one like it–if he could afford it.

"Just under fourteen hundred dollars."

"Not bad, not bad" The sheriff was thinking that maybe. "That's not much more than a Model T."

Hank, couldn't tell the sheriff about the gambling that got him the Ford first and then he traded for the Studebaker. He couldn't tell how he had schemed with his best friend, Attorney Bennett. *No sir, not telling that story, how they'd planned to work together and break Mel's game, palming the Jack of Clubs and adding an Ace as well–working his way to the big pot. No matter that ole Mel thought he'd had a winning hand with a Straight Flush, "I knew that my Royal Flush would top that." The game had gone on too long anyway, and all that Mel had left was his Model T–his pockets were empty. He bet the Ford on the last hand–thinking he'd beat out his archrival, Hank Schultz.*

Mel was a poor loser–always has been. Hank remembered in grade school when Mel came into the room; Hank would squeak, "Oink Oink"–then under his breath whisper, "What is that awful smell?" That would rile up Mel. Once at recess, he came punchin at Hank. Hank was a full head taller, but still took a bloody nose and a black eye from Mel. Hank knew he'd out smart that pig farmer, but Papa Paul sat him down one night.

"Son, you have to stop being mean and bullying kids at school. I've heard from your teacher that you can be pretty mean to younger kids. I think it's a moral issue. A good Lutheran boy needs to be kind and loving. Can you change your ways?" asked Papa Paul. "Yes, Papa, yes, I'll be better. I really will," Hank answered. And, he meant that for a day or two. Then he planned how to be a better schemer–thief–liar–whatever.

For he was Hank Schultz!

Actually Mel Otto did not smell–except of money. Hank had to reconcile that Mel had a pig farm–a big one–a good wife, "I'm goin to kill you some day, Big Hank. Some day you're going to get it when you're not expectin it."

Yah, Mel had sputtered those words again a couple days ago, as he threw the keys to the Ford and asked his neighbor, Chet, for a ride home. "You'd better watch your back. Someday I'm going to kill you–if it's the last thing I do," shouted Mel. Everyone thought that he might someday keep that promise.

Hank was not worried–"Why worry over some little pig farmer? For I'm Hank Schultz."

But here he was, staring at the badge of a sheriff he didn't know: a badge on a burly chest and a holster with a gun.

"Are you OK, Mr. Schultz? You look kinda upset. 'Everythin OK?" Sheriff Blake couldn't help remembering that about a year ago he'd found a neighbor, Joe Wright, sitting in his car, but with his brains blown out. Shot himself–just depressed they said. It was a mess and really sad, too. Hope that's not what this guy is up to– see what I can do.

"How about lettin me buy you a cup of coffee in Red Cloud– only about 15 miles further–got a good café there with good coffee."

"Sounds OK," says Hank, not really knowing what he was going to do.

Hank followed the sheriff's car, as it pulled in to park by Rosie's Café: homemade pies every day. The two men ordered their coffee and slid into a booth. Hank's face was still pinched. "It's like this, I just lost my girl. She got married a couple years ago, and it's still hard to take. She even had a baby by the squirt of a man."

"Sorry to hear that, young man, love can tear you apart. Were you sweethearts for long?"

"A couple of years," Hank lied. "I'm a farmer, a good farmer."

"And, the other guy?"

"He's a farmer, too," never mentioning that Will was his brother.

"Some times ya don't always know what goes wrong. You lookin for a new one? Is that why you're drivin 'round? In that car you should be findin a fancy gal anytime."

"Yah, do you know any gals here worth looking at?"

Hank couldn't believe he was telling this story to a stranger–a sheriff no less.

"Well, let's see. Yah, there's Rosie over there"–pointing to a middle aged woman with tight, little curls–like a new perm–and weighing, oh, maybe 210.

"Aaah. Thought maybe I'd find a widowed farm girl."

"Well," the sheriff laughed, "you've come to the right place." He slapped his hand on his thigh, laughing loudly. "We've got Widda Penelope. What a dish!! –she's been a widda a couple years now–married old Herman Stanton–better'n twice her age. He was a toddlin old fool to think she'd love him, a beer drinkin, tobaccy chewing fart–but rich, rich, rich–owned a bunch of wheat land–hey, it's over there–near Fairview.

"Penelope grew up here in Red Cloud–good folks–then she came back from college with high falutin ideas–givin the eye to ole Herman–ole widower hisself. She brought him cake and pies, and gave him sweet talk. Married her in two months–like real fast. She'd go walkin through town hangin on to him as if she was the Queen of Sheba. It was funny to see. She's quite a looker, if you know what I mean. Ha, never could 'magine them makin love, that slim little looker and that big flabby fart." Then he laughed again.

"Lots of folks thought that maybe she'd done him in–you know knocked 'im off with a bunch of arsenic. I looked into it, as sheriff, seeing if I could smell somethin dirty, but didn't find a thing. She cried and cried at the funeral, made a mess of 'erself. And she doesn't go out much now–'cept to the Methodist church where she sings in the choir–and looks purty saintly on Sundays. So maybe she really did love that ole man. But she does have the land in Colorado. Don't know how's it doin".

Hank looked curious, "I think I'll check out the town tomorrow. Methodist you say." He face brightened up, just thinking of a new conquest. "Thanks for the coffee; is there a decent hotel here?"

"Right next door, the Stanton Hotel –purty good, purty plain you know. Yup, it's owned by Widda Stanton, too. Check it out."

Hank ambled over and checked in for one night. The hotel was two-story brick, with a window for each of the ten rooms and a shared bath for some–private for others. Hank rented a private room, dollar and fifty cents a night with coffee in the morning. He yanked up the pull-down shades to look out to the near empty street–just a bed frame and decent mattress was all he needed. Sleep came quickly. He didn't once think about Will and Julie.

Hank woke up already planning his church-going, and meeting Widda' Stanton.

First thing Hank went back to Rosie's café, then drove around town—about 550 people lived there, stop signs and dirt roads, had a Rexall drug store, Sam's grocery store, filing station, and a hardware store. Pretty typical—nothing special except for the Stanton Hotel. Unusual to have one of those around, must have traffic through the town. He drove by three churches, St. Paul's Lutheran, Holy Mother Catholic and First Methodist.

Yes, that's the one.

He noticed the worship times and saw a fellowship hour after the 11:00 AM service.

Bingo, good time to be charming.

Driving around Red Cloud for another ten minutes, *I think I've found a gold mine. I need to check with the county assessor about some land that might be held in the name of Penelope Stanton. Yes, a real gold mine.* Hank began laughing and singing at the same time, as he headed back to Colorado.

Monday morning Hank drove straight to Hopetown to check with the county assessor, "Hello, Assessor Peetz, I'm looking to buy some land, I've been told it's held in the name of Penelope Stanton. Could you check your records to see if it is near the homestead?"

"Sure, let me see," said the assessor, "why yes, it's this Section, 118 on County Road 36. Why, Hank, that's close to your mom's homestead."—Checking further, "Yup, it's close, just has the Updike's place between the two—looks like a good piece of property." The assessor didn't mention that the property taxes—were unpaid for the past three years. He saw that a little over seven hundred dollars were owed. *That's a problem,* thought the clerk, *two more years and it's turned over to the State.*

Hank's trip back home went fast as he was singing or humming the whole way back. "A rich widow—is just what I want—and they say one not too bad looking at that."

"Where have you been, Hank?" asked Mama Rose, looking disturbed when Hank arrived around noon. "I needed help with all the milking. You didn't tell me that you weren't coming back. That is too much for me to get done, as well as feed all the livestock. Please stay home more, so we can get the chores done."

"I'm sorry, Mama, I thought Pete and his boys were coming over to help."

"They all were down with the croup –just nasty stuff."

"I'm sorry, Mama," as he kissed her cheek. "I got carried away in Red Cloud as I went there to look for some land to buy."

"We never talked about buying more land. What? Where did you get that idea?"

"Well, since Will and Julie now have started a family of their own, they need to have more land to farm, too."

"I think we have enough for both us and for Will and Julie, You never want to be greedy with God's land."

Hank had heard that message over and over again. It came from Papa Paul and that crazy Cheyenne guy–always being sure that you don't take more than your share!

"We can hardly manage to care for the land we have now," Mama continued.

"You're probably right, Mama, but I think it's time that I think of finding a wife, too."

"Why, Hank! Have you found someone special?" Mama could see in his eye that he was up to something. She knew that look meant that he was scheming.

"As a matter of fact, I plan to meet someone very soon, in Red Cloud. I'm going to meet her at church next Sunday."

"Church? Oh, that's good." Mama said hoping that her wayward son was renewing his faith. Sadness still hit her heart when she recalled finding out about his ex- communication–being thrown out of the church–never to receive the sacraments again.

"Yes, Mama, I was told about it by the sheriff who stopped to look over my papers for my new car. He said the church has a good choir."

"But, Hank, please, please don't leave me with all the chores to do. I am too old to milk all those cows. Will can do the milking next week, but he has his own cows and livestock to take care of, too."

"I won't, Mama, I won't–it was just that things happened so fast–" Hank stuttered.

All the bad things that had happened, like the ex-communication, seemed like long, long ago. Hank was ecstatic, but he still cringed and felt sad when he disappointed mama.

Chapter 27

EVIL PLOT

Man is the cruelest animal
  Friedrich Nietzsche

The next Sunday morning Hank looked mighty fine in his navy suit and sparkling white shirt when he drove his new, yellow Studebaker up to the First Methodist Church. The edifice was regular size, gray brick, and had stained glass windows showing "Jesus as Shepherd" and "Jesus Teaching the Children." The pews held about 75 worshippers facing a plain altar. Curiosity caused several older women, their hats draped with veils, to crane their necks for a peek at the tall, handsome, auburn-haired stranger in their midst.

A couple of children embarrassed their moms by whispering, "Who's that, Mommy?"

"Shush, shush," came the reprimand.

Mr. Winston, the preacher, entered wearing a black suit and carrying a Bible. He welcomed everyone and looking around asked, "Any newcomers or visitors in our midst today? Ah–yes, sir, please stand and tell us who you are?"

Hank obliged, "I'm Hank Schultz from Fairview." Ah–could be heard, and murmurs, as the 6'4' young man stood erect, tossing his reddish brown hair slightly to indicate warmth and cheer.

"Welcome, Welcome," said the minister, and others smiled and nodded. "Please join us in the fellowship hall after services, so we can get acquainted."

Mrs. Johnson, grey-haired with firm arms and ample legs, pumped the organ and began with a strong chord–and in walked the choir–black robed with white stoles–probably fourteen or so–mixed group–mostly gray-haired women wearing heavy glasses, a couple of men–also gray, with glasses, and –and–a true beauty. She was tall with dark hair in a puffy bun, and her porcelain white skin–in the black choir robe–added to her mystery.

That must be Penelope Stanton, Widow Stanton–gee whiz. Hank's heart was pounding thinking of the prospects–no, not of love–but of land–of money–of power. After the choir's anthem, done with too much soprano and few dynamics and a bass that seemed out of tune, the sermon, the dismissal finally came–then shaking hands with the minister and another invitation to socialize–coffee and cake in the fellowship hall.

Several older men introduced themselves and asked Hank his reason for coming to Red Cloud. "I'm speculating on some land," Hank answered.

"Please join us for coffee. We got some good farming land around here," they all commented.

"Yah interested in ranch land or farming?" an older, lanky man asked.

"Oh, definitely farming, I'm into wheat farming now." Hank wasn't really interested in buying land, but had his own ideas of how to speculate on farmland. They chatted a bit longer, and then the mystery widow–Penelope–walked in–dressed again in striking black with a younger man walking beside her. They were conversing. Hank overheard the man say, "Well, maybe another night then, Penelope, I'd really like to take you to the dance."

Penelope smiled sweetly at him, "Oh, Jack, you know I don't dance and don't go out much–yet."

Jack replied, "It's about time, Penelope; it's been two years." He looked like a forlorn dog waiting for a bone.

Pitiful thought Hank.

Just then Hank caught a glimpse of the most beautiful brown eyes he'd ever seen. A smile spread across her crimson lips, "This must be Mr. Schultz from Fairview," remembering the minister's welcome.

Mr. Jack crossed over and shook Hank's hand, although you could see Jack didn't welcome any competition for the lovely widow's hand.

Hank bowed deeply, "I am, and with whom am I honored to be speaking?" He smiled deeply knowing that his straight, white teeth and magnificent looks would get any woman. *It always works, he* thought.

Penelope stepped back slightly and smiled. *Such perfect diction, such gallant manners.*

"I'm Penelope Stanton."

"The Penelope Stanton, owner of the famed Stanton Hotel. Why I was a guest there last week," Hank said.

"I do hope it was comfortable," Penelope was also teasing, as she fluttered her long, dark lashes and tilted her head shyly. "And maybe you'll stay there often. What brings you to Red Cloud?"

"I'm looking for available land to buy. I'm farming across the state line, and hoped I might find some property for sale near to it."

"What a coincidence, as I own some acreage on the Colorado side, but it isn't for sale," she laughed. "In fact I was looking to buy some more land on that side. Maybe we should look together!"

Hank was more intrigued each moment. Here was a woman to his liking, a shrewd, cunning businesswoman.

Jack, noticing that he was now not part of the conversation, excused himself. Penelope continued, "How much acreage are you looking for and what purpose do you have for it?"

"I'd like about a section of good soil for wheat farming. That's what I have now–dry land, nice and flat, easy to cut."

"If you have time today, I could take you around the country to look at some of the land that might be for sale, but I'm not certain there is any."

"Do you have time? A husband–children?" Hank already knew the answer but wanted to extend the talk.

"I have the time, today. I'm widowed without children, but have family living here in Red Cloud. Perhaps you could to join us for Sunday dinner. We can talk more about your plans then, and maybe drive around some with my father and brother."

Too good to be true–and meeting her family as well–this is my lucky day.

Hank hadn't once thought about Julie.

Penelope said, "Do you have a car here?"

"Yes."

"Then just follow me about a mile south of town. I'll go slowly so you don't get lost. I have a black Model T Ford," she laughed, "like everyone else in the county." Penelope looked up at him, this time her brown eyes were laughing, and even her lips looked as if they wanted to be kissed.

Penelope said goodbye to others and walked ahead of Hank to the parking lot where she got into her car, and looked surprised–and–pleased when Hank pulled up behind her in his yellow Studebaker.

Now this is what I've been waiting for –a wealthy man–with class–not like beer-drinking Herman, Penelope mused.

Penelope's family was pleased to have a Sunday guest, and treated him as royalty. Their home would be considered to be of an elevated lifestyle. Little did they know that Hank's farm was a homestead–owned by his mother–and his car was a gambling debt payoff. And Hank didn't know that the Hardin's were behind three years in paying their property taxes–potentially losing their farm and a whole section land. Both parties had something at stake in this new friendship–and both knew ways of scheming to get it.

After a two-hour trip into the countryside with Penelope's father guiding them, Hank gave Penelope a warm goodbye, and asked if he could come again next weekend for more speculation.

"I'd be delighted and hope that you find the Hotel comfortable again." She definitely wanted to go slowly with this, although already she had some feelings for this man that were not all business. She felt she'd really like to invite him to stay with her–in her big, fluffy, empty bed.

When she reentered her parent's home, Mr. Hardin said, "Do you know who Hank Schultz's grandfather was? Why, he was that famous Seed Man! Paul Pinot. Farmers came from all over the state just to see his way of farming. He was a master–learned it all when he lived in Germany.

"You really have a catch now, as those crops are still the best in the area. You go decent and slow, but you want to catch this one before too long. I hear his mother, Widow Rose, is gettin to be of that age–'n Hank is in line to inherit the whole thing. Oh, there is another brother, Will, I think his name is, but Hank is sure to be the one chosen."

Hank's trip back to Fairview went fast again, singing or humming the whole way back. *A rich widow is just what I want, and one really hot for luvvin, I can tell.*

"Mama," Hank said as he kissed her cheek. "I did go to church in Red Cloud and found a lovely widow there who seemed interested in me. Maybe as my wife."

"Why, Hank, don't you think that will be a long way off. You're only 22 now. But if you found someone special Mama could see in his eyes that he'd been scheming again. She knew that look.

"It's a Methodist Church with a decent service. Afterwards I talked with some farmers and then one of the choir members, a woman."

Ah, the church going–not for salvation–but for some woman. Mama knew him well. "Penelope Stanton–she invited me to her parent's house–the Hardin's–for Sunday dinner." Hank wanted the set-up to be logical–and natural. "I went and we talked, and then took a ride around the farmlands. She is very intelligent."

Mama knew this was not the whole story "Tell me more."

"She's a widow–for almost two years–hasn't any kids. I plan to go and see her next weekend."

"A widow–that's wonderful. Maybe you can bring her here for Sunday dinner sometime. I'd like to meet her. I know something about being a widow, but I had children."

Hank hadn't remembered to compare Penelope with his own mother. *It's hard to think of Mama as a married woman, been a widow for so long. That's right, I need a woman like Penelope Stanton with money and land–someone I can marry. That sounds pretty dangerous; don't know if I can only have one woman–but then again I'm 22. I've had my flings. I've had my fun, and maybe I've even left a few little reds around. Like with Daisy in North Platte. She wrote me once saying that she was having my baby. Couldn't be, but there it was in black and white–my baby. Then all that gushy stuff about loving me and hoping it was a boy, and looking like me. I didn't write back, just a note saying, 'Take care of it'. I stuck in a hundred dollars and added, 'Don't contact me again or I will bring a law suit–or some threat like that!' Never heard from her again. Oh, she was one sexy bitch–but a wife? Never–for a wife.*

Penelope had been known in Red Cloud as the daughter of Randolph Hardin.

Here I was, Randolph Hardin always the best farmer in the area until about ten years ago. Drat it anyway. I just bought too much land at too high of a price. Then I couldn't pay the taxes and got behind 'cause I bought a Fordson tractor. Just stretched my money too far, and I couldn't afford to buy good seed crop. Just went down hill from there.

I sure was smart to advise my beautiful, scheming daughter to try and latch onto ole Stanton. He had just been widowed and was looking pretty needy. I knew that Penelope could fit the bill. I told her 'now don't be gentle with that ole man, give him more than he ever had before, make it often and if possible feed him lots and lots of fat meat and really stuff him before bed, if you know what I mean. Get him all riled up every night, and you'll wear out the old bastard's heart. 'Sure enough, it didn't take long, only 18 months. The poor bastard picked a Sunday church service to keel over and die right on the spot in the middle of the sermon. But they say he had a big smile on his face, as Penelope had given him a wild night with lots of wine and a juicy steak. Sure brought that to a quick end. Penelope has been a perfect, rich widow. She saved our house, but not the farm. Maybe this new dude will be the answer. I hope so.

By marrying that ole, beer-drinking, fat Stanton, Penelope didn't take long to do the math, and figured she had gained over ten thousand dollars in land, the Hotel, gold coins, and some money in the First National Bank. She was well to do, but wanted more. She began looking almost immediately for another mate, one with ideas as greedy as hers. *It's time to throw off my widow's weeds.*

In fact while Hank was looking for a rich widow, Penelope had been inquiring in surrounding towns for a single man–bachelor–or widower–she didn't care if he was handsome or not–just that he had money.

So the church meeting on Sunday hadn't been accidental. They were alike in character, alike in disposition, and both intent upon gaining wealth. Both knew what they wanted in this relationship, and it wasn't about love.

Chapter 28

'TIL DEATH DO US PART

Intensely selfish people are always very decided as to what they wish. They do not waste their energies on considering the good of others.

Ouida Wanda

No need to do all that silly courting thing, thought Hank and apparently Penelope agreed. It was 1927, and the world was prosperous. On New Year's Eve and just seven months after meeting they were married in her parents' home. Her father and mother, one brother, Mama Rose, Margaret and Pete–and Julie and Will–were there. Hank tried not to look into Julie's eyes, for he knew he would give away his feelings of love for her. Will didn't suspect anything from his younger brother. *He's too naïve,* thought Hank.

"You're a lucky man to find someone so much like you, Hank. May your marriage be as happy as ours," Will said.

Julie added a hug, and said, "Be happy." Hank's heart nearly burst at her touch.

Penelope looked lovely in her white velvet dress, and Hank handsome in his black suit. And by marrying on the last day of the year the new Schultz's slightly improved their income tax picture for that year. They planned it that way. Their honeymoon was a whole week at a lovely resort in Glenwood Springs. It was now time to move in their plan for wealth.

Hank and Penelope settled into the homestead house–the home Mama Rose had sacrificed so much for. She left behind the memories of living in her first dugout home, but the tender presence of John William was in her mind every night. She often shared thoughts with him about the happenings of the day.

Dearest husband, now our last child is married and happy. The wedding was simple, somewhat like ours, and hopefully will be lived as fully as ours was. Somehow I don't get the feeling that they are soul mates as you and I were–or as Julie and Will are–just a feeling. The bride was married before, but widowed. He was an old man when they married and died in church from a heart attack.

Sometimes I see a glance in her eyes that doesn't seem tender, but rather searching out, like she is conniving. I could be wrong, but Hank has always had that trait–clever–always looking out for himself, so maybe she has that, too, after being widowed. They are still on their honeymoon, but when they get back perhaps I will get to know more about her character, as we'll share this house. Maybe I soon will be with you, my beloved John William–oh, to feel your arms around me one more time. To see the yellow roses you used to pick for me. John William, I've missed you every day. Some day–someday– and then sleep came.

Mama Rose didn't have to wait long before finding out what Penelope was really like. The night Hank and his new bride arrived back home; they had tea with Mama and described adventures of the honeymoon. As young people they obviously enjoyed each other.

"Well, it's time for bed," said Hank, "see you in the morning."

Their bedroom was above Mama's. Shortly after they went to bed, the bedsprings were making a pounding sound and squeals could be heard. Not gentle lovemaking–no way! Mama was embarrassed to be a witness to that. *Should be private,* she thought, so she covered her head. But several times during the night she was awakened again to the bounce and bumps of the bed against the wall and floor.

As morning came, Mama tried to avoid eye contact as Hank burst into the kitchen. "Oh, am I hungry, Mama, what is there to eat?" His eyes were laughing and his cheeks red.

"I have scrambled eggs and some toast. Is that enough? And when will your lovely bride be getting up?"

"Oh, Penelope likes to get up around 9 o'clock."

"Really!" Mama gasped, "never heard of someone–who wasn't sick or dying–sleep past 7:00 AM."

"Oh, she has to get her beauty sleep," and he laughed again. "I'll go out and milk the cows and feed the livestock. Does Will come over every day, and when?"

"He'll be here about now, usually comes after he milks his cows. Not much to do until the snow is gone. Inspecting all the barns, sheds, chicken coops, the tractor and other equipment takes more time. Usually he checks the house for leaks, but you can do that since you live here."

"You're right, Mama. I'll help with all that, too. Will Julie be coming, too?" Even mentioning her name made Hank's heart beat faster–*Got ta get over that. I'm a married man now.* Hank grabbed his coat, gloves and left to work in the barn.

Penelope came down stairs about 9:30 AM. Mama was shocked to see that she wore a startling scarlet, satin robe, not tied in the front, nor buttoned, nothing. As she entered the kitchen, she said, "Good morning, Mama"–the gown opened fully–exposing a completely naked body with tits swinging bravely, looking perky enough, but still shocking, and her tummy rounded and pubic hair as thick and black as the hair on her head!

"Whoops, better tie myself up–just in case somebody comes in," she laughed wickedly.

Mama was too shocked to say a thing, but thought, *As if I'm not somebody.* "Yes, I think it's better to come downstairs fully dressed in the winter, it's pretty chilly in the downstairs–and living on the farm–you never know who might be here. Hank and Will are working out in the barn. Do you want to have any breakfast?"

"No, think I'll just have a cup of coffee if you have any. And smoke my morning cigarette." Penelope pulled a package of cigarettes from a pocket in the gown and looked for a match around the cook stove. Finding one, she lit up and blew smoke toward the ceiling, again startling Mama–who began coughing.

"Whoops, I should have asked you first if it was OK to light up, but these are the days of women's freedom, and smoking is one good sign of that."

"I've never seen a woman smoke, before–just on magazine covers. I don't think it is good for you–all that smoke in your lungs."

"Oh, I think it looks sophisticated–like a movie star."

"Why don't you go out on the porch to smoke, then no one else has to breathe it, too?" squeaked Mama, coughing a bit.

"Maybe when it's not so cold–maybe in the summer time, but for now I want to stay inside." Penelope didn't apologize. With that she took a few more puffs on the long cigarette.

Mama just stared out the window.

Chapter 29

MAMA MAKES A MOVE

I change myself; I change the world.
Gloria Anzuldua, *Borderland/LaFrontera The New Mestiza*

Mama knew that now her home would be a place of conflict–of challenge. *I don't need trouble anymore–perhaps its time to move on.*

"Mama, please come and live with us. You know we've wanted you to come for years and years. It's so much easier for you, since you don't have to go outside to the toilet. Now that the newly weds are home, they probably want some privacy," Margaret's face turned a bright red when she said that.

If she only knew that they didn't seem to notice if they were private or not thought Mama Rose, remembering the nightly squeaks and squeals. With that memory, Mama made up her mind to move in with Margaret. Her daughter's house was only three miles to the east of the homestead. Pete, was a man of many talents–a farmer, a carpenter, and an inventor.

"Why, Pete can build anything," Margaret said. "He built our brick house. It has a fireplace and a whole basement. The best, to me, is the indoor Johnnie. I hate to go outside in the dark and the cold. He got this flush toilet through Monkey Wards; it has water in a tank and flushes everything down and out to the septic tank. The cistern holds water from the windmill, so we don't run out of it either."

"We also have electricity."

Margaret was the only Lutheran woman to have both conveniences. One Methodist lady in a nearby town had a flush toilet, but no electricity. Mama said, "It's a mark of the times to come." Mama and Margaret had always been close as mother and daughter. Margaret was a true farmer's wife, doing the chores as needed, but especially busy with raising chickens, must have over 100 laying hens.

"Can you believe? They even have in-door plumbing–a rare thing, Pete has developed a system of electricity using the windmill as a generator. It's quite unusual–gives them light at night. Now our kerosene lamps don't compare with his–even the Hurricane Lanterns aren't as good, even with new wicks, they have to be cleaned all the time, and a globe is always breaking. Someday we'll all have that electricity," Mama said.

Other changes were happening with Julie and Will. Serena was born in August 14 1929, with a wistful look on her face, long tapered fingers and a thatch of red hair. Will and Julie were thrilled.

"My little violinist and as beautiful as my grandmother, Frieda," Will said.

"Or my mother, Serena," Julie added.

"You're right, she's a miracle mix of both of them–and maybe Mama Rose, our Promise Seed." So they named her Serena Rose. She, indeed, would some day become a great violinist, but that would be a long time from now.

Julie and Will, with their two babies, had the same routine– Saturday night dance, Sunday morning church, dinner with Mama, Margaret and Pete and their young boys. They were a popular couple. Will's baritone voice had such passion, so he sang for many occasions–like funerals and weddings.

"I have this gift from my dad, so I share as much as I can– makes me feel closer to him."

That summer was very busy getting the wheat cut, stacked, and then thrashed. Nights would come at last. Julie and Will would talk about their dreams and twine their bodies into loving cocoons.

Hank and Penelope lived a different lifestyle. "I hate this old, creaky house–so far out from nowhere. We must move to Hopetown. At least there we can see our friends," Penelope whined.

So Hank hired the best builders in the county. Many of the carpenters were disappointed, as Hank alleged they didn't do this or that right "No pay for poor work," he'd say.

"No one can challenge Hank, the Almighty," said one man cheated out of his pay. Hank just ignored their threats and challenges. "I'm always right," he'd say. Eventually Hank and Penelope had a spacious, elegant house, in Hopetown and seldom visited the homestead again.

Sadly it gradually grew dismal and showed signs of neglect. Paint peeled from its sides and shingles were never replaced; one window on the west side cracked when hit by hail; it wasn't repaired. Most deplorable were the yellow climbing roses on the outside fence, left untended, they faded and withered away.

In contrast the Schultz's Hopetown house was a lively place where Hank and Penelope entertained only the wealthy of the county. Why they even had several visitors from overseas! These 'Schultz's' were considered the "beautiful couple," sitting in their library with cigarettes and wine each evening, chatting happily as they searched travel maps for their next overseas trips. Surprisingly it became obvious that the Hank and Penelope were really devoted to each other.

"That's all that counts, I think." Will said, and Julie agreed.

"No one can criticize their lifestyle–they are getting what they want. I'm not envious at all."

Julie's first attempt to make friends with Penelope didn't work out at all. Penelope, a college-educated lady, tried to impress upon Julie that she was going to live with more sophisticated taste.

"I just hate to cook," she said, "and to wash a dish!" Not in her lifetime, as she left stacks of dirty dishes in the sink until there wasn't a clean one in the house.

"Oh, dear Molly, please come over and help me. I've had my female troubles again," she'd whine, and Molly, the good-hearted neighbor, would bring her scrubbers and buckets, and wash the dishes, floors, and straighten the whole house. "Just don't know what I'd do without you." Penelope would say as she handed Molly two old apples for the day's work.

But Julie simply moved on with her own style of class–never reminding Penelope that Mama Rose was also college-educated, a gifted violinist, plus owner of all their land and their crops. Also Mama was respected by many of the women leaders in Denver, the capitol of the new state.

Perhaps the superficial style of the new bride would have been overlooked, but when Julie came by with her new baby, Serena, Penelope's only remark was, "Why, she doesn't have any hair, how strange. I hope I never have a baby–they are just too messy and noisy." With that remark Penelope took out a cigarette and began smoking–in front of Julie–and the baby and little Ernie.

"Well, come over sometime, please do." With that Julie left, carrying her babies to the Model T. Although no friendship ever developed between the two women, Julie always invited Penelope to every family gathering at their house.

Chapter 30

MAMA'S TIN LIZZY

And forget not that the earth delights to feel your bare feet and the wind longs to play with your hair.
Khalil Gibran

Moving into Margaret's home freed Mama Rose from all chores, like cooking, cleaning, tending her chickens, and sometimes milking the cows. Mama drew in fresh vigor for life. "It's like a vacation! I can work in the garden; talk with Margaret, or just do nothing all day. But I want to do more! Let me think– what can I do that's new and exciting? I feel like I'm sixteen again. You can't just let yourself stop growing."

Mama's black hair still thick and shiny had only a few streaks of gray; it was hard to believe that she was nearly sixty. On Saturday nights, she went dancing with Margaret and Pete, joined by Will and Julie. Mama would never sit alone on the side lines, as men loved to dance with this petite, happy person. She'd also play her violin like a fiddle, as Will sang dance songs. You could hear her tinkling laughter throughout the night.

"It's time for me to learn to drive," she announced one morning at breakfast. "I will buy a Model T and drive myself wherever I want. I plan to drive to Denver and join the Governor's wife and women leaders to deal with many issues in the State needing a female perspective."

Margaret and Pete smiled; they knew any advice they'd give would be ignored for this was Mama talking. So, Mama Rose and Margaret went car shopping in Hopetown.

"I'm going to buy groceries, I'll be back in 30 minutes." Margaret left Mama to go shopping.

"That's the one for me," Mama laughed. "I want that flashy black one, over there," pointing at one among all black Fords. "That's my Tin Lizzie."

Mama hopped right in with Rudy, the 17 year-old salesman, sitting beside her on the right side. It never occurred to him that she'd never driven before. She'd watched Will drive many times and certainly had driven the Fordson tractor! Mama confidently turned the starter key and jerked forward quickly. She never depressed anything – like the clutch.

"Whoops!" yelled the salesman. "Push the clutch, yes the pedal to the left. His face had turned ashen. "Get it into gear – yes with that stick in the middle– the gear shift– then the accelerator– yah that one. Let out the clutch slowly – slowly.

Mama looked straight ahead, her hat slightly askew.

The first time it was anything but slow, as the Tin Lizzy jerked and sputtered and jerked again, gaining speed as she went down a side street in Hopetown.

"Slow down, slow down," shouted Rudy as his hands flew to the top trying to grab only to anything.

Mama looked straight ahead with a grim smile on her face. Finding them selves near the end of the dirt lane, the petrified salesman shouted, "The brake, the brake," point at the right pedal. With that Mama looked down at her feet trying to locate the brake pedal and served into and out of a shallow ditch. "Whoops, Whoops," she shouted as the car came to a sudden, shuttering stop! At that point Rudy jumped out of the car and ran to the driver's side, shaking his head and his whole body.

"Have you ever driven a car before?" Rudy asked with a squeaky voice at a near panic stage. He looked like he might lose his breakfast.

"Why no, I never have–how did I do?" asked Mama innocently.

The salesman slumped against the car and didn't answer just motioned for Mama to exit and move to the passenger's side. He then leaped in. Without a word Rudy drove the Ford back to the dealership and swayed helplessly into the building, leaving Mama to come in by herself.

The manager, Mr. Wilson, who knew everyone around came to meet Mama and said, "Why Mrs. Schultz how brave of you to drive this little Ford! It sure will help you out this winter when you want to go visitin. How about calling Will to come over and drive this wonderful car to Margaret's where you can practice and practice all the driving." *I sure don't want Mama to be driving around Hopetown*, thought Mr. Wilson.

"Why young man, that would be a foolish thing to do. Will is busy in the fields, now you show me some more tricks to driving and I'll drive home quick as a wink, I can drive a Fordson, so why not this little Tin Lizzy?"

"That's very good, Mrs. Schultz, but a car is different and when you drive the Fordson there aren't any other tractors around, are there?"

"You're right, but I can see other cars coming and stay to the right side of the road, right?" Mama's eyes were now flashing, so look out!

"Yes, you're right; stay in your own lane– to the right –keep your eyes straight ahead, no looking at your feet." Mr. Wilson knew that he was not going to win the argument, and since no one would be out driving in Hopetown right now, he knew that this widow would drive home.

"Best I show you some tricks on how to drive your car, since you already know how to drive a tractor."

With that said, he and Mama drove farther into the country road where he showed her the way to calmly shift the stick shift, let out the clutch, gently press the accelerator. "And when you want to stop gently press the brake so you don't fly through the windshield," Mr. Wilson said

After several jerky attempts, Mama began to drive slowly and smoothly. "I've got it; time to go home," she said confidently. "It's only a few miles, and the sun is still shining. Better get going. Let me write you a check and be on my way, thank you very much. Her hat was on straight again, and her thin lips, without a smile, told of her determination.

"Isn't Margaret coming back after her grocery shopping?" Mr. Wilson was a bit uncertain about having Mama drive without any help.

"Oh, my yes. I almost forgot about Margaret. I just got so excited about my new freedom. Better wait for her."

In about ten minutes Margaret drove up to the dealership and hopped out, looking for Mama Rose. "Why you're sitting in your own car!" she said with a great swoop of her hands.

"I'm so excited. Mr. Wilson taught me how to drive." Mama looked like a little kid with a new bike. "Why don't you follow me home, so if I make a bad turn you'll be there to help me," Mama said.

Margaret, knowing her mother, never argued.

Mr. Wilson looked away quickly as Mama started her car and slowly, smoothly sailed down the street with Margaret following behind. The trip of ten miles home was without any trouble until Mama reached the turn into their yard. Miscalculating her speed, Mama did not slow down–at all–but turned too quickly–and the car sailed into the shallow ditch and into a low fence and then back on the road again, correcting the turn like a veteran.

But then Tin Lizzy entered the yard where chickens were running freely.

Never heard so much squawking, screeching, and feathers flying as the flock scurried to get out of the way of the mad driver! Thankfully none was hurt, just that the scared hens didn't lay any eggs for a day or two. Ending the maiden voyage with a screech only a few feet from the barn door, Mama hopped out, smiling, with hat still on straight.

Margaret followed closely behind.

"Look out," Mama shouted every time she'd drive into the yard, but she didn't need to bother as the chickens would glance her way and scuttle to the hen house.

Widow Schultz had her freedom and was seen almost daily visiting old friends or even driving to meetings in Denver with socially active women (even though it was 180 mile on dirt roads). Of course she spent the night with good friends or even at the elegant Brown Palace, a famous Denver hotel.

That was until the sky grew angry by noon–and the dust storms began, and the world turned dark and dangerous.

Chapter 31

THE EARTH RISES UP

Black blizzard they called it, with an edge like steel.
Timothy Egan, *The Worst Hard Times.*

The deadly deed had already begun–Europe, on the brink of war, needed wheat and corn, so prices rose. Every farmer in the county planted more and more wheat.

"Remember how fortunes are made," Hank remarked. "On just one section we spend only about forty cents to plant one bushel–and sell it for a dollar thirty; that's a profit of over three hundred percent!"

Will was more cautious. He urged farmers at a meeting, "We've got to put a halt to this madness, as everyone is planting more and more wheat–yah, we're making a lot of money–as much as possible–just going nuts, but it can't last."

"But, Will, we got ta make as much as we can. Some of us are just beginnin our farming, 'n everything costs way too much," whined a neighbor.

"He's right," claimed Hank, "the only thing we can do is plant more, so what does come up, we can sell. Feed ourselves–and the livestock. Will, we can't quit planting now."

Will had a steady, cool head, perhaps because he was Papa Paul's grandson. "I just don't see that," said Will. "This grass–the prairie–was never meant to be plowed. We made the mistake of digging up what had been here for thousands of years, and it's time to stop over-planting. Together we can save the soil, but planting more and more, the soil is going to grow weak and soon nothing will grow.

"If you plant, you must rotate the crops; plant alfalfa or oats, not wheat every year. Heaven help us if we get a drought; this place will blow away. We've got to work together–if not, we'll all fail. Help each other; when we have extra hay, we need to share. Some land must lay fallow for a few years, or all its strength will be sucked out, soon there will be nothing."

Will continued, "And the other side of the coin, if we plant too much wheat–we'll have a surplus–'n the price of wheat will drop." Some nodded their heads in agreement, while others shook their heads. A few sided with Will–but most with Hank–so they plowed everything in sight–and planted more wheat.

Just as Will had warned–too much wheat and price of wheat plummeted–then banks failed–Tuesday the 29th, October 1929–the Great Depression began. But farmers–planted more–and incomes fell even more–there was no chance to recover. No one could reverse the direction–it was too late.

"Guess you were right, Will. We should have listened," men would say at the pool hall or at church, but they couldn't turn back the clock. To add to the tragedy, the winds began to change the face of the earth.

They had made their own devil–even more powerful.

Drought seared the land to powder, which the wind picked up. Black clouds formed–thousands and thousands of feet higher than anyone had ever seen. Day turned into night–it was dark all the time.

Lightning strikes were fierce and the air dry. Even the animals began to panic–running wildly for protection.

There was none.

"I think it's the end times–the end of the world," cried one farmer.

The days of dust didn't stop. Waiting for rains to come was like dreaming a trip to the moon. Looking up at the skies in the morning, seeing no clouds, only the sun beating down was troubling. Faith began to fail. Farmers walked in the fields, seeing no growth, no germinating seeds, they'd murmur, "Can we go on?"

One year, two years, and even into three, the ground remained parched and gray. Will said, "We'll never give up."

Wells dried up. Windmills stood still and haunting. Mama Rose looked to the sky, "Please, dear Lord, just a breeze to help us now. Livestock are crying just from thirst, not to mention how hungry they are growing–you can hear them all day and night–shaking their heads and pawing the ground."

She had lived through so much and now this. *What would Red Sun say? What would Papa Paul say? Have we so misused our Mother Earth to be punished? Why this?* Mama Rose never lost her faith, but her heart would nearly break when she looked across fields gone barren and gray. *Oh, John William, what is going to become of our beloved home?*

Some desperate farmers began feeding their livestock tumbleweeds, just to fill their stomachs–but that only caused a type of colic. Those who plowed up all the prairie sod now saw the results–no green shoots of plants–of any kind–the land was stripped. Papa Paul said 'plant in the late summer, so snow could cover the fragile shoots', but it was too late; just the winter winds. No snow. The soil was ripped apart like paper Mache.

Nothing held.

When the spring winds came it was even worse. There was no topsoil left. Only the memory of earth remained. It was bare-naked. The disaster grew day by day. Even those that left a few acres of virgin sod found that soil couldn't be held, as the winds grew fiercer. Neighbors who had selfishly plowed too much demonized other neighbors with tons of smothering dirt onto their fields. Now there was no stopping the growing destruction.

The treeless horizon became hazy with dust. People began to die of dust pneumonia–dust was everywhere. No wonder the era was called the Dust Bowl Days. No one was safe. Every morning a shovel was needed to clean the kitchen floor, and the bedding was covered with a layer of dust.

Ernie and Serena ate breakfast quietly, knowing their cereal was filled with flying dust. Julie put dampened cloths over their noses and tried to keep their nostrils open, free of the dirt-filled mucus.

"We can't go on," several said. "Let's go to the West coast by the ocean, where there's no dust bowl." Families pondered leaving, and a few did.

One family, the Updike's, with Dutch roots, put everything into a wagon and just left–leaving their house and the barn–already torn apart by the unending wind. They had no livestock left–all had died. Growing up near canals and the low land in Holland, the Updike's thought the drought was work of the Devil.

Sometimes Julie felt the same, as her mind wandered back to the green lands of Denmark and her childhood. *"Though I walk in the valley of the shadow of death, I will fear no evil–for You are with me, Thy rock and Thy staff they comfort me–."* She held onto her faith and hope that the rains would come again.

Will did, too.

"We should buy the Updike farm from the bank, don't you think?" asked Will. "It's right next to the homestead, and the land could lay fallow for a couple of seasons. The rains will come again, then we could plant, and surely we will have rain–sometime," said Will.

"Yes, I agree. And our family is growing," Julie said, being eight months pregnant with their third child. "We can seize on it. Let's bargain for a good price. The house is nice; it's bigger than the one we now have, and that's a good thing, too."

So Will approached the banker to buy the land and house. Mama Rose was in support of the plan, but Hank objected as the land lay between the homestead and Penelope's land–*I want it. I want it all,* he thought.

Late in March Will and Julie moved from Gus's house to the Updike place; "Ours at last."

No one saw it coming.

That gigantic dust storm hit almost out of a blue sky, right after church services in mid-April 1934-April 14th to be exact. As the black cloud approached some said it was six miles high. Darkness engulfed everything at midday. Clamoring to get home and to safety, everyone rushed from church. The livestock were frightened, moaning, and bellowing loudly.

"Come on, Ernie, help me close the barn doors. We've got to shut the sheds as tightly as possible."

"Daddy, Daddy, I can't see you. I can't see my hands. I can't breathe."

Just in time Will grabbed him and shouted, "Hold on son; hold on to each other–don't let go." Finally groping their way along the clothesline, they reached the front door–and hurried inside. Serena was helping Julie cover the windows with the few towels left.

"We've got to cover the doors, too." Julie was worried, but tried to hide her wavering voice.

The blackness continued until what would have been sundown. No one could breathe. Static electricity shocked you when touching any thing. "Ouch, Mommy," Serena cried. Will tried to calm everyone by singing hymns, but no one could sing along.

The dust was too thick.

"We'd better just go to bed. Everyone sleep here with me and Mama," said Will, worried that one of them would just stop breathing. Coughing interrupted sleep. The next morning the sun rose reluctantly, bright red in the still dust-filled sky.

"I've checked the livestock. We lost one calf and two pigs, looks like they just choked up on dust. It's too hard on all the animals. The chickens look like they all have turned gray, and they aren't laying any eggs."

Will phoned Mama Rose and found that she was OK but having trouble breathing. "I feel so helpless, but Margaret is here." Mama, the woman who had gone through so much–only once before had she felt so helpless. Will remembered.

"We're going to be OK. I'm checking now with Hank and Penelope. I think they drove off a couple days ago before the big fellow hit. I think they drove away–somewhere. We'll just hope for the best for them. Stay inside today."

Yes, he found out, they had taken their car to California–to the ocean–away from the dying prairie.

Ernie and Serena couldn't go to school, as the sky still looked threatening. After checking the livestock, Will stayed inside, too. They all huddled together. About noon another dust storm began in earnest. The howling winds left no doubt it would be another bad one.

Something else was happening–unplanned–the third baby was not waiting anymore.

`"Will, Will, I think our baby is coming. Oh my God, can this be! It's three weeks early."

"I'm here, darling, I'm here, my sweetheart," Will hugging her, called to Ernie and Serena,

"We'll manage this together. Birthing is something that happens all the time on the farm." He looked at the children; they were very frightened.

"You'll be OK. You've seen kittens born, and this will be just like that, only one baby–not a litter."

Serena knew some details about babies being born, and said, "I want to have a baby, too."

Julie said, "That's good, but you'll need to get bigger so you can lift a baby and help your husband. Just like seeds in the field you need to plant them at the right time, and you should not plant any until you have a partner, a house, and a nice bed for the baby to sleep in."

"Oh," was all Serena said, seemingly satisfied to know that she was to wait a while.

Will said, "Don't think we can get Dr. Burns out here–roads probably closed to Hopetown, with the drifts of dirt–and it's hard to see–the dust is really thick–and Margaret can't come as their road is closed, too."

"We'll make it, darling Julie," he said, calmly.

"Yes, we will. You are my Buddy, my love." Julie groaned as another contraction began. She leaned on Will's arm as they walked around the kitchen, trying to calm the contraction. Will boiled water for the scissors, and got string for tying off the umbilical cord.

Julie, with help, got up onto the kitchen table, now a birthing table.

"Oh, let me hold your hand, Will," she squeezed hard as the contractions came closer and closer together. Her panting grew louder. Within ten minutes the baby's head showed, and with a groan and big push, out "it" popped–off-white, slimy–and surprised to be in this world.

"It's a boy!" Will. "He's a big guy–look at him–he's breathing and crying at the same time."

Loud and boisterous cries came for the new infant brother. Will laid him on Julie's tummy, where she wiped off his face.

"I have a brother," Ernie laughed.

After waiting about fifteen minutes the afterbirth came out, Will took the twine and tied the umbilical cord in two places about three inches apart. One big clamp of the good scissors cut the cord in two. "There young fella, you'll have a good little navel. You're free–and what a voice!! A baritone for sure!" Baby Boy was free from Mama Julie for the first time in almost nine months.

Will took the little bundle into a blanket and began singing, "Rock a bye, Baby. Oh, you are a big guy." The little guy stopped crying and stared at his daddy. Will kissed Julie and placed the baby near her breast. Snuggling in the baby knew what to do–"a miracle of life, my beloved Will," whispered Julie.

"Let's call him David," yelled Ernie from the parlor, "He slew Goliath and became a King."

"That would be fine, David Paul, after his grandpa Papa Paul," said Will, "indeed a good name for him, King David," Will said proudly.

"I think a good nickname for him would be 'Dusty'" said Ernie. "He's bound to be a farmer, 'cuz he has enough dirt on him to grow crops right now."

And so that name would stick for the rest of his life–Dusty– born in the middle of a dust storm, and yes, he would be come a farmer–but that was many years ahead. Dusty was born at a time of crisis, so he was always a curious, observant child. With his curly brown hair and soft brown eyes, he probably looked the most like Will.

"He weighs around eight pounds," Will said, estimated from weighing chickens. "David Paul Schultz, you are a quiet one and observant–always checking out how others were feeling" and that was the way Dusty grew up–a sensitive boy, seldom crying.

Each child was different–Ernie, the oldest, the intellectual, was taller than average with brownish red hair and brown eyes–like Will. Serena, at her young age, was a red head with blue eyes, "Like my Grandma Frieda," but she has such exquisite, long tapered fingers–much like Grandma Rose–perhaps a violinist?" And David, what would he grow up to be–

"Whatever he wants, as he is king," laughed Will.

In her heart Julie remembered that horrible Mr. Pedersen, who would beat his wife and blame her for bringing into the world 'another damn kid'. How different her beloved Will was in all respects. Yes, it was a blessing, at a difficult time, but a blessing,

—

The three children were the only things that grew in 1934– except for farmers who grew more desperate, as the winds continued to blow. The dust storms blocked out all sunlight, nostrils filled with dirt. Their lungs caked inside, and they choked to death; it was called 'dust pneumonia'. Death was everywhere.

Troubles would continue–but the Schultz family kept faith and trying to stay afloat. Franklin Delano Roosevelt, FDR, had taken charge as President in 1933, vowing to make changes–and so he did–the New Deal began.

"Beginning of socialism," warned Hank. He detested FDR and all the economic leveling he stood for, yet Hank was the first to accept Land Reclamation money and any welfare he could. "When one fool puts money on the table, it takes another one to leave it there!" he said.

Chapter 32

AS SHE LAY DYING

There is a time to weep and time to laugh; a time to mourn and a time to dance.
Ecclesiastes 3:4

The dust began to settle and life went on. Rains came and small crops again survived. The Great Depression still wounded nearly everyone. Will and Julie worked hard trying to keep the Updike farm, bought when the bank repossessed it. Autumn set the leaves turning gold, brown, and then falling off. Thanksgiving would come in another week.

One morning while Mama Rose was gathering eggs, she was walking slower and seemed to even to be shrinking. Mama was sixty-five years old. Suddenly while carrying the eggs Rose fell to the ground, just sort of slid downward; she didn't cry out, no words, just looked at the eggs spilled all around her, many broken.

"I–I– I," she was trying to yell, but no words came out. Her mouth was pulled to the right side, and her left arm bent at a strange angle. Margaret had just looked out of the kitchen window, wondering where Mama was. She hurried to the chicken coop– Mama was struggling– trying to get up with broken eggs all around her skirt.

"Mama, Mama, what happened?" Then Margaret knew–a stroke–all alone–*Pete is out in the field–sons are at school. I can't leave Mama alone, but I have to.* She covered Mama with her apron and ran out toward the field and shouted for Pete, then into the house–rang the doctor's number– four long rings. "Hello this is Mrs. Hereford. Mama Rose had a stroke."

"I'll be right out," was the response. Dr. Burns knew it was serious.

Pete heard Margaret's yell, so he put the tractor into full speed racing s fast as he could across the field. Picking Mama up he carried her into the bedroom. "There, there Mama, you'll be OK, as he gently laid her down. "We're all here."

Pete phoned Will and Hank– they came within a half hour shaken, white, and perspiring.

Dr. Burns came and said, "This is serious, just keep her comfortable, make sure you turn her so she doesn't get bedsorcs."

Little could be done in 1935, but wait.

And so it was. Mama lay in her bed while Margaret bathed her, fed her, and managed a bedpan under the tiny, old body, who didn't weigh much. Every day Julie came with special food, but Mama couldn't eat solids–only liquids.

"I–na–.un–gr," she tried to say. Her right eye watered and irritated her cheek. Mama understood everything. She just couldn't talk, walk, or even laugh–so unlike Mama. Will brought her violin, "Mama, here touch your violin–the one you played so well–and sang with Daddy."

More tears and Mama closed her eyes–to sleep–or slip into a coma–it was hard to tell–sometimes.

Mama's condition didn't change as weeks went by–Christmas was coming. She grew weaker day by day, but still tried to talk to everyone who came to visit. "I–I–luv–ooo–a–" trying to say the words, "I love you all." They all understood. Ernie and Serena touched Mama's arm and said, "We love you, Grandma–" Dusty tried to say the same and smiled.

The snow finally came–the farmers were ecstatic. "Maybe the drought is gone; maybe there will be rain in the spring."

Mama could hear the excitement–*I won't be here to see it, but praise the Lord. Oh–to see the shoots of green turn to golden wheat.* "Ga–.sss gooooood" as she tried to say, "God is good." . *Three weeks, they say. I've been in this bed, can barely move my leg and hardly at all my right hand, but I can write–a little–can't see worth anything, as Margaret put my glasses way over there. They say I had a stroke–right before Thanksgiving. Just a little headache, and there I was lying by the chicken coop with eggs spilled everywhere. I couldn't get up. Couldn't yell, but in a few minutes Margaret saw me all sprawled out. Pete came running and picked me up like a rag doll–put me in my bed–been here ever since. The doctor came; looked sad, so I knew it wasn't good. He said, "Just make her comfortable–darn–how could that be??? Comfortable? Easy for him to say–does he have a brain? As I'm all crumpled up here in this bed? How can I be comfortable lying paralyzed in this bed? Perhaps he means others–my family–should be–comfortable–let me go–in peace? Makes me want to laugh. What does he know–about my life?*

Then Will and Hank came in their cars–looking pretty scared and saying, 'Mama, Mama, you're going to be alright' and they were crying–my big boys crying. All my children–grandchildren come by every day and give me a hug and kiss. I love them all. I'm glad we live so close together. Can't talk to them much, as I just dribble. I cry sometimes–but it's time to go–to go home–. Don't know how long it takes to really die–maybe a long, long time. I want to go to heaven, to be with John William. It's been 28 long, long years since he held me to his heart. Each day I miss his kisses, his singing–his laughter–but dying is a slow thing.

Will and Julie came each night to help with any of the personal care chores. Margaret, the eldest child, gave her all to Mama. She cried only in the kitchen, where Mama couldn't see the tears.

"I'm going to have Christmas dinner just as if all was OK," said Margaret firmly.

"I'll bring rolls, salad, and pies and, of course, cookies." Julie said. "We'll celebrate Christ's birth–as always–knowing that Mama may be celebrating with Jesus in heaven."

"Yes, everyone come after church in the morning. Are you all going to church tonight–Christmas Eve?" Margaret asked.

"Sure, after the chores are done," said Will. He stroked Mama's cheek holding out the hope that she could sit up and sing Christmas carols.

"Julie will be staying home with Dusty and Serena since it's pretty cold out. But Ernie will come with me to say goodnight, OK?"

Mama tried to smile and nod.

When Margaret called Hank to come for Christmas Dinner; Penelope answered, "We have a few people dropping in for Christmas, but Hank will bring cookies for the afternoon."

Penelope never came to see Mama, "Dying just makes me sick," she grimaced.

*A stroke–how impossible–*Rose continued thinking–*I can always overcome–just get up and walk. How helpless I feel. Margaret even has to change my diapers–like a baby I am–this is worse than cancer–oh, dear Mother, no, I can't say that–you suffered so. But I'm not able to say anything–no one can understand me. That's the worst. Oh, please dear Jesus, take me home–I can't move, I can't kiss my beloved grandbabies–I've held little David Paul–just once–little Dusty, and now I have no way to tell him all about his daddy and his grandpa, and his great grandpa. I have no way to tell him the stories of how his grandpa built the house that Uncle Hank lives in–lived in. I have no way of giving him cookies when he comes to visit.*

Oh, dear God, it seems there is much yet to do. I want to tell each of my children: Margaret, Will and Hank–how proud I am of them and how much I have loved them–but my voice is gone. Perhaps it will come back if I just pray enough. Or rest enough.

*I know that God holds us in the palm of His hand and He knows the very hairs on our head. We're not alone. We are part of His great plan. Remember how Old Timer would talk about Mahoe and how the coming of the white man was predicted, all part of God's good plan. We have a new President–a good man, FDR– new things will happen. I can see it coming, but first I must get well so I can help. Christmas is here and I have lots to do, but now must rest–ow must—.res. –..*Rose slipped in and out of a dreamless sleep.

Christmas Eve–that magical night–Oh Holy Night–Silent Night, and the images of sweetness, gentleness, goodness–but not to everyone. Snowflakes gently fell as a plot was being hatched–an evil plot by two crafty men–Attorney Bill Bennett and Hank Schultz.

"I tell you–there isn't much time–we have to act tonight!" Bill blurted out. "I've seen the will, and you are only to be a servant person, one without any decision making power whatsoever. Will is to have it all–and he is supposed to share. I know that won't sit right with you–you two are not from the same seed."

"We are, but Will sees the land as something sacred, spiritual, and to be saved or something. I know it can produce so much more–more tons of wheat and who knows what else. We have the right to use it–God said so! Will listened to ole Papa Paul way too long–and then that crazy Indian," Hank groaned.

Attorney Bill shook his head, "Doesn't make any difference what he believes or not. You have to act now or you'll be out of any inheritance forever. A will is a binding legal document, but it can be changed and that's what we must do–now before your mother dies. The doctor told you she only has a day or so, but what if tonight?"

"I hear you, Counselor. I hear you, but somehow it just doesn't seem right–on Christmas Eve."

"That's the best time; no one will suspect why you'd made such a visit tonight. We need to go before it's too late. We'll bring George Williams along–he'll be quiet about any bottom-of-the-deck stuff, as I've done lots for him–he wouldn't want the public to know that. You know my legal fee will be ten percent of all you have, and that is already in a signed legal document. You haven't forgotten that, have you, pal?" Bill warned.

"Of course not, we've been partners in business for a long time, and you know I always keep my word."

"You're right. I trust you. But this needs to be done right now. Are you ready?"

"Guess so. I'll drive."

Off the two went; they picked up George Williams on the way to Margaret's farm.

Rose, spunky Rose, lay flat on the bed, drifting in and out of to sleep–as death was slowly creeping in.

The sun had set; it was Christmas Eve. Shades were drawn; the room was quiet. The smell of pine needles and Christmas baking seeped in under the door, as Margaret prepared turkey, potatoes, cranberry sauce, and Christmas cookies for the family dinner. Everyone was coming–except Penelope–bringing all the special foods–the family recipes. They knew how to handle losses–simply live on–keep on working.

Mama Rose awakened at a knock at the door.

In came a shadow of a man. "Hi, Mama, I came to wish you a blessed Christmas," he rasped raggedly. "It's me–Will."

"Will?" She was surprised, "Will?" Rose tried to turn her head slightly toward the door. "Will? g to 'ch r ch?" she tried to mutter. Will had just been here a few hours ago and was coming back after the Christmas Eve services.

"Oh, I caught a terrible cold, can hardly talk." He rasped again.

"R' OK. befuur ?" she was confused, as he didn't seem to have a cold when he came earlier. "'Sss mell–cigs?" Rose tried to query, knowing that Will didn't smoke.

"Yah, stopped at the Pool Hall to pick up some candy for the kids, and you know how smoky that place can be!"

Rose knew that Will always took candy to his kids on Saturday nights–a special treat for them. But this was Christmas Eve–so, she was questioning. "Op'n–'mas Eve?" she whispered–doubtfully.

He didn't answer. "Sorry to have to come on Christmas Eve, but your will–your will has to be re-signed–nothing changed, but it got water on it from the leaks in the roof with all the melting snow," he rasped. "The attorney called me to have you sign it again–of course, no changes–just the water ruined your signature on the last page."

Rose knew that a signed will would be important–*but why now–tonight? They must suspect I'll be going soon, something is wrong. .I'll just play along.*

He placed the signature page of the will, on a tray and guided Mama Rose's hand with the pen to the right spot. Then he walked quietly to the window, opening the shade to the west–noting the two attorneys watching–and witnessing–as planned.

"That'll help you see better where to sign," he added.

Rose knew that opening the shade wouldn't help her see any better. *I can hardly see in the bright daylight, so–I wonder what's going on. I know this not Will, I think it's Hank–but I'm not sure.* Feeling the pen in her hand, she dutifully signed the will.

"Will–feelin ver'y weak–soon–gone, ple'se, dear Will, 'ing– fa'rite–'Bide ' Me"

"Sing your favorite song, "Abide with Me?" he repeated. "Gee, Mama, I may not be able to squeak out a sound." Knowing that he couldn't sing–like Will, he began to hum the tune, just a line or two.

Yes. It's Hank. Rose's heart sank, not knowing why this was happening. *Why? Hank has always been conniving, selfish, and somewhat evil. But why change the will–on Christmas Eve–and when no one else is around?*

"I'll be back around noon for our Christmas dinner. We even baked some cookies for the celebration. We'll celebrate by being all together with you," he said–barely whispering, after kissing Mama good night, said goodbye to Margaret.

Rose knew it was Hank–he couldn't sing and he was a smoker, too. Rose had a premonition that she wouldn't see Hank in the morning. He'd already left the room, the house. Outside the two witnesses waited, then they hurried to the car, parked down the road. They drove quickly away without their lights on.

Rose pondered again, *Why? The will had been clear. The eldest son, William John Schultz was to have it all, and then to share and share alike the profits from–the homestead and the land. She had worked so hard all these years, made sacrifices. Hank had Penelope's land; why would he want more? Why would Hank want to change the will? I'm sure that's what he did–but I couldn't read it–at all. I hope I've done the right thing–God's will be done!*

Just as she dozed back into sleep, there was another knock on the door.

Will and his oldest child, Ernie, came in. "Hi, Mama," said Will in his usual soft manner. "We just finished the Christmas Eve program at church. You know how excited all the kids are to see what Santa has brought. We'll be back tomorrow for the Christmas dinner. Julie is baking the rolls, making pies and salads for the dinner. Dusty and Serena are sound asleep–waiting for Santa."

He's so much like John William. Does he know that Hank was just here?

Rose could hardly whisper, "ing ''bide–Me'"

"Sing 'Abide with Me'?–Sure; I know it's your favorite–and Ernie will sing, too." Will's robust baritone was just like beloved John William's voice. Ernie was sounding almost the same with his young changing voice. A tear slipped to the pillow, as Rose knew that this was Will–the real one–that gentle one–that favorite son–who saved her life at one time–long, long ago.

When they finished, Rose whispered again, frantically. "Ange–will." Puzzled Will replied, "You want me to change, Mama? In what way, Mama?" Rose tried to shake her head–impossible–

"'Ank–.c'ange will" she tried again, but Will didn't understand. "Aak? Will?"

"I'm sorry Mama, I can't make that out. Do you want your pillow changed? What?"

So tired, Rose tried to shake her head, but couldn't so she didn't try again, just accepted the kiss both Will and Ernie gave her as they left, "See you tomorrow–after the morning chores."

The lights were growing dimmer and dimmer for Rose, as she drifted toward the Light–onward and onward–into her final sleep.

When Margaret slipped in for her final check on Mama, she found that she was no longer breathing, but had–died with a small smile on her face, even in her paralysis–the smile was there. And laid on her chest, by her heart was a fresh, beautiful–yellow rose!

"Oh Mama, Mama, you've gone," sobbed Margaret. "Pete, Pete come here! The rose, where did it come from? Did Hank or Will bring it? I didn't see them have anything like that!" She continued crying as Pete came in, and together they gently covered the valiant, courageous woman, called Mama– Mama Rose.

In the meantime, Bill Bennett took the signed will and put it into his safety box in his office. Hank was smiling. "I alone will own the homestead and all the other land as well. It was the right thing to do, because I, Hank Schultz, am the smartest, strongest, and wisest of the Schultz children. I alone rightly deserve to become the ruler of more and more land–the richest man in the State."

In a hurry to gain the wealth, neither Hank nor Bill Bennett had read the signed will. If they would have they would have been surprised to see that Mama Rose had outsmarted them–as usual– for the will was not signed by Rose Pinot Schultz but rather signed by–

Santa Claus.

Chapter 33

DILEMMA AND CONSPIRACY

Murderers are not monsters. They're men and that's the most frightening thing about them.
Alice Sebold, *The Lovely Bones*

Bill Bennett's jaw was clenched, rigid. His eyes narrowed and his throat parched–dry. In his mind he planned the conspiracy. *How could she have outsmarted–both of us!–she–old, dying, yet there she was full of her faculties and outdid us in one stroke. 'Santa Claus' damn that was clever. But Widow Rose always was smart and knew her farming. It was known around the county that Rose ruled. One tough prairie farmer, never ceasing to amaze all the others with her sense of future–what should be plowed–what should be left to fallow–to regain the nutritional strength for another bumper crop. The way she made the fields rich through uneven rows, those that went this way and that. Damn, how did she know that would hold the land? Of course nothing held the land with the dust storms, but she was right. Damn, she was smart–she triumphed over all.*

Maybe she learned it all from Papa Paul–or that Indian chief. People still talk about Paul and his gift of sorting seeds, using only the best for the next crop. He was persistent, never accepting second best. Here was his daughter, the Widow Rose–damn– dammit!

Maybe it was the old wizard Indian guy–that Red Sun in Hair– Old Timer–Old Fart. He seemed to have a sense of the land. They say he even talked to it–like it was alive–did really spooky things, like talk with horses. Wise beyond words I've heard and had a degree from University of North Carolina.

Glad I never had to deal with him. Guess he even went to DC, talking to President Lincoln, challenging the US government to return the Indian lands they were giving away to homesteaders. He wanted them to honor the treaties as legal documents! by not sending the natives farther and farther from their lands–into fenced off lands with no hope of feeding themselves. Glad I didn't argue that case. Nothing helped them at all; they just don't get it! This land is to be developed, not something crazy like talking to it. Giving it honor, all that bullshit. Heard Old-Timer even saved the Schultz boy when a rattler bit him on the neck–used some mumbo jumbo and some crap from his medicine bag. Some said they thought he was an angel who walked among us! Really weird. Gads!! Hank is right–he should have the land now and really make it produce–like it is supposed to. Will is just like his mother–filled with ideas of keeping it sacred and resting every other year. Bullshit! Hank rightfully deserves it all, not to share like Widow Rose said. That defeats the use of the land–breaking it up into little bitty pieces that can't be farmed to the hilt. Use it. God gave us dominion over the land and asked that we produce from it–to feed all the people. It's right there in the Bible.

What was Rose thinking–Santa Claus–Guess we could plead that she had lost her mind? No, that won't work as there are just too many witnesses that knew she was alert to the end–that she was always the shrewd and intelligent. A woman with class–smart– went to college and played the violin like a pro. No, she had her sharp mind even to the last. Why she even had all of her papers together including her taxes for this year. No, we cannot claim she was incompetent–that won't work.

How about not disclosing the contents of the will? They'll never even bother to record a will, with copies at the Court House. No one needs to know that this will–signed by Santa Claus–is null and void. Couldn't we just read the will and not expect anyone to ask to see the signature? They won't need to know there is another legal will signed by Rose Pinot Schultz, less than a year ago. Will is honest to the core–he won't even look at the will. Ahh he'll be disappointed to just give up the land to Hank, but he'll just turn the other cheek and say, 'Nothing will come between brothers. This is the way Mama wanted it to be, 'Keep the land together'. Little will he know that he was to have all of it! Rose already figured that

Will would work honestly–share with Hank and Margaret. No, he will never know.

Folks came from counties around to Widow Rose's funeral. Governor even sent a special message about what Rose Schultz had done for the women's social issues. People came out of respect for the widow who'd raised three children and ran a farm, even farming another half-section bought by Papa Paul from a desperate homesteader.

That farm had been a show place, with trees for a windbreak, vegetable garden with straight rows, and beautiful roses that lined the fence. Rose loved roses–yellow ones–remembering when she was being courted by John William he would often bring her a favorite–yellow rose. Inside the homestead had been equally as gracious, with fine furniture and china, reminding Rose of her childhood home. She even drove a Model T Ford. Very much ahead of her time–that Widow Rose.

That was about to change.

Chapter 34

NOTHING COMES BETWEEN BROTHERS

Thanks to the resilience of nature, and the indomitable human spirit, there still is hope.
Jane Goodall, *Hope for Animals and Their World*

But Bennett had no regrets–knowing that Hank had promised him ten percent of the crops produced on the land. But Hank really has no land of his own–not a speck. All he has was Penelope's fields, and she wouldn't share a dime–a peculiar bitch. So Bennett had reasons why he would never let anyone see the signature–Santa Claus. *I know Hank is more conniving than I am. Remember some of the shady things Hank did–like cheating when he played poker. Oh, that was slick. Hank never just played the game–he played to win! He was in it for the money. That night when Hank won Otto's' car was one of his best schemes!–stacking the deck with clubs so that he eventually had a Royal Flush–poor old Otto really was right when he shouted 'Hank's a cheat', but I stood beside my old buddy. I knew there was something it for me, too.*

Hank had a reputation of being a popular, available bachelor–but not in Fairview–he had them all and needed to look for fresher pastures. He found the women of Scottsbluff, North Platte, and Ogallala far more appealing–and available. *He'd even to go to Omaha, where he claimed there were the most beautiful women–and exotic dance hall damsels. We sure had some wild time, wow! Glad my wife never found out about my 'business trips'. That was until he met Penelope; talk about an equally conniving partner! No, Hank is a selfish, dishonest man, and we think alike.*

When Bennett shared the crafty idea of non-disclosure of the faulty signature, Hank was ecstatic. "That's the way. Poor Will, he's so naïve and trusting. He'll never ask to see the will. I'll have all the land," Hank shouted triumphantly. "And I'll make it really produce, twice as much as now, with all these crazy ideas of letting the damn soil rest. That it has a soul–a spirit! It's our duty to make it work–for us! What happens if I die before Will?" questioned Hank.

"Won't happen–he's older–and if you do–well–maybe you'd better have some kids, too–so you can know that it's being properly farmed?"

"You're right, but that was my agreement with Penelope–no kids! I think she got rid of one–don't know for sure, but she was pretty cranky for a while and left for Denver. When she came back, she didn't want any fooling around for a couple of weeks," pondered Hank.

—--—

The will was to be read by Attorney Bennett at Margaret's house. All were present. Surely Will was to be named as owner of the homestead. It was he who saved the land after John William died, quitting school and all. Everyone knew that Will would share any profits.

Bennett began the formal reading, by noting that on May 14, 1935 he had completed and had signed by Rose Pinot Schultz, her last will and testimony. "I've kept the will in my office safe to be read upon her death to all of her children: Margaret, William, and Henri."

Bennett began with a senatorial voice, "I, Rose Pinot Schultz, being of sound mind and will, do hereby leave all my holdings of land and property to my youngest son, Henri Jonathan Schultz, to be farmed faithfully, and any profits he sees fit to share he should do so." Signed Rose Pinot Schultz

Will gasped, and turned suddenly a chalky white, with his mouth opened, but no words were spoken. Julie, seated beside him, groaned. Margaret sat upright, staring at Hank, and said, "You did this, you skunk!" In a harsh rasp, she hissed, "You were always the cunning one, the selfish one. You are plain evil–and now this! I can no longer call you brother." Her voice rose to a high shrill.

"Nothing will come between brothers, dear sister, nothing," responded Will in a near whisper.

"But it isn't fair," she shouted.

Julie grasped Will's hand, and began to cry. Hank said nothing, just got up and quickly walked to the door where his coat hung and put it on. Bennett followed. Without saying a word, they left–taking the will with them.

"I said it would work, didn't I?" snickered Bennett. They got into Hank's car and sped away.

"I have no regrets," replied Hank. "Did you see the stupid look on Will's face. Absolutely priceless! He is so naïve, so trusting, serves him right, always the good son. Dang, I'm now the owner of it all!"

"Bring on the champagne," laughed Bennett, "there really is a Santa Claus."

"Penelope, we did it; I'm the sole owner of the Schultz estate."

She glowed with greed. "I knew you could do it; let's celebrate."

Will, Julie, Margaret and her husband, Pete couldn't move for minutes, simply staring at the floor.

Finally Will got up and said, "Guess it's time to go do the evening chores." His voice was quivering slightly.

Julie said nothing.

"Will, you've got to fight this! It isn't fair," Margaret pleaded.

"No, it isn't fair. But it must have been what Mama wanted. She knew the value of keeping the land together, not splitting it up into portions, smaller and smaller."

"But she never would have given it to Hank! She knew Hank was lazy and conniving. She didn't like Penelope and found her equally as dishonest. Mama never said bad things about people, but she said that Hank's wife had an evil side to her–now we know. All they want is money, money, money," Margaret cried.

"Maybe Mama changed her mind." Will spoke softly, not really believing this either, but knowing that he needed to leave so that the big tears beginning to form in his eyes didn't spill over.

"Come children," said Julie as she put coats on the three. "It's time to leave."

"But we just got here," said Ernie.

"I know, but we must go home before dark to feed the animals," Julie said confidently.

And they drove away.

At home, it was quiet. Neither Julie nor Will spoke. The children knew something was very wrong and quietly went about their chores. Little Serena picked up her doll and hugged it, knowing in her young mind that there was sadness.

Will remained quiet for a week. He seldom came into the house directly from the barn, but could be seen sitting on the south side, simply staring out to the horizon. The winter blizzards came and went. He, Ernie, and Dusty went down to the homestead every day–as usual–assuring the livestock that they weren't abandoned. Hank and Penelope had gone to warm Arizona but returned late in January, never saying a word to anyone.

It was February 1st when Will called, "Ernie and Dusty, let's go to the auction in town and see what livestock we can buy. We have to think of tomorrow and build up our stock. Maybe there will even be some pregnant cows, as calving should soon start. Spring will soon be coming!" He sounded light hearted, as his old self emerged.

Neither Will nor Julie ever talked about that afternoon reading of the will. They began to build a future on the ruined land they'd bought. They never looked back.

"That skunk–that cheat. Hank will some day get his due, just wait and see." Old farmers and friends of Will who heard the news were dumbfounded. "And for a brother yet–can't imagine how it'd feel to hurt a brother. Mama said that Hank's wife had an evil side to her–now we know. All they want is money, money, money," Margaret cried.

People knew; shaking heads, they looked ashamed, so when one hurt, they all did.

PART IV

BENT NOT

BROKEN

Chapter 35

WINDMILLS AND GRASSHOPPERS

They swallowed everything–until nothing was standing–some attacked him–leaving not a flower or leaf or a sprig of grass standing.
Timothy Egan *The Worst Hard Times.*

Even Hank admitted that there wasn't enough moisture to plant wheat or corn that Fall–1936. "We've barely enough hay for the livestock through the winter. Maybe we'd better sell off what we can and save a few cows–just hoping for next year."

Will pointed to the bare prairie, shaking his head, "I'm glad Mama Rose isn't here to see the ground, just gray everywhere. Trees barely have any leaves; it's like when Papa Paul first came, nothing then but the prairie sod."

"Don't start that argument again, Will. What's done is done."

"I'm sorry–you're right–we–can't go back. With more water–we could make it. Remember Old Timer would tell us about there being a whole, big lake of water underneath this ground. He called it Mother Blue Water or something like that–."

"You didn't believe that ole Indian?" scoffed Hank.

"Well, he was right about a lot of things–remember how Old Timer said there was lots of water under ground? Maybe if we had enough windmills going we could pump water to irrigate the land. Let's see if we could do some planting just around the windmill. Want to try?" Will's eyes were now shiny and had an excited look on his face.

"That might work, let's put down another well or two and see how much we can bring up and spread around. The wind keeps blowing and blowing, so we know the windmills will run." Hank was now also involved.

Four windmills went up in three weeks. The wind blew night and day, and so the rows of corn and wheat within about half a mile–all around the homestead and Will's own land. Soon small green shoots were coming up. Neighbors came to see what the Schultz brothers had cooked up. "We've got ta do the same," they said.

"They irrigate all over the world, why not here? But we'd better check with someone who knows how much water there really is." Will said with caution–remembering Old Timer's words, "Don't take more than you need. Keep everything in balance–harmony. If you don't, someday the whole earth will fly to the sky–just like a speck of dust."

"You're right, we might use up all the water and then not have any for the livestock," echoed a neighbor.

Hank said, "Who needs livestock? Why wait, let's get started; another day and it may be too late."

No expert was called; neighbors all around began putting up new windmills and trying to irrigate the rows of corn and wheat. The wind was still blowing, but the irrigated land held moisture.

"Will–thank you for this one!" the neighbors shouted.

Seeing progress, Will cautioned, "Not too much–leave some of the land to rest.

He continued, "Hey, the land, yes, but let's not rest now–let's celebrate–how about a barn dance? Been a long time since we had one. Time we have some fun–who has the home brew!"

"I do–you're right," chimed a trio.

"I've brewed enough beer for all–might have some dust in it, but still packs a wallop," laughed a fourth.

"Use our haymow," invited Will. The old Updike farm had the largest barn in the area. "We'll need some fiddlers, a drum, an accordion, banjo, I can call the squares, and sing a tune or so. Let's check with the women folk to see what they want–then do a general ring on the phone. Let everyone come. Let's celebrate!"

The long, dark days and nights of blowing wind were not forgotten, but for right now, it was going to be fine. That's how farmers faced challenges–the best gamblers in the world. A few fall rains had come and with the windmills' irrigation, green blades of wheat had sprouted. It was time to laugh again.

Water was pumped up, lots and lots of it, filling A full, red moon rose. After doing chores, the neighbors gathered–over 75 came–with their children. Fiddles, banjoes, mouth harps, accordions. Folks had checked their attics, trunks, and found old musical instruments. Coffee, pie, cakes, and cookies appeared–into the haymow everyone went. Lots of space, but not much hay.

"Let's dance!" yelled Will.

"One of the best nights we can remember," neighbors said.

Beer even helped some forget they had lost nearly everything. Others had lost loved ones, too–especially children from dust pneumonia. The times were still hard. But, dance they did. Everyone–old and young danced. Two-step, waltz, polka, and, of course, square dance. There was no microphone, but Will had a big–enormous voice and could call the dance like a pro.

In that area of Colorado dancing was a common thing. Dads and moms taught the young ones. Children who hadn't laughed for a long time were now having fun. There was hope. Not long into the night the youngest toddled off to sleep in the hay. Older folks danced until the moon was high in the sky, then stopped for coffee, cookies, pie, and cake. All had morning chores to do and of course, Sunday services. But for one night in September they remembered only the fun of music and dancing and seeing each other laughing, not crying.

Two average-sized rainstorms came the first week in October; they helped calm farmers' nerves. The dust stayed on the ground. Hay around the windmills and even in the fields was thriving–perhaps enough to feed the livestock through the winter. Winter came, but little snow. The start of 1937 seemed ominous, but a few spring snows coaxed the winter wheat to show that it had survived.

Also came a new little Schultz; Rachel Marie, the fourth child, was born on March 27, 1937, and was declared to be the prettiest one of all. Will couldn't get over how perfect her tiny face was, just like Julie's. "Even her mouth is the shape of yours." He was ecstatic now with two boys and two girls.

The spring promised change, until one day in May–just as the grass was greening and new plants in showing promise. It was a warm day. The wind stopped blowing. Windmill blades poised, motionless. The silence was eerie. Three years of dust and wind–

now it was deathly–quiet. Clear blue skies stood empty, not a cloud to be seen.

People walked outside, saying, "Something isn't right. What's happening?"

Then to the west a cloud appeared, close to the ground–dark–black–as wide as the horizon–but no higher than a three-storied barn–coming closer–and closer. At first not a sound, but then–a deep, droning, buzzing–roar–coming from the cloud–growing louder and louder as the black cloud came nearer. Then without warning–the sky darkened completely–it was not a dust storm–it was dark and threatening–what was it?

Worse than any dust storm!–swarms and swarms of grasshoppers–filled the sky with their beating wings. They averaged about 25 million per acre. More and more came, swooping down to the growing grass, corn, and wheat. The sound of their munching and beating, beating, beating wings–was worse than thunder, more frightening than fire. The cattle, the horses, chickens, moms, dads, children, all seemed to be screaming–lashing their arms at the intruders, but to no avail. Nothing stopped these creatures from Hell. They swooped down again and again, ate everything in sight.

Crunching, crunching, crunching even the fence posts, the outhouses, sides of the house–doorways–all the leaves of the fruit trees, even their bark. Julie and Will took brooms and cornhusks, anything to beat and beat–into the air. They were able to create enough resistance that the ugly creatures didn't enter their house–as they did other farmers'.

The ugly creatures poured into clothing and hair. The children who were inside the houses were terrified as the crunching grasshoppers broke through and under the door, and under the linoleum–crunching, crunching. Chairs and table that had been standing in the kitchen–were now sawdust on the floor.

The struggling fields that once held hope–were now filled only with empty sticks. Huddling together, people crying. "The garden, it can't be–no, not all gone–not when we just had a glimmer of hope–no, please God, don't let us starve–no." Crying children had never seen such a horrible sight, nor heard such deafening roar from grasshoppers. It was far more frightening than even the dust blizzards.

The grasshoppers ate everything. Their ugly eyes searching, searching for more prey, but then–suddenly they were gone. A black cloud swirled eastward and they moved on to another farm– another field. Piles of rubble remained–that's all, but the sturdy windmills–all metal–stood. Thank God, Will and Julie's stood! Will drove the Model A crunching over dead grasshoppers on the road–rushing to the homestead. Arriving, his eyes were deceived! He thought, Not a blade of grass or stock of corn was disturbed. The grasshoppers had left the homestead untouched. Will's heart wrenched. *"What did this mean? Why is one field destroyed and another left untouched? Am I, Will, being punished for some wrong I've done. Why? Why?*

Will couldn't help but feel bitter, as he and his family were the ones who suffered the most. But he turned his eyes to the heavens and said, "I am your faithful servant. Thank you, Lord, for saving the homestead. Thank you, Lord, for saving my children, my beloved Julie and me."

And then he set out to work–hard–to forget what he was seeing. Returning home, Will was uncertain what he'd tell the family. Seeing Julie–she was more beautiful than ever–standing there with open arms. *What can I say? Maybe she should have married Hank.* Will always knew that Hank would've taken her in a minute. The crush Hank had on Julie–the first day Will brought her to the homestead, Hank's look gave away any secret about how he felt–and with all his girlfriends–none measured up to Julie. But Julie never looked at Hank the same way, for her eyes were only on Will. But at times Will could only wish for the luck that Hank seemed to have–no grasshoppers!

No, no, I mustn't let those thoughts come into my mind. I must stay focused on solutions. What to do next? I'll never blame God. Mama always said, 'He'll guide your ways, and blessings will follow. Lo, I'm with you even to the ends of the earth.' Well, Lord, this may be the end.

As he stopped the car in the driveway, Julie came rushing out, "How are things?" She could see by his face that he'd been through a terrible turmoil.

"Miracle of miracles, all is safe–not one grasshopper touched the fields." Julie could see his jaw tighten, as he looked again at the sticks standing in their fields.

"Only the homestead was saved. It's Hank's land now," said Julie, tears flowing down her cheeks. She stopped and looked to the heavens and said, "No, it will never be Hank's land, that land is Mama's, Daddy's, and Papa Paul's; it belongs to all of us. We're the keepers of it, to honor the land as Papa taught us, to respect it as Old Timer showed us. If it's to prosper, we're the hands to make it pure. Let's begin. Don't you dare think bad thoughts."

Will laughed and gave her a hug and a long, sweet kiss.

"I'm taking Ernie with me. We're going to do some dangerous work in the morning."

"What, my darling, what?"

"Poison those damn creatures–to hell and back!" he cried triumphantly.

With that he called all the neighbors who'd lost their crops. He called the governor, who ordered the National Guard to spray all the fields with the deadly ingredients: molasses, arsenic, sorghum. "We must get busy, very busy, to treat the fields so if those damn creatures return, they'll feast on poison–that'll teach them to stay away."

Over the next three days Julie stayed in the house. She didn't see Will or Ernie. When they returned, they scrubbed and scrubbed removing all the dirt and poison from their bodies and clothes– leaving the sun to kill whatever else might still be on their skin. They stood naked as jaybirds facing toward the sun, until dried, then came inside the house. You could see by their determined expressions that the deed had been done.

Experts explained that because of the last years' dry hot summers, grasshoppers hatched at enormous rates, but that the plague of them was unusual. The grasshoppers did return a week later–the evil ones tried chomping as before, but dropped dead in place–the poison worked. And, seeing their fallen comrades, other grasshoppers never landed, but sailed over to other fields–perhaps into Nebraska–but their trail was gone, for now in eastern Colorado. The homestead was saved.

When Hank and Penelope returned from their stay in Arizona, Hank said, "Dang that was good of you, Will. We heard that you and Ernie worked with the National Guard to spray all the land. I know it's been really hard for you and the family, and I want to do all that I can to help you over this rough time."

"Thanks, Brother," replied Will, knowing that he had to accept any help he could get. "I've been thinking that what I read in the newspapers about our new president's plan to help us farmers could really help you and me. He wants us to let land rest, to be fallow, and to pay us for land we don't plant. He's called it a Soil Conservation Act, and the Congress has passed a law for the feds to buy back land they gave away to homesteaders. I think that would be a big help until at least we can get the land fertile again. What do you think, Hank?"

"I think he is trying to take over the farms. I think he is power hungry and wants all of it to himself. He's a socialist. Why if we don't plant, then how do we live? Do you believe he is going to pay us not to plant forever? And, to buy back the homesteads? Crazy idea. He just wants to have more for himself. No, it's a trick. He's a trickster, but we'll take some of that money, as we can't plant some of the fields anyway. Yeah, we'll take the money," Hank sneered.

"Well, if we believe we have elected a good, wise president, then we, as the people, shouldn't be afraid."

Will continued, "I've been thinking that maybe it's time for me to start over–let the bank have my farm. I can't stand to hear the cattle and horses cry when they're hungry and thirsty. We lost our crops to the grasshoppers, and I can't make the mortgage payments. Just don't have it in me–anymore. Sell all our livestock and go west."

Hank really perked up. *What if he does let the bank take over, wow–I could buy up that Updike place for pennies on the dollar. Then I'd have all my land together–for as far as the eye could see– all mine.*

Will continued, "I hear that you can make a lot of money out on the west coast. We can start over in California or Oregon. We have nothing here, anyway. Take what we can from a sale–just start over–we have nothing to lose!"

"You're probably right," Hank smiled.

Chapter 36

WESTWARD BOUND

"–and in the eyes of the people, there is the failure and in the eyes of the hungry, there is a growing wrath. In the souls of the people, the grapes of wrath are growing heavy.
John Steinbeck, *The Grapes of Wrath*

The smell of grasshopper poison–arsenic, bran, molasses–a stinging, sweet smell–still filled the air. June had begun–hot. And dead grasshoppers now and then crunched between your feet and still needed to be swept from the outdoor privy seat. Morning came–too early as dawned the day of departure. The sun rose red and warning. Mixed feelings were all around, as Will and Julie placed the last cardboard box of clothes, underwear, socks, pants, a couple of dresses–for all ages from three months to thirty-nine years–into the wagon, covered with a canvas. Not much, but all they had. Will checked the tires, looked one last time at empty fields, empty barn, and soon to be–empty house. Joy complicated with fear of the unknown, dreaded memories of the past twenty years–had come to this.

With only two hundred twelve dollars in his billfold, safely kept in his pocket closed with a safety pin–his mouth was dry–eyes dull and red–Will turned away. The law had stopped those short sales when someone could be the only bidder and get a whole farm for a dollar or so they could later sell it back to the real owner. And bankers risked their lives going out into the countryside, as some had been lynched. *Is this all I have to show for years of work, prayer, sweat, and tears.* 'THE SALE–it stated–moving'. But only a few–maybe–twenty–came to the sale–unlucky ones? Losers? Who knows–those staying put–waiting for another bumper year–or just–left behind–without hope. Those who did come to the sale had only a few bucks in their pockets. A sad sight–salt in the wound. Hank never even showed up. Why should he–he didn't need a hog–a fine pair of horses–he had it all. And Will didn't know that Hank had already bought the mortgage from under Will by paying off the Updike house and farm for only two hundred dollars. Margaret did come, thank God for her–hogs sold for five dollars each.

Hank had asked, "Just in case you need to come back why don't you leave your two cows with me –? And I'll give you ten percent on the land we lay fallow for the government. Just in case."

"Thanks, that's a good idea," replied Will. Hank just smirked thinking of 'his free' cows and who would ever think of claiming the money for unplanted crops!

All day precious possessions moved into new hands, and pennies, dimes into Will's pocket. Fallen nesters–like Will and Julie–just picked up and moved–not far away–five miles at the most but–away from the grasshoppers, the endless empty fields– hope had failed. "Let me check one more time," Julie's face told it all. *I can't look back–our farm–our dream but now–a new start.*

Standing alone near the stairway to the upstairs' bedroom where all the children had slept–now Julie couldn't hold back the tears. "So sleep in Jesus name," sobs came–more sobs. Her mother Serena's last words–'Sleep in Jesus name'. Wiping her eyes, Julie crushed her arms around herself, then she walked through the kitchen door, shut it, and out to the car, now filled with the children, Will, and their dreams.

Her head held high–never looking back.

The Model A started easily; pulling the wagon was not too hard. Slowly they left the yard, with the children staring back–but silent. Will looked straight ahead–his eyes filled with tears, but not a word spoken. Driving on the graveled road toward Fairview, passing the homestead, the sun caught the windows in a glittering farewell–no one said a thing. There were no yellow roses growing by the gate. Grandma Rose's garden was gone. Hank and Penelope never kept it weeded or even watered–just left it to die. As dreams too often, did as well.

Remembering Grandma Rose's will, *"All property goes to my youngest son, Henri,"* Julie's stomach turned–*No, I must not look back–what was done–is done.* She looked tenderly at Will's sunken cheeks and patted his knee remembering his words, *"Nothing will come between brothers."–some times that's hard to bear as Hank only cares for himself–oh yes, he is charming–but always looking out for himself. Here we are: Will–and I–starting over–is this really what Mama Rose wanted–why?*

The road ahead wasn't long or unknown–Hopetown. Reaching the junction where they usually turned south, instead the Model A turned north heading for Wyoming. They kept to the lower Highway 40 to avoid climbing mountains. No events interrupted their slow, long ride through Wyoming.

"It's a bit longer, but the car can't take the big mountains. We'll go through Salt Lake City, so we can see that big lake filled with salt water. Glad that we got the good word from Joe Klammer before we left. He said, "Come make a fortune, come to Idaho or Oregon. California is too full already, but lots of work up here in Oregon." We'll call him as soon as we get to Boise, maybe even stay overnight at his house. Says he has a big place and we're welcome."

Whenever they stopped to fill the gas tank and check the oil Will would ask, "How about work around here?"

"Not good," would be the usual answer. "Country is going broke, no work."

"Sure don't like what I'm hearing," Will told Julie.

"It'll be OK, just keep your faith." Julie would answer.

Almost into the state of Utah, Will saw a sign, 'cabins for rent'. "Let's stop here." It was Crested Junction, and the place looked clean–a dollar a night.

"We'll take it. How far to Boise?" Will asked the owner.

"Just about ten hours drive on a good day, as you need to go through Salt Lake City then take a straight northwest angle to Twin Falls. It's quite a stretch."

"Do you have a telephone we can use?"

"Sure, long distance will be about two dollars for three minutes."

"Wow, that's expensive, isn't it?"

"Yah, we're far out and don't have good service out here. You have to talk fast."

Will called his friend, Joe Klammer. "Hello Joe, this is Will Schultz, how're you doing?"

"This is a surprise. Are you here in Idaho?"

"Almost, and wanted to know if we could stop and stay at your place in a day or two. You said that we'd be welcome."

Will heard a slight gasp. "Guess you didn't get my last letter. I mailed it a week ago. Sorry, but things have turned very sour. I told you not to come, but stay put in Colorado."

"What!" Will's voice sounded alarmed, "No, I didn't get your letter. That's bad news. Isn't there any work?"

"Hardly any. Have you seen the signs on the road, 'Go home, Okies', 'No work'? Yah, it's bad all over the place. And to make it worse, we have a houseful now, as two of our kids and their families had to move in with us this last week. They lost everything and had no place to stay. So it won't work for you to come to stay with us, either. I'm really sorry, as you stood by me many times. Will, I'm sorry."

"Sorry to learn about all of this." You could hear Will's voice begin to crack. "What about work, any ideas?"

"Not much, as you'll see the signs around as you come into the state, 'No work'. But there is one place you should try–Fruitland. It's almost July and I know that they're pickin peaches and soon will be pickin apples. It's a big place, not far from Boise. Try that."

Just then came the warning, that the two minutes were nearly up. "So sorry, Buddy, for the bad news. Good luck." Click. It was over.

"Goodbye, Joe." Will held the receiver for some time, looking very sad–anxious. "Now what to do?" Will spoke to the sky.

Chapter 37

FRUITLAND CAMP

Once the fear started and the wave of collapse started to spread, it was hard to let a buck go because there might not be one to replace it. The economy was a pool of glue.
Timothy Egan *The Worst*
Hard Times

Chugging slowly, it seemed the Schultz's would never reach Fruitland. Three days later and nearly broke, they finally arrived.

"Yes. We're hiring. Got lots of peaches are really ripe. Can use good workers."

"How about my son, Ernie? He's twelve."

"If he's a good worker. He looks strong."

"He is; we're farmers from Colorado."

"OK, start tomorrow. You can occupy the cabin that's empty. It's # 9."

With that Will drove the Model A closer to the cabins and saw #9. "Here we are–our new home."

Just remember the grasshoppers–crunch, crunch. Julie's mind settled on how they could manage in this little cabin on the property of Zeke's Orchards, Fruitland–anything would be better than those grasshoppers.

"Just think one day at a time–one day at a time–not about school, not about church, not about a cook stove–one day at a time," said Will.

The cabin had been used before–many times. It seemed to remember struggling families, just like the Schultz's–heavy smells of cooking grease, old coffee, spilled milk, musty flour, rotten eggs. The floor was filthy–although colorful–some type of Chinese designed linoleum–yellow, red, and blue–primary colors. But it hadn't been swept–perhaps ever.

The one bed frame held nothing, not even a spring–nothing else–but the floors were meant for sleeping. Four wobbly wooden kitchen chairs were various colors of white, yellow, green, all favorite colors of some previous passersby–and chipped, so they resembled confetti. Sad curtains of yellow daisies–or was that just old grease–and pull-up shades that were in pieces, but perhaps they would hold the secrets of the Schultz's from public view. The stove, a pot-bellied antique, had two lids, a shifter for ashes, and a pipe that leaned to one-side crawling up and out the roof.

Their new home.

Bare walls and bare studs made any decorating a challenge. One wall had three shelves and a metal wire strung across projecting nails to hold clothes, if the owners had any. A dresser sat in one corner with a large, wavy mirror on the top. A sink of sorts clung to the wall with a type of cupboard surrounding it with worn, yellow oiled cloth as a cover. Several open shelves waited to be filled with dishes, pots, pans, and maybe sacks of sugar and flour. There was no place to hold tableware.

Pictures? None. A calendar of Washington DC, was stuck on–January 1931. No clock, better not know, here where time stood still. Windows, ah yes, fresh air–there were three. They looked out to each side and then the door. All are screened–good–no flies–no grasshoppers.

"This will do–no–it'll be great. We can camp here for months and be free to explore the wonders of Idaho." Julie declared in triumph. "Let's bring in all our things from the wagon and car, then fix some supper for the night. We'll buy something–build a fire–even in this heat–and have a feast."

Serena joined in the happiness, Rachel–three months old needed to be held. She was sucking her thumb–a comfort thing.

Dusty said, "I love it already–and I can hear the birds singing." He was the usual chipper guy–forgetting how homesick he had been.

"Baths for all!" Julie called after supper. Ernie carried water from the tank at the center of the circular camp, filled the tub and put it on the stove–burning full blast even on a hot summer evening "We all need a good soaking, but that'll wait–just quick baths–everyone. First Rachel, then Dusty, they should be the cleanest–then Serena, and finally Ernie."

Dreading the thought of being last in the line of bathers, Ernie warned Dusty, "Please don't pee in the water–I have to bathe in that, too." Dusty squeezed his face into a frown–"Won't do!" A blanket stretched over a corner wall served as some privacy. By 8 o'clock everyone had some type of bath and soon all were sound asleep in bedding on the floor. Meeting neighbors would have to wait until morning–the Schultz family was exhausted.

By 6:00 AM, all were up. After bread, jam, milk, and coffee, Will and Ernie left for the orchards. Julie, Serena and Dusty began to sort their belongings; Rachel napped in her buggy. Soon the pile of "things" had been sorted, all neat and tidy.

Serena, now eight, sat for a few minutes looking at her slender hands, beautiful, artistic, like Grandma Rose's. Almost six when Grandma died, Serena remembered well; "Someday you'll play Papa Paul's violin–someday you'll be a famous violinist as your great grandpapa Pinot was in Germany." Grandma loved to hold Serena's slender fingers and wrists. "Someday. I'll always believe." She closed her eyes and in her mind could hear Grandma Rose playing, 'Claire de Lune', and feel Grandma's guiding hands showing the little redheaded granddaughter how to hold the bow and violin. "Someday, not yet."

Julie laughed, "Nothing could've spoiled this adventure–nothing, but this cabin does need some paint, pictures, some attention!" Now her artistic talents were to be tested–without money and paintbrushes–how? She'd find a way.

Julie had never lived around so many people–living out on the prairie. Within minutes there was a knock at the door. Julie answered it. "Welcome" she called out to several gray-haired women dressed in worn-out, wrinkled housedresses. "Come in, come in," said Julie. For a moment she felt queasy–now she had neighbors–lots of them. The women sat on the four chairs, looking quite comfortable.

They gave their names. "We look out for each other–that's the Golden Rule here–the only way we can make it. Times are tough."

"What do I need to know about how things are done here, like where do you go to get your kindling and throw your wastewater?" asked Julie.

"We have an organization," said a tall woman with a slight German accent. "We keep the place clean–no flies–and quiet. You can help on Mondays, if that's OK with you. Take a turn; making certain all is clean, tidy. Then we meet on Friday afternoons just for us to talk–for tea, coffee, and maybe cookies. We want you to come, too–this Friday; it's at my house–#14."

Suddenly Julie was feeling included, useful, and less lonely. The women all looked old and beaten. Julie could see in their eyes the same story that was in hers–losses, fears, and little hope. They talked briefly about the conditions of the economy. "We're all tryin to make it–a day at a time–as pickers. There's no other work." Each woman looked down at her worn shoes and worn-out hands.

"Ellen, the boss's wife is a good woman; she understands, but look out for Zeke, the boss, he has an eye for the women. Just be careful–we all stick together on this. We had one newcomer about a month ago, who really did upset ever'thin when she went for him–it was nasty. We got rid of her–them–poor husband–Joe, didn't know why he got fired."

Julie had a sense of forewarning; perhaps they warned every newcomer. Each place had its rules, and she wasn't going to break any. "I'm glad you told me about that, as I don't want any trouble for my family–or for me–." she smiled slightly. Julie thought, *Won't be a problem for me, as I know how to handle those creepy creatures*–remembering her close call when just a hired girl in Nebraska.

"Do you have any thing that you do special?" asked the tall German-speaking woman.

"Oh, mostly just being a good mom, but I do love to paint. I know how to do some healing things, if someone is sick."

"Painting! We really need that around here–and we always have someone who is sick. Can we call on you?"

"Of course, I know how to handle bleeding, births, and some fevers. I also know that it helps in a place as crowded as this, if we know when someone is ill–so we don't spread the sickness. You know what I mean. We can all help each other in crises–like when there is an accident."

Petra, the tall woman in charge, smiled, "Why yes, that's what we try to do here–as women. I keep a little chart of those who are sick, so we try to help each other. No one has family here–so we are family. No one has money. Pay is just a few dollars a week. And, jobs won't last."

"Really? That's not good news," Julie's face drained of color.

"Well, the peach season is almost over, and the apple season is short. Then it will be winter. So most of us plan to move south for work–we hope." The women looked worried, and suddenly sadder–older.

"Best get home, get dinner ready." Everyone scattered. Cans of beans and hotdogs were all most of them had for dinner, and supper was even less.

"You did fine, son, but oh, it's hard work–don't know if I can do it." Will and Ernie came home, walking slowly down the dusty path, looking tired, carrying a sack of something.

"Here, honey, some peaches; we get to take some badly bruised ones home."

"How was your work?"

"Rough," said Will. "It's tough work, picking as fast as you can, and I'm not fast. Think we earned about a dollar today."

Will's face showed his weariness, "You have to be really careful not to bruise a peach. I had two whole boxes rejected–Ernie had none. He's more careful than me. My big hands aren't good for peaches." He looked down in an ashamed way. "We'll get the hang of it."

Ernie was excited to tell of their earnings. Julie described the visit from neighbors, the rules, but said nothing about Zeke, the boss.

"Bad news was that the peach season is short, and apple pickin doesn't start right away. It's short, too." The Schultz's were too tired to think ahead.

"What can we do?" asked Julie after the bigger kids were asleep. "It's so hot, with mice and bugs; hope we don't get sick. We'll make it, but how?"

Will counted their remaining money, and worrying about the next months.

Will whispered, "I've heard that all the camps are about the same. Seems we're lucky to have heard about Fruitland. Some guys wandered around looking for work–and had to leave their families, penniless–just don't want that to happen."

"It won't!" Julie reassured him. Sleep was upon them and sometimes–nightmares.

Early–after Will and Ernie had gone to the orchards, there was a surprise knock at the door. Answering it, there stood a large woman with gray hair, a pug nose, a double chin, bright red lipstick and a touch of rouge. She smiled.

"Hello," said Julie, "won't you come in?"

"Well, yes, Mrs. Schultz, I guess I can call you that. I'm Ellen, and my husband, Zeke, is the Manager. He told me that you had just moved in. Thought you might like to do some work for me– like help me bake bread and some pies. I always need help, as there's so much to do managing the camp!" She laughed heartily– even her large tummy jiggled–pulling herself up to disguise her overweight.

Just then Rachel began to fuss, so Ellen went right to the buggy and picked her up.

"Oh, I love babies," said Ellen, "have three of my own–not babies now–all grown up and out of the house.

"Can you come tomorrow? I have bread to bake and several pies for Sunday's dinner. All the children are coming over. It's Zeke's 42nd birthday–I'm older than he is." Her tummy jiggled again as she laughed. "How much do you want for pay?"

"Why I've never done this before? I would just like to help you," Julie said.

"How about for every loaf of bread you bake you make one for you, too, and the same with pie and cakes," Ellen said smiling.

Startled, Julie could hardly believe it, "Why that would be wonderful, and just cooking in a real kitchen, it's been so long." *Having some bread and pie, will make us all feel better*

"Then you'll come over in the morning. Oh. I can hardly wait," replied Ellen.

Chapter 38

THE FIGHT

Above all be the heroine of your life, not the victim.
Nora Ephron

Around 9:00 AM Julie wheeled Rachel in the buggy around to the manager's spacious house. She carried the buggy up three steps and knocked on the door. Instead of Ellen, Zeke answered it. "Well, well, well, look who's here. I heard that you're going to bake me a birthday cake. I hope you can jump right out of it yourself, pretty little lady."

Startled and before Julie could answer, Ellen appeared around the corner. "Come in, come in," she called, smiling broadly. "Oh, Zeke, you are always such a tease," she gave him a hug, as she pushed by him and opened the door widely.

Julie wasn't so lucky, as he stood too close for her to pass without rubbing against his belly. She could hear him breathe heavily. Zeke helped carry in the buggy and tickled Rachel's chin–she laughed. He seems quite harmless now–perhaps the gossiping women were wrong.

Spreading her arms and laughing, Ellen grabbed Julie's arm and showed her the big kitchen–with a gas stove and refrigerator and said, "This is my kingdom–and why I'm so fat." Again, she laughed, looking at Julie's slim figure said, "Don't you get fat like I did–you're so slim–even after having four babies, too."

Julie smiled, "Your kitchen is beautiful–and orderly."

"Zeke wouldn't have it any other way. Right, Zeke?"

Zeke was staring at Julie's figure.

I wish he didn't do that–and would stay away! Julie thought.

"You're right. Everything in its place makes for easier moves."

Julie knew he wasn't just talking about the orderly kitchen. After putting Rachel down for a nap Julie went to the sink and washed her hands under running water. *Oh that feels so good!* Julie thought. "What do you want me to make, first?"

"How about bread, that takes a while to rise." Ellen said

"Good. Then we can do the pies and cake. How many for dinner tomorrow?"

"We'll have six, three kids and one husband–other than Zeke," Ellen laughed again.

Without talking more, they set out flour for bread and pies. Zeke left for the orchard. Julie liked Ellen–feeling a little sorry for her with a husband so openly flirtatious.

Might be better than one sneaking behind your back, thought Julie.

"Let's get some dinner together for Zeke, and us, too, if you'd like?"

"I'll make some fried potatoes, peas, and pork chops if you have them on hand," Julie offered. "I'll need to feed Rachel at sometime, if you could let me use a bedroom or parlor." Julie thought it might be too open to breastfeed in the kitchen with Zeke staring, although it was customary for women to breastfeed just about anywhere.

"Oh, just do it right here, when you're eating if it works for you. I like having another woman around. With families coming and going so fast, sometimes I actually get lonely. Tell me about yourself and your family. Why are you here?"

"It's a long story. Yes, I'll tell you and hope you tell me your story and how you got started with this orchard."

The women shared stories and worked together like sisters. It was a good feeling to help someone, and also to get fresh bread and two pies for the family. Zeke's chocolate birthday cake was tall with perfect frosting.

"Can't tell you how much fun this was," said Ellen.

"Do you want me back next week?"

"Why yes, could you come three times a week?–just in the mornings would help. That would give me such a boost. Maybe you can go grocery shopping with me sometime. That would help us both. I know where the best bargains are. It's hard for the family to make dollars stretch."

After coming steadily for two weeks, Ellen said one day, "Let's go shopping, tomorrow, OK?"

"OK, I'll leave Rachel with Serena tomorrow, so we can get around easier without the buggy."

Next morning they left about 9:00 AM Ellen drove a newer Ford to a grocery store about five miles away. Julie just looked on and made some suggestions. She felt Ellen really wanted to talk–maybe girl talk.

"What do you think of men in general, Julie?" Ellen asked as if she felt Julie might have some insights.

"I've only loved one man, so I don't have many ideas," Ellen. "Why do you ask?"

"Oh, you're so pretty. I thought that maybe you'd had lots of boyfriends," the overweight woman looked pitifully sad.

"No, I have my Will, and he's all I ever want. What about you, Ellen?"

"Oh, I'm not attractive now, but once upon a time I was–I think–I did have lots of boys in high school with crushes on me 'cause I developed early–you know what I mean. I did kiss a few, but that was all. Guess they wanted more.

"When I met Zeke, he was a lady's man. He was so good-looking and was a great dancer. I wondered why he chose me. Sometimes I thought that it might be because my daddy owned lots of orchards. Zeke's been a good husband, mostly, but sometimes when new pickers come in to camp, I can tell he checks out the prettiest ones. I knew he had an eye for you."

"Oh, dear Ellen, I don't think so, do you? I really never noticed. What makes you think that?"

"Oh, I know it isn't you. You work so hard and are with your kids all the time, but you are the prettiest one this year. I just wondered if you had noticed him–has he ever tried to come to your house for something?"

"Never. I've never seen him, except right here; how sad for you to worry. I mean that. That isn't right, partners for life. I'd never look at another man, and I'd never hurt another woman. We're sisters. Please never worry about Zeke around me. I'm sure he loves you very much," Julie was shaking now, concerned that the shopping trip was only for Ellen to check up on her.

"I like you, Julie. Just wanted to make sure." Ellen's eyes were still filled with suspicion, but also with tears; she looked like an unloved woman.

"Guess we should get back, fix dinner for Zeke," Ellen said, as they went to pay for the groceries, then to the car and back home.

Zeke came home at noon. Julie stayed as far away at the sink as possible, not looking at him at all. She could feel Ellen's eyes on him during the whole time. It was a strained time, and one that Julie didn't like. She was glad to leave and go home.

"Want me to come day after tomorrow?" Julie asked.

"Yes,"

Julie walked quickly home, not feeling very secure with a jealous wife–a lonely friend–

Julie left Rachel with Serena the next time she went to Ellen's. It was easier to get the work done. When she arrived Ellen was busy fussing around in the kitchen, laying out all the flour and sugar for cookies and bread baking.

"I forgot to tell you that I have a luncheon at church I need to go to today," Ellen laughed. "Sometimes I forget, as it's only once a month. Can you fix dinner for Zeke–just some meatloaf, potatoes and green beans? He'll like that."

"Sure, no problem, if I don't need to stay too long, since I left Rachel at home with Serena." Julie felt trapped and shaky. *Wish I would've brought Rachel today. I hate being in this house alone with Zeke. I wonder if Ellen forgot about our conversation?*

"Oh, that is such a big help to me. I hate to miss my church meetings and all the news I hear."

After baking bread and three pies, Julie set the table for Zeke's dinner and had it ready to serve to him when he came in.

"Oh, my little cream puff is here all alone. Oh, how lucky can I be," Zeke said smiling.

"I love meat loaf–and other things, too. Now that was good." Pushing away his plate, and leaning back, looking longingly at Julie, as she picked it up and went to the sink to wash it. "Now for a little dessert, don't you think, pretty lady?"

"Here's your pie," Julie eyed him coldly.

"Come over and sit on my lap, just a little bit–and I'll tell you a story." Zeke reached out to grab her hand.

"That won't be necessary, I need to go now," Julie responded.

"Now, now, just remember I'm the manager, and your husband works for me. When I want something, I get it; do you understand, little lady? I could make it very hard on your husband and your boy, if you don't cooperate. You get what I'm saying?" Zeke's face was flushed now and his eyes were filled with desire. Julie could see that between his legs a large lump was forming. Her heart was pounding, just as it had at the Pedersen's home so many years ago.

With that, Zeke stood up and grabbed her by the shoulders and tried to kiss her on the lips. Julie turned her face quickly, and the kiss landed in the air. Quickly he pulled her back against his chest and tried to raise her chin up with his other hand. "Now let me kiss you or there will be trouble."

Julie relaxed briefly and then with the swift action of a cat, she squirmed under his arms and away from his grip. She smiled, thinking of all alternatives, "You are such a strong man, Zeke, and so handsome. I don't think you need to force yourself upon a stranger. Let's get acquainted a bit more, so I can serve you just the way you like it," she purred, smiling wickedly.

"Why you little minx, you're really quite a clever little lady," Zeke was taken back by her quick thinking. "What 'ta you have in mind, little lady?"

"I'm thinking a better place wouldn't be in your house. Ellen is a friend. She's so generous and kind. This would hurt her a lot, and she loves you so much." Julie's face was now calm, and her eyes never leaving his face. She was carefully moving toward the sink where she knew a large knife was laying, yet to be washed. *Steady, don't take your eyes off the skunk–move like a tiger–silently.* She reached backwards and could feel the handle of the knife and was about to grab it and plunge, but then–

A car could be heard in the driveway, a door slammed shut. Ellen returned–just in time.

As the door opened, Zeke was quickly leaving the table–his bulge retreating as he walked to the door.

Ellen came in.

"Well, how about that, the meeting was next week–not this one. I'm always getting those dates mixed up! Zeke, I see you've already had your dinner–except your pie–did you save anything for me?" she laughed.

And Zeke responded, "Oh course, Ellen, I never take it all. Better get back to the orchard." He left without looking back at Julie, but he knew–she knew–there would be another time.

"Oh, thanks Julie, you made my favorite meatloaf and freshly baked bread. You're so good." Ellen sat down and began eating all that was left over.

Julie's heart was still pounding, realizing that she'd been close to doing something hurtful–that wasn't who she was. Oh, if she could just tell Will what had happened, but then he wouldn't let her come over again–the jobs were so important. *I must keep this to myself and not breathe a word to anyone. We must keep working. I know I can do it–but how? I hate the sight of that evil man–I could've killed him with one strike–he doesn't know how strong I really am. But I must play the game–for us all.*

"Julie, would you mind very much if I send a roasting chicken home with you? We've way too many. The kids would love some meat with their bread."

Julie's eyes filled with tears, as it'd been nearly a month since the family had any meat at all. A wish come true. *How'd Ellen know we were in dire need?*

"Thanks, Ellen, you're very kind." Looking back at Ellen standing, on the porch, Julie saw the look–a look of gratitude–a look of knowing what nearly happened–women know.

"Dear friend, I know now how strong you are–I won't let anything happen to you or your family."

Ellen's face told it all–sagging–from knowing a husband's betrayal, her own jealousy, but a fierce determination to test a friendship.

As Julie strolled back to the cabin–she wondered–*did Ellen really have a church luncheon–or did she merely say so–to test how I would control Zeke?* She wondered, too, *could I have used a knife to hurt Zeke?* Julie had never hurt anyone–resourceful, but never hurtful. Shaking still, she entered the cabin–and laid down on the bed–when Will and Ernie came home–she got up–as women do–and simply carried on–getting supper ready. Julie never told anyone, nor did Ellen; for the next two weeks, they worked together, laughing again. Ellen never left the house when Julie came to help–and Julie always took Rachel with her–a safety measure. Silence was the best defense. The peaches were picked and now on to the apples, as the weather was cooler in the evenings. Will and Ernie needed a rest–badly–but that wasn't to happen.

"We've got to talk about our next steps," Will said one night, as they cuddled in their lumpy, crowded bed.

"I think there is only one solution–to go back home–to Colorado."

"I think so, too–hard to do that–like a failure–and we haven't much money for the trip," Will said.

"I know, but we'll find a way–we always have–'Ask and ye shall receive; God's promise is true.'"

Will drifted off to troubled sleep. Julie lay awake for another hour, planning, praying, how could she earn money for at least the gas to get home–*how could I?*

Chapter 39

RESCUE

Every action of your life touches on some chord that will vibrate in eternity.

Edwin Hubble Chapin

One night a loud pounding on the door awakened all. "Help, help, my daughter is bleeding. Come quick! Come quick, Julie," the voice had that Petra's German accent. Julie grabbed her housecoat and covered her pajamas. Opening the door, she heard Petra crying again.

"She's had a baby and is bleeding really bad."

Putting on her slippers, Julie said, "Goodbye, Will, I'll be back soon."

The two of them ran to Cabin #14 where Virginia, Petra's seventeen-year-old daughter, lay on the table where she'd delivered a healthy baby girl.

"I can't stop the bleeding."

Immediately Julie began kneading the tummy–the womb–of Virginia–hard.

"Where is the afterbirth?" Julie called, "I've got to see if it has a tear in it."

"Emil threw it out in a newspaper."

"Get it quickly."

Emil, Petra's husband, ran out to the trash bin, and returned with the bloody afterbirth, still wrapped in the newspaper. Julie kept kneading Virginia's womb to stop the bleeding.

"Open the newspaper, so I can see the whole afterbirth," Julie shouted. He did.

"AAAaahh just as I was afraid of–look there's a big tear along that lining–some of the placenta is still attached inside her womb.

We've got to get Virginia to the hospital right away–or she will bleed to death. Run, find someone with a car–that works."

Emil ran next door to Oscar who had a big old Oldsmobile, and drove it to Cabin #14.

"Carry her out in the blanket with the baby. Help her nurse the baby–that'll help stop the bleeding." Julie was giving the orders fast at the same time she continued kneading the womb. As they drove out of the camp, others opened doors to see what the commotion was.

"Any one know where there's a hospital?

"Yes, it's about two miles away, St. Mary's." Good. Hurry but no accidents–don't run out of gas".

The young mother's lips were turning blue, and then she shut her eyes. The baby was nursing, as if it knew it had a job to do.

As they entered the hospital lot, Julie told Emil to run to the emergency entrance. "Tell someone that we had a bleeding new mother. Quickly."

A robust, tall nurse opened the emergency door and had a gurney for the men to put the mother and baby on. The nurse rushed to the telephone.

"Dr. Johnston, we have an emergency, can you come right now? Yes, it's a young mom who has been hemorrhaging. Yes, the baby is here, too, and a couple of neighbors. Yes, I'll get the OR room ready for a D&C."

It was now 2:00 AM.

"I'm Nurse Jordan. Come with me." They all hurried to the operating room.

"Just you," pointing to Julie. "Come in–keep kneading the womb. Someone take the baby–a girl? How beautiful!"

Nurse Jordan immediately went to the medicine cabinet and got a syringe and needle, grabbed a vial of clear liquid, pulled up some of it, and gave Virginia a shot.

"That will help–stop the bleeding."

Just then Dr. Johnson rushed in. Scrubbing his hands as did Nurse Jordan. They both get gowned and gloved with surgical masks on. Julie stood to the side.

They put Virginia's legs into the stirrups, and covered her with sterile drapes.

"Your friend, here–Julie? Did the right thing. Probably saved your life."

Soon he had scraped the womb and removed the tissue. The bleeding began to stop. "I want you and the baby to stay overnight, so we can keep checking on you, Ok?" Virginia nodded, as did Emil and Petra.

Dr. Johnson thanked Nurse Jordan. Pointing to Petra, he said, "You're lucky Mrs. Jordan was here tonight. She usually is the supervisor in the daytime–was filling in for another nurse tonight. You were just lucky, as she is the best in the whole state of Idaho."

Nurse Jordan blushed and said, "Thanks. I'm glad I was here, but it was that young woman over there that really saved her." She pointed to Julie.

"You did, indeed. How did you know what to do?" asked Dr. Johnson.

"I've helped with a lot of babies being born, but mostly I learned about bleeding from helping on the farm."

"Well, you certainly did all the right things. Where do you live?"

"We are fruit pickers' and live in the Zeke's Orchard's camp near the highway."

"How are things going for you out there? Are you making good wages?"

"We hardly make it and hear that the picking season is almost over. We don't know what to do when the apples run out. We're all in the same boat."

"May I ask my wife and a couple of her friends to visit you tomorrow and bring some food for all, but mostly for the young mother–Virginia–she'll need to build up her blood."

"Yes, that would be nice; but my family is managing OK." Julie knew everyone in the camp could use help, but no one wanted charity.

The trip home was quick; they arrived around 4:00 AM. Petra hugged Julie so long. "You are an angel sent by God," she said.

"We are all family," Julie responded, realizing that she was still in her pajamas, robe, and slippers. She was exhausted.

Near midday Julie heard a knock on the door, and when she opened it, there stood four well-dressed women from Fruitland.

"Hello, I'm Mrs. Johnson," said one brown-haired woman of middle age. "My husband, Dr. Johnson, told me of your heroism last night. We've come with some food and baby clothes."

"Oh, I just did what any mother would do; we're one big family."

"Indeed, and that's what's important–to do unto others–We're wives of doctors in town and wanted to help if you need some food and clothes for the baby."

"I'm sure she could use those things, and yes, the food will help all of us. How kind of you all," Julie's voice was cracking– tears flowing. The boxes were filled with meats, chickens, potatoes, rice, cookies, oranges–the gift was overwhelming.

"I can't thank you enough–; we will share."

Looking around in the cabin, the women noticed many bright paintings covering the bare walls.

"These are magnificent! Who did these paintings?" the women asked.

Julie shyly said, "I did. The place was so drab, so I added a little color."

"You're really a fine artist–these resemble the famous artist Georgia O'Keeffe!" They explained, looking at four large colorful flowers and waves.

"I don't know who he is, but I love to paint–as my mother did, too."

"Immensely talented."

"Thanks. I just wanted to remember the beautiful things I've seen–like the flowers in the summer and the waves of the ocean– waves of wheat–God's beautiful creations."

"Are any for sale?" inquired one younger woman.

"Oh no, but I'd like each of you take the ones that you like, as we will soon be moving out. Take them–as thanks for your generosity," Julie smiled.

The women looked carefully at them, and each took one, carefully rolled up.

"These are wonderful. Thank so very, very much." They continued to murmur as they left.

When they were gone Julie looked at her newly blank, empty walls; their barrenness mirrored her own sense of privation, and for a moment she allowed herself to feel the sadness.

"I'll paint some more when we get home."

Then she spied the sugar bowl–filled with bills–five and ten dollar bills, from where? She then knew that the women had left money for the paintings.

But oh, no, thought Julie, *these were gifts*! She counted the money and was astonished. "Fifty-three dollars–just enough with what we've saved for the gas to get home–Ask and ye shall receive!"

As the Schultz's prepared to leave the camp, Julie had one last visit to make–to Ellen's home. She knocked on the door.

"Well, such a surprise, Julie. Come in," Ellen said, "What do you have in your hand covered up with paper?"

"It's a portrait of you. When I was breastfeeding Rachel I saw your photograph–so beautiful–so I painted a likeness, do you like it?"

Tears washed across Ellen's fat cheeks. "Yes, that's what I looked like when I met Zeke–I'd almost forgotten."

"Don't forget it anymore. You are a beautiful woman and my friend. Goodbye, and may God protect you and fill you with peace."

With that, Julie and family left Fruitland, on their way back home to the prairie.

Chapter 40

WAY HOME

Courage is being scared to death–but saddling up anyway.
John Wayne

"Father, we ask that you lead the way as we head home. All things work for the good of those who love the Lord. We don't question the wisdom of coming this far away from home. We need so much. Our money is almost gone; we have no farm, no livestock, no house, and no work. Please guard and protect our children first and foremost. Keep us always in Your tender care. We ask this in Jesus name. Amen." Will prayed with head low, as did Julie. The children looked downward, with mixed emotions.

"We want to go home! To go to school and be with our old friends," said Ernie and Serena.

"I want to stay. I love these big trees 'n want to find more seeds. I even planted some," said Dusty.

These tiny things that grew into big things mystified this grandson of Papa Paul. And Rachel was getting too big to sleep well in an infant's buggy. It was time to go home–if they could just make it.

"Winter is coming; we can't make it. It's the end of apple picking. At least we have family and friends in Fairview. I really don't care what others think as long as you and I are together–nothing else matters. I'm tired, tired," groaned Will.

"I'm so tired, no decent kitchen, no place to call home–it feels so hopeless." Her voice trailed off, and her hands covered her face.

"Oh, dearest Julie, so many dreams died. Now we have to go back to the country of dust and grasshoppers. I had such dreams. Everything I touch turns to dust. Promises I've made to you–to care for you. Here I am nearly forty, as old as my dad when he died. It's all over–so fast. If only Mama"–he didn't finish the sentence–

But Julie knew–and she still wondered, too. *Why, Why, Why was Hank given the homestead? Don't look back–some things can't be changed.*

"Don't say that, please, Will. It just happened. Like to all of us–look around us–we're just part of the pack–hungry, with nothing, and going home. We do have a place to go to; some don't. Remember after your dad was killed–your mama became the leader of the county. She showed how strong the Schultz blood really is.

"You have the Promise Seed like your dad and Mama Rose. You became head of the house–at age of seven. Remember that– the homestead, and buying more land, built it up for over twenty years. That was because of you. Not Hank. He had little to do with the success. He just reaped the benefits. He's lazy and conniving– but that was what Mama wanted–I guess–to keep the land in the hands of only one. God will direct us–you–in perhaps a new way–a way of your heart. Come on, let's get on the road!"

"You're right, Julie, you're strong. You've made such sacrifices. I'll love you always."

Dusty cried, "Let's go–'ome."

They all laughed. Leaving the camp seemed like the period at the end of a sentence. With that, their Model A Ford pulled the cumbersome wagon out of the camp. They left, to retrace their path across Idaho–then the windy state of Wyoming–home to Colorado. Sailing through Boise felt familiar and seeing the Snake River, no surprises–they were feeling increasingly confident as Fruitland got farther and farther behind them.

"We'll make it to Pocatello by tonight, if we don't have trouble," Will called out.

No one answered; they just kept their eyes straight ahead– toward home. The stops were infrequent–and talk even less. All seemed lost in their own thoughts–even the kids were thinking.

"Hope Baby–my little pet goat–is still there–maybe I can have her back," said Serena.

"Didn't realize that you missed your little goat so much," Julie sighed.

So many memories were left behind in Colorado. *Would the memories be scars throughout life?* Julie wondered–*like my last memories of Mama no more breaths and turning blue–and cold. And, waiting for Daddy when he went fishing at night, and never came back. Some things I can't forget–I wonder about Will–about his dad–he doesn't talk about that. Did he see his dad's charred body? And how did he help his mama when she cried? Lots of memories–and now more of them–our lives in Idaho.*

At each stop for gas Will would ask, "How are things in town?"

"Gotten worse–we're all in this boat. The Nazis are trying to take over the world –marched right into some place called the Soo Daten Land or some such. There's war in China–more trouble–people are starving, and there're bread lines in the bigger cities. So far FDR's kept us steady, and out of war."

This news was ominous. What could they expect back home? Will at times seemed to shudder–as he drove–ever onward. *I'll do anything at all, so the kids have food–I will find something*! Not sharing his worries with anyone.

Julie, too, was thinking, as the lump in her throat got bigger. *It feels like when I was four years old and Tanta Mary came to our house when Mama was sick. She was in Mama's room and came out, and said, 'It's going to be OK–you will come and live me.' I just had my dolly in my arms and nothing else. After Mama went to sleep in her bed, she was cold. I tried to cover her up so she wouldn't shiver. She wasn't right, as she didn't say she loved me, as she always did. Her hands were cold, and her eyes were shut. I never saw her again–somehow I feel like that again–like I need to hold someone's hand again, but whose? Will is too troubled himself.*

The familiar search for a cheap cabin, the cold bread and butter some warm milk–crackers–the tummy felt full enough for sleep, and then the morning again.

"If all goes well we'll make it to Creston Junction tomorrow. Remember staying there? 'Heaven in the Red Desert' I think it was called. Want to stop there?"

"Yes," cried they all, and Serena said, "Yes, the owner had a violin–she let me touch it!"

"I didn't know that," remarked Julie, "when was that?"

"You were feeding Rachel, and I was in the kitchen with her, she let me touch it, said it had been her husband's. She used to play, she said, and tried to play it little–it was very out of tune." Serena's eyes were shiny.

Julie looked straight into her daughter's eyes and said, with the passion of a mother's will, "You will play–someday you will be great."

And, Serena knew things would be different.

As the Model A struggled up one hill and then another in the desert of Wyoming, the car didn't overheat; it was struggling–but cool. As the car crested another hill, and started down, the car seemed to be gradually gaining speed–slow, then faster, faster, faster–faster–the fence posts were whizzing by. Will seemed tense, turning white as a sheet, keeping his hands gripped on the wheel. Nothing happened until they reached the bottom of the hill–the car slowed to a crawl, then stopped completely, still on the road.

His voice shaking, Will stuttered, "The brakes failed." He jumped out of the car and vomited into the ditch. "Brakes failed– we almost crashed."

"Oh, my God," cried, Julie, "failed?" She jumped out, too, and hugged him to calm him down.

"I couldn't pump and get anything; they were shot." He walked around–looking dazed and still pale. "I couldn't control the car, but someone did it for me. I felt the strength in my hands. That was a miracle. The car was going at least 75 miles an hour being propelled by the weight of the wagon. We could've ended in the ditch–all killed. Thank you, Lord, thank you angels–thanks." Will still leaned against the side of the car, still shaking.

"Daddy," said Ernie, "I can run ahead to a filling station, get some help to fix the brakes or give us a pull. Saw a sign back there, 'Creston Junction 3 miles'. I'm fast. OK?"

"Guess you'd better. I can't run as fast as you. We have water enough for the wait."

With that, Ernie sped away, running. His worn-out shoes were flopping as he r

Soon he was a speck on the horizon. No other cars came by– although Will was ready. It was almost two hours before Ernie returned, but then–in a dark brown, old pickup, a broken window on the passenger's side. It was the motel owner's son, Ron, driving.

"Howdy folks, sorry you've had some trouble. Let's see what we can do to pull you all to Creston," said the awkward-looking kid. "We have a garage in town that might have the parts to fix the brakes, and if not we'll go on to Rowling's where I know they have help. These brakes do get old and break. I know how to fix some, so I'll look at them when we can get it off the road."

With that they unhitched the wagon and pulled it to the side of the road. Julie wrote a note, saying. "We'll be back in 10 minutes," knowing it would be longer. With the hard times people seemed more honest, not stealing since all were poor, in the same boat. Pulled by Ron's old pickup, the car needed to be steered very, very carefully, as there were no brakes.

When in Creston Junction, mechanics began to look over the brakes. "You're lucky only the linings are worn out, the brake lines aren't broken. We have the right linings here, too. Yup, indeed you're a lucky bunch–could have been dangerous–really luck'."

Will smiled, as he knew it hadn't all been luck. By sunset the brakes were fixed. They drove back to the wagon, hitched it up, and returned to the 'Heaven in the Red Desert.' The owner had a surprise–she'd fixed a chicken supper for them with a treat–cherry pie–(Dusty whispered to Mama Julie, "Glad it's not peach"–all were tired of peaches).

"Someday you'll come to our house in Fairview," Julie said, not knowing if that would ever happen. Serena touched the violin again, looking at it with love in her eyes, just as Papa Paul had looked at his violin. Just fixing the brakes cost another bunch of money and left only forty-four dollars.

"We'll make it–I'm sure," Will said.

The motel owner, and Julie sat and talked until almost 10:00 PM while all others were fast asleep.

"You've had a very tough time, my dear. I wish I could help you out. You'll find your way. I know you can. I'm not charging for the room tonight, you need to keep all that you have."

"Thanks. Someday I hope you come to visit."

"I will, I think I will. You're doing the right thing. With all the trouble in the world you've got to be close to family."

In the morning, the Schultz family left early, "Bye, thanks again for all your help."

Each time the gas level tipped to empty, Will hated to see their dwindling bills in his hand as he filled the tank to the top. Carefully he counted out each bill. Gratefully all the tires held steady, so when they crossed into Colorado with only 37 miles to go, Will had the grand sum of forty four left in his pocket.

The brown gray of the harvested wheat and corn was mellow and reassuring to the family. The prairie was beautiful, even without any trees or rivers. And, the wind still blew. Driving to Margaret's house–they passed by the homestead. No one looked that direction, but straight ahead–to the future, not the past.

Turning into Margaret's farmyard, it was familiar–welcoming. Will was the first to get out, and Margaret met him with wide open arms, "Brother Will, Brother Will, you are here, safe and sound. And there you are, Sister Julie, come in, come in."

Those words were like music to their ears. The kids rolled out and Margaret's son, Jim, came running out. "Play you a game of hoops," he cried out, glad to have a family to play games with again.

"Oh, the kids have gotten so brown, and Rachel, so big," Margaret said. "Pete is out in the field, he'll be in, in an hour or so, so make yourselves at home, and I'll finish the potatoes for supper."

"Let us help," said Julie and Serena were glad to see a kitchen again.

"You won't have to stay here but overnight, as we found a place right in Fairview you can rent–if you think it would work. It is the Prottsman's place, just got vacant about three days ago. It's that yellow house on the corner; I think it has 2-3 bedrooms and a big kitchen."

"You mean that basement house?" Julie looked surprised.

"Yes, that's the one; it's been fixed up inside," Margaret said with hope in her voice, "and only fifteen dollars a month. I checked even in other towns, and it seems, because of the hard times, folks aren't moving around. You can move right in, and it's only two blocks from the school. School started about three weeks ago, but I believe your kids can catch up."

"I'll look into the W.P.A. (Works Progress Administration) program tomorrow. Think that's about the only job around," said Will.

"You're right–bread lines all over. It's the toughest time we've seen. Sit down and tell me all about Wyoming and Idaho. You must have seen so much."

"Yes, we sure did, but nothing looks as good as the prairies of Colorado," said Will.

Julie said, "We made new friends–and all of them as poor as we are. The work was hard–like all over I guess." She began to shudder slightly. *I don't know if I can stand to live in a basement– under ground like a mole. Can I pretend it's a regular house? We'll have to see in the morning–and I can be strong.*

Julie shuddered again.

PART V

CHANGES

Chapter 41

DECEIT

There is no purpose more inspiring than to begin the age of restoration reweaving the wondrous diverse life that still is surrounding us.

E.O. Wilson, *The Diversity of Life*

"Two milk cows are yours–I'm sure of that," Hank said. "When you left, I hadn't done the numbers yet. We had just a little crop."

"Let's figure it out," Ernie said.

Ernie, now twelve, brought out his pencil and on a board started to put down the figures. "Hey, young fella', you're right on top of things."

"I'm learning; had a chance in Idaho to do calculating for the boss. Zeke was honest, but sometimes made mistakes," Ernie said.

"Good, OK, let's figure. You've got your two cows for sure."

"And one calf. . . you can't separate calf from its mama."

"You're right."

"But you'll pull them over in your wagon?"

"No, you'll have to pick them up. And you can have the cows and calf, or if you want I can keep them and pay you for them." Hank was smiling widely–he liked the challenge of this youngster. "I will throw in a dozen laying hens; how's that, young man?"

"Yah, we'll take two cows and the one calf, and thanks for the hens. How much did you make on the crop?"

"Well, you can look at the books, but it was a hundred and one dollars."

"And, for the land that the Land Restoration Grant paid?"

"Now, listen here, young man, that was not in the plan?"

"Why not, that land was part of the ten percent agreement. The hundred sixty acres you weren't to plant for two more years. That would have paid another hundred sixty dollars at one dollar an acre."

"Don't think that's right, but if you insist," Hank was laughing now.

"It's not funny," Ernie's face was growing red, It's honest, that's what it is–honest," looking Hank straight in the eyes. Taking his pencil, Ernie calculated: "10% of 101=$10.10 and 10% of 160=$16.00 or $10.10 +16=$26.10; is that right?" Looking at his dad, then at the Uncle Hank.

"That'd be right. I'll make it an even $27.00 for all, and put it straight into First National Bank, where I keep my money." Hank wasn't amused by the last challenging comment. *Honest? Little does this punk know! I don't want him snooping around in my affairs.*

"Good, we'll come and get the cows and chickens tonight," Ernie affirmed.

Will was thoughtful about the exchange and wondered if he had miscalculated Hank. He knew his son–this was the man who would take charge someday.

The two milk cows and calf went into the sturdy little barn on the Fairview rented property. In the hen house, a dozen chickens sat in nests of new hay. Serena and Dusty were in charge of chickens. Rachel was just six months, so wasn't much help,

A new beginning, thought Will.

"What about that Hitler fella? He seems to want to rule the world. That's their problem. Yah, some of us have family over there, but we can just send money and not get into that ole war." Conversations such as these swirled around in the pool hall.

The German pastor at the Lutheran Church stopped preaching in German–said it might be suspicious, like to be preaching in an enemy's language. Some folks stopped coming to church–they didn't think that God spoke in any other language but German. But some even tried to change their names, so they sounded more English–not so German. A family named Radke became the Hanson's–and others did likewise.

"What if we have to go to war–what if then? What if our boys would go to war? Who'd farm the land?"

"Don't think that's a good idea," Hank would argue.

Hank and Penelope had no children, so needn't to worry about that. Hank had wanted sons–begged Penelope to "Please, please try to get pregnant." Knowing their love-making was frequent and passionate–he was sure she'd get pregnant right away. But Penelope had other plans.

With her beautiful face made up in lipstick, powder and rouge, she shouted, "Oh, NO, NO, No. that wasn't in the agreement." She even showed her long fingernails, like claws at Hank. "We're to have fun, travel, have a nice home–but with kids, that's all gone. No, I don't want all that mess of diapers and that breast stuff. I would hate that–just hate it–fussing in the night."

Penelope screwed up her face into a horrible frown–looking ever so much like a witch. "Can you imagine what my hair would look like in the morning if I didn't have it shampooed and shiny! I'd be fat and ugly–like all the women around Hopetown–and forget Fairview–they are pigs–just awful. If I get pregnant, it'd be your fault. I'd find some way to fix that!" Penelope threatened. She stormed into the bathroom and slammed the door.

Looking down at his feet, Hank didn't bring up the subject again. He was disappointed, but also hated to think of cutting up his/their land–even sharing it with a son. *I've worked too hard for this to let it out of my hands. No, it's better to be free; no kids.*

In about an hour Penelope came out of the bathroom, still in a huff, but looking all made up again. "Let's plan a trip to Hawaii, my sweet Hank," she purred, "get away from all this war talk." It was December 1, 1938 when they booked a cruise to Maui–to stay three months, until March, when the crops needed to be supervised.

For now Will wasn't worried about any fighting in Europe. WPA didn't pay much, but it did put food on the table. Will drove to Hopetown to apply and found a long line of men spilling out of the courthouse–all of them signing up for work with WPA, as did Will. All their faces and the way they shuffled–showed the strain of being out of work–like beaten dogs with tails between their legs. Sad.

"It's no worse than pickin peaches, and it pays almost the same, five dollars a week." In just two weeks, Will was made foreman, and the pay increased by two dollars a week–to twenty-eight dollars a month. Rent was nearly half the paycheck.

Damn, I've got to ask the landlady to reduce the rent. Swallow my pride–the kids are growing and eat more and more everyday–got to do it, he thought. Knocking on the landlady's door, Will felt bad. Opening the door she looked stern; he felt even worse.

"Can you cut the rent to ten dollars a month?"

"It's already dirt cheap."

"Well, I just make $7 a week for a family of six."

"Not my problem," she said, with a wicked smile, but then softened. "O.K. that's ten dollars a month; but pay on time!"

Will saw the image of Papa Paul, standing tall and afraid of nothing.

So, he held up his head–and walked away, murmuring "Thanks.*" Some day–some day.*

Her head was lowered, as Julie looked into the flour bin and saw nothing. Only four dollars left to buy flour and sugar for cooking–for a whole month. *We asked for protection and guidance. We are living like moles–how can I take it any longer–give me strength, give me courage, please, Lord. I hate living in this hole.*

Julie stood in the middle of her kitchen in the basement house. Only a small front door pointed out of the dungeon, and hardly a window in the house to open. Yes–like the dugout Mama Rose despised. Three tiny bedrooms, a closet for storing coal, and a kitchen; no toilet–that was a privy outside's–next to the pump for water. The steps were steep as you walked down into the hole–their home–it was dark, crowded, like a tomb–not a home at all.

Julie's depression seemed uncanny, like a dark cloud from the other side. She didn't usually feel like this. *Anything but a hole–I feel like a cornered rat–I feel like I'm disappearing–down, down, down. There's no bottom–just more falling and falling. Maybe Daddy felt like this when he was drowning–I've got to stop and pull myself up–but with what?*

Just then Ernie and Serena came rushing down the steps from school; they were happy. "It was good to be back–everyone but ole snotty Oscar was glad to see me," said Ernie.

"I have my old friend Jane, still here. She's says I can buy Baby back–for a quarter." Serena's eyes were sparkling as she anticipated seeing her pet again.

"We'll find a quarter–somehow," said Mama Julie. Dusty proudly said, "I planted seeds."

Mama Julie had nearly forgotten that Dusty had taken some seeds he'd found next door from old apples that had fallen, and planted them along the fence toward the road. "Yes, you really did, and in a few years we'll have fruit–like apples."

"Don't forget I planted some peach pits, too, from Idaho."

"Wow," said Ernie and Serena "That's really good."

"I missed you, Ernie, and 'Erena" His brown eyes looked sad. Rachel just cooed–happy.

Each had more stories to tell, and Julie felt content, again.

"We've got the best new principal, his name is Mr. Carlotti from Boston–he speaks really funny," said Serena.

"Yah, he even played the violin this morning when we sang the National Anthem. And he has three big sons–two are twins, they go to high school and are really good football players, so they said," remarked Ernie.

Julie's heart skipped a beat when she heard about the violin playing–*perhaps, perhaps–maybe there would be a chance for Serena to learn to play. Grandpa Pinot's Steiner violin was kept at Margaret's for safekeeping. They said it was worth a fortune– maybe there will be a time.*

"I must go to the PTA meeting next week and meet all your teachers.

Ernie told more about the new principal–"Mr. Carlotti, he loves to tell stories–about everything. He's so smart. He says that our president sent expert teachers from the east coast to teach out in the rural areas, so the kids would have a better education. I like that. He teaches American Literature, Social Studies, and music."

"That's a lot of subjects," Julie remembered her year in high school and how she loved literature–especially poetry–it reminded her of her father recited poetry to Mama Serena–*Funny how I remembered that–I was just three-years old–so long ago.*

"Some day we'll invite Mr. Carlotti and his sons over for Sunday dinner," Julie remarked, forgetting there was no flour in the bin.

"I told him that you were a painter, a real artist, and he wants to come and see your paintings," Ernie said.

And so he did; Mr. Carlotti visited each home and when he saw Julie's paintings of sunflowers and wheat fields he remarked in a serious tone, "Why you paint like Georgia O'Keeffe!"

Julie laughed, "Someone told me that when we lived in Idaho. I don't know who he is."

"No, Georgia is a woman, a famous artist in New York who also lives in New Mexico. I've admired her works for a long time. She was born in Wisconsin, somewhat like here, and began to paint those beautiful scenes of wheat fields and flowers. It's an amazing story, perhaps you will meet some day."

And so they did, many years later.

Julie's depression began to lift and she even tried to feel better about her basement home. *It seems so hopeless every day in this dark coffin. I must stay strong for all–especially for my Will.*

Chapter 42

ELECTRIFYING

I believe that luck is preparation-meeting opportunity.
Oprah Winfrey

Dusty came running down the steps saying, "Uncle Hank is comin. He's drivin really, really fast."

Anticipating some news, they heard screeching wheels. Down the steps leaped Hank. "Come on, Will, I've got to take you to Hopetown. Right now! Don't ask questions; just come. There's a chance for a real job, a real chance, but we have to beat ole Mel Otto, that bastard. Come on. Can't wait!"

"I'm with you," Will yelled.

As they sped out of Fairview down the dirt road, Hank shouted, "I just learned about a new program, the Rural Electric Association, called REA. It's a big program from the feds. It will change the west, and they need a foreman. It's a chance for you to get out of the WPA." He floored his new silver Studebaker. A rooster-tail of dust and dirt flew up, and their speed was at least 60 miles an hour–maybe more.

"How do you think I can be a foreman?"

"Cause you are one right now!"

"But of electricity?"

"Doesn't matter. You know how to make people work together. You always have–you smart bastard." Hank laughed, getting his kicks from the thrill of competition, as he wasn't nearly as interested in getting Will a foreman's job, as beating an old enemy, the pig farmer. This chance was too good to pass up.

In less than ten minutes they pulled up to the County building and, not looking around, dashed in and Will filled out the application forms. When they finished and the county supervisor, said, "Will, you have the job! You're just the man we need."

Then out of breath ran in Mel Otto. Looking frustrated and angry, he made a motion with his third finger, right hand. "Someday, you're going to get it, someday." Mel knew his enemy beat him–again.

Hank just sneered, "You've said that before. Oink, oink. Get out of this foreman's way."

Mel left, seething.

Will and Hank stayed for two more hours, listening and learning about the job.

"Can't quite believe it; I'll be supervising all the wiring for hundreds of farm houses even street lights in Fairview!"

"Yes, it's the biggest thing ever to happen in the rural area, to have electricity wired throughout the country, one end to another. We'll light up like the 4th of July," Supervisor Johnson claimed.

Everyone in the county knew that Will was the man for the job–this gentle, smart, and honest man.

"The best part, too, is the salary, one hundred twenty dollars, a month with Social Security benefits. Quite an increase from only twenty-eight dollars a month, right? And you'll have that new Roosevelt program for your retirement. You start in the morning with an office right here in the courthouse. Right here by all the big shots," laughed Joe Johnson.

Hank's eyes were glistening as he saw his big brother gasp, "Can't believe it. One minute I'm digging ditches earning seven dollars a week and paying most of it for rent. Can't thank you enough, Hank, and you, Joe. Can't thank you enough. Let's go tell the family, and I'll be here tomorrow at 8:00 AM."

The trip home was a buzz of talk about how Hank had heard the announcement about the program. "I'm on the Board of Directors of the Greenland Elevator, and we hear things first." Hank said proudly–being in the know was having the power. Hank loved that.

Will and Julie hugged and did a little two-step around the kitchen. "Just think, maybe we can even buy a house in Hopetown–or here in Fairview–a real house–our home–so different from living in the dungeon or the cabin in Idaho.

Julie remarked, "The kids may not want to move to a big city–over a thousand people."

"I start tomorrow, so I have to resign tonight as the WPA foreman. Who wants to ride with me to Sheriff Bill's house? He's the one who keeps tabs on all of this?"

Even Julie and Baby Rachel hopped into the car, and when they returned it was already dark. It was the end of 1940–life was going to change–for them–for the whole world.

Chapter 43

A RUSSIAN MISSION

We sleep safely at night because rough men stand ready to visit violence on those who would harm us.
Winston Churchill

"I hate war as only a soldier who has lived it can, only as one who has seen its brutality, its futility, its stupidity," proclaimed General Dwight David Eisenhower.

No one wanted to go to war. No one wanted to lose a son–or a daughter. It wasn't a war that people in the United States felt a need to be involved in. There was the Pacific Ocean–and the Atlantic–they were protected, and Europe was a long, long way off. Let them handle their own problems. But it wasn't to be that way.

President Roosevelt, pressured by Winston Churchill on one side but flanked by determined pacifistic politicians on the other, chose not to join the European war. As the Nazis increasingly invaded friends and allies, America passed them guns and tanks, but otherwise stood idly by. After Pearl Harbor, Sunday, December 7, 1941, there were no oceans or mountains that could shield the land of the free. It took until then for the USA to engage in the European conflict, and make it World War II. So War was declared on Monday, December 8th, 1941. Its European front ended in May of 1945.

Little Fairview, so far removed, yet so patriotic, saw men and–boys signing up to serve. No questions asked, they just went to war–some in the Pacific, others in Europe.

Ernie completed high school in June 1943; he was almost eighteen.

"Dad, Mom, it's the right thing to do–to enlist. Please give me permission to go."

"Yes, son," they both said, sadly.

Dusty, now eight, wanted to go, too. Serena was thirteen and Rachel, six. Each said, tenderly, "We don't want you to go."

Mama Julie talked nervously and found herself repeating things she had told Ernie when he was just a youngster. "Now don't get a cold, and brush you teeth." *I'm so silly, that's not what I want to tell him. Please Lord, keep my baby safe–let him come home–soon.*

Will simply put his arm around Ernie's shoulder and said, "Be brave; come home."

After basic training Ernie arrived at Fort Bragg, North Carolina for his assignment. A captain called him into his office. "We need good men willing to put their lives on hold. It's a risky assignment; you can turn it down, but we think you're one of the only men who can do this special job. Let me describe it for you and see what you think.

"You may have heard of the Lend Lease Program. It's a program to help our Allies face the Axis with more military equipment, tanks, trucks, airplanes, and submarines. We're building all this equipment and lending it to our Allies. It's a big program, but it needs lots of help. We need mechanics to teach the allied folks how to use the equipment we send to them. Some of our technology is so different that when something breaks down they can't fix it. We've sent over lots of trucks to the USSR. But, when the stuff arrives, no one knows how to keep 'em running. Breakdowns are really a bitch. In some ways it'd be better if we never sent 'em anything."

The captain looked very disgusted, "But then they have to face huge fire power from the Nazis. It's a mess. They have the Nazis stalled just outside Stalingrad. And they're tough; the Red Army started an attack called Operation Uranus, and have actually trapped the dang German 6th Army. Russians have a tough General called Vasily Chuikov. He's pushing as hard as the Russians can, but their trucks are falling apart. We've sent over hundreds and hundreds of the M29 Weasel Studebaker truck, but no Russian knows how to repair that special gasoline engine! Your job will be tough; you have to go where these trucks are and help repair 'em. You are to teach the Russians how to do that, perhaps while under fire. It will be very risky."

"OK? Now, here's the plan. We need farm boys–men who have used Studebaker trucks and already know how to repair 'em. I've checked on you 'n you're one of those farm boys."

Ernie nodded, "Yes, sir, I am."

"Did y' ever work on Studebakers?"

"I did, Sir. My uncle had one, and I got to work on it every now and then. I know the Stoody has a great engine; it had a mammoth block and is the best made. It's different than other makes of trucks," Ernie smiled.

"You're exactly right! That's what makes this problem so dang troublesome. The engine is different. Not too many guys know that–but you do–great! Gads they need help–really they're so behind–might lose the War–and for us, too. This job is that important."

"Next question, can you speak German?"

"Can speak some, Sir, not much, but I heard a lot around our home. My Dad spoke it and Grandma Rose, but she died before I could learn much from her. But I heard it in church, too."

"That's good, Private Schultz, good enough–it tells me that you have some language skills, so we'll send you to a Russian language school, total immersion for a month. Then you'll pick up more when you're in USSR. And you'll also be learning some about the equipment. What do you say, Private?"

"Sir, I would be honored to do whatever is needed. Where will I be doing the teaching?"

"Over in the USSR, on the far side of Jerry. We know that the Russkies have factories in the Ukraine and rail lines to Moscow and other big cities. That's the tough part; you'll be with just seven others–eight of you all together, but on your own–no protection except your own wits. You'll have to be looking like civilians to blend in. It may be dangerous–dang–I know it will be! You may be left there–even captured–we don't know. The Red Army isn't well equipped–'n the Germans are fighting to take Stalingrad and keep moving eastward–fast. Their tanks are deadly."

Six dizzy weeks passed. Ernie wasn't allowed so much as to think in English. When he casually mentioned one morning that he'd dreamed in Russian, the First Sergeant shooed him out the door and down the hall, along with several others. "You've made it–you're ready!"

"Welcome aboard! We'll fly you first into Iceland; they declared neutrality, and, in fact, we've had Army posts there since '40. You'll go via private aircraft with a WAF (Women's Auxiliary Ferrying Squadron organized 1942) pilot, also dressed civilian. Don't want the–a Jerry spies –and they're everywhere, men–to see any khaki or notice anyone saluting. From there you'll go in a deep-water fishing boat across a patch of the North Atlantic. Then you'll travel close to the fjords around Norway to the Baltic Sea and cross toward the south. You'll be Danish fishermen.

"The objective is to avoid being detected by the Finns. Those bastards hate both the Jerries and Russkies so much they can't figure out which side they're on! From Denmark you cross to the Estonian coast. That's a rough call, as Estonians are about like the Finns; they stay afloat by putting their noses up the crack of whoever's ahead–the Russians or the Germans. Gads, you won't know until you get there.

"Once ashore you'll be met by the underground. They'll put you on a train to Moscow. That's where you become mechanics. They'll start you out in the factory. That's where you teach other mechanics to repair Studebaker trucks. When you're done, you'll send a message through the underground as to where you can be picked up, and then make your way back to the U.S. Army–that is if you can tell when you're done–and if you have survived," said the captain in a somber tone.

"We were eager to go, to help. Our tongues could make Russian words after the total immersion–no speaking English–just Russian–we could get by. Our instructor, an old Russian professor, told us, 'You have good ears for language, but your accents aren't perfect. You need to work on that–talk to native speakers as much as possible.'"

"My grandpa had uncles in the Ukraine–the Steppes, so he probably spoke some Russian, too. I talked with him a lot before he died. I'll be listening to the accents, see if my ear can pick it up."

"You will do fine, but you'll probably starve. They don't have food for themselves–let alone the U.S. Army. And prepare for the cold–you may freeze before anything else kills you," the professor added.

"No one sounded at all positive, but I'm maybe going see the Volga Steppes that my dad told me about. Grandpa Paul was from that area. He was a great scientist. Sure would be a good chance for me to learn how the Russians made that treeless desert produce so much."

In the meantime back in Hopetown, Dusty asked, "Mama, why are there people living behind those big fences with barbed wire all around? They can't get out, and Army soldiers are walking around pointing guns at them. What did they do?"

"Nothing, that's the problem–they haven't done anything at all. Just that they have the wrong last name and look different! It's a crime in my estimation," Julie said grimly. "Those people are Americans–who just happen to be of Japanese birth, like I'm of Danish birth and your dad of German. They should be free to go home–to California." Her usual smile was gone–only an angry line from her lips, and her blue eyes were not bright.

"War does strange things to people. They make people become suspicious of every little thing–fear. Like our last name Schultz, some people say it sounds 'too German' and that we should change it to make it Smith–baloney–I'm as American as anyone–so are you.

"I remember not many years ago when our German Preacher, Pastor Schmidt, was asked by the sheriff not to preach in German any more. That was an order from the County Commissioners. 'English only is to be spoken,' they ruled. That might be in public places, but this is a free country, and you can speak in any language you wish. I guess–a church is a public place–so maybe that's right–these rules are so confining–war makes you not trust your neighbor–how sad."

Eight soldiers, clothed as fisherman, split into two groups. If one group didn't get there, perhaps the other would. Each man took his place on the fishing boat as they passed up the East Coast from Baltimore to a point on the Newfoundland shore, the way any fishing boat would. The Wolf Pack, the feared German submarines, was to be avoided at all times. The Pack even came to the shoreline of New York City. Undetected until they were right in the harbor!

These eight brave volunteers were farmers; none had ever been at sea or up in an airplane. This first leg was just the cap off the bottle of the courage they would need to complete their risky mission. Four climbed into the Grumman Twin amphibian plane.

"It's a new plane, just built a year ago in New York. So far the record is one hundred percent safe."

Out of how many trips? thought the huddled soldier-mechanics.

"Since we'll be flying mostly over water, the amphibian nature of the plane will be a better assurance that we'll make it." The female pilot tried to sound convincing; she looked completely capable, but still –a woman.

They gritted their teeth.

"It only holds four to five passengers, so we have two of these babies here. See those straps? Buckle yourself into a seat so we can take off."

Mama and Will read Ernie's first letter until it nearly fell apart. They cried each time:

Dear Mom and Dad, brother and sisters,

I miss you all very much and hope everyone is well.

We crossed into farm country. I felt so close to the soil and knew how the farmers were struggling with so few males around– all the men are off fighting. No livestock to be seen. My sympathy is overwhelming. I know we have to be here. Can't write much except that I'm safe and with other farm boys. Thanks for raising me to see all people as the same, all beliefs as valuable.

Everyone is hungry. I try to give some to the kids–they look so starved. How can humans–kill each other? I could never have had better parents, and family. If I never get back home, you'll know that I carry your faith in my heart. I know that Jesus is with me every day.

Keep praying for me, as I do you and all my brothers, sisters, aunts, uncles–know that I am your faithful son.

Ernie

Ernie wrote many letters; only another one got through to Hopetown–after the War was declared over:

Everywhere we go people wave flags and say "Thanks" 'Spasibo' in Russian. Just hard to see all the buildings down and the people starving. So many women are widowed. I have lots who want to marry me and go the U.S., but I'm not ready for that. I do feel just awful that many are starving and their crops are ruined from all the bombing. The people need all the aid we can give. I see sacks of corn and wheat and wonder if they might have grown by you! I am going to Denmark tomorrow to help them with the telephone lines that were broken–and see the place where you were born, Mama.

I got to a place called Buchenwald –"Book wood" in English. But it defies Christian words. And I saw the gardens and house where Hitler and his wife committed suicide. The Black Forest is bigger than I thought and really beautiful. Hopefully the land will replenish. Land is forgiving; we've seen that on the prairie. I am a changed person, perhaps not so casual as before. I've seen so much that must be done to heal this world, and hope to be home soon.

Ernie

Chapter 44

BRONZE STARS

Be strong–be not afraid–for the Lord thy God is with thee.
Joshua 1:9

Ernie came home, October 16, 1945–a lifetime for Julie and Will and his brother and sisters. Ernie walked in the door late one night. He was home!

On his uniform he wore the Bronze Star for Bravery as did each of the other five. Bryon's and Timothy's farmer parents and family in Wisconsin and Indiana received theirs posthumously. Several times Ernie's family and friends, and even complete strangers would ask him to tell his story.

"I just can't, sorry, but it's too deep and I have nothing to brag about. All the soldiers were heroes and most deserved more medals than I did. In fact, the dead deserve all the medals." Ernie would bow his head in silence.

Ernie could only share his story with other returned soldiers, as they did with him, at the local Veterans of Foreign War (VFW) hall. This is what he told his fellow warriors:

"Early morning August 11, 1942, we crossed the northern Atlantic at about 8,000 feet. That gave us a chance to really see the ocean, all the waves. The flight was kinda smooth; only one of us, Chuck, got airsick. Shit, he puked all over the place, poor bastard. About mid-afternoon the plane landed in what looked like a snow pile–it was the eastern coast of Greenland, actually the only place– almost–where a plane could land on the ground, not a damn sheet of ice. Unbelievable, but we got to take a goddam shower–a hot one and had really good grub–and lots of it.

"The next jaunt was to Rejkjansbaer, Iceland. Did you know it's much warmer there, with all the volcanoes and crap? Man, were the people friendly. They actually gave us hugs and those Iceland women were really hot (laughter–) and they even served us their beer hot! Everyone became very happy. Really happy."

All the vets were clapping their hands and roaring.

"The next morning, bright and early, we got to be real fisherman. Damn, perhaps that was the toughest part. We sailed in two little half-assed fishing boats, basically an oversized rowboat with a smelly little shitty diesel in it, across a lot of open water. The boat's skipper called it the Norwegian Sea and then the Baltic Sea. Boy! Did he have the balls!

We passed by a shitload of them Norwegian fjords, but we stayed close to the coastline. We kept our fishing nets always out, in case some bastard Nazis spotted us–and maybe sent us a little deeper into the water! We were all land people–farmers. Shit, we were sick as dogs. No one could keep any food down. Pukin all day 'n night. The damn sea was so choppy and brackish, not pretty at all. And the daylight–almost no night! That made it really tough.

"I don't know how fast we were going, but we finally hit the coast of Estonia. Probably a week, but, damn, it seemed like forever. Getting back onto land was a relief, but then our captain said, 'The next part is the most dangerous time, 'cuz we never know exactly how to read the damn Estonians. Let's hope it's one of the fuckin times when they're for the goddam Russians!'

"A couple of our guys went white-faced, with buggy eyes. We couldn't turn back, but what was ahead? We were all scared shitless. I stayed as calm as possible, "Let's pray."

Everyone bowed.

"We are in Your Hands, Dear Father. Protect us with your mighty army of angels. We ask this in Jesus' name."

"AMEN," they all said–even that tough fuckin bastard, the captain--he knew what shit we faced.

"Our Estonian underground guy, in broken Russian, told us we had to hurry to St. Petersburg. He said German scouts were everywhere, and we should just keep goddam quiet. Our Yankee accents would tell 'em right off that we're not from those parts.

"Our guys all nodded. You could see the sweat on our faces. Goddamit, were we scared shitless.

"We huddled down into a wagon full of hay and covered up as best we could. Then we rolled down a damn cobble stone street to the St. Petersburg train station–bangin our butts. The wagon came right up to the track, and when the coast was clear we skipped onto the closest train car. A different guy, a prick Russki, with a real stiff face, said the train would take us to Moscow. Him, we could understand–thank God we had our total immersion that would save our shit–at least for a while.

"It was a hospital train, all box cars clearly marked with a white cross on top. It was supposed to be safe from bombers–but not always. Damn, we could be sitting ducks crossing the plains to Moscow, but that, pals, was the safest way to travel.

"Now came the shittiest part. I got separated from the other guys in a car full of damn crying kids, maybe orphans. They definitely didn't have any moms or dads in the car. Two nurses were trying to calm them. I asked if I could help, and a worn-out looking, really pretty nurse understood my broken Russki. Just like that she put a crying toddler into my arms and told me the story. Damn. His aunt was supposed to come to the station in Moscow and get him, but only if she got the word that the little fellow's mama was killed in a bomb raid. 'If not, he'd go into an orphanage. They're all overfull already, we can just pray his aunt comes,' the pretty nurse said.

"Gads that was a half-assed reason, but she looked so bushed – no, more than that. Her eyes told the story she'd seen too many fuckin casualties of war, and they weren't all soldiers. I really do hate war, just do," Ernie continued. Others nodded or just stared into space.

"So I tried to buddy up with the kid, but he wouldn't have nothing to do with this stranger who talked funny. He kicked and screamed like anything, but after while he relaxed and finally went to sleep. That evening the hospital train pulled into Moscow.

"Pitiful conditions –carts and wagons pulled up to the train and anyone who could walk out, did. Lots of them on crutches, all bandaged up, and weak. But those who could do it on their own got onto a cart and got carried away–to what? Damn.

"That pretty nurse scanned the crowd, but aunty didn't show up. What to do? Dammit. Could I just let the tyke go to an orphanage? But I was under orders; join ranks or go AWOL.

"Sometimes you just can't keep from hating yourself. Shit!! Goddam it!!" Ernie paused for a while.

"We had to hop a new train, to Stalingrad. Just when I was about to hand the kid off to anyone handy that tired-eyed nurse came running, 'She's here. She's here!'–then the nurse took the kid and ran off. I could see her hand him to a sobbing woman. Oh, the narrow escapes and the hit-or-miss of heartbreak. Sometimes God puts you at the fuckin edge, then saves your sorry ass. Shit!

"I caught up with my buddies just in the nick of time and made a running jump onto the train for Stalingrad, a good 500 miles southeast. It was night so you couldn't see a shitty thing. But the next morning we were in flat land like my Grandpa Paul must have seen, the Volga Steppes. That area was about deserted, and most of the houses looked bombed out. That was a goddam fuckin bitch. Before we got to Stalingrad, our 'leader'–the Russki contact person, came to our seats and whispered to get off at the next stop and wait for a Russki soldier. He was going to take us in a truck to a warehouse full of the M29 Weasel Studebakers. We jumped off at the next stop, I think Dubovka, and sure enough a uniformed Russki soldier was there. He spoke clear and slow, for us to understand. He was a stud, took us for some grub –we couldn't remember the last time we'd eaten. Damn that was great borscht, full of cabbage and some kind of meat, and lots of hot, fresh bread. We were in fuckin heaven. Shit, they even gave us thirds.

"Next we went to the fuckin warehouse. It was lit pretty good and crammed with trucks, probably a couple hundred in all. There were plenty of tools and–us–we were the teaching instruments.

"It took four fuckin days just to set up the classes. Then the students showed up. They were all young guys, about our age. Damn, they looked skinny next to us Yanks. But soon we got to learn about starvation, and shit, we grew skinnier by the day. Everything shrunk except our cocks and balls!" Everyone laughed.

"We worked goddam day and night, with small groups first and then one on one. Pretty soon the Russkis knew enough to get to work repairing the hundreds of fuckin broken-down trucks. That's where time seemed to stand still. These trucks came up by slow barge, up the Volga River under stacks of hay and corn stalks. We really knew we were in a damn war zone.

"Each day was about the same. The soldiers were focused, no fuckin nonsense. This was their Great Patriotic War. Most of them had lost close friends, and family, or both. They didn't talk about the war, just kept working. Shit, so did we.

"There was one really scary night–probably February of '44. We heard bombs close by, and the soldiers hurried into shelters and dragged us along. Shit, we could only understand them saying the Germans had broken through a defense line and were just two miles away. The soldiers were armed, but not us. One of 'em threw me a goddam rifle; Thank God I knew how to use it. We doused the lights–waited. Nobody bitched we knew the fuckin war had come calling, and we were soldiers. But just the way the explosions came on fast–they went fast. We heard that the goddam tough Red Army had waded in and pushed the bastard Germans back. The next morning we could see how close it had come. Mother Fucker!! But for the time being the Germans were retreating, so we chased them. What a goddamn mistake!"

Ernie's voice almost became a whisper. Every vet sat still. "Never going to forget the destruction we got to witness. Hardly one house in fifty stood untouched in the whole city. The people looked just as broken-down as the buildings, mostly women and whatever men hadn't been able to get the hell out. The streets were lousy with maggoty remains of horses!

"Believe it or not, the goddamned Luftwaffe dropped them, fuckin shit, and everything else possible from the sky–dead birds, horses, rocks, old rubbish, and even outhouse poop. Yes, indeed, they dumped shit onto the streets of Stalingrad. It was the middle of winter –that helped keep the stinking dead and shit stench down –and everyone was cold. There was no firewood and people were just starving. Fuck. It's hard to talk about that part of it, y'know?"

The fellow vets sat and stared at Ernie. He just stared into space, trying to gather his thoughts. "This meant even the damn Germans, young guys just like us, had no way to retreat, and thousands of 'em died same as the Russkis. A lot just froze to death–the Germans had it about as rough as the Russians. Goddam, it was ugly. I try to forget; my mind can't hold that many ugly things for very long. But we kept on repairing those trucks–never ran short of broken-down trucks. Just pluggin onward, like sitting ducks.

"So there we sat, eight fuckin 'fisherman' wearing rags, cold as hell, and starving. The Russkis were kind and shared what little food they had. Some days we were lucky to find a potato to eat. Other times we'd just sit and sing the National Anthem, or anything else to remind us of some goddam human life that we once had.

"Maybe we all coulda made it to the end of the damn war, but two of us didn't. Damn, I can hardly bear to think of that day – somewhere in May of '44." Ernie stopped for a minute looking at his hands. No one spoke.

"We were taking a break, sitting around drinking what could have been a cup of tea, from one bag we all shared. Suddenly a goddam sniper fired through one of the windows above us. He got Bryan and Timothy. Both shot in the head, one-two! At least they didn't suffer, thank God! We scrambled to take them away from the sunlight and hold onto them. We hoped to God to bring 'em back to life, but that wasn't gonna happen–we all cried. Goddam motherfucker got our men.

"Russki soldiers heard those shots. They came and surrounded that building, ran up the stairwell shooting all the way. You could hear them fuckin holler when they found the hiding shit-head sniper; I've never heard anything madder. It seemed like forever before they returned. One soldier had a bloody severed head and two more each had a severed foot. Goddam! Only war can change Christian men into crazed animals. Oh, my god, how could we change into such fuckin beasts."

No vet spoke. Many looked shocked, but they also knew–they also knew.

"All that time, all that hardship –our first time to see a GI so much as get more than a goddam, bunged up knuckle. How do you tell Bryan and Tim's next of kin–? Both guys were farm boys, from Indiana and Wisconsin. We just slouched over and cried–us– grown men. This was so fruitless, so stupid. Like Ike said, 'war is stupid.'"

Not a word was spoken by the veterans sitting, listening. You could hear a sniffle, a cleared voice, but silence. Too many had experienced the same painful loss.

"The Russians kept pushing the damn Nazis back, back, back. We trailed along with 'em. It was hard to feature that we, eight, now six, hadn't worn a uniform since Baltimore, and couldn't. When Berlin fell, we–Yanks–let the Russkis get there first. They needed to taste their special fuckin victory over the Nazis, who had done such destruction to Mother Russia. We finally got to the west side of Berlin, and saw an American commander looking us up and down, then he gave us a salute. He knew we were 'out of uniform' and might not be easy to recognize from our enlistment photographs.

"Nothing can touch the pride, the power, the goddamn joy it gave us to see that American flag and Americans in uniform! We marched up to the commander, and we all had tears flowing down our cheeks–even me–shit! We saluted. God bless the U.S.A.! We were on our way home–to America, and finally to our families. No one should ever go through this fuckin war." Nodding heads and closed eyes said it all. Memories fade, but emotions? Never.

Chapter 45

ECOLOGY

I know of no restorative of heart, body, and soul more effective against hopelessness than restoration of the Earth.
Berry Lopez. *The Spring Nature Heals*

After the War, things were different. The country had changed and Ernie had, too. His baby face had hardened into manhood. He had grown three inches–now well over 6'4". He even talked differently; Ernie was more serious–contemplative. Even during the many dinners held in honor of those who had served, Ernie's face would look stressed. What was he thinking? Why had he become so quiet?

One night about two months after returning, Ernie said, "I've been thinking that I want to do something different in my life than simply farm. I know how to do that, and that is what I want to do, but I also want to be a leader in changing how we farm and how we care for the soil, and for each other. I don't want to be part of a world that tears things up and spits it out helter skelter. I want to be part of the world that honors life that builds up rather than tears things down. I want to go to the University of Colorado and learn new ways of thinking–and maybe farming," Ernie said pensively.

"Then you will, son," both parents echoed.

Julie added, "With the GI Bill you'll have a chance that you never would have had without that support. Go, study, learn, and become the leader you've always have been".

It took five years, but Ernie earned a civil engineering degree with a minor in botany. But his real interest flowered when he read of the unfolding science called ecology. Some ecologists focused on plant communities and others on the links between culture and biology or integrative medicine, the link between healing and spirituality. The new field looked at the connections between all things–spiritual–reminding Ernie of Papa Paul's and Red Sun's beliefs and practices.

Around the campus Ernie stood out. His height put him above most, but the look in his eyes made the real impression. Ernie was elected to several campus-wide organizations and began to speak for change in the government–especially the Department of Agriculture.

"We have to set standards and limitations on use of land, without taking away the rights of the individual farmer. We have to make farming a recognized industry in this country. Each individual farmer must become a keeper of records, so that each knows why and how the harvest flourishes or fails. And we can't just let land go to big corporations who don't care about the land–just about profits. Keeping the farmer on his –or her –land has to become a national priority."

Then there was his high school sweetheart, "Yvonne, Yvonne, make me the happiest man on earth." Ernie proposed. They were both now 24 years old; Yvonne, too, was an engineer.

"Strange about your family, Ernie, everyone seems to marry the only gal they've ever dated. You must be a band of wolves! Of course I will and will love you forever."

So Yvonne and Ernie were married. He became a local director of the County Soil Conservation Corps, and she established a pioneer-consulting firm on water conservation. Together they began to shape policy protecting the natural resources, especially in vulnerable ecological areas like the desert and the prairie. They continued to fight against the legal and economic forces that helped corporations accumulate farmlands, to the detriment of the small family farmer.

One target was their Uncle Hank's the High Prairie Corporation. Hank and Ernie had many heated arguments–both seeing the situation from different points of view.

Ernie took the lead. "All I see is that you take more than you ought to and sell it at higher prices to the international market. Since the War, prices are skyrocketing, and you're riding the crest of that wave."

"Ernie, we have starving folks to feed. You've seen that somewhere?" Hank argued.

"Yes, but it's not going to feed the people, that's the problem, it going to feed the big oil companies and bargaining for oil. You only use hybrid seeds, and you know that they don't reproduce the following year, so the small farmer gets caught in the web of buying more and more hybrid seeds; and some day when overseas people, like in Africa, try to plant what we send them, they'll be caught, too.

"What if some great disaster happens and there were no more seeds–what then? How would crops reproduce? Some seed crops must be saved, even in vaults somewhere, just in case there is such a disaster.

Hank retorted, "But that wouldn't work; those seeds would contaminate the hybrids, and there are patents on those. No, that would be the actual disaster, and you're talking to one of the old time experts."

"I respect that, Uncle Hank, but I also know you're not following the rules to let the land lie fallow every two years. You're planting every year and claiming to be letting it be fallow. You change your charts. I've seen them! You are cheating the government."

"You're calling me a cheat!"

"I'm saying you're not reporting the accuracy that is expected," Ernie tried to make his point, but be respectful.

"Just prove that, young man, just prove that."

But Hank knew that he was caught, so he changed his charts– again. Ernie continued to drive past Hank's land season by season, but he had no authority to do anything but teach the proper methods and to oversee the introduction of good practices. But an incoming sheriff could make the law stand–and he would.

Chapter 46

SHERIFF WILL

All that is necessary for evil to triumph is for good men to do nothing
Edmund Burke

The open spaces, the prairie sod, the treeless landscape were all long gone. Electric lines and telephone lines ran down every country road, and now the interstate highways had sliced through farms with one big swath and went around tiny towns leaving them isolated.

"Can't really be good for the country," you'd hear old timers say.

"Why–you don't know who your neighbor is. Some of the owners don't even live in Colorado. I've heard some are even from overseas."

"Yah, and some ain't even farmers. It's a bunch of business men in New York, trying to suck life out of the land."

"Everything's goin mega, like tall elevators, seed operators, and guys running around in air conditioned tractors. Them ain't farmers!"

"How about them guys don't even keep cows or hogs no more? Just plant the seed and run off to Arizona or California for the winter, then come back and rake the grain in and go off again. Cain't be right! They don't' touch the land at all; how's it to feel cared for."

"–and it's not rich like it used ta be. Just feel it–and smell it. Why, that's not soil any more –that's just fertilizer!" cried an old man, reaching down to pick up a handful of soil.

"–and crop dusters with all kinds of death. Ain't right, just somethin wrong 'bout that," the old man continued.

"Don't even have farmer names any more!"

"Heard that the Kafka's, Miller's, Schmidt's all sold out to big companies named Wheat Consolidated or Farm Friends or some such –came in and tore down all their houses and barns and now just stretches of wheat as far as the eye can see. No fences. 'Cause it's all that Conglomerated crap."

"They'll keep the little guy out–control it all."

A dozen or so old men in overalls and billed caps sat around every morning at Bessie's Café on Main Street in Hopetown, talking about old times. After the morning coffee they'd wander out to their pickups and drive home, hardly three or four blocks away. All had retired, having made their fortunes; none was poor. Insurance against hail and flood kept the income predictable. Social Security made retirement easier, too.

Uncertainties abated; and with them, old customs of knowing everything that was going on–for your own protection and others– also faded into the past.

"You have to watch out now. All kinds of strangers come whizzing by on the interstates–could be any crook or killer–so lock your doors, pull down your shades–and keep to yourself."

It was a change in time; before, the neighbors were your police, and the doctor and lawyer were personal acquaintances. Now it was different.

"Yah, it was Tom Bailey, caught out by the sand hills –just minding his own business drinkin his morning coffee, when these two guys in a big new Chevy drove up out of nowhere, we think, pulled out guns and shot him straight bang in the head. Died right there. The bums took all 'is money that he kept in that thar big box by 'is bed. How'd they knowed where he kept his cash? Somethin's going on here."

"But if good ole Will Schultz hadn't been out there checking on the REA poles we'd never knowed what had happened to poor Tom.

"Will was lucky. He got suspicious when he saw that out-of-state car, took down the license plate number, went about out by the barn, as if he was checking the lines. Had the big REA truck sittin right out by the hen house. He'd gone up in Tom's haymow to get a better view of what was goin on.

"When the rascals came running out to their car–they'd looked around–see'd no one took off, makin clouds of dust, Will said. He ran into the house, called for Tom, then saw his body flopped over by the kitchen stove, jest starin out, two eyes wide open 'n a hole in his forehead. Will knew he was a goner. Ran to Tom's telephone 'n dialed that number into Sheriff Ben's office. Ben formed up a posse right 'thar. State patrol stopped the car just this side of Brush. Bastards got almost a hundred miles, thinkin they'd never be caught. Bastards! Killin 'n innocent man who'd worked hard all his life."

"Seems Sheriff Ben decided not to run for the office ag'in after being sheriff of Benson County for twenty-plus years. He said, 'It's time to hang it up. All the newcomers make it hard to keep the law. It's jest not like it used to be. That's when we the People–even though most of us 'r Republican–asked Will, a Democrat, to run for office. He said "I'm sixty years old, too. Am I too old?"

"Never! –Look at you–trim as any twenty-year old and twice as handsome," Julie commented. His wavy hair was still beautiful, and turning slightly gray–and sometimes in the wind still stood straight up–like horns–or was it a crown? Julie laughed, remembering.

"You're right. I really could help and I'm not afraid of anything–after Idaho and coming down that mountain with no brakes."

So Will became Sheriff Will–known for his no nonsense approach and his sense of fairness. High school students–teenagers–feeling their oats, if caught playing ditchem or racing too fast, were brought into the jail and given a jawing, made to order for each one.

When telling this sort of story Will might add, "Sometimes I even take them on a trip back to the jail cells where they can look at the bare springs on bed frames. They might spend a night there, if the Judge finds them guilty. That scare does most of them all the good they need," the Sheriff chuckled. Will and Julie liked being the big parents for the County. They appeared often at the County Fair, rode on floats in the parade and were symbols of good people.

Chapter 47

EMBEZZLING

The want of money and the distress of a thief can never be alleged as the cause of thievery, for many honest people endure greater hardship with fortitude.
William Blake

But other problems were brewing for the Sheriff of Benson County. "Will," the District Judge said. "I had a strange call from a guy who wouldn't leave his name. Said there was someone in high office that was siphoning off money from the town. That's all he said."

"Well, let's see what the DA might know–Bennett is on top of everything."

"Will, I hate to say this, but I just don't trust Bennett, not for many years. He seems to cover up things that a DA should investigate. Just a feeling I sometimes get. He always says, 'that's just the way things are done here'."

"You mean he might be the one involved?" Will could only think back to when Bennett had read his mother's will. There was always something strange about that whole deal.

"How could we find out? It's like looking for the mouse when the cat is at your elbow."

"I think there might be a way. We might use Jane Franikow. She audits the State's budget. Bennett maybe hasn't met her, and he damn sure can't impress her. See if Jane can uncover anything. Make sure it's legal, but still a way of getting to the books. OK?"

"You give the order, Judge, and I'll carry it out."

State of Colorado Assistant Auditor General Jane Franikow found the opportunity quaintly interesting and cleared her busy schedule. She came unannounced to the District Attorney's office with an order to audit the books. Jane took everything more than a week old and set two assistants working in an empty room at the local hotel. They took two weeks, and never let the materials out of their sight.

The DA was furious. "How can you justify bringing an expensive attorney all the way from Denver to audit our books! I'm contesting this order." Bennett brought his complaint to the District Judge who quickly overruled it–so the audit began.

Jane Franikow and her team traced a web of wholesale fraud, misuse of public funds, a second set of books, and casual daylight theft. She said, "There is a scheme of illegal filings, illegal use of foreclosure, and other representations clearly contrary to facts that go back over 30 years. It was cleverly done, but the District Attorney is an embezzler of public funds. It seems he involved his secretary, Miss Jenny, in the fraud. It is possible that others may have known about the fraud, but those facts are not clear. He should be tried as well as his secretary–Miss Jenny–."

Both were tried and found guilty.

Sheriff Will was taken back but had some questions; he thought, *Could it be that Bennett had something to do with Mama Rose's will? No, that would mean that Hank was also involved–not my brother–never!*

Will put those ideas out of his mind, but Bennett himself was another matter. Two deputies helped escort Bennett to the State Prison in Canon City. Will drove, one deputy sat in the front seat, and one stayed in back with Bennett, who wore handcuffs.

"He's not to be trusted; I was offered five thousand dollars to accidently let him loose somewhere around Pueblo," said one deputy, "Sure didn't take that!"

"This is really serious. I just have too much faith in people, but it takes all kinds of people I guess; but why has he been my brother's best friend all these years?"

The District Judge looked dismayed, then said, "You know Will, I hate to say this, but do you think that 'anonymous' caller might have been Hank? Could that be? They were always the best of friends, but it sounded so much like Hank, I almost asked him–Hank has that little rasp at the end of each sentence–have you noticed?"

"Nope, that couldn't be. They're best of buddies. And I never heard Hank's speak with a rasp–must have been someone else, but someone who really knew the truth!" Will replied.

The Sheriff drove carefully and the deputies stayed very alert as they neared Pueblo, rumored a possible holdout for members of the New York Mafia. Nothing came amiss; within an hour they pulled up to the State Prison, Canon City.

"Hello there," greeted the warden, "we'll make certain he serves his time–at least 30 years; stealing from your own people doesn't go well with me."

Back in Hopetown Will called brother Hank to see how Penelope was doing. She'd fallen rapidly into mental decline; the doctor called it 'Alzheimer's disease.'

"How's it going for you, Hank? Penelope doing, OK?"

"She doesn't know me now, or anyone else. She's just has gone down hill the last month or so–stayed about the same for the last seven years–but now it's worse." His voice sounded so sad– and Will noticed a slight rasp at the end of each sentence.

I wonder. Will shuddered.

"Yes, it's sad; Julie stops to see her at least once a week, and you know that Rachel is her main caregiver."

"Yes, Rachel, her nurse practitioner–is an angel. I talk with her every day. There isn't anything that Rachel doesn't do for Penelope. But, she's slipping, though. Doesn't eat much, chokes a lot and can't swallow."

Within a week Penelope choked on her soup and could not be revived. She had died, still a beautiful woman, at the age of 68. In her will she gave all of her property and belongings to her husband, Henri Pinot Schultz. She was buried in the Hopetown cemetery, in an ordinary plot, like everyone else. Her tombstone wasn't ordinary; it was sizeable and very expensive.

Chapter 48

THE PROMISE SEED

"–we, all of us, inherit everything, and then we choose what to cherish, what to disavow, what to do next; which is why it's worth trying to know where things come from."
Jill Lepore

The concert hall suddenly grew silent as the house lights dimmed. Breathlessly, the overflowing crowd waited for the long expected performance by the violin virtuoso. They burst into thundering applause as the tall, beautiful redheaded woman in a long, forest green satin dress walked gracefully toward the conductor. The sudden beginning of Paganini's Concerto for Violin in D Major split the harmonics in the concert hall. The overtones of the mellow Steiner violin echoed throughout. As the violinist raised her head, red voluminous hair fell down across her right shoulder.

Awe from the audience could be felt, not heard. Each crescendo reached a new peak of miraculous tone, and the perfection of fingering seemed to slide effortlessly. As the end approached, you could feel the audience bending forward anticipating the final arpeggio and tonic tone. The whole room seemed suspended for a moment. Then thunder broke loose as the crowd rose to their feet in a standing ovation. Their applause cascaded in wave after wave.

The violinist smiled victoriously, bowed and bowed, left and returned for three more standing ovations. On the fourth the virtuoso placed the violin again under her chin, as the orchestra and she broke into the complicated, technically difficult Rimsky-Korsakov's "Flight of the Bumble Bee."

Suspended between heaven and earth was the description given by the music reviewer in the New York Times. Serena Rose Schultz seemed connected in spirit with her great-grandfather, Henri Pinot, a violin virtuoso of the late 19th Century, and concertmaster of the Strasberg Symphony. Her interpretation and technique have made her one of the most sought-after, critical artists of the Twentieth Century. Standing tall with stunning red hair flowing down her back–she may have resembled Great Grandma Frieda, but she played like Great Grandpa Henri Pinot so many decades ago.

Her proud parents, Julie and Will, were amazed with their talented daughter who once only played on an out-of-tune, warn-out violin, that belonged to the motel owner in Creston Junction, Idaho.

"Indeed she's got the spirit of Mama Rose and the beauty of Grandma Frieda," remarked Will. Julie agreed.

Not only had Serena inherited the unique talent, but she also studied with great teachers at the Lamont School of Music at Denver University. Later their daughter studied under the great master teacher, Raymond Montavi, at Julliard School of Music. The virtuosic violinist travelled throughout the country playing the priceless Steiner family violin.

Another moment of pride came when Will and Julie read in the Denver Post an account by a reporter: *Something new and miraculous is happening in Fruita, Colorado, not the usual fruit orchard, of which there are many in that area, but a unique one called, Schultz First Fruits. Mr. Dusty Schultz, a successful organic fruit grower has been awarded the Farmers of America (FOA). For over twenty years, Mr. Schultz has been growing peaches, pears, apricots, and cherries without the use of pesticides or herbicides*

Asked how he got started doing these 'so-called organic orchards' he replied, "I got a degree from Colorado State University, but I really learned most from my grandfather, Papa Paul. He was known as The Seed Man and his friend, Red Sun in Hair, a Cheyenne/Scottish man would come every spring to bless the land that for centuries had belonged to the Cheyenne tribe. I call our orchards First Fruits, because this land does not really to us but rather to our Creator.

Mr. Schultz may be ahead of his time, but it is a practice we need to support, said the reporter.

And their youngest, Rachel, the beloved nurse practitioner in Hopetown, was so much like Grandma Serena that Mama Julie would often say, "You have that healing touch that your grandma had."

One day Rachel said, "Mama, do you think I can fit into Grandma Rose's wedding dress?"

So it was that Hopetown celebrated the wedding of Nurse Rachel and Widower Gerald Freeman. All the town folks attended the wedding at St. Paul's Lutheran church and danced throughout the night in the Schultz barn, just like Julie and Will had done so many years before. Will's still strong voice sang to the newlyweds, "With Someone Like You." Sister Serena played the fiddle and other players joined with banjo, drum, and another fiddle. Square dancing began as whole families danced to the calls of Will. Even Gerald's two young children joined in the fun. Now stepmother of two, Rachel slightly taller but with the same sparkling black eyes, looked stunning in Grandma Rose's wedding dress. It seemed as if the world stood still returning to the time when Rose and John William first began their journey to the formidable prairie.

Yes, indeed these children: Ernie, Serena, Dusty, and Rachel each carried some part of the genetics, the inheritance, from their parents and grandparents. They were The Promise Seed and would carry on the knowledge and skills grown on the windy prairie of eastern Colorado.

Now instead of a treeless, gray land, homesteads grew into mansions with green lawns, rose bushes, and even some swimming pools. Livestock was gone, as were the barns that held them. No longer did only two tiny ruts link neighbors where wagons had pioneered the roads that now were covered with black asphalt, Large grain elevators rose as giants on the horizon holding the 'bread basket of the country'. Oh, a few old timers remained remembering when dust covered the sun, and darkness of night came too soon, and the cattle moaned for water.

The wind of long ago, never ceased. One day Ernie said, "Remember how Uncle Pete hitched up those generators to the windmill. He made his own electrical power plant, storing the electricity in batteries in the basement of their house! No one had done that before in our county! Let's see how we can to use this damn wind. It blows all the time. What say we do that?"

It would take many more decades before the wind would become harvested for the emerging energy crisis, but the seeds for such ideas were planted long ago.

PART VI

THE GRAVE

Chapter 49

A MYSTERIOUS DEATH

It is said that your life flashes before you just before you die. That is true; it's called LIFE.

Terry Pratchett *The Last Continent*

Rain had fallen steadily for a week, one of those dreary, gray weeks of early spring. The dirt roads were barely passable, leaving no trace of a passer-by, as the ruts merged into one long, muddy run. An odd feeling, almost dread, hung in the air. It was March 21st ; those millionaires, some multi-millionaire farmers, wanted to be out in the fields. Much needed to get done, but now the rain!

In Hopetown, where most of the old timers lived, rather than out on their farms–homesteaded by their risk-taking parents in the early 1900's. Here they sat every morning in their usual places at Betsy's Café. Dressed in striped overalls and bill caps pulled straight on, they made the get-up look like a uniform–Marching to Order of the Farm. Their billed caps covered the white rim on tops of their foreheads, above the summer sun's brown paint across wrinkled faces.

About a dozen farmers now waited 'til the rain stopped.

"This damn weather–either too much rain–or not enough–the Devil has his hand in this."

"It's all a gamble–but I been farming too long to think of another way of life."

Mumbling continued as the men sorted through the grain prices and what cattle and hogs were bringing per hundredweight. Every morning they gathered–checking in on all the latest news around the county–sizing up each other's bankroll and in general just enjoying the morning ritual of having coffee.

"Sure wonder where Hank is. He's usually the first one here, now that his ole lady passed," one uttered curiously.

Hank Schultz, the handsome, richest bastard in these parts, was not well liked by most.

"He sure changed his ways after he married that rich widda'. Why I remember when Hank got ex-communicated from the Lutheran Church 'cause he was chasing and fornicating with every woman, single or married," reminded another.

"Yah, I never played poker with him, too risky, cheatin 'n all," retorted one.

"Some folks don't forget," chimed another, "like when he did some finaglin to get Widda Rose's homestead. Don't forget 'bout the whole thing, even if it happened a long time ago."

"Nope sure don't forget," another said.

Just then Sheriff Will, now in his twentieth year as sheriff walked in.

"A good man," they all agreed, "no matter if he's a Democrat, he's one damn Democrat you can talk to. And that gun in its holder might be loaded, but never had to use it but once, for those ornery out-of-town teenagers who robbed the hardware store. Those rascals caught ole Will 'tween two haystacks 'n fired pellets at him hadn't worked up to the rifle they also had.

"He was a lucky son-of-a gun," All nodded.

"But oh, to tangle with Sheriff's son. Why Ernie grabbed 'em kids like they were sacks of 'tatoes. Sure he dropped them on the ground a time or two and tied them up like pigs in a blanket," The fellas chuckled.

"Man–that Ernie was mad?"

"Think he woulda done those kids in, if Sheriff hadn't yelled, "Stop!"

Lots of stories–maybe myths surrounded the legend of Sheriff Will, even had the national news coverage on him a couple of times during the twenty years for his ideas about law and justice– a mighty find man–all would agree.

"Hi there Sheriff, what's up?"

"Hi yah fellas. Hi, there Betsy, how about a cup' a your best? How's it going?"

"Hi, Will caught any bank robbers lately?

"Nah, just a bunch of no-good, lazy bums. I'll catch a lotta 'em sitting around drinking coffee."

Poking fun at all, Will sat down and drank his black coffee, and asked, "Say, any of you guys seen Hank around? He was supposed to come for supper last night. Now that he's a widower he doesn't miss a home-cooked meal. Wonder what happened to him?"

"Nope, haven't seen him or his white pickup around," they mumbled.

"Maybe he went out to 'is machine shop. It's time to git the tractor set up for spring harrowing. He's always on top of that. Better go check on him, as he coulda gotten stuck in all this mud."

"Yah, that's right," murmured Will. "I'd better go and check him."

"Want me to go along in case you get stuck? It's pretty nasty out there near the Nebraska state line. They had a good two more inches last night. I'd heared on the radio." said Jake, an old friend of Will's. "I'll go with you ya. Haven't much to do around here 'cept shoot the bull with these ole losers."

They all laughed.

"Take it easy 'n call on us men if you boys need some help," they all laughed. A tight knit group ready to stand by each other.

"See yah," Jake and Will left the café.

"Thanks for offering to ride along. It's pretty nasty on those side roads."

"Glad to do it, as Hank could be in trouble by hisself. He's just not the same since Penelope died, just sort of hangin around. He went everyday and sat by her side at the Morningside Nursing Home. Drat, that Alzheimer's is the baddest thing. Can't believe it happened to such a pretty lady, 'n smart, too."

The men drove on in silence, with a close eye on slippery roads. Will drove slowly and carefully. It took half an hour to cover ten miles. As they were turning the corner to go in, Jake said, "Hey, I think that's Hank's white pickup. He must've come out early."

"You're right; that's good to see."

Will stopped the car and with their heavy rubber boots sloshed through inches of mud just outside the shop. The door was slightly ajar as Will, then Jake went in.

They saw something they didn't' want to see. Hank, or what was left of him, was splashed on the west wall of the she, with red–blood–lots of it. And Hank's chest looked crushed.

"Oh, my god, look at Hank," cried Will. He got down on his knees touching Hank's face and muttering, "Little Brother, Little Brother, I wasn't here to help you–" Patting Hank's cheek and pushing the graying auburn hair to the side. Will sobbed like a baby.

Hank's face was frozen; his eyes were wide open, his mouth was, too. He had an expression that Will had never seen on his brother's face–fear. Like maybe–he'd seen something, a ghost or worse yet–the tractor charging right at him, and crushing him into the wall. Squashing his chest, so that his heart burst and blood squirted everywhere. Stomped right into his body, so no breath could be taken. But his eyes! His eyes–seeming to say that he'd seen something– terrifying!

"Something evil did this to him–I feel it– something powerful–eerie, unspeakable– horrid."

Jake shaking said, "He must have had the engine running and got down to fix something in the front–when it slipped into gear 'n smashed him. Just an accident, an accident."

"I only hope so–but Hank would never leave the engine running when he was working on it in front. He would have shut off the engine–not take a chance even if he had the brake set."

Will ran back and looked into the front of the tractor. "Yes, the brake was pulled clear back. He had set the brake and the ignition was off! Someone slipped in and set the engine going and put it into gear before Hank could rescue himself. We'll get to the bottom of this. We'll know.

"Now I have to call the coroner and get an investigation. Not me. I'm too close. I'm his brother for god's sake. I can't do an investigation. That would be seen in the court of law as 'conflict of interest.'

With that Will pulled himself up, after all he was the sheriff.

Stiffly he walked back to his cruiser and called on the radio. "Help. There's been a terrible accident or something. And Hank is dead."

The dispatcher picked up the message. "Oh, Will, I'm so sorry the call is in right now, and I'll call Julie –if you want."

"Yes, yes, do that."

Now Will was shaking and Jake put his arm around Will's shoulder.

"But why were the keys still in the ignition and the brake set. This couldn't have been an accident.

"This is tough –tough."

"I don't want to be sheriff anymore. Twenty years of seeing these kinds of things, even out here, and it does get to you. Especially if, if –" He didn't finish the sentence.

Will sat down in the police cruiser, and thought–*There are no tire tracks anywhere. With all the rain they would have been swept away. And neighbors? Hank didn't have any. But maybe someone saw Hank's pickup yesterday and maybe even stopped in –or maybe –maybe. That's all there is, maybe.*

Noon came and a bright sun with it, drying off some of the mud, but there would be no clues.

The coroner arrived around 1:00 PM, been on the job for thirty years–always reelected because no one else would run.

"Looks like he left the ignition on and forgot to set the brake, and the engine just too off and hit him square in the chest and burst his aorta. He went fast, didn't suffer at all."

"But why that scared look on his face–like he'd seen someone–or something. Why would he have that look?" asked Will still shaking.

"Sometimes when folks die in an accident, their muscles just crunch up."

"But his eyes they look scared–like he saw something–or somebody."

"Can't say the look any different from others I've seen when the impact is sudden like this. Just pops out the eyes like that–the pressure."

"But then the key in the ignition wasn't turned on and the brake was set. So what about that?"

"You guys didn't change anything did you? Like run in and do the natural thing, before you even saw Hank against the wall?"

"Nah, couldn't miss that blood on the wall."

Jake was not quite certain, as it all happened so fast. "I just don't remember what happened first or second. I don't think we touched a thing."

"Oh, Jake, you were right there when I ran in, we didn't touch a thing. We just rushed over to Hank."

"Not sure 'bout that. Will, really, I was slower than you. I kind of got caught in the mud and didn't follow as close as you may have thought. Don't you think you might have automatically shut off the engine? If it was still running'–guess it couldn't have been 'cause the gas would be gone–like runnin all day. But maybe you did do that, just in a flash, like'n you would have any other time–or maybe.

"Geez, Jake. I'd know if I did or not. I wasn't that dazed and I'm the sheriff. Besides I've seen accidents the twenty years I've been doing this. I just think this was no accident. I think someone did Hank in."

"You're, right, Will," the coroner commented. "We need to have an investigation just to set the record straight. Accidents should always be investigated." The coroner spoke as if reading from some manual he'd absorbed years before.

"I think the district attorney should appoint an investigative team, and you can be a part of it, if you want, Will."

"No, not a good idea," Will said automatically. "But not now, we've got to get his body to a funeral home. It's been here long enough for rigor mortis to pass and real decay to get started." As hard as it was, Will, Jake, and the coroner, covered Hank's 6'4" body and then got it into the coroner's stations wagon–now a hearse.

"Where do you want me to take him?" the coroner spoke softly.

"Johnson's Mortuary. That's where we've all gone. All the Schultz's, and thanks for coming, Dr. Moss. You were always been someone I could count on. Thanks, and well, thanks.

Will's mind was wandering off from the overwhelming sorrow of losing his brother, his last sibling. *Margaret's been gone five, six years back. Now I'm the only one of John William and Rose Schultz, three children left. I feel so alone.*

As they left the shed, the sun suddenly caught the shadow of an arrow plunged into the sod wall near where Hank had been pinned. The arrow was not just an ordinary arrow –it was a Cheyenne Red Arrow–not the white one for peace, but the one with the red feather–the eagles' red feather–a symbol for war or revenge.

How long had it been there? Wasn't that part of the original machine shed? That west wall was all that was left as part of the sod shelter.

A strange sound, a whisper was heard. "Remember Daddy built this shed, as he knew that the livestock couldn't survive underground as we did, into the dugout. This wall was to remind us of our beginnings as homesteaders – how we triumphed it will remind us of our roots and spiritual covenant with the land." The room grew cold, the whisper ceased, a dry leaf blew against the wall.

Had the arrow been there all the time–or was it placed there recently? A reminder of Old Timer's warning was, "Don't abuse the land, give thanks and praise–for we are the keepers of the land–we are just passing through.

No one saw the arrow–no one, perhaps it's still there.

"May I drive the cruiser for you," asked Jake, knowing the shock must be dimming Will's reactions.

"That's a good idea. I deputize you right now.'1040' over and out."

Wills tears fell without shame, as they drove carefully through the muddy roads back toward Fairview, where word spread quickly about Hank's accident or untimely death.

Clusters of people whispered their opinions and also how close Will was to his younger brother. They brought salads and rolls, covered dishes to Julie and Will's house, knowing that soon the funeral would be planned. Children assembled with their families, and friends would call. It was custom for all–woven throughout to give respect to Julie and Will. In small towns joys and sorrows are shared. The funeral would bring an end to all.

But would it? What would the inquest show? Was this really an accident?

An answer was never found–some suspected Mel Otto. Many had heard him threaten Hank's life–when he lost the poker game and knew animosity had between the two since they were grade school kids. But no one had any evidence that Mel was even close to Fairview when the accident happened–let alone–near the machine shed–yet people wondered–Some suspected that Attorney's Bennett's Mafia might have come back, if they found out that Hank had made that call to the judge about Bennett's embezzlement. Many thought about all the women Hank had had and perhaps a vengeful woman or man could have done him in.

No one remembered what Red Sun in Hair–had told them that the Red Arrow was only used for revenge against an enemy. No one remembered, but no one believed this was an accident–no, not one

Chapter 50

HANK'S WILL

Life without love is like a tree without blossom or fruit.
Khalil Gibran

Clouds hung low, heavy gray rain clouds. They held sway over Hopetown. The Hanks memorial service was at the First Methodist–a closed casket, because there was no way to put a peaceful look back on Hank's grimaced face. Shock had hit the town. Many were there to give testimony to their friend Hank and to recall his long, colorful life. No one came who had been on the short end of one of his crafty business deals.

Later that afternoon sole remnants of Hank's kin–Julie and Will and children, Ernie, Serena, Dusty, and Rachel–gathered at the probate judge's office. The sudden and violent death left many questions regarding the succession of Hank's estate–childless and a widower. How would Hank want to be remembered? Since Penelope's death from Alzheimer's disease, Hank had spent more and more time with Julie and Will, dropping in for dinner, supper, or coffee whenever he passed by their home in Hopetown. He seemed so lonely, so eager to be with them.

It seemed that Hank had, indeed, loved strange Penelope. Her death had been long in coming. Hank was at her side–day and night, trying to help Penelope cope with all the losses of memory and bodily functions. It felt like an empty place in the room now that he, too, was dead.

It was hard to believe.

And the will–yet to be read. No one knew Hank's worth: the homestead, the many sections of land–over ten in all, including his inheritance from Penelope, or the high-priced farm equipment on the land itself. Perhaps Hank had accumulated stocks and bonds.

No one knew–it really didn't matter, as Will was certain that the estate would go to some important person in Hank's social life– maybe to some charity to be named in his honor.

Attorney Martin, dressed in a dark grey suit, opened the sealed envelope.

"We are here today for the reading of the will. It is dated and signed by Henri Jonathan Schultz, January 17, 1982. Martin began to read:

I, Henri Jonathan Schultz, do leave all land holdings, farm equipment, cash, back accounts, and bonds at First Bank of Hopetown and Bank of Nebraska, Ogallala, and every other earthly thing in my possession, jointly to my brother William John Schultz and to my sister-in-law Julie Serena Schultz whom I have always loved but could not have.

Signed,

Henri Jonathan Schultz

After finishing, Mr. Martin, looked up and saw startled faces– faces in disbelief.

"Before going on, I also have something of importance to share with you. While examining Henri's legal papers I found an envelope containing another will. It was dated **August 14, 1935,** prepared by Mr. Bill Bennett and signed by your mother, **Rose Pinot Schultz.** This signature is authentic from my comparisons to other legal documents. But, there was still another supposedly amended will as of **December 24, 1935**, the day of her death, not with her signature, but–signed, Santa Claus.

Gasps seemed to such all the air in the room and shake it. Will spoke first. "What do you mean? What was in the first–legal will?"

Mr. Martin, said, "If you will permit, I will read it and give you the document:

August 14, 1935.

I, Rose Pinot Schultz, do hereby leave all the homestead property, all my personal belongings, all my accumulated bank accounts, and all personal effects including my Model T Ford, to my beloved first-born son, William John Schultz. He has for all these many years been a faithful servant to the soil and loved the land. He is instructed to use this land for the good of all. When there are profits to be shared, he is to share these with his sister Margaret and his brother Henri.

I know William John is a child of God as is his wife, Julie Serena. Each of their offspring is a worthy servant as well. To Ernie: you must strive to become the overseer, a co-manager of the farm. Dusty, you are to be the keeper of the Box of Promise Seeds. Serena, already interested in the violin, will have Great Grandpa Pinot's Steiner violin. If any other children are born to Will and Julie, they shall be given what their journey needs. (Note: Rachel was not yet born when Mama died)

I will go soon to be with my Maker and my beloved husband, John William. He has been waiting for a long time. I love you all.

Signed,

Rose Pinot Schultz

Shaking visibly as color drained from his face, Will whispered, "It'll take a while to think this through."

Mr. Martin continued, "As you know, your brother had no heirs. And being a widower he was also bequeathed all land and personal wealth of his wife, Penelope, to you. These possessions are now part of his –now your –estate."

Will, still gasping for breath, asked, "Why did Hank keep that fake will at all? Why didn't he destroy it as evidence?"

Mr. Martin, answered, "I wondered about that myself, then thought perhaps Hank regretted this act, especially lying about his mother's real intent. That may have worn on him. Perhaps he had a little bit of conscience. Perhaps."

Ernie turned to Mr. Martin, and said, "Thanks, we're going to have to put all of this together." His face, too, was tense and angry.

"We just didn't know that anyone could be so dishonest to his own kin!"

Her face covered by her shaking hands, Julie recalled the time she first met Hank at the Saturday night dance and the time he'd taken her on the buggy ride. "I can't believe he did this! How could he have been so cruel seeing how we struggled–living with nothing and having to leave it all behind–as we left for Idaho–with nothing.

"How could he have done this? Why? They lived in luxury while we beat off the grasshopper invasion. Oh–I'm simply livid. Oh, that smell still lingers in my mind and the hoppers never even munched on a blade of the homestead–their land–because of Will and Ernie's work–saved it! That skunk bought our Updike farm for a pittance without ever giving us a penny to save it."

Her shaking voice was now nearly a shout. "He could have paid for it and given it to us–but no. No. No. No!"

Then Julie pulled herself up, sitting tall. "No, no, don't try to remember it all. They lived in luxury and we–right next door–I remember when our kids needed new shoes–or to the time when Will's weekly wage was seven dollars a week from working long hours with the WPA–or how I worked for three dollars a month for food for the family–cleaning the church. During those hard times Hank and Penelope vacationed in Hawaii and–No–I must not be angry–I must not–I must not."

Julie said, "Thank you for reading the will–we'd like to see the original will–and Grandma Rose's signature."

Ernie sat quietly, his eyes blazing–"That bastard," he whispered.

"Bennett knew about this all along," hissed Will. "I'm glad I put him away–and if he ever gets out–" His hand was now in a fist.

"It must be hard to take it in, and I understand. I think it will take a few days or weeks to get a handle on it all," remarked Mr. Martin. "I'll have the documents recorded and then you can decide how you wish to handle the estate. The accounts are all in order."

Then he left.

Slowly, the tension lifted.

Will held Julie's arm as he straightened up to walk. Ernie came up on the other side and put an arm around his dad. Turning to all, Will's mellow, strong baritone voice was suddenly small and far away.

He said, "If you don't mind, I'd like to visit–alone–the cemetery where Mama and Daddy are buried–in Fairview."

The family silently went back home.

Will drove his old car to the small cemetery. He shuffled out of the car across the plots to reach the headstones of–John William Schultz: March 21, 1910 and Rose Pinot Schultz: December 24, 1935. Will's knees buckled beneath him, and he laid face down on the graves–sobbing–"Mama, Mama, Mama. I knew you always said I was to care for the homestead. You always said that. I always wondered why you changed your mind. What had I done to disappoint you? Now I know." Sobbing like a baby–"Now I know– now I know."

Will laid for several minutes. Gradually he got up on his knees, then stood up and raised his arms to the heavens.

"Please, Lord, forgive him–his jealousy was evil, but wash his sins as white as snow. If I, a sinner in my own way, want Your blessing, I freely ask that grace be given to my brother."

Back in Will and Julie's home each sat like stones. Ernie had a look of disbelief–softly whispered. "He did know–that bastard."

Julie stood–in her heart remembering how Mama Rose always flung herself across the grave of John William, crying for him, "John William come back!" That sorrow is so deep that sometimes nothing can make it go away. And now another sorrow so deep– would it ever soften?

She felt a deep wound in her heart, as she had never known Will to be angry like this. The power of revenge was so close to the surface. And, what about her own feelings? Could she put them into a place of forgiveness–what would it take?

"Let's take it a day at a time–a day at a time," was all Julie could say. "Let's just get to work that always helps."

And so they did.

For almost a month, no one spoke of the will. Sometimes you'd see someone begin to form a question, and then see Will's distorted face and then pull back. People didn't ask, but people wondered.

The holidays came–and went. Will read the original will, signed by Mama Rose, over and over again. It was as if he needed to be reassured again and again, now almost fifty years later, that mama's love remained on those old faded pages.

PART VII

SAVING

MOTHER EARTH

Chapter 51

REVOLUTION

This is a call to revolution. The Earth is under threat. It cannot cope with all that we demand of it. It is losing its balance.

Charles The Prince of Wales,
Harmony: a new way of looking at our world

One day in mid-March 1984, when winds of promise were waving flags, kites were flying, and smell of welcoming earth spread through Hopetown and Fairview, Julie heard a whistling in the back yard–something she hadn't heard for almost a year. Then suddenly the burst of song, loud and clear, "With someone like you–a pal so good and true. I'd like to leave it all behind and go and find–some place that's known to God alone." (Brennan, 1919) Will was standing, feet wide apart and his arms lifted to the sky. Julie ran to him, and they whirled around and around–like old times.

"Nothing should come between brothers. It's time to bless the land–it's March–and Old Timer will be waiting for us," Will cried out loudly. "Let's get to work!"

Ernie's son, Paul, went immediately to the barn to check on the horses.

"I'm going to ride Babe II, Grandpa, and see if I can find some gophers and nesting birds," said little Paul.

"That's a good idea, just say hello to them, don't hurt any of them, as they are part of our family!" said Grandpa Will.

After about half an hour the small boy, seven years old, about the same age that Will was when his father died in the prairie fire, came riding fast on his pinto pony.

He flew to Will's side. "Grandpa, Grandpa, I saw a strange thing on the southeast corner of the field. It looked like a man, but I'm not sure. I was too far away, but I think I heard a drum beating, and the man's long hair was flying in the wind–as I rode closer I saw him raise his hand to the sky, and there was a big, big bird, maybe an eagle flying way, way high. And the man waved to me, but didn't say a word except something I couldn't understand like–sort of a mumble–Maaaa–something. I rode closer, as I wasn't afraid–but he suddenly disappeared–like right before my eyes!"

"What could it have been, Grandpa? Come look with me–please, Grandpa."

Will gathered up the bridle and slid onto his black mare's back, and with Grandson Paul rode to the spot where the young boy had seen the man.

"Is this where you saw him?"

"Yes, Grandpa, right here."

Grandpa Will looked around, "I don't see anything, do you? Wait–there's something over by that bush, a white thing."

Will got off his horse and walked slowly to the spot where it lay–perfectly still–perfectly white–an arrow with a white-feathered shaft–the Cheyenne Sacred White Arrow–a symbol of peace.

Will stood perfectly still, gazing upward, as a smile slowly crossed his face and in a small voice said, "Yes, yes, now I know–now I know. I remember the Red Arrow of Revenge in the sod wall of the shed–now this Arrow of Peace. Now I know what killed Hank. Yes, Red Sun's Revenge!"

"Lord, please forgive my brother." He looked up at the blue sky and remembered Papa Paul and Red Sun in Hair.

"Someday, you, too–will know."

EPILOG

2018

The winds still blow across the prairie but now they power wind machines that bring electricity to surrounding towns. Rain still is scarce on the desert, but farmers have tapped into the Ogallala underground water resource that Red Sun in Hair talked about. Their irrigation pumps spill rainbows across the fields. The tractors are air-conditioned while hired contractors do the harvesting. Where once men (and women) on horseback checked the fences and all land within the property lines, drones now fly around collecting data about the seed supply, the need for fertilizer. Once, the farmers checked the fertility of the soil by examining it by hand, even tasting it. Now computers accurately record the data.

The Schultz family still manages one of the best farms in the country, and foreign visitors learn more about modern farming than they can from books. Will and Julie have gone to their heavenly home, joining Papa Paul, Red Sun in Hair, Mama Rose, John William, and Ernie who lost his life flying in Africa as a consultant on water issues for the United Nations. Serena still performs for special groups on the valued Steiner violin. Dusty still operates his famous organic orchards and writes a column in a statewide journal about the power of using natural products instead of chemicals. Rachel teaches nurses the special skills of healing, but she has retired from active nursing and shares her life with her husband, adult children and six grandchildren.

Each March 21st the whole family gathers at the homestead to bless the land, The Promise Seed, and to keep the covenant long ago begun by Papa Paul and Red Sun in Hair.

Prairie as seen 1909

Fairview's grain elevators 2016.
Photo used by permission Phillips County Museum

About the Author

Born on the barren prairie, Glittenberg still finds peace by returning to those endless miles, unhampered by hills, rivers, and lakes. Touched and inspired by the giant expansive star-lit nights, no risk is too great to tether her flight. As a cultural anthropologist and a psychiatric nurse, Jody has brought worldwide attention to social justice needs in slums, prisons, and issues of torture. She has studied people, from continent to continent, ever exploring the face of humankind. Jody is a recipient of numerous honors in nursing and anthropology.

Dr. Glittenberg retired in 2003 as Professor Emerita of Nursing, Anthropology, & Psychiatry, U. of Arizona, Tucson, AZ.

Mother of two children, five stepchildren, grandmother of a mix of ten grandkids, one great grandson, and one rescued dog, she and her husband, Joel Hinrichs, are writers and musicians who passionately pursue bringing justice into the world.

A Note from the Author

Dear Readers,

Thank you for reading my story of the five generations of courageous homesteaders. I hope that you found that their story of honoring the earth and sustaining generative seeds, precious water, the harmony of music and art, is a call for each of us to become more aware of our responsibility and connections to all. Perhaps resilience and love are the greatest lessons instilled by these pioneers who needed to overcome the weather and selfish people, as well as to forgive one another.

If you have questions or further thoughts about how each of can become more involved in honoring each other, the earth, the sky, and all living creatures, please let me know. You, too, can become part of the revolution.

The Promise Seed

Jody Glittenberg
Email jglitten@msn.com

Bibliography

Egan, Timothy. *The Worst Hard Times: The untold story of those who survived the Great American Dust Bowl.* (2006). Houghton Mifflin Harcourt: New York.

Goodall, Jane (with Thane Maynard and Gail Hudson). (2009). *Hope: for the animals and their world.* Grand Central Publishing: New York.

Prince of Wales (with Tony Juniper and Ian Skelly) (2010) *Harmony: a new way of looking at our world.* Harper-Collins Publishers: NY/NY

Walker, Nancy. (1993). *Spirit Walker.* Bantam Doubleday Dell Publishing Group, Inc. New York.

Music Attributions

"Red River Valley" (first published by James Kerrigan 1896, a folk tune) North Carolina Music Archives Center: Chapel Hill, NC.

Brennan, J. Keirn, (songwriter) Let the Rest of the World Go By. (1919). M. Witmark & Sons: New York (recorded by many leading western singers since publication)

All other quotations used in this novel are available in the public domain through Google: famous quotes